I0817665

PRAISE FOR IMOGEN CLARK

An Unwanted Inheritance

'Brimful of emotion – a wonderful plot and characters that you are rooting for, even when you know you shouldn't. *An Unwanted Inheritance* is that gem of a thing: a story to truly lose yourself in. I LOVED IT!'

—Faith Hogan, bestselling author of
The Ladies' Midnight Swimming Club

'What happens when you drop a bag of cash right in the middle of three siblings and their families? A whole lot of good fun and drama. *An Unwanted Inheritance* delightfully explores the flaws that come with being human as Clark plunges us into a story about what is right and wrong and what it means to be a family. She ratchets up the tension as the story races to its surprising and oh-so-satisfying conclusion.'

—Boo Walker, bestselling author of *The Singing Trees*

'A gripping tale about money, greed, and what really matters.'

—Anstey Harris, bestselling author of
The Truths and Triumphs of Grace Atherton

‘Imogen Clark deftly peels back the layers of loyalty, family secrets and moral dilemma to examine a family that must make a choice between need, greed and integrity. Pacey, thought provoking, and with characters that test the ties of blood, marriage and friendship to the limit, *An Unwanted Inheritance* will have you wondering how far you'd go to uphold your own principles – and how much, or how little, it would take to betray them.’

—Julietta Henderson, author of
The Funny Thing about Norman Foreman

‘Lovingly crafted, with flawed and nuanced characters, this riveting story will stay with readers long after the last page is turned.’

—Christine Nolfi, bestselling author of *A Brighter Flame*

Reluctantly Home

‘Connected by loss, a friendship blooms across the generations in this compassionate and nuanced story of endings and new beginnings.’

—Fiona Valpy, bestselling author of *The Skylark's Secret*

‘Imogen Clark is a master at creating flawed, real, lovable characters and exploring their emotions. This novel cleverly weaves together the past and present, and will leave you thinking about the story long after you finish the final page.’

—Soraya M. Lane, bestselling author of *Wives of War* and
The Last Correspondent

The Last Piece

'This is a wonderful novel about the secrets we keep from the ones we love the most. Imogen Clark has a real talent for shining a light on the idiosyncrasies of family life and revealing past traumas, present hurts and future hopes.'

—Victoria Connelly, author of *The Rose Girls* and *Love in an English Garden*

'*The Last Piece* is a beautifully crafted, insightful tale about family and the cracks below the surface of seemingly perfect lives. Clark's characters, with their various secrets and flaws, leap off the page. A most enjoyable and riveting read.'

—S.D. Robertson, author of *My Sister's Lies* and *Time to Say Goodbye*

'I couldn't resist going on this journey with the Nightingale family. With emotion on every page and mystery swirling around each character, *The Last Piece* explores how the past can be as unpredictable as the future. I raced through this life-affirming book, which left me buoyed with the promise of second chances.'

—Jo Furniss, author of *The Last to Know*

Where the Story Starts

'Once again . . . Imogen Clark urges readers to turn the pages as the delightfully pleasant facade of her characters' lives begins to crack when the mysteries of the past come to call. Both soothing and riveting, *Where the Story Starts* asks: what if your greatest secret is the one you don't even know exists?'

—Amber Cowie, author of *Rapid Falls* and *Raven Lane*

The Thing About Clare

'Warm and emotionally complex . . . A family drama that's hard to disentangle yourself from.'

—Nick Alexander, bestselling author of *Things We Never Said*

In Another Life

ALSO BY IMOGEN CLARK

Postcards From a Stranger

The Thing About Clare

Where the Story Starts

Postcards at Christmas (a novella)

The Last Piece

Reluctantly Home

Impossible to Forget

An Unwanted Inheritance

In a Single Moment

A Borrowed Path

Writing as Izzy Bromley

The Coach Trip

Table for Five

The Bed in the Shed

In Another Life

Imogen Clark

LAKE UNION
PUBLISHING

This is a work of fiction. Names, characters, organizations, places, events, and incidents are either products of the author's imagination or are used fictitiously. Any resemblance to actual persons, living or dead, or actual events is purely coincidental.

Published by Lake Union Publishing, Seattle

www.apub.com

EU Product Safety contact:
Amazon Publishing, Amazon Media EU S.à r.l.
38, avenue John F. Kennedy, L-1855 Luxembourg
amazonpublishing-gpsr@amazon.com

ISBN-13: 9781662528972
eISBN: 9781662518058

Cover design by Will Speed
Image credits: © fstop Images © Alexander Korotich © dadedi1 / Shutterstock

Printed in the United States of America

For Mum

1

2022 – Ripon

'Are you sure we haven't forgotten anyone?'

Bronte stared at the list, her vision blurring slightly. She wiped the tears away before Marc could see and pass comment. There was always a comment.

'Don't see how we could have done,' said Marc. 'The whole town is on that list.'

He was right. The announcement of the death had been in the paper and that, combined with the local grapevine, meant there couldn't be a soul left in Ripon who hadn't heard about it.

'It's going to be standing room only,' said Annie.

Marc threw her the look he reserved for when people were being particularly stupid.

'Don't be ridiculous, Annie. It's a cathedral.'

Annie pulled a face at him.

'You're so bloody literal, Marc. You know what I mean. Mum knew the whole town and everyone adored her. They'll all want to say goodbye.'

'There will still be enough seats for everyone, though. That's all I'm saying,' chipped in Marc, unable, as usual, to allow anyone else to have the last word.

'Whatever,' said Annie, turning her back on him. 'You can be such an arse, Marc. You know that, right?'

Bronte, used to zoning out the bickering of her siblings, continued to focus on the list in her hand. It was very long. There was barely an organisation in Ripon that wasn't represented. Her mother really had been the proverbial pillar of the community.

But there was one obvious omission.

'It's such a shame that there'll be no family coming, not from Mum's side at least,' she said thoughtfully.

'Well, she hasn't got any . . . didn't have any,' said Marc.

'I know. But it's still sad.'

Marc tutted impatiently.

'We've just established that it's going to be "standing room only".' He made air quotes with his fingers and Annie snarled at him. 'Don't worry, there'll be plenty of mourning. And there's us, and Dad's family. No one can say she won't get a decent send-off.'

'I know that. Do you think I should increase the catering order, just in case?'

'No,' chorused Marc and Annie loudly and Bronte shrank a little at the force of it. 'There's always too much food,' said Marc. 'And if it runs out then people can just wait until they get home. It won't kill them.'

Bronte stared at her brother, disbelieving.

'Sorry. Poor taste,' he said, dismissing his comment with a toss of his head.

'Dad said that loads of people have been in touch wanting to say a few words in the service,' said Annie. 'They all have stories about her. It's so cute.'

Marc frowned. 'We can't have that. It'll get completely out of hand.'

'But if people want to pay their respects . . .' objected Annie.

'Then they can, just not in the service. Imagine if everyone decided to stick in their two penn'orth. It would go on all night.'

This had the makings of an argument and Bronte, ever the diplomat, stepped in to keep the peace.

'I'm sure it will all run like clockwork,' she said appeasingly.

'Of course it will,' said Marc, as if there could be absolutely no doubt. 'The cars are coming at ten thirty. The service is at eleven. I've spoken to the vicar and he knows what he's going to say. My eulogy is written. The readings are all printed out. The orders of service are in a box in the hall. The hotel is primed and ready. I don't think I've forgotten anything.'

Marc was doing that thing he did, the oldest sibling thing that told everyone he was completely in charge and that no one detail had fallen through the cracks. It made Bronte want to run away. She was in the middle, falling squarely between Marc's confident competence and Annie's devil-may-care insouciance. The middle child, neither one thing nor the other and not really sure about any of it.

'And,' he added, 'it's not going to rain.'

He made a little ta-dah gesture with his hands, as if he could take credit for the weather on top of everything else, but then dropped them to his side, seemingly recalling what it was that he was organising so capably.

'Where's Dad?' asked Annie, looking around as if their father might have been hiding behind a door.

'He's gone for a walk,' Bronte replied. 'I told him that we . . .' She shot a glance at Marc, tacitly acknowledging his organisational skills. '. . . have everything under control and that he wasn't to worry about a thing.'

'How's he doing?' Annie asked, her tone more gentle.

She and Marc both turned to look at Bronte. As the only one of them to still be living in their home town, she was best placed to know. Bronte considered before answering.

'I think he's still in shock.'

'Well, he's not alone there,' said Marc.

'No, but we have lives of our own, away from home. Dad only had Mum. And now she's gone.'

Bronte's voice cracked as the emotion that she'd been trying to keep in check threatened to escape.

Annie wrapped an arm around her shoulder and pulled her in close.

'Oh, Bront. It's okay. You can cry. You don't have to be brave all the time.'

Bronte wasn't being especially brave, but she feared if she started to cry she might never stop. She leaned into her little sister, burrowing her face into her jumper, its soft fibres tickling her nose, and let out a shuddering sob.

'It's just not right,' she mumbled. 'She was so young. Sixty-two is no age. She had so much she wanted to do. And to die from a sting. A bloody bee sting. How is that fair?'

'How do you get to be that old without knowing you're allergic to bees?' said Marc, as if somehow their mother had been complicit in her own death.

'Well, if you've never been stung, then how would you know . . .' began Bronte.

'But that's what I mean. I've been stung loads of times. And you were that time we were playing Twister, remember?'

Bronte did remember. Being stung had hurt, but her nine-year-old self had been more upset knowing that by releasing its sting into her, the bee had caused its own death.

'I haven't,' said Annie. 'Do you think I should get tested? Now we know about Mum.'

Bronte stepped out of Annie's embrace.

'Maybe,' she said. She didn't have the energy for what she knew was coming. Annie and drama were never far apart. 'I think I'll go for a walk, get some fresh air.'

She left them to their allergy discussions and headed for the front door of their family home without much idea of where she was going. Just away, she thought.

The evening was bright, the spring sunlight still with a bit of a kick to it, and she squinted as she stepped out. She could put on her sunglasses, but she was bound to see someone who had known her mother and they might think she was being dramatic, like a bereaved celebrity perhaps. And anyhow, her sunglasses were in her bag, which was on the kitchen table. She didn't want to go back. She wanted to be outside in the fresh air where she wasn't answerable to anyone.

She walked down the steps, opened the gate and set off towards the town. The urge to text Joel was overwhelming. There was nothing that happened to her that didn't prompt a need to tell Joel all about it. It was like a compulsion, as natural to her as having her own thoughts. Have an idea, share it with Joel. That was how it had been for the last five years. That was how she had assumed it always would be.

But Joel had blocked her number. It was for their own good, he had said. Just whilst she got used to everything. She wasn't sure she ever would.

She would go to the shop instead. That was where she always went when she needed to feel safe. Her little shop, with its baskets of discarded trinkets and curios, things no longer required by the people who originally bought them but lovingly given a second chance by Bronte. It was her refuge, her port in any storm.

She snuck along the pavement, hoping that no one would notice her. That was unlikely. If you lived in a place for all your life then bumping into people you knew was unavoidable, especially when you most wanted to be on your own.

But Bronte couldn't face any more conversations today. It was lovely that everyone she met wanted to tell her how wonderful Loretta had been, a linchpin in the community who would be painfully missed. They meant well, Bronte didn't doubt it, but these conversations left her wanting to scream. She didn't care how much they would miss her mother at the Brownies, or the WI, or on the parish council, or the very many things that seemed to require her mother's attention and would evidently barely survive without her.

None of them would miss Loretta as much as Bronte did. She was already missing her mother more than anyone could possibly imagine. In fact, Bronte had no idea how she was expected to keep moving through day after day without her mother at her side.

It felt impossible.

2

On the morning of her mother's funeral, the best Bronte could say was that she was functioning. She got up, showered, dressed, and made a stab at applying a little make-up. She took in her reflection in the mirror. Her hair had lost its shine, her skin was grey and half-moons of stormy purple sat beneath her eyes.

She had not been looking her best before her mother's unexpected death. Joel had dropped his bomb into her world three months, two weeks and four days before and the fallout from that had still showed on her face when she suffered the second crushing blow. She could barely remember how she used to look and wondered whether she would ever be the same again.

But her sallow complexion and hollow eyes were the least of her concerns as she stared at herself. The greatest affront was her dress. It was a screaming fuchsia, so vibrant that you almost had to look at it side on. It glowed.

Not wearing black to the funeral had been a family decision.

'Mum wouldn't have wanted us to be sad,' said Annie.

Bronte stared at her sister and shook her head, unable to fully follow her meaning. Of course they were going to be sad. Their mother was dead, for goodness' sake.

'She'd have wanted the funeral to be a celebration of life,' Annie pressed on, glancing at them each in turn to urge their agreement.

'Not us sitting around weeping and wailing. She'd have hated that. And she hated black too.'

Bronte thought her sister was probably right, but she couldn't begin to contemplate wearing anything other than the darkest, most mournful clothing.

'So, nothing dark, then?' asked Marc. 'Is that what you're saying?'

Annie nodded enthusiastically. 'Precisely.'

Bronte looked at her father. He was older than their mother by seven years, a gap she had barely noticed before, but now he suddenly looked like the kind of old man who struggled to prise open a jar or use the self-checkout: grey, lined and bewildered by how things could have changed so much in such a short period of time.

'What do you think, Dad?' she asked. 'Would you prefer people to wear black or colour?'

Garth sat slumped in his chair, shoulders hunched and spine rounded. Everything about him screamed broken.

'I'll wear a suit,' he said in a voice that was barely audible. 'And they're all dark, but I have a jazzy tie, the one with the pink and blue flowers. Your mother bought it to cheer my wardrobe up a bit. She said that just because I was an accountant there was no need to look gloomy.'

His face blossomed into a sad smile briefly before slipping back.

Bronte reached out, took her father's hand and gave it a little squeeze. She felt no echoing response.

'So, we're agreed then?' asked Annie. 'No black?'

They had all nodded even though none of them looked fully convinced except Annie.

Now, Bronte stared at the fuchsia monstrosity in horror. She had chosen this dress because it was the brightest, boldest item she could find, hoping that wearing something so intense would signal the depth of her sorrow in Annie's topsy-turvy no-black world. But now the day had arrived, she wanted to rip it off. It screamed her pain too loudly when all she wanted to do was shrink into herself and never come out.

It was too late, however. Nothing else in her wardrobe was smart enough, or clean enough, or brightly coloured enough. She didn't even have a decent black dress. Dressing in pink felt all kinds of wrong, though, as if she was going to a wedding not a funeral. She should have stood up to her siblings, objected to the plan when she had a chance, but, as ever, she had let them get their way. She could hardly complain now when she hadn't done so then.

She made her way downstairs to wait for the time to pass. Food was too much to contemplate but she made herself a cup of coffee, which she then let go cold. Her phone buzzed endlessly. Many were messages from Marc, confirming details that she already knew, and then Annie complaining about Marc's officiousness. Then there were some from friends of her mother's sending yet more condolences, explanations why they may not be at the funeral but would get there if they possibly could, as if Bronte needed to know or would notice. They meant well, she knew that, but she couldn't bring herself to care.

Picking up her phone, she flicked to the last message from Joel. He had temporarily unblocked her to send a short and formal note expressing his sorrow at her mother's passing. Bronte had been unable to read anything in the twenty-five-word message beyond what he had intended, despite her attempts to unearth a hidden meaning.

For what must have been the thousandth time, she determined to delete the message thread. What good was it doing anyway? Reading over all the messages from happier times just made her feel more desolate and it wouldn't change the situation. Yet every time she went to remove it, she thought about how final that would be and changed her mind. It would feel like deleting her dreams, the life that she had thought lay ahead of her. She wasn't delusional – she knew he was never coming back to her – but she wasn't ready to say goodbye to all those plans. Not yet at least.

When it was time to leave for the funeral, she picked up her bag, checking for the hundredth time that it contained enough tissues. Marc had said the car would pick her up en route but parking was tricky on her little terraced street and her house was five minutes' walk from her parents'. She would make her own way there, she had told him, and he had sniffed as if this decision were breaking some unwritten funeral rule.

Avoiding her jarring reflection, Bronte left the house and pulled the door closed behind her. Outside, the day held promise. The sky wasn't quite blue but the clouds weren't very convincing, as if one decent breath of wind would see them all off. On any other day, Bronte would have enjoyed a circuit around the Seven Bridges Valley, a favourite run of hers, but there would be no running by the river today. She took a deep breath and set off towards her parents' house, keeping her head down.

As she approached, she could see a pair of sleek black cars already parked outside and her heart began to race. Was she late? Would Marc have cause to complain? She checked her watch anxiously, but no. She was exactly on time.

She averted her eyes as she walked past, not wanting to catch a glimpse of the coffin. It was silly. She knew her mother wasn't really inside – not the vibrant, capable, loving woman that she knew at least – but her body was and that was an image Bronte didn't want in her head. It would come, she knew, but she wasn't ready to face it just yet.

She turned towards the house and went up the stairs to the front door.

'Only me,' she called as she let herself in.

Marc was in the hallway, smoothing down his eyebrows in the mirror. He was wearing a red jacket that Bronte had never seen before.

'Hi,' she said. 'You look nice.'

He looked down at himself with a little shrug and then looked at her properly.

'Bloody hell. That dress takes no prisoners,' he said.

'Is it too much?' Bronte asked fearfully. She knew it was.

But Marc shook his head.

'No, it's perfect. Mum would have loved it. She always liked pink.'

This was true.

'That's what I thought,' Bronte replied, her voice barely above a whisper.

Annie tripped down the stairs in a yellow sundress covered in a daisy print, looking like she'd stepped out of a shampoo commercial.

'Morning, Bront. Great dress.'

'Thanks,' Bronte muttered. 'Is Dad okay?'

Annie squeezed her lips together and nodded tightly, making it immediately apparent that their father was far from okay.

'We'll look after him,' said Bronte, and suddenly the thought of having someone else's pain to deal with made her own feel more manageable. And then he was there on the stairs, looking so fragile and vulnerable that she had to fight the urge to go and take his arm. He gave them a thin smile.

'Don't you all look lovely,' he said. 'Your mum would have been so proud.'

Bronte felt a sob building in her chest and she closed her eyes and concentrated hard on keeping it where it was.

Finally, Marc's wife, Sara, appeared. She was wearing a trouser suit in a powder blue. It was classy and understated, and immediately made Bronte hate her choice of dress even more. Why hadn't she thought harder about her decision? Sara had a phone pressed to her ear and acknowledged them with a raise of an eyebrow as she continued her conversation.

'I know, but if Grandma said it was his turn then . . .'

She pulled the phone away from her ear and Bronte heard a child, she assumed one of her nephews, shouting the injustice of something down the line. Sara remained calm.

'I know, but I can't deal with it now. Grandma is in charge. Please do as she says. I'll see you later. Can you put Grandma back on?' There was a pause. 'Hi, Mum. Yes . . . Thanks . . . We're just leaving now . . . I'll be back around seven . . . Good . . . Will do. Bye.'

She slipped the phone into a convenient pocket in her powder-blue bag and tutted as if her children were a nuisance.

'Mum sends her love,' she said to no one in particular.

Bronte suppressed a scowl. If she had children, she wouldn't tut at them. Not that there would be any children. Not now.

'Right. Shall we go?' asked Marc. 'Might as well be waiting there as here.'

Bronte would rather have waited until the last possible second before leaving, but what was the point of that? And anyway, Marc was already outside, working out who would sit where in the car.

3

Annie had been right. The cathedral was full to bursting. Bronte stood alone on the threshold and stared at row after row of heads. Colour predominated, a veritable rainbow of shades, albeit with varying levels of commitment to the theme. One or two people were in dark coats, as if they hadn't heard, or had but couldn't bring themselves to shake off the old traditions.

Marc, her father and Annie were all pallbearers, Bronte precluded by being a head shorter than Annie, and she felt horribly at sea with no clear task to perform. Sara shuffled about next to her, muttering about what a good turnout it was, how beautiful the cathedral flowers looked, but Bronte wasn't listening and Sara quickly gave up, picking up an order of service and studying it as if she hadn't already seen one.

A couple of faces turned to look Bronte's way and offered sympathetic smiles, which she tried to return. Still people filed in. Bronte recognised her former geography teacher, the woman who coordinated the litter picking, the man who ran the hardware shop in the market square. There seemed to be no end to them, the great and the good of the city, all people whose lives her mother had touched in one way or another. It was a wonderful tribute to her, or it would have been if it wasn't so very sad.

A lady in a floral shirtwaister dress stopped, head cocked to one side, and gave Bronte the empathetic look that she was beginning to recognise. The woman was something to do with the parish council, although Bronte wasn't sure what.

'I'm so very sorry,' she said. 'Your mother was an amazing woman. So much energy and drive. She put us all to shame. It's all such a terrible shock, her passing like that. A bee sting. Honestly, who'd credit it. I can't quite take it in. I'm not sure how Ripon will manage without her.'

'Thank you,' replied Bronte weakly. 'And thank you for coming.'

'The very least I could do,' replied the woman and then bustled off to take one of the few remaining seats.

Gradually, a hush fell over the echoing space as one by one the mourners realised that the family had arrived. The organist, who had been playing something generically mournful, brought the piece to a pleasing cadence, paused, and then began to play the Chopin that the family had chosen for the entrance of the coffin. The music was unfamiliar to Bronte, a point in its favour as it had no previous associations, and she thought she was unlikely to remember it afterwards.

She could hear whispering behind her and then shuffling footsteps as the pallbearers found their rhythm, the coffin steady on broad shoulders. Bronte stepped to one side to let them pass and then fell in behind them. They walked so slowly that she worried she might overbalance. Concentrating hard on putting one foot in front of the other without wobbling, she kept her head bowed to avoid making eye contact with anyone.

Finally, they reached the front and Bronte watched, her heart in her throat, as the coffin was balanced carefully on the catafalque. Then the undertakers withdrew and the family turned towards the row of seats that had been reserved for them at the front.

Bronte's view had been blocked by the coffin but now she saw that there was someone sitting there already.

'Who's that?' whispered Annie, raising her eyebrows and nodding towards the woman.

Bronte frowned. She didn't recognise her. She had an angular face with strong bone structure and dark eyes. Her hair was white and cropped short in a spiky pixie style and she was dressed in Lycra leggings and trainers with the kind of fleece jacket that you might wear to walk a dog. Her clothing was all black but that was the only concession to the occasion.

Bronte looked at Annie and then at Marc. Marc shook his head and rolled his eyes.

'For God's sake,' he muttered under his breath. He liked things to run according to his plan and getting someone to move seats would interfere with his sense of decorum.

Bronte was less concerned. It was clearly a mistake. The woman had obviously seen a free row of chairs and sat down, not realising that this space was meant for family only, and so before Marc could be rude Bronte took the lead.

'I'm sorry,' she said quietly, 'but this row is reserved for the family.'

She expected the woman to leap to her feet, apologising wildly, but she didn't move.

Annie chipped in. 'I think there's some room at the back,' she said, gesturing with her arm, but the woman showed no sign of getting up.

Bronte, not wanting to make a fuss in front of a whole cathedral of people, sat down next to her. What did it matter who sat where anyway? The main thing was that they had a seat.

Annie frowned hard but then took her place next to Bronte, and her father sat next to her, leaving seats for Marc and Sara on the end.

However, Marc was having none of it. He tutted and muttered under his breath, unhappy with this wrinkle in his carefully curated plan. Instead of sitting down, he stood in front of the woman, looming over her.

'I really must insist that you move,' he began. 'This row is for immediate family only.'

The woman stared up at him coolly, unintimidated.

'I am immediate family,' she said.

Marc's eyebrows knotted together. 'I don't think so,' he said with the air of someone playing the winning card.

The corners of the woman's mouth turned up into a sad smile, her eyes meeting Marc's angry glare.

'I'm Etta's sister,' she said.

4

1981 – London

The world was Loretta's oyster and it felt amazing. Twenty-one years old, recently graduated from a top university with a first-class degree in journalism and a job lined up with the *Daily Chronicle* on Fleet Street. It really didn't get much better than this and Loretta was riding the crest of the wave.

The best part was that she had done it all herself. When she'd said she wanted to work on a newspaper, her mother had assumed she wanted to be a secretary and had been delighted by her daughter's aspirations. When Loretta explained her true ambitions, her mother had been doubtful. 'Are you sure, love?' she'd asked with concern in her voice. 'People like us don't do jobs like that,' which had made Loretta all the more determined to succeed. No one was going to tell her what she could and couldn't do – she didn't care who they were.

And she had made it. She didn't want to brag and pulled her face into as neutral an expression as she could manage when talking to her fellow graduates who were still searching for a position, but inside her heart sang. Loretta Halliday, daughter of a welder and a laundress and hailing from a council estate in Barnet, was on her way right to the top.

But the job didn't start until September and today was her graduation ceremony. Loretta was the first Halliday to go to university and so her parents' pride in what she'd achieved was mixed with a fear of showing themselves up in front of the other families. There had been huge consternation over what they should wear so they 'didn't let our Etta down'. Loretta wasn't sure what was expected but she thought her mother's hat might be a step too far and was relieved when it was left behind, although she was touched by how seriously they were taking her big day.

Loretta's main concern was whether their rusting Austin Allegro would make the journey without overheating at the side of the road, which was a regular event. So far, however, all was well. Her parents were in the front seats and she and her younger sister, Natalie, were in the back. Natalie sprawled, her head resting in Loretta's lap and her bare toes sticking out of the window. The rest of her was folded in a way that was clearly uncomfortable if the way she wriggled and squirmed was anything to go by.

She groaned quietly.

'I am never drinking again. Don't let me, Etta. Promise.'

Their mother turned round in her seat.

'What was that?' she asked.

Natalie widened her eyes at Loretta, imploring her not to tell, and Loretta grinned back. Natalie's secrets were safe with her. Her own teenage years had had their fair share of high jinks but she had been positively angelic by comparison. However, what their parents didn't know wouldn't hurt them and Loretta was always on Natalie's case, making sure she didn't get in any serious trouble.

'Nat was just saying . . .' Loretta began, her mind working hard to make something up, but her mother cut across her.

'Oh, Natalie. Sit up straight, would you. You're creasing Etta's dress. And put your feet down. What will people think?'

'They'll think that they wish they could ride along with their toes in the fresh air,' replied Natalie, but she shuffled herself up to a sitting position and then slumped down the other way so her head was resting against the door.

'Are we nearly there yet?' she asked their father in time-honoured tradition, but he ignored her. 'Now, the letter says we get a drink on arrival,' said her mother, peering for the hundredth time at the details for the ceremony.

'Do you think they'll have beer?' asked her father.

'You'll take what you're offered and not make a fuss,' said her mother. Her eyes dropped back to the very well-thumbed letter. 'And you have to collect your cap and gown, Etta. Where do you go for that then?'

Loretta could feel her mother's panic starting to bubble up again.

'It's fine, Mum. I'm sure it'll all be clear when we get there. And I can just ask someone if I'm not sure.'

Her mother looked horrified at this, as if asking for help would reveal the extent of her ignorance, but she refolded the letter and put it back in her bag.

'What's it matter if we do the wrong thing,' said her father. 'We're the Hallidays and we have just as much right to be there as anyone else.'

He turned round in his seat to nod at Loretta and her mother nudged him in the ribs.

'Watch the road, Bob,' she hissed. 'You'll have us all dead in a ditch.'

Her father turned back round.

'What about you, Natalie?' he asked. 'Do you fancy all this university business?'

'Yes, maybe you can have a look round, Natalie,' suggested her mother. Now that she had got used to the idea of one of her children at university, she wasn't entirely averse to the other one going too. Loretta knew how she liked to brag when she was at the laundrette.

'Face it, Mum. I'm never going to uni,' replied Natalie tetchily. 'I probably won't even pass my exams.'

Her mother made an exasperated clicking sound with her tongue.

'Well, I don't know. Your father and me never had these opportunities. We left school at fourteen, you know, and straight into work.'

'There weren't two and a half million people on the dole back then, Mum. Things are different now.'

'All the more reason to get some good qualifications behind you like our Etta has done.'

Loretta smirked at Natalie in the back of the car and Natalie mimed putting a gun to her head and pulling the trigger. Their mother was still going on but neither girl was listening.

'Blah, blah, blah,' Loretta mouthed at Natalie, who squeezed her lips together to stop herself laughing. Then Natalie put a hand over her forehead and groaned quietly.

'Don't make me laugh,' she whispered. 'It makes my headache worse.'

'What was that?' asked their mother, turning round again, this time with an expression that said she knew they were up to something but didn't quite know what. It was an expression that was very familiar.

'Nothing,' they both chorused.

'A bit of radio, I think,' said her mother and turned the car stereo on. 'Oh, lovely. David Jacobs.'

With the music on they were safe to chat without being overheard. Loretta eyed her sister, who looked decidedly wan.

'Where did you go last night?' she asked. 'After I saw you.'

Natalie looked up as she thought about it.

'I saw you in The Midland?' she said, apparently not at all sure about the shape of her evening.

Loretta nodded encouragingly.

'So, after that we went to The Crown, and then The Cottage, and then The Star, I think. It's a bit hazy.'

'The Star?! Bloody hell.'

Natalie groaned again.

'I know. Shoot me now.' She slumped a little further down the door but then she seemed to rally.

'But I'll be fine by the time we get there,' she said. 'I won't do anything to spoil my big sister's special day.' She beamed at Loretta, who rolled her eyes and shook her head.

'There'll be fizzy wine,' Loretta said knowingly, and Natalie pretended to vomit.

'Seriously though, sis,' Natalie said. 'I'm dead proud of you. You are going to be the hottest newshound in London. You'll be sniffing out all the big stories. The others don't stand a chance. In fact, they might as well just give up now.'

Loretta threw her a grateful smile.

'I don't suppose I'll be doing much more than making the tea to start with,' she said.

'Yeah, but you'll be there, though. That's the thing. On the spot.'

Natalie's face slipped and Loretta grabbed her bare foot and began to massage the arch, rubbing hard with her thumbs.

'You'll find your thing, too,' she said. 'I'm just lucky because I know what I want to do.'

'There's no luck here, Etta. Everything you have is because you worked so bloody hard to get it.'

There was no point denying what they both knew to be true.

'You'll work it out, Nat,' she said.

'Or I can just sit around on my backside scrounging from the state like the rest of the working class. Or shouldn't I believe what I read in the paper?'

She winked at Loretta.

'Wait until I'm writing it,' Loretta said. 'Then you can believe it.'

5

The graduation had gone well. Despite her mother's misgivings, her parents hadn't put a foot out of place, although they had been the only family to whoop when the Vice Chancellor handed over the certificate. Loretta was just pleased that she'd managed to get up on to the stage without tripping over her gown and had taken possession of her Bachelor of Arts (Hons) without mishap.

After the ceremony, she had posed for endless photographs, which she doubted anyone would ever look at again. There had been the obligatory one with her and her parents, the photographer staging the photo so that nothing about it looked natural, but then Natalie had crashed into the group.

'I'm part of this family too even if I don't have a fancy degree,' she said in a mock-indignant tone and dropped to her knees in front of the three of them, arms akimbo. 'So, go on, Mr Photographer Man! Take our picture.'

The photographer had looked horrified at this break with decorum but, probably anxious to get this unruly creature away from his cubicle as quickly as possible, had obliged. Loretta didn't doubt that of all the photos taken that day, the one of the four of them, with her and Natalie creased with giggles and their parents looking somewhere between proud and mortified, would be the one she would want to keep when the envelope of proofs thudded on to the doormat.

And now she was back at home, her student life, which had passed in the blink of an eye, completed. She was ready to move on to whatever was coming next, but not before a long, lazy and hopefully hot summer had drifted by.

Their family home, never tidy at the best of times, was in a state of chaos. Loretta had returned with boxes and bags, the detritus of three years living away, which were still piled up in the hall and on the landing whilst they worked out where the duplicated kitchen equipment, bedding and all those books would go until she moved out again.

'It's hardly worth unpacking,' said Natalie. 'You'll be living in some smart flat in Highgate by the end of the summer.'

Loretta thought that a single room in the depths of Kentish Town was more likely on the pittance she was going to be earning, but she liked the idea of having a place of her own rather than commuting from home. It made her feel like a grown-up.

Adding to the mess she had brought with her was her parents' holiday packing. They were going away for their twenty-fifth wedding anniversary – a road trip around Brittany in France – and seemed to be planning to take everything they owned with them.

'You do know that Brittany is barely any further south than we are?' asked Natalie, picking up their father's Speedo swimming trunks between finger and thumb and dangling them in the air.

'We might be lucky with the weather,' their mother said. 'You never know.'

'We're always lucky,' chipped in her father. 'It's the Halliday way. The sun shines on us wherever we go. It can't help itself.'

Loretta rolled her eyes, but there was a grain of truth in his words. They did seem to be blessed, the four of them. Nothing ever happened that they couldn't deal with by pulling together. She had been brought up with a strong sense of Team Halliday and the older she got, the more she appreciated just how precious that was.

'I don't think you need a travel kettle, Mum,' she said, suppressing a smile. 'I'm sure they have kettles over there.'

'Well, your father likes a decent cup of tea in the morning so I'm taking PG Tips too.' She waved a box in the air. 'And Marmite. There may be no Marmite in France.'

'I think they have shops,' said Natalie. 'And tea. Honestly, Mum. You're never going to get all this stuff in the car. And you'll never squeeze any duty-free in on the way back. Can't pass up all that cheap booze.'

Their mother straightened her spine as if she had been issued with a personal challenge.

'Where there's a will, there's a way,' she said.

The next morning, everything bar the kitchen sink was packed into the car and they were ready to say their goodbyes. Just before they left, Loretta's mother pulled her to one side.

'You'll look after your sister, won't you?' she said. 'Try to stop her getting in a state about her exam results and don't let her go out drinking every night. She thinks I don't know but . . .' Her mother rolled her eyes.

'Don't worry,' Loretta replied. 'I'll keep an eye on her. You just concentrate on having a wonderful holiday. Send us a postcard and take loads of photos.'

Her mother's head spun round to look at her father in horror.

'You did pack the camera?'

'And five rolls of film,' he replied, giving her an indulgent smile. 'Now come on. Finish your goodbyes and let's get going or we'll miss the ferry.'

Natalie appeared at her side and they watched and waved until the car drove out of sight.

‘Fancy still wanting to go on holiday together after twenty-five years of marriage,’ said Natalie as they went back inside the house. ‘Bloody miracle.’

‘I think it’s romantic,’ replied Loretta. ‘Brittany though. When I’ve been married for twenty-five years I want to be going to Barbados.’

‘You always did have ideas above your station,’ laughed Natalie. ‘What’s wrong with Southend?’

6

The next day was gloriously hot, in London at least. Loretta hoped it was the same in France for their parents. Their house had a backyard rather than a garden but it was south facing and Natalie had taken most of the bedding from her bed and repositioned it on the concrete slabs. There she lay, wearing a bikini made from less fabric than a handkerchief and a pair of their mother's sunglasses, a bottle of Coppertone sun oil at her side. She raised her sunglasses lazily as Loretta appeared.

'Two whole weeks,' she sighed. 'Two weeks without anyone mentioning exam results, or jobs or my future.' Then she propped herself up on an elbow and stared at Loretta with narrowed eyes. 'You'd better not start on with all that.'

Loretta lay down next to her. The quilt was warm from the sun and smelled lightly of Natalie but the concrete beneath that was hard and unyielding.

'Not my job, Nat,' she said. 'What you do with your future is up to you. I've got my own life to think about.'

She gazed up at the sky above their heads. It was a piercing blue and streaked with gauzy clouds, so high they were barely there at all.

'God, isn't this bliss?' sighed Natalie. 'I've been dreaming about the summer all year. Just lazing about doing nothing.'

'Me too,' replied Loretta, thinking of the days she'd spent in the library revising for her finals and the guilt that had dogged her when she'd given herself any time off.

They lay side by side in silence for a while, just soaking up the warmth.

'I can feel myself getting browner,' Natalie said eventually. 'This summer I'm going to get really, really tanned, proper Mediterranean brown. Like the woman on that advert. You know.'

Loretta did but she wasn't really interested in tanning. She didn't have time for it. The world was full of stories that she needed to investigate and she couldn't waste her whole summer on something as trivial as lazing around in the sun.

'I think I'll switch to baby oil tomorrow,' Natalie mused. 'That suntan lotion's nearly run out anyway.' And then, out of nowhere, 'Let's have a party.'

Loretta briefly considered the pros and cons of the idea although it didn't really matter what she said. Natalie would go ahead anyway.

'Okay,' she agreed, 'but we'd better do it sooner rather than later in case anything needs fixing afterwards.'

'This Saturday then?' suggested Natalie enthusiastically. 'I'll see who's around. We could have a barbecue if it stays like this. Sharon's got one at her house. I'll ask her if she'll lend it. What do you reckon?'

'Why not?'

Loretta stood up. Natalie didn't move but opened one eye.

'Where are you going?' she asked.

'Inside to get a pen and paper. This requires a proper list!'

'You're so bloody organised,' said Natalie and closed her eyes again.

Pretty soon they had the makings of a decent party.

'People can bring their own booze and whatever they want to barbecue and we'll just buy bread buns and ketchup. That won't cost much. We can take it out of the money Dad left us.'

'If we live on baked beans for the rest of the two weeks,' laughed Loretta. 'Do you want to make some tapes, then we won't have to bring my record player outside.'

Natalie pulled her knees into her chest and squealed. 'Will do. It's going to be ace,' she said with a broad grin. 'I need something to look forward to.' Then her grin slipped a little. 'I'm not going to go to uni.'

She was trying to sound casual, Loretta could tell, but she suspected this was the first time the idea had been voiced out loud. 'I know you liked it but it's not for me. No one else is going either. Most of my mates didn't even stay on at school. I'm going to travel instead, see the world. I might go grape picking in France. People do that, don't they? Or maybe get some bar work. What do you think?'

She looked up at Loretta and Loretta understood that her sister was seeking her support and approval.

'Sounds good,' she replied obligingly. 'When do you want to go?'

Natalie shrugged. 'Don't know yet.' She paused, biting at her knuckle. 'Do you think Mum and Dad will be upset?'

Loretta didn't hesitate. 'No. They'll understand. But you need to have a proper plan. You can't just drift about.'

'I know. I thought I could get a job here for a bit, save up and then maybe go next year.'

Loretta tipped her head to one side and considered her baby sister. At eighteen she still looked like a child, certainly not old enough to go off and explore the world on her own. Then again, Loretta must have looked this young when she left home three years before, and she had known she was grown-up enough to cope.

Natalie was different though. There was a fragility to her, a vulnerability that Loretta didn't share. No, it wasn't vulnerability, she corrected herself. It was more wistful than that. Natalie was a dreamer, imagining her way into fantasy worlds that only touched reality here and there. And really, what was wrong with that? Just because Loretta was driven to an end goal didn't mean Natalie's lack of a plan made her any more fragile.

'Etta?' Natalie said, cutting through her musings. 'Could I do that, do you think?'

'Yes,' replied Loretta. 'I'm sure you could.'

7

The day of the party rolled round. The fine weather was holding, and Loretta had set the borrowed barbecue up on the back wall. The kids from the street came and peered at it, many of them not having seen one before and not sure why you might want to cook outside when there was a perfectly good oven in the kitchen.

The houses on their street were all so close together that everyone knew everyone else's business. They might have a guest list but basically anyone might turn up to the party and it would be hard to turn them away.

They put the kitchen chairs out in the yard and borrowed a wallpapering table from next door, throwing a ticking sheet over it to hide the paint splatters.

Loretta hoped that with a bit of luck the only reason their guests would have to go inside would be to use the bathroom, but she had been to enough parties to know that things seldom worked like that. Still, their parents weren't particularly precious about the house. As long as nothing got completely ruined it should all be fine.

Natalie came out carrying her huge portable tape player and an extension lead.

'Where am I plugging this in? If we run it on batteries it'll only last five seconds.'

They threaded the cable through the open kitchen window and Loretta took it and stretched it over to the tape player.

'Perfect,' she said. 'Are those the tapes?' she asked.

Natalie nodded. 'Me and Chrissie have done loads.'

Loretta picked a couple up and ran her eyes down the inserts. Madness, Blondie, Bowie, The Jam, a few disco standards. She approved.

The party started small, closest friends arriving first. They stood in the yard, bottles in hand, edging round to stay in the sun's glow until it slipped below the roofs of the surrounding houses. Gradually, more guests arrived and soon the yard was full of people and sound. Those that couldn't fit in spilled over into the alley behind or sat up high on the walls, their legs swinging.

'Turn it up,' shouted someone when Toyah's 'I Want to be Free' came on. Loretta could hear Natalie leading the singing, blasting out the lyrics with gusto as if it had been written with her in mind.

They were mainly Natalie's friends. Loretta had lost touch with most of hers after she went away, their lives diverging. Some of them were married now and a couple had children, a prospect that terrified Loretta. She didn't mind. She would make new friends, she thought. And she wouldn't have to tell them anything about her past. She could reinvent herself to match her new life.

She knew it probably sounded pompous if she were to say it out loud, but Loretta wanted to use the news as a force for good. She saw herself seeking out the stories that really mattered and giving a voice to the ignored and overlooked. It wouldn't happen overnight, she was well aware of how hard the road ahead would be, but her intentions were clear. The press was the backbone of a strong democracy, providing clear information to discuss and challenge the issues of the day. And she was going to be right up there with the best of them.

'Penny for them?'

Loretta looked up to see Liz and her face broke into a grin. Liz was her oldest friend. Thrust together on the first day of primary school, they had stuck together ever since.

'I was just thinking about what's next,' Loretta replied. 'You know. Dreams. Life goals. Trivial stuff like that.'

Liz sat down next to her and they clinked bottles.

'Who'd have thought it?' she said. 'Loretta and Liz all grown up and heading out into the big wide world.' She punched Loretta playfully on the arm.

'It's a long time since warm milk in the infants,' Loretta said.

'Isn't it? Did I tell you I've got a new job? At Radio Rentals, so if you need a new telly I'm your woman.'

'Congratulations! That's great.'

Liz pulled a face. 'Not as great as your swanky new job but the pay's not bad for a girl with only four O levels.'

They chattered on, sharing gossip about the people they knew until close to midnight when Liz left to go home.

'See you soon. Don't forget us,' she said, wrapping Loretta in her arms and pulling her in for a tight squeeze.

'As if! Liz and Loretta forever!' she replied, and meant it, but actually this whole evening had an end-of-era feeling to it. Loretta was moving on and whilst she didn't want to accept it there were bound to be some changes, some things that got left behind. And some people.

It was almost two o'clock when Loretta heard shouting from inside the house where, inevitably, some of the partygoers had drifted. A few people had left, but the party was still going strong, as if the remainder were pushing on through to morning.

'She's outside,' someone said. And then, 'Where's Nat?'

Loretta looked over but didn't get up. If someone wanted her, she wasn't hard to find. There seemed to be a little gaggle of people tipping out through the kitchen door and into the yard.

‘That’s Etta, in the red top,’ someone said, pointing at her, and then she saw that there were two uniformed police officers at the centre of the group. One of the neighbours must have complained about the noise.

Loretta stood up, raising her palms in supplication as if they were coming to arrest her.

‘I’m sorry,’ she said before the police had a chance to ask her. ‘Is it too loud? We’ll turn it down. Nat! Can you turn the music down.’

The policemen kept approaching, nothing about their demeanour changed by her clear capitulation, and Loretta wondered what else might have brought them to the house. She was pretty certain there was no pot but she had a surreptitious sniff just to check.

‘Loretta Halliday?’ they asked.

Loretta nodded.

‘What’s this about?’ she asked. ‘Is there a problem?’

The older of the two officers was closest to her but he ignored her questions. ‘Is your sister, Natalie Halliday, here?’ he asked.

Loretta’s mind was racing. She was certain she hadn’t done anything to merit a visit from the police but she couldn’t guarantee that Natalie hadn’t. She decided to play things very politely until she knew what was going on.

‘Yes,’ she said. ‘She’s over there. Nat! Can you come here a minute?’

Natalie, who had been sprawling against the wall, stood up and began to walk towards them, clearly concentrating hard so she didn’t appear as drunk as she presumably was.

‘What’s up?’ she asked when she got close enough. She was slurring a little and her eyes were glazed and slightly unfocused.

‘Is there somewhere private where we can talk?’ asked the policeman. His tone didn’t suggest that they were in trouble, but

Loretta had read enough about police brutality to know that you couldn't drop your guard.

'Whatever it is, you can say it here,' said Natalie. Her tone was more aggressive than Loretta thought wise and she tried to signal as such, but Natalie's attention was on the policeman.

'I think it would be better if we went inside,' said the policeman.

He had kind eyes, Loretta thought, and there was a kind of meekness to his partner too, a woman, that she hadn't seen when they were further away. Something wasn't right.

'Okay,' she said.

The policeman gestured towards the back door.

'Thank you,' he said. 'I'm afraid we have some bad news.'

8

Loretta's heart was thumping in her chest as she led the officers into the house. The group of friends who had gathered to see what was going on parted to let them pass and she could hear their whispered questions. Natalie had questions too.

'What's going on?' she kept asking, each time louder than before, but Loretta had no answer for her.

'Let's just see what they have to say,' she said quietly, trying to appease Natalie, but really she was just as desperate to know.

There were party guests everywhere, many not having noticed the presence of the police, and Loretta stood in the kitchen, not really sure what to do next. The policeman pushed through the crowd and headed back into the hallway.

'Is this the lounge?' he asked, putting his hand on the door handle. He was missing the top joint of his middle finger, Loretta noticed, and she started to wonder how that might have happened. She forced her mind back to the present situation.

She nodded and he opened the door. There were people in there too – so much for keeping the party outside. She was about to suggest they try the dining room when the policeman spoke.

'Can you all please leave this room,' he said in a tone that suggested an order rather than a request, and the guests moved without question. Someone mouthed 'Okay?' at Loretta as they passed and someone else touched her arm and squeezed it gently.

'What do you want with them?' snarled one of Natalie's mates. 'You can't just come barging into people's houses when they ain't done nothing.'

Loretta put up a hand to show that it was all okay and they didn't need defending, but she knew the people round there were naturally suspicious of the police and would always assume some kind of fit-up, and she was grateful for the support, however misguided.

The female officer closed the door behind them and the world fell quiet, the music and chatter muted.

'Shall we sit down?' asked the older one.

Loretta had questions, but all her newly learned journalistic techniques deserted her and she was left unable to articulate them. Natalie was still wittering about unwelcome interruptions and getting back to the party but her objections were losing steam.

They all sat, she and Natalie on the sofa and a police officer perched on each armchair, a pair of unlikely bookends. Loretta's curiosity was starting to swamp her anxiety. What on earth could be justifying all this fuss?

The officers exchanged glances and then the older one spoke.

'You are Loretta and Natalie Halliday?' he began, which irritated Loretta as that much was obvious. She nodded quickly, urging him to move on.

'We received a telephone call from the British Consulate in France . . .'

Loretta didn't know anyone in France.

'They were calling to say that two bodies have been found in a guesthouse in the Saint-Malo area. We believe the bodies to be Robert and Patricia Halliday.'

He paused as Loretta took in what he was saying.

'That's our parents,' she said. 'They're on holiday in France. For their twenty-fifth wedding anniversary.'

So this couldn't be them, she wanted to add, but it was dawning on her exactly what she was being told.

'They were found by the guesthouse staff. Their absence was noticed when they failed to attend their meals and someone went to check. The scene suggested that they had died in their sleep the day before yesterday. The French police believe that it may have been carbon monoxide poisoning.'

Loretta stared at him. Blinking seemed to be the only movement she was capable of. Beside her, Natalie was also unnaturally motionless, as if the entire scene were a still from a film.

'It can't be them,' she said. 'Can't be.' And then, 'Are you sure?'

It seemed to be a struggle for the policeman to maintain eye contact but he didn't let his gaze drop. He swallowed.

'Their passports were amongst their possessions. They were identified from the passport photographs. There is no doubt. I'm so very sorry.'

Nobody spoke. Loretta could hear the dull beat of the party music and outside a girl screeched playfully, others laughing in response.

'Is there someone we can ring for you?' the female officer asked. 'A relative?'

Loretta shook her head. Their parents were both only children, one of the things that had brought them together in the first place. There were just the four of them. Team Halliday. They didn't need anyone else.

'You shouldn't be alone at a time like this,' said the woman.

Loretta gestured towards the door.

'We're hardly alone,' she said.

'Yes, but an adult . . .'

'We're both adults,' Loretta snapped at her.

The woman backed down, mumbling an apology.

Natalie spoke then, her voice calm with no hint of a slur.

'What happens now?' she asked.

'This is the number of the Foreign and Commonwealth Office. They will be able to give you more details. The line is open twenty-four hours a day, but perhaps it might be better to wait until morning . . .'

He held out a printed card. Loretta stared at his hand with its missing joint for a moment, fascinated by it, and then, realising that she was supposed to take the card, she leaned across to reach it.

Suddenly, she wanted them to leave. They had done what they came for. They were no longer required. She stood up.

'Thank you,' she said. 'You can go now. We will ring the . . .'

'Foreign and Commonwealth Office,' the policewoman offered.

'Yes, them. In the morning.'

Natalie stood too but the officers seemed reluctant to move.

'We'll be fine,' said Loretta.

'Shall we ask your guests to leave?'

Loretta had no idea. She didn't know what to do or say.

'No, thank you,' said Natalie quickly. 'We can do it. We can do everything.'

The police muttered their condolences again and allowed themselves to be steered towards the front door.

'We will be in touch tomorrow,' said the woman. 'And once again, we're so very sorry.'

Loretta could sense that the woman was looking at her, wanting to make eye contact, but she didn't raise her head, not wanting to see the pity in her expression.

'Thank you,' she said and closed the door behind them.

Word that there were police in the house seemed to have spread, so when Loretta turned away from the front door a small crowd of people had gathered in the hall behind her, looking expectant. Natalie's friend Chrissie was the first to come rushing over to ask what was going on. But she took one look at their faces and pulled them both into a hug without asking any questions. Loretta felt Natalie release into her friend's embrace, convulsing in sobs almost at once. Loretta stood very still, aware of the warmth from Chrissie's body seeping into her own.

'Mum and Dad are dead,' Natalie managed to say between gulps.

'What?' replied Chrissie, pushing Natalie to arm's length and staring at her, confused by the news.

'They're dead,' Natalie said again. 'In France.'

'No.' Chrissie took a moment to let this sink in. 'What happened? I mean, how?'

'They think it was carbon monoxide poisoning,' replied Loretta numbly.

'Oh my God.' Chrissie's mouth fell open. 'Shit.'

Loretta was aware of muttering growing louder around them as the story was repeated for those who hadn't caught it first time or couldn't believe what they'd heard. Chrissie spoke over them.

'Right. You two go in the lounge. I'm going to make some tea. Everyone else, the party's over. Let's clear everything up so Etta and Nat don't have to deal with all this mess in the morning.'

Loretta started to object, but then she saw the sense of this and let Chrissie take control. Blindly, she allowed herself to be guided back into the lounge. She felt Natalie grasping for her hand and she clutched at it as if they were little girls once more. Natalie was squeezing so tightly that she could feel the bones in her fingers crunch together but she didn't pull her hand free.

They dropped on to the sofa, almost sitting on top of one another.

'They can't be dead,' whispered Natalie. 'Not dead.' And then, 'What are we going to do?'

'I don't know,' replied Loretta.

What else was there to say?

9

They must have fallen asleep because when Loretta opened her eyes it was no longer dark outside. Natalie was curled up against her, her head resting on Loretta's chest. She was sleeping so peacefully and it took Loretta a moment to work out why they weren't in their beds. Then she saw Chrissie asleep in an armchair and she remembered.

The party. The police. Their parents.

A wave of something she couldn't quite identify engulfed her and she struggled to catch a full breath. Her parents. Her lovely, funny, hard-working, reliable, proud parents were gone. It was such an unbelievable concept. How could it be true? And what was she meant to do now? She was twenty-one. She knew nothing about anything. And there was Natalie. She was basically a child.

Loretta squeezed her eyes shut, took three deep, calming breaths and then opened them. Nothing had changed. She had to cope. It was all up to her. Her back was stiff and she eased herself into a different position carefully so she didn't wake Natalie. She had to be practical. There would be time enough for emotion later but right now she had to work out what they needed to do. Natalie wasn't good at that kind of thing at the best of times, which this most certainly was not. So that was that. It was all down to her. There was no one else.

There was no one else.

She let these words settle for a moment. The two of them were entirely on their own, tossed into the depths of the adult ocean when she had only been dipping her toe in the water.

It was up to her to take control. She was the elder sister and was far better equipped after three years away from home to deal with the practicalities. And she could do it. She would start by ringing that number on the card the police had given her. Somebody there would tell her how this worked. They would fly her parents home, she assumed. She had no idea who *they* were. And what about the car?

The thought that she might have to go to France herself panicked her. That felt impossible. She couldn't leave Natalie and anyway, what would be the point? Her parents were dead. Going wouldn't change anything. There would be questions, an investigation, blame to apportion, but none of that was for now. Now she had to deal with one step at a time.

However, her mind wasn't working in a one-step-at-a-time kind of fashion. It leapt from one impossible obstacle to the next. What about the funeral? How would they find the money to pay for that, to pay for anything, in fact? There was the house, the bills? Loretta had no idea where to start piecing it all together and once again she felt her chest start to constrict.

Next to her Natalie began to stir and Loretta stroked her sister's hair, hoping it would feel soothing. She didn't want her to wake up frightened.

'It's me,' she whispered. 'I'm here. Are you okay?'

Natalie sat up and stared straight at her. Her eye make-up had smudged down her face and she was deathly pale, the hard-won suntan lost overnight.

'It's not true, is it?' she asked. 'Tell me it didn't really happen, Etta. They're not really dead, are they?'

Her eyes, wide and imploring, searched Loretta's face for a different reality, but what could Loretta say?

'I'm sorry,' she replied, her own eyes brimming over with tears as she saw Natalie's face collapse. Then Natalie threw herself into Loretta's arms and they held each other tightly, Natalie murmuring that it couldn't have happened and there must have been some terrible mistake.

Chrissie woke then and took Loretta's place comforting Natalie whilst Loretta went to make them a drink, more for something to do than because she was thirsty. She thought about digging out the brandy that her mother used for the family Christmas cake. There would be no more of her mother's Christmas cakes. The thought pummelled into her chest, blow after blow, each landing directly on top of the last.

Not brandy, she decided. Coffee instead. There would be time enough for brandy.

The house was tidier than it had been before the party. Chrissie must have coordinated a huge team. The washing-up was done and put away and all the rubbish cleared from the yard. Someone had even mopped the floor; Loretta could smell the clean scent of Ajax. Mum would be pleased, she thought.

And then she remembered again.

They stumbled through that day, and the next and the one after that. Kathleen at the Foreign and Commonwealth Office was wonderful, calmly steering Loretta through the procedure for the repatriation of the bodies with just the right blend of efficiency and sympathy. She and Natalie coped without any histrionics, both of them staying resolutely stoical. It was almost as if there were an unspoken fear that if they gave any indication of not coping, some official channel would swoop in and take control.

However, that wasn't going to happen. They were both grown-up and deemed capable of dealing with their own business. The world didn't care that they had suddenly become orphans overnight. They were simply two adults dealing with the deaths of other adults; an everyday occurrence with nothing remarkable about it, bar the unfortunate location of the deaths.

Eventually, the bodies were returned. Investigations, inquiries and the stamping of forms meant that this seemed to take forever and by the time they could finally hold the funeral – a modest affair publicised by word of mouth only and with no wake because organising one was beyond what they had to give – the starting date for Loretta's job was upon them.

There would be no little flat in Kentish Town. How could she leave Natalie now? But she found that she was almost relieved to have an excuse not to move out. She had no stomach for yet more change, couldn't dig deep enough to uncover the resources necessary. And she was fine at home, for now at least.

Gradually, the administration of death was dealt with, each piece falling into place like a macabre jigsaw, until the two of them would eventually subsume their parents' affairs entirely. The house, the bank accounts, the car would all be transferred as if they had always belonged to them. To the outside world, nothing at 27 Solomon Street looked any different.

But inside everything had changed.

10

The day Loretta was due to start work, the heavens opened. The outfit she had thought to wear looked too lightweight and she had to have a last-minute change of plan. She hoped she looked the part – serious but with a sense of humour, stylish but practical, fitting in yet standing out. Was that too much for one set of clothes to convey? She would try nonetheless.

She reached the *Daily Chronicle*'s offices on Fleet Street, her stomach churning. She had pictured this: her standing on the pavement and staring up at the frontage of the building that represented all her endeavours until now and everything she hoped to achieve in the future. In her imagination, the moment had taken on an almost reverential significance, something that would stay with her for a lifetime and that she would recount to young recruits when she herself was a grande dame of journalism.

However, reality did not live up to the movie-worthy scene she had created in her head. She found herself being bundled inside by a man in a mackintosh with a large black umbrella.

'Don't just stand there in the rain getting in the way,' he said, not unpleasantly. 'You're coming in here, are you?'

She was flustered and wet and this wasn't at all how she'd pictured stepping over the threshold into the hallowed offices, but she offered the man her best smile and then there was an unsightly dance as he tried to negotiate his umbrella whilst holding the door open for her at the same time.

Eventually, they were both inside and dripping on the chequered linoleum. The man shook out his umbrella, droplets of rain landing on her sopping coat, and began to furl it efficiently. Loretta took a metaphorical deep breath and determined to begin as she meant to go on. Confidently and with an air of being in control.

'I'm Loretta Halliday,' she said, thrusting her hand towards him.

He looked at it then up at her but had no hand spare to shake it with.

'Pleased to meet you,' he said instead, with what she feared might be an indulgent smile. 'I'm Malcolm Penn. I know. Great name for a journalist. I call it fate. And what brings you here, Loretta Halliday?'

Loretta tilted her chin upwards ever so slightly.

'I'm starting work here today,' she said. 'Apprentice in the newsroom.'

'Are you, by God,' he said. 'Well, you'd better come with me. This way.'

He set off in the direction of the stairs, clearly expecting Loretta to follow. She wasn't sure what to do. She had been told to announce herself at the reception desk, which she could see at the far end of the hall. As she dithered, Malcolm Penn had reached the double doors that she assumed led to the staircase and he turned to see where she was. Finding her still standing where he had left her, he called over.

'Are you coming, Miss Halliday?' he asked.

Loretta's glance flitted between him and the reception desk and he seemed to grasp her dilemma.

'Susan,' he called over to the reception desk. 'This is Loretta Halliday, starting here today on the apprentice scheme. I'll take her upstairs with me. Tell the powers that be, would you?'

'Right you are, Mr Penn,' replied Susan and immediately picked up her telephone.

'There. That's sorted. Now, are you coming or am I destined to hold this door open forever never quite being able to get my teeth into whatever juicy story awaits me, like some kind of modern-day Tantalus?'

'Sorry,' said Loretta, and virtually ran across the hall to him.

As they climbed the stairs – 'the lift can be temperamental' – he quizzed her on her life thus far including where she was from, where she'd studied and what her main ambitions were. As she fired back answers, it occurred to her that she was witnessing a real journalist in action, relieving her of information as easily as breathing.

He was puffing a little by the time they reached the top.

'Not as fit as I should be,' he confessed. 'Too many fags. Not enough apples. Right. We're through here.'

Loretta still had no idea why he had taken her under his wing and whether his actions were appropriate, but she was committed to them now and just had to hope that he wasn't going to play some terrible practical joke on her and leave her locked in a stationery cupboard all day.

He didn't seem the type for that kind of caper, though. He was old, for a start – forties at least – with soft frog-like features and thinning, slightly greasy hair that was pushed off his wide forehead but kept flopping forward, forcing him to scrape it back almost constantly. His John Lennon glasses were smeared but that might just have been the rain. He looked fundamentally benign.

They reached a half-glazed double door, which he pushed open and then paused on the threshold.

'Behold! The newsroom.'

Loretta stared, awestruck at this veritable hive of frantic activity.

The first thing that struck her was the noise. Typewriters clattered on almost every desk and people shouted back and forth at one another to spare themselves the effort of getting up. Piles of papers were scattered over desks, and in-trays overflowed on to the floor. Everywhere people were striding about with a sense of purpose, as if there were somewhere they should have been five minutes earlier. The atmosphere was alive with electrifying energy and thick with cigarette smoke, butts burning in ashtrays on almost every surface.

Along the far wall was a string of offices, all with glass fronts. Venetian blinds hung at jaunty angles at some and were fully drawn at others. The only women she could see in the room were stationed directly outside each glass-fronted office. There seemed to be no women in the central space at all.

'Welcome to the madhouse,' said Malcolm, raising his voice a little so that he could be heard over the racket. 'Let's go and speak to Anthea. She knows everything. She'll sort you out.'

Loretta followed him across the room. One or two men looked up from their typing as she went past but no one seemed interested in her. She tried to look confident but she could feel her pulse pounding.

Sitting at the far end of the room at a desk that commanded a view of the entire space was a woman who Loretta guessed would be in her fifties. Her short hair was dyed an unconvincing chestnut and set into rigid waves, and she wore a beige twinset. She didn't appear to have changed her look for thirty years.

'Anthea,' shouted Malcolm over the racket. 'This is our new recruit, Loretta Halliday.'

'Don't bellow, Malcolm,' Anthea replied. 'It's noisy enough in here without you adding to the hullabaloo. Now. Miss Halliday. Welcome. I'll take it from here, Malcolm, thank you.'

Malcolm, clearly dismissed, retreated with a casual salute and Loretta thanked him for his help.

'I'll bring your paperwork in due course,' said Anthea, 'but let's get you settled first. You'll be working with Mr Redpath. He's one of our most experienced reporters on the crime desk. He's not in yet but that means we can get you settled before he arrives. Follow me.'

She said this as if it would be preferable to his already being at his desk and Loretta's stomach clenched. She had noted how first names were adequate for Malcolm but apparently not for her new boss. The crime desk, though. That sounded exciting. She had been worried that she'd be placed on something dull to cut her teeth, but it seemed she was going to be thrown straight into the melee.

Anthea bustled across the floor. Loretta followed in her wake, stepping around piles of papers and chairs that had been pushed away from their desks as if the occupants had left in a hurry. Almost in the middle of the room was a desk that stood out from the rest by virtue of its neatness. There was a telephone, its curly cable fastidiously unknotted, a typewriter, ready loaded with paper, a pen pot, a tower of three in-trays and a shorthand notebook. The desk next to it, half its size and about six inches lower, was completely clear except for a telephone.

'Mr Redpath is a stickler for tidiness. A lone voice in this wilderness,' said Anthea. 'This will be your desk. I suggest you sit there and look busy until he arrives.'

And then she turned and made her way back to her own desk.

Loretta sat down. Look busy? Busy doing what, precisely? There wasn't even a typewriter to type up a story. She thought about picking up the telephone handset but who would she be talking to? Her eyes scanned the space, desperate to find something useful to do, and she didn't see her new boss approaching.

'Well, you're off to a fine start. Can't even use your time productively, I see.'

'I'm sorry. I've just this second got here. I was just . . .'

'You'll find that I'm not interested in excuses. Sit down. Tell me you can take shorthand at least.'

Loretta nodded. They had learned the Pitman system and she had practised until she was up to one hundred words per minute. Mr Redpath opened a desk drawer and passed her a dog-eared notebook and a Bic biro.

'Good. Now write this down.'

11

Loretta took the lid off the pen and opened the notebook, flicking through to find the first clean page. The pad was full of shorthand, some examples neater than others, but before she could fully take that in, Mr Redpath had started to speak. Flustered and trying to hold the start of his sentence in her head, Loretta found a page and began.

'It is a phenomenon worthy of note,' he began, 'that in newsrooms up and down the country apprentices who turn up bright-eyed and bushy-tailed on their first day invariably disappoint by the end of the week. Many fail to make it to their first payday. It is not clear what makes the current generation of recruits, particularly the girls, so unsuitable for the task but one has to consider whether in the absence of national service we as a nation are breeding young people with little initiative and even less backbone.'

He clicked his fingers at her and held out his hand.

'Show.'

Loretta passed him the notebook, the sense of what she had been asked to take down slowly washing over her now she had time to think. She pulled her lips between her teeth in a mixture of nervousness and anger.

Mr Redpath read over what she had written, his face set in a scowl.

'Bushy-tailed isn't clear,' he said. 'And initiative is incorrect.'

He handed the notebook back to her but Loretta wasn't sure what he wanted her to do. Was she supposed to rewrite those two words, or do the whole piece again, although what would be the point of that? But before she had time to ask, he spoke again.

'Not brilliant. Not terrible,' he said. 'Mine's a tea, milk two sugars.' He opened a desk drawer and passed her a plain white mug. 'This is my cup. It is to be kept clean at all times and never to find its way into general circulation. Do you understand?'

Loretta took the mug, nodding.

'Don't just nod. I know you have a tongue in your head. Answer me properly.'

'Yes, Mr Redpath,' she said.

He stared at her.

'Well, go on then. A man could die of thirst.'

Loretta was on the point of asking him where she would find the kettle and supplies but then she stopped. This was a test. He wanted initiative. She would give him initiative. He lifted his hands to the keys of his typewriter and began to type, steadfastly not looking in her direction.

Feeling panicked, she glanced around the newsroom to see if she could see where the tea station was, or at the very least someone with tea that she could ask. As her eyes cast around, she saw Malcolm Penn watching her. She gave him a tentative smile and he tipped his head towards a door on the far wall. She looked over and then looked back at him questioningly. He nodded.

'Thanks,' she mouthed and set off confidently in the direction he'd suggested.

The door, when she reached it, opened on to a small kitchenette with a hot-water boiler, a fridge and a cupboard that contained various stained and chipped mugs. She could see why Mr Redpath insisted on using his own. There was a box of PG Tips on the countertop, teabags scattered around it where people had removed more than one and not bothered to return the spare. There was also a huge jar of Nescafé and an open bag of sugar. Teaspoons littered the surface like little boats.

Loretta made the tea, carefully stirring the sugar in to make sure it was all dissolved. She decided that she shouldn't make one for herself at this point. She considered making a cup for Malcolm but she didn't know what he drank or how he took it. She would return his kindness when she got a chance, though.

Then she took the cup of tea and delivered it to Mr Redpath. He was still typing when she got back to the desk and she placed the cup of tea on a coaster at his elbow. With a flourish, he pulled the paper from the typewriter and she saw that it wasn't a single sheet but a few all fastened together. He handed them to her.

'Remove the carbons,' he said. 'Then the top copy goes to the news desk, the second copy for the copy taster, the third for the picture desk and the last one is for your files.'

Was this another test, she wondered. Was she expected to distribute each copy to its rightful home? Not sure what to do, she looked down at the paper and let her eyes skim the words.

It is the role of the apprentice to listen and learn. Questions are permitted but not encouraged. A good junior reporter can use their initiative and deduce what is expected of them by reading the signals around them. And making a good cup of tea is essential.

She looked up. If she'd hoped that Mr Redpath would now be smiling at her, test passed with flying colours, she was sorely mistaken. He looked just as implacable as he had done before. So she sat back down at her desk, picked up the notebook and pen and glanced up at him expectantly. From the corner of her eye, she thought she saw a thumbs-up sign from Malcom Penn but she couldn't swear to it.

12

At one o'clock there seemed to be a general downing of tools for lunch. Mr Redpath, who had spent much of the morning explaining the finer points of newspaper production to her, all things she had covered in depth at university, opened his briefcase and took out a square packet of sandwiches wrapped in greaseproof paper. He opened it on his desk and Loretta got the unmistakeable whiff of egg. She hadn't brought any lunch with her, not being sure of the form, and now she wasn't sure what she was expected to do.

She supposed she should ask to be dismissed, or at least if she was allowed a lunch hour, but the prospect of interrupting Mr Redpath and his egg sandwich was too much. She'd rather go hungry. She could probably last all day without any lunch anyhow. She resolved to have a bigger breakfast the following day.

And then Malcolm was at her back.

'Don't mind if we whisk your apprentice away, do you, Redpath? Take her to the pub, show her where the real work happens.'

Mr Redpath looked up disdainfully. He had a tiny morsel of egg yolk lodged in his moustache. This was so at odds with his fastidious behaviour thus far that it made Loretta want to giggle, probably a stress release from her terrifying morning.

'As long as she's back here by two I don't care where you take her,' he said, without making eye contact with Loretta.

'Come on then, Loretta. Grab your stuff.'

Oozing gratitude, Loretta put her coat over her arm and picked up her handbag. Then she followed Malcolm across the newsroom to the door to the stairs. On the way they picked up a guy a few years older than her and a girl who had been sitting at a desk directly outside one of the glass-fronted offices.

'Loretta, Dave. Dave, Loretta,' said Malcom as they walked.

'And I'm Tracey,' said the girl, rolling her eyes at Malcolm. 'Pleased to meet you. How's your first morning been? Awful, I'd guess. He's such a boring old bastard, that Redpath.'

Loretta didn't want to be overheard criticising her boss on her first morning so she just smiled and hoped that would do, but Tracey was having none of it.

'Did he make you take dictation and then go on about how rubbish he expects you'll be? He did, didn't he? He does that to everyone. I don't know why they put the new people with him. It hardly gives a good impression. The rest of us are all right, aren't we, Malcolm?'

Malcolm didn't seem to feel the need to reply and Loretta held her tongue too. They were on the stairs now and she was less anxious, but she'd be happier when they were out of earshot of anyone who might report back to her new boss. 'Don't worry,' Tracey continued. 'You're only thinking what we already know. He's a miserable sod.'

'But a great reporter,' said Malcolm, holding the door open for them. 'You can learn a lot from him as long as you don't rub him up the wrong way.'

Loretta smiled again. She wasn't sure what response was expected of her but she definitely didn't want to rub anyone up the wrong way, especially not on her first day.

There was a pub right next door to the newspaper offices and Dave led the way. Inside, it was almost as noisy as the newsroom.

Men were standing three deep at the bar, each with a cigarette in one hand and a pint in the other. Loretta had heard stories of the Fleet Street pubs, where golden nuggets of information melded together into stories, and here she was, right in the middle of it.

'I'm buying, seeing as it's your first day,' said Malcolm, wagging a finger at her, 'but don't get used to it. What'll you have?'

Loretta looked around her. Everyone had alcohol of some kind or other but that didn't feel right when she was working.

'Orange juice?' she suggested tentatively.

'Don't be ridiculous,' said Dave. 'You'll never make a reporter if you don't drink at lunchtime.'

'Okay. Half a dry cider then, please,' she said, capitulating without a fight.

'That's more like it. Trace?'

'Cinzano and lemonade please, Dave,' she said, and then without warning she bolted across the room to secure a table from a group who were leaving.

'*News of the World*,' said Dave under his breath. 'Lightweights.'

Loretta took her place at the squat wooden table with Tracey to her left and Dave opposite her, leaving the stool to her right for Malcolm, who soon returned from the bar, a tray of teetering drinks in his hand.

'So,' he said after he'd sat down and taken a gulp of his pint. 'Tell us about yourself.'

Loretta shuffled in her seat and pulled at her skirt.

'Not much to tell, really. I'm twenty-one, fresh out of uni. I live in Barnet with my sister, Natalie. And I want to be a journalist.'

Malcolm looked slightly disappointed, as if he had been expecting something more explosive.

'It's a start, I suppose. But what about you? What are *you* like?'

He cocked his head to look at her and his hair flopped down over his forehead again. He brushed it back.

Loretta thought for a moment.

'Okay,' she began slowly. 'Well, I'm intensely curious. I'm calm under pressure. I'm persistent. I have good attention to detail. I like to think I'm empathetic. I'm pretty courageous. And my favourite band is Joy Division.'

Dave let out a little sound of approval.

'Yeah. Love them,' he said. 'Shame about Ian Curtis.'

'What makes you think you're courageous?' asked Malcolm.

Loretta met his gaze. His eyes behind his glasses were pale grey, almost without colour at all. There was a pause whilst she considered. This was none of his business, but something told her that if she wanted to be taken seriously then she needed to be more than the latest apprentice who may or may not stick the course.

She decided to press on, not because it would elicit sympathy – she really didn't think it would from Malcolm – but because what had happened over the summer had become part of who she now was. She couldn't hide it away.

'My parents were both killed in an accident in July,' she said, without breaking eye contact. 'My younger sister and I are all that's left of our family.'

Dave blew out a low whistle and Tracey's hand shot to her mouth but Malcolm continued to stare steadily. She stared back. If he wanted courageous, she could give it to him. He broke away before she did. He took another gulp of his pint.

'Okay,' he said. 'That's courageous.'

13

Loretta's first week of work seemed to go well. Mr Redpath didn't lighten up but he didn't get any darker either. When he set her a task, she worked hard to complete it asking as few questions as she could. He was head of the crime desk, it turned out, and so the stories he reported on were interesting and horrifying in equal measure. She heard about devastating house fires, men accused of rape, and plenty of theft and fraud. It was only a few months since the Yorkshire Ripper had been imprisoned and once or twice she heard Mr Redpath bemoaning the loss of the story, but Loretta thought there seemed to be plenty more crime to get their teeth into without the need for a new serial killer.

When she got stuck she had a quick word with Malcolm or Dave, making a detour on her way to wash up or fill her boss's pristine mug, but only staying for a moment before steering back on course for the tea bay. She appreciated how they seemed to have taken her under their wings and she wanted to prove herself worthy of their attention.

So she took shorthand and filed Mr Redpath's copy with the appropriate desks and listened to him talk. He had yet to take her out of the office with him, which was disappointing, but she assumed he was waiting to make sure that she was fully house-trained before he presented her to the outside world. But that was all right. Loretta had time. She could wait.

At home, things were less positive. Only six weeks had passed since the accident and it was perfectly natural that they would be grieving, but Loretta had her new job and with the excitement and the adrenaline that it brought, she found that hours and sometimes an entire working day would go by without her thinking about her parents once. When she did remember she felt dreadful that she could let them leave her mind so easily, but then she knew they wouldn't have wanted her to do anything to scupper this opportunity. The job at the newspaper was what they had all been moving towards for years and Loretta felt she owed it to her parents to give it her best shot.

However, Natalie was a very different story. With school over and no university place to go to, Natalie was lost. Loretta didn't know what time she dragged herself out of bed but sometimes she hadn't managed it by the time Loretta returned home from the newspaper. She didn't get dressed for days on end and there was every sign that she wasn't even washing.

Loretta, thinking it might help if she had a focus for her day, suggested that Natalie might cook for them in the evenings. In fact, there was a whole range of household duties that Natalie could turn her attention to and which Loretta would have dealt with if she had been the one at home all day, but Loretta could see that Natalie was struggling and didn't want to burden her with too much.

One Friday, after they had eaten a meal of fish fingers, chips and peas, a Loretta post-work staple, she took Natalie's hand and led her to the sofa. Natalie drifted along after her like a zombie and flopped into the cushions, her hair dark and hanging in greasy clumps and her eyes sunk deep.

'This is going to sound stupid,' Loretta began, 'but what's up, Nat? You can't carry on like this. What's the matter?'

She understood her sister well enough to know that Natalie would get what she was really asking. This was more than grief. There was that, of course there was, but there was something far more desperate at play here that Loretta was struggling to grasp.

When Natalie finally raised her head there was a blankness to her expression that frightened Loretta. Where was the fun-loving, live wire of a sister? There was not one iota of that person still visible in Natalie's demeanour.

Natalie closed her eyes, as if she wanted the world and everything it contained to leave her in peace. Loretta hoped this didn't include her. She tried again.

'I can see something's not right, more than just Mum and Dad,' she said. 'And I want to help. But I don't know where to start. I need you to give me a clue.'

Natalie sighed deeply and for a moment Loretta feared that was all the response she was going to get. But then she spoke.

'I don't get it either,' she replied, her eyes focused on the pattern on her nightdress. 'I just can't seem to . . . It's like something has emptied my brain so all that's left is one room with nothing in it. And I can't find my way back to how it was before. I'm trapped on the wrong side of the door. Does that make any sense?'

It didn't. Loretta couldn't imagine anything even close to what Natalie was describing.

'Why don't you try doing something with your days? Maybe you could go and see Chrissie or your other friends.'

Natalie shrugged.

'What would I say?' she said, and Loretta could see her point. What news did she have when all she did was lie in bed or on the sofa?

'Well, how about looking for a job? You said you wanted to go grape picking and that you'd save up first. I know there aren't many jobs around but there must be something.'

Natalie's expression was of genuine confusion.

'Grape picking? Did I say that?' she asked. 'I can't remember. It doesn't sound like me.'

'Oh, it does!' encouraged Loretta. 'It sounds exactly like you. Wanting to go exploring the world on an adventure. We could get Mum's atlas out and have a look, plan out a route.'

Loretta half stood up, ready to whisk the atlas down from its shelf, but Natalie didn't react at all so she sat back down.

'I'm worried about you, Nat,' she said gently. 'I know that you're really hurting but I don't know how to make it stop.'

Natalie looked up at her with so much sadness in her dark eyes that Loretta wanted to hold her tight and never let her go.

'Don't worry about me, Etta,' she said. 'I'll sort it out. I just need a bit of time.'

'Shall I run you a bath, with lots of bubbles like we used to have when we were little? We can wash your hair and get some clean clothes on you. That'll make you feel better.'

Loretta was pleased with her suggestion. Whenever she'd been under the weather for a few days it always helped to get fresh and clean. She stood up, tugging at Natalie's hand to take her with her, but Natalie resisted and stayed where she was.

'Maybe later,' she said.

14

2022 – Ripon

'I'm Etta's sister,' the stranger said slowly, her eyes meeting Marc's angry glare.

Bronte could see the thoughts flit across her brother's mind. They were all there on his face for her to read. First they said, 'Don't lie to me. My mother didn't have a sister.' Then, 'How can I get this woman to move without causing a scene?', and finally Bronte saw resignation that there was nothing he could do in that moment as their mother's funeral was about to start. He tutted under his breath and took his seat next to Sara, his wife.

Then the vicar stepped forward and the service began and Bronte's attention slipped from the woman who claimed to be her aunt and on to her mother. It was only when she became aware of the woman shuddering with sobs next to her that she remembered she was there. Prepared to let her mind wander at will rather than concentrate on the sadness of the funeral, Bronte thought about what the woman had said, which was almost nothing.

She was Etta's sister.

This was peculiar on two counts. Their mother was an only child. They knew this to be true. She had had no sister, or brother for that matter. And no one had ever called their mother Etta. She was either Loretta or, more commonly, Lori. In fact, now she came to think about it, Bronte had a vague childhood memory of her mother being quite sharp with someone who had addressed her as Etta. Bronte had just assumed she didn't like it and wanted to make that clear before the shortened name stuck. Weird then that this woman, who claimed to be her sister, would choose to call her that.

Marc stood up to give his eulogy and Bronte pulled her attention back to the service.

'Our wonderful mother, Loretta, was a mainstay of this community,' he began. An appreciative murmur hummed around the cathedral. 'I'm certain that somehow or other she or her deeds will have touched every person in this little city of ours. Whether you were in the Brownies or appreciated the flowers in the market square. If you used the bike sheds outside the library or enjoyed one of her fabulous creations at a school cake sale. We, her beloved family, were never quite sure how she achieved so much. She was clearly gifted more hours in the day than the rest of us . . .' – a little laughter rose up from the congregation – 'and what she accomplished on a daily basis puts us to shame.'

'Hear, hear,' called out a man behind Bronte.

Marc continued along this vein for a while and then moved into family anecdotes. There was barely anything about Loretta's life from before they were born, no details of her early years, her education. This didn't strike Bronte as odd. Their mother always said that her life didn't really get going until she moved to Leeds and met their father. Until then she had lived in London, with her parents, who had died before Loretta married. She'd had an unremarkable office job after she left school that she said was so unmemorable even she had forgotten the details. She hadn't gone to university either and had made such a huge fuss when her children had got the grades to go, even though Garth's family had all attended higher education.

There had been no mention of any siblings. Bronte assumed one of them must have asked at some point, although she didn't think it had been her. It would have been Marc, being the eldest, and then when there was nothing to learn on that score they had stopped wondering. Their mother had no family except them and that was that.

As she thought about it now, Bronte realised she had liked that her mother had always seen herself in terms of her husband and children without being an entity on her own. And it was far nicer to believe that she'd had no life before them. It made Bronte feel important, special. So she hadn't enquired any further about her mother's past. If there had ever been anything more important than the three of them and their father in Loretta's life then she hadn't wanted to know.

Bronte realised that she had stopped listening to her brother's eulogy and pulled her attention back to the present. Before the service, she had assumed it would be the thought of her mother lying just feet away in the coffin that she would have to distract herself from, not the arrival of a mysterious mourner. Either way, she was grateful. Anything that made the funeral easier to get through had to be a positive of sorts.

And then it was all over. Those who had wanted to speak had spoken, the readings had been read, the hymns sung. The committal was for family only, giving anyone who wanted to escape the wake an opportunity to slip away discreetly in the gap between the two. Should she invite this woman? If she really were her mother's sister then she ought to be there, but the idea that she could be was so ludicrous that Bronte was having difficulty making sense of it. And then there was Marc, who most definitely wouldn't take kindly to such a suggestion.

Her father, Marc, Sara and Annie were gathering themselves for the sombre procession out of the cathedral. Annie blew her nose noisily on a tissue and Bronte reached over and squeezed her arm. Annie looked at her through watery eyes and suddenly seemed much younger than she was. Looking out for her little sister helped to ease Bronte's sorrow, albeit temporarily, and Annie so rarely required any help that it made the moment even more poignant.

Sara looked as composed as ever. Cool, even. She really wasn't part of this, Bronte thought, not a real Ashton, despite being married to Marc, and then she chastised herself for thinking it. She watched as Sara slipped an arm around Marc, pulling him close. He leaned into her, whispering something into her hair.

Their father looked utterly broken and the sight of him sent Bronte to his side.

'Are you holding up okay, Dad?' she said quietly.

He turned to her, face pale and eyes red-rimmed, and nodded bravely.

'Shall we go?' she asked him, more a statement than a question because the answer was clear.

Then she turned to speak to the stranger. She wasn't sure what she was going to say, whether she would insist that the committal was family only or invite her to come along. But as it turned out, which she would have chosen was immaterial.

The woman was gone.

15

Bronte scanned the cathedral, her eyes searching for the woman with the pixie haircut. She had been at her side just a moment ago and now she was nowhere to be seen. All around her people were gathering themselves to leave, tissues and orders of service being stuffed into pockets and bags, but there was no sign of the stranger. She had entirely disappeared.

Turning to face the front once more, Bronte concluded that the woman choosing to leave of her own accord would make things simpler. There would be no confrontation later in the day and that suited her. She pushed the incident to the back of her mind and focused on supporting their father through what was still to come.

It was only later, when the mourners and those well-meaning but slightly overbearing women who had stayed behind to tidy up had all left, that Bronte thought about the stranger at the funeral. With peace restored in the house, Annie and her father were slumped on the sofa. They both looked wrung out by the day. Their father had a tumbler in his hand but the level of whisky hadn't dropped all afternoon as far as Bronte could tell. Annie had kicked off her shoes and cried away all her make-up. She had the slightly dazed look of someone who has been woken abruptly from a deep sleep.

Marc was in an armchair, not the one their mother favoured, which no one would ever be able to sit in again, but the one nearest the window. Sara, who was clearly itching to leave, didn't sit but hovered by the door sending increasingly frantic signals to Marc, which he was failing to pick up.

'Well,' he said. 'I think that went very well.'

He probably wasn't consciously seeking praise for his organisational skills, Bronte thought, but that was how it came across. She obliged.

'Yes. Well done for pulling it all together, Marc. You did a great job.'

Marc accepted her words with a small shrug and a modest dropping of his head.

'I'm just glad it all went off without a hitch,' he said. 'And Mum would have been pleased, I think.'

They all agreed that Loretta would, indeed, have been delighted by her send-off. All her favourite people in one place would have thrilled her, even if it was for such a sad occasion.

'What about that woman, though,' said Annie. 'At the start. That nutcase who said she was Mum's sister.'

Marc let out a little huff.

'You often get that type at a funeral. Sad little people who are just looking for attention. Annoying that she sat with us through the whole thing, but I don't suppose it matters really. She disappeared fast enough at the end. Wanted to get out of there before people started asking questions, I assume.'

'Did anyone see her go?' asked Annie. 'Was she there for the whole service?'

'I think so,' said Bronte, 'but I didn't see her leave. I turned round and she'd just disappeared.'

'In shame, no doubt, for trying to ambush someone else's day,' added Marc. 'Anyone for another drink? Dad? Annie?'

Bronte heard Sara suck in a deep breath from over by the door.

'We really should be going, Marc,' she said. 'I told Mum we'd be back before seven. It'll have been a long day for her.'

It's been a long day for us, Bronte thought but didn't say.

'I'm sure she's fine,' Annie said, the snip in her tone barely concealed. 'The boys will be in bed by now anyway. Not much point you racing home.'

Sara glowered at Annie but then seemed to remember where they were and why and pulled her face into a smile of sorts.

'Yes, you're right, Annie,' she said tightly. 'I'm sure they're okay. I might just ring Mum though, to warn her we'll be late.'

'Lucky to have a mum to ring,' Annie said under her breath and Bronte winced. This wasn't the moment for Annie to pick a fight.

'I think I'd actually like a cup of tea,' said their father as if Annie hadn't spoken.

'I'll make that for you, Garth,' said Sara. 'Anyone else?'

Everyone raised a hand and Sara left the room, a woman on a mission to make tea and then leave.

'You don't suppose she might actually have been Mum's sister?' asked Bronte when Sara had gone.

She had been toying with this idea all day, letting it play out in her mind, with all its unlikely connotations and consequences.

'Don't be ridiculous,' replied Marc dismissively. 'She was just some woman wanting to cause bother. I mean, did you see how she was dressed for a start? Do you really think that an estranged sister meeting the family for the first time and at the funeral would turn up looking like she'd come straight from the allotment?'

He did have a point, Bronte supposed. It was odd not to make an effort with your appearance, particularly if you were going to plonk yourself in the front row.

'Did Mum ever mention a sister to you, Dad?' she asked.

Their father shook his head.

'Your mother had no family,' he said. 'That's why she moved up here. She fancied a change and there was nothing keeping her in London, no career to speak of and no family ties there.'

'And then you got married in Gretna Green, just the two of you,' added Annie.

Garth's face brightened at the memory.

'That was your mother's doing. It wasn't as if we were underage. Lori was twenty-eight. But she thought it would be fun, romantic, to just run off and do it, so we did. No one minded. Her parents had already passed away. Mine were a bit disgruntled, but they didn't really object. I was thirty-five by then. I think they were relieved someone was taking me off their hands.'

They all smiled encouragingly at his weak joke.

Marc shook his head, as if he had reached a conclusion in his own head. 'If Mum had had a sister, she'd have invited her to be a witness at the very least. You know how big she was on family,' he said.

'Maybe they fell out,' said Annie with a hint at naughtiness. 'Perhaps there was some big feud.'

Garth shook his head.

'I hardly think that's likely. When did your mother ever fall out with anyone?'

This was true. One of the reasons Loretta had been so widely liked was that she was just so lovely to everyone.

Sara reappeared with a tray of tea. Bronte noted that she had used Loretta's china cups, which held significantly less liquid than the everyday mugs, and wondered whether this was a considered move on Sara's part to get away earlier, concluding seconds later that of course it had been. Small amounts of tea were much more quickly consumed and that fact wouldn't have been lost on her sister-in-law.

'I don't believe a word of it,' said Marc. 'There is no long-lost sister. It was just someone playing a sick joke. And the fact that she disappeared as soon as the service was over just proves my point. If she really were Mum's sister she'd have stuck around to meet us all.'

He sat back in his chair – QED.

Bronte had to agree that he was probably right. But there had been something about the energy coming off the woman that belied that version of events, and those juddering sobs had felt very real.

16

After the funeral, the huge outpouring of grief that there had been over Loretta's untimely death dried up quickly as the people of Ripon got on with their lives. The number of callers bearing casseroles declined significantly and the telephone in the hall of Bronte's parents' house no longer rang all day long.

Marc had returned to Leeds and Annie to London, so it was just Bronte and Garth left. Bronte contemplated moving in with her father, just for a few nights so that he wouldn't be alone, but when she proposed the idea, Garth had assured her that it wasn't necessary and she felt relieved. She loved being in her little terraced house, and dealing with her grief was hard enough without drowning herself in the memories that the family home held.

Her house wasn't perfect either, mind you. It had ghosts of its own, with Joel and their plans for their future together so recently imploded. At least the tragedy of her mother had brought some perspective into the catastrophe in her own life. She wasn't dead. She had to be grateful for that at least. And yes, the rug had been pulled out from under her, forcing her to entirely reconsider her life, but what was her life going to be anyway? Her plans had always been modest. She had seen herself settling down with Joel and starting a family. That wasn't going to happen now but maybe it hadn't been her destiny anyway. More fool her for daring to dream.

Bronte had always seen herself as a small, unimportant kind of person. Marc had the brains and Annie was the free spirit and she was . . . well, she was the spare, the middle child of whom no one had ever had many expectations. Neither firstborn nor baby. Neither forthright nor wayward. She had moved through life without making many ripples in its surface. And now that was likely to continue.

But she did have her shop. That was something she had achieved on her own. Bronte's Bric-a-Brac was possibly the smallest shop unit in Ripon, tucked away up an alley where there was barely any passing trade, but those who knew about it were loyal and told their friends and so she earned a reasonable living.

The shop frontage looked like a house, with an ordinary unglazed door and a bay window with heavy panelling beneath. All the woodwork was painted in a deep green that looked black on a dull day, and Bronte's Bric-a-Brac was written across the top in a Victoriana-inspired font.

The old-fashioned bell tinkled as she pushed open the door. It caught on a few days' accumulated post and leaflets and Bronte bent down to pick them up, inhaling the familiar comforting scent of the place as she did so – dust, wax polish, lavender and the smell of things well used.

Her hurriedly scribbled sign – CLOSED DUE TO FAMILY BEREAVEMENT – was still stuck in the window, held in place by a strip of packing tape, which was all she'd had to hand when she'd locked up and fled to the hospital. She pulled it down and screwed it up without reading the words. The tape left a sticky mark on the window. She would clean that off later.

She dropped the post on to the chair where she sat in the long gaps between customers. The larger part of her business was online these days and so her time was spent on the laptop, posting the most valuable of her acquisitions and dealing with sales and enquiries. Marc had told her that it was madness to keep the shop open when it barely wiped its own face, but for Bronte the shop was at the heart of what she did. Without it, she would just be another person selling vintage stuff online, anonymous, soulless. That wasn't what she was about.

As she rearranged a few of the shelves, she reassessed where she found herself. Piece by piece she was picking up her life again – running club on Wednesdays, drinks with her friends on Fridays, cosy nights in with a film and a takeaway on Saturdays. She was getting through the days with white lies and fake smiles, hoping that soon everyone would have more or less forgotten that her mother had recently died in such extraordinary circumstances ('A bee sting! I know. Can you credit it?') and her lover had left her without warning.

Yet she couldn't shake thoughts of the bogus sister from her mind. Her head told her that Annie and Marc were probably right, that the woman was just attention-seeking, or maybe mentally unwell. She wondered whether she might even be wanting to make a claim on her mother's estate, although with three children and a widower ahead of her this felt a little ambitious for a would-be con artist.

However, her heart was telling her a different story. Would someone with no real connection to her mother sob like the woman had done? It was hard to reconcile this image with Marc's theories.

She'd called in at her father's house after work and found him pottering around his garden. The garden was beautiful, the product of many hours' work on her father's part when her mother had been busy doing all the many things that filled her days. Each summer, he opened it up to visitors for a day or two, her mother selling cups of tea and cakes for charity and her father chatting for hours about which varieties he had planted and why. Would he still do that now that he was alone? Bronte didn't like to think about it.

He was cutting back the forsythia, gold-speckled branches in a heap at his feet. He looked gaunt, Bronte thought, and older than he had a month before. Her mother had generated so much vitality around her and without her Garth seemed to have shrunk, the age gap between them suddenly appearing wider than it had before.

Bronte pulled the wheelbarrow over and started to load the trimmings into it.

'Good day?' asked her father without stopping what he was doing.

'Not bad. Same old same old, you know. Listen, Dad . . .' She paused, not sure how to get to the question she wanted to ask. 'I've been thinking about Mum.'

He stopped snipping and eyed her, eyebrows raised as if to say, haven't we all?

'It's just I realised that I don't really know much about her life before us.'

'No, I suppose that's the way of things,' Garth said. 'We generally think about people in terms of our own experiences of them, so there are huge parts of their lives that we never discover. Sometimes I only find out interesting facts at a funeral and then wonder why I never asked more when the person was alive.'

'That's just it,' Bronte continued. 'I didn't learn anything from Marc's eulogy because he started with Mum's life here. I suppose if she was still in touch with anyone from her childhood, they would have been at the funeral?'

She added a question mark, hoping that her father would answer it, but he just replied, 'I suppose they would,' and Bronte wanted to scream. They had made the list for the funeral together. There had been no one on it who she didn't know or know of.

'Was there anyone she talked about when she was reminiscing? Childhood stories? Everyone has those, don't they?'

This was true. Everyone she knew, including her father, had anecdotes from their past that they tripped out from time to time, some of them with a dull predictability. But not her mother, she realised now. Her present had been so vital, so full, that Bronte had never really noticed the omission of anything much from her past. Maybe that was because they had never asked, but now Bronte thought about it she wondered whether her mother had just been particularly adept at deflecting any questions, turning matters back to her, Annie, Marc or their father.

Garth continued to snip at the branches. 'There was one friend she talked about. A girl from primary school. Her name began with an L like Lori's.'

Bronte was starting to feel exasperated with his vagueness, but she needed to stay patient.

'Lisa?' she suggested. 'Or Laura?'

Her father shook his head.

'No,' he said. 'That wasn't it.'

'Lorraine? Linda?' Bronte racked her brain for L names from approximately the right era.

'Liz!' Garth said with sudden triumph. 'It was Liz. Liz and Loretta. She said the teacher sat them next to each other on the first day of school and they were never apart after that.'

'Did you tell her about Mum?' Bronte asked. 'About the funeral?'

'I wrote,' her father said. 'I didn't have a phone number but I found her address in your mother's book. It was listed under L&L. I'd have missed it if she hadn't told me about the Liz and Loretta thing.'

'And did you hear back?' Bronte asked, anxious that this tiny little clue to her mother's childhood shouldn't have ended in nothing.

'I did. I have the card somewhere. It had a phone number, I think. She was on holiday for the funeral so couldn't come. Pity.'

He was starting to ramble and Bronte cut across him.

'Where did you put the card, Dad? I might get in touch.'

'It's on your mother's bureau,' he said, but then his expression changed. 'Is this about that woman? The one at the funeral.'

It was but Bronte could sense that telling her father so wouldn't help.

'No. Not at all. I think we're all agreed that she was just some oddball who crashed the service. It's just that I realised I don't know much about Mum's childhood. I'm curious, that's all.'

Garth turned back to his forsythia.

'I'm really not sure there's much to learn,' he said. 'I was married to your mother for over thirty years. If there'd been anything remarkable about her life in London, I feel sure she'd have told me.'

17

Bronte left her father to his pruning and went inside, ostensibly to make them both a drink but actually to have a rummage through her mother's bureau to see what she could find.

It was in the corner of the dining room, an antique writing desk with a flap that came down to reveal endless little drawers inside, each too small to be of much use other than to house stray paperclips and elastic bands. It was always tidy, her mother dealing with any correspondence and then filing it at once. Most of her correspondence arrived digitally, but for letters that came through the post there was a series of pigeonholes below the little drawers and this was where Bronte started her search for the card from Liz. It was to no avail, though. There was no sign of it.

Then she realised that it was her father who had dealt with the card when it arrived and not her mother. She opened the main drawer and there it was, sitting on top of her mother's stationery where he had dropped it, out of place.

Bronte felt her heart pump a little harder. Even though she had a good idea what the card said, it was the possibilities it opened up that excited her. The front had a watercolour sketch of a quayside on it, with a tall grain store towering over the little fishing boats.

She opened it up. Inside, someone had started to write on the right-hand side of the card but then ran out of space and so had moved to the left so that the card read backwards.

Dear Garth
I can't believe your news. I'm devastated, to be honest. Loretta was my oldest friend and has always held a very special place in my heart, even though we haven't seen each other for years. It was great when she found you and then had Marc, Bronte and Annie – her own little family. She deserved one of her own after everything that happened.
I'm so sorry but I'll be away for the funeral and can't rearrange my plans but I'll be thinking of you all. If you ever want a chat then my phone number is below.
I'm so sorry, Garth. Etta was a fabulous woman and I'm sure you're all going to miss her loads. I know I will.
With love,
Liz Cooper (née Young)

Seeing her mother's name written there made Bronte's chest ache but she tried to steer beyond the emotion to consider the card. She read it again and then for a third time. She turned the card over and saw the picture was of a place called Wells-next-the-Sea. She had no idea where that was but it couldn't be on the coast anywhere near Ripon or she'd have heard of it.

She wanted to ring Liz immediately and unleash all her questions, but she knew that was the wrong approach. Instead, she took out her phone and snapped a photo of Liz's message and the phone number. She put the card back where she'd found it before picking it up again and slotting it neatly into one of the pigeonholes, just as her mother would have done.

Then she headed for the kitchen to make the promised drinks.

Later, sitting at her own kitchen table, Bronte googled Wells-next-the-Sea. It was a little seaside town on the North Norfolk coast. She looked up Liz Cooper and then Elizabeth Cooper and millions of hits popped up immediately. She added a location but the only thing was a local newspaper article about a litter pick that a Liz Cooper had been involved with. Bronte peered at the tiny photograph that accompanied the piece but it was of a group of people and when she tried to zoom in, the image lost its definition.

The doorbell rang and when Bronte opened it there stood Helen, Bronte's friend from the running club. She was dressed ready to run. Wednesday.

'Shit. Oh Helen, I'm so sorry,' said Bronte before Helen had said anything, gesturing at her own clothing. 'I totally forgot.'

'No worries,' replied Helen, stepping around Bronte and making her way into the house. 'I'm not feeling it today anyway. Make me a cup of peppermint tea and we'll call it quits. How are you doing anyway?'

Helen dropped down into Bronte's hand-me-down sofa and started to unlace her trainers, slipping out of them and then tucking her legs up under her.

'I'm okay,' replied Bronte, keen to avoid more post-death-of-mother conversations. 'But I'm in the middle of solving a mystery.'

Helen sat forward. 'Ooh! What kind of mystery?'

'There was a woman at the funeral. She sat in the front row with us. Really irritated Marc.'

'Oh, I like her already,' chipped in Helen.

Bronte threw her a rebuking look and then smirked.

'Anyway,' she continued, 'she announced that she was Mum's sister and then left before any of us got to speak to her.'

Helen frowned.

'Didn't you tell me your mum was an only child?' she said. 'Which was why she had three kids herself?'

'I did. Hence the mystery.'

'Have you spoken to this woman?'

'No. She appeared and then just disappeared, like I said. Annie and Marc think she was an attention seeker but I'm not sure.'

'And you're trying to track her down,' finished Helen.

Bronte nodded.

'Ooh! That is exciting. Tell me.'

Bronte screwed up her nose.

'I've only just started,' she confessed. 'But Dad told me about Mum's oldest friend. I'd never heard of her either, but Dad remembered Mum mentioning her. I've got a phone number for her.'

'So you'll ring her?'

Bronte bit her lip.

'Yes, but I can't just blurt out my questions on the phone. I think I need to meet her.'

'Yeah, maybe,' agreed Helen. 'Where does she live?'

'Wells-next-the-Sea.'

'In Norfolk? Nice. Will you go and see her?'

Bronte hadn't got this far in her thinking.

'I don't know. I suppose so. I could go at the weekend if this woman is around and happy to see me. Fancy a road trip?'

Helen tutted. 'I can't this weekend but if it's another time then definitely.'

This was all moving quite quickly and Bronte paused to take stock.

'I suppose I should probably go on my own anyway,' she mused. 'What do you think?'

Helen nodded. 'Probably. Wouldn't want to ambush the poor woman. Take your running kit, though. There are no hills in Norfolk so you can get some big miles in. What are you going to ask her?'

'I really haven't thought. I'd just started investigating when you arrived. What I really want to know is whether Mum actually did have a sister.'

Helen looked thoughtful. 'If it turns out she did and never mentioned it then you have to wonder why not. They might have had a falling-out. Then again, surely she'd just say they'd lost touch, not hide her existence entirely.'

Bronte agreed. She hadn't thought her mother was the type for a family feud so that scenario felt unlikely.

'Maybe she wanted to keep her hidden for some other reason,' said Helen. 'Or maybe it was her whole past she didn't want you to know about.'

Again, Bronte couldn't see it. But then a few days ago it would never have crossed her mind that her mother might have a secret sister.

Helen looked at the sports watch on her wrist, ready for the run that hadn't happened.

'It's only just gone seven. Why don't you ring her now? No time like the present.'

The thought horrified Bronte. She couldn't just ring up like that without any preparation. Or maybe she could . . .

'What should I say?' she asked Helen.

'Explain who you are and that you're going to be in Norfolk and would like to call in to chat about her memories of your mum. It's almost true.'

Bronte still felt doubtful.

'Go on,' encouraged Helen. 'What's the worst that can happen? She says no and you don't get to talk to someone you didn't even know existed until yesterday. But she won't say no.'

Bronte breathed in deeply to give herself courage.

'Okay,' she said.

She dialled the number.

18

Liz said yes, she would be delighted to meet Bronte and why didn't she call in on Sunday afternoon for a cup of tea as she was passing. Bronte thanked her and then put her phone down.

'Well?' asked Helen, her eyes wide. 'What did she sound like?'

'Nice. Surprised to hear from me but she knew Mum had three kids so she knew who I was. London accent, I think. Well, southern at least.'

'Was that where your mum was from?' asked Helen, and when Bronte nodded she added, 'That makes sense then, doesn't it? How far is it?'

Bronte opened up the map app, had a look and pulled a face. 'About four hours' drive,' she said.

The distance felt overwhelming, like she was being asked to trek to the far side of the moon. She knew this was ridiculous but when had she ever driven herself so far before? She couldn't think of a single occasion and her head spun at the idea of doing it now.

Her apprehension must have shown because Helen gave her an understanding smile. 'It's not that far if you take it steady,' she said encouragingly. 'It'll be an adventure!'

◆ ◆ ◆

As it turned out, Bronte quite enjoyed the drive. She bought a new audiobook to listen to and it felt comforting to have Juliet Stevenson's calming voice in the car with her. It was almost as though the actress was sitting in the passenger seat next to her as heavy goods vehicles thundered past on the A1. Sometimes they drove so close that her little car shook in the downdraught, and at one point Bronte almost commented on how imposing they were to Juliet before she remembered that she wasn't actually there.

After a couple of challenging roundabouts, which she had to circumnavigate more than once before she identified her exit, she found herself driving down smaller and smaller roads until they were not much more than farm tracks. Finally, a quaint sign featuring a fisherman's rope and a beach scene announced that she had arrived at the seaside town of Wells-next-the-Sea.

Liz's house was a bungalow in a quiet cul-de-sac of other bungalows. Bronte pulled up outside and checked her appearance in the rear-view mirror. Her heart banged against her ribs and her hand shook as she applied some lip balm. She couldn't decide if she was more nervous about meeting a stranger or what that stranger might tell her.

The bungalow was semi-detached, and there was a paved area with a little red car parked on it. Someone seemed to be in, at least. The front garden had been gravelled and was spotted with pots of newly planted bedding flowers that promised to blossom into a riot of colour once the summer took hold. Interspersed between the containers were various concrete figures – some gnomes, a meerkat or two and a little pond with fairies at its edge. Bronte tried not to judge the display, but it was tricky.

She had run through what she wanted to say a hundred times but now she was here her nerve was failing her and it was all she could do not to start the engine and drive away. But then the front door was opening and there stood a woman who she assumed must be Liz.

She was striking, tall with ashy-blonde hair pulled up into a straggly ponytail. She was wearing a pair of linen dungarees in a faded sea-green and had black Crocs on her feet. She didn't match the impressions that her house created at all.

'Bronte,' she called. 'Hi. Please. Come in.'

Bronte stepped out of the car, smiling broadly and telling herself that there was nothing to be nervous about.

'Hello. You must be Liz,' she said. 'So nice to meet you.'

She walked towards the woman with hand outstretched ready to shake but as soon as she was close enough, Liz engulfed her in a hug.

'I've heard so much about you,' Liz said.

Bronte let the embrace wash over her and resisted the urge to reply that, by contrast, she had heard absolutely nothing about Liz.

'Come in, come in,' said Liz with genuine enthusiasm. 'I'll stick the kettle on.'

Bronte's eye was drawn to the occupants of the garden and Liz caught her looking.

'My kids keep buying them for me,' she said by way of explanation. 'I think the first one was supposed to be a joke but then they just haven't stopped. I hated them to start with but I'm growing quite fond now.'

She grinned in a way that drew Bronte to her. Everything about this woman seemed to Bronte to be entirely open and honest.

Bronte followed her inside and to the back where a light and airy conservatory ran the width of the bungalow.

'Please. Take the weight off, darlin',' said Liz, indicating the wicker chairs topped with plump but faded floral cushions. 'What will you have? Tea? Coffee?'

'Coffee, please,' replied Bronte. 'What a lovely home. Have you been here long?'

'Me and Rich moved up here just before Covid. He was in the haulage game and sold the business to a competitor, so we retired to the seaside. Bit of a cliché but it's lovely here. I'm a bit too young to be retired, though, so I do some holiday let management to keep busy. There are a lot of holiday lets in Wells.'

She disappeared and Bronte could hear her moving about the kitchen.

'And where do you live?' she called through.

'I'm in Ripon, just down the road from Mum and Dad. Dad,' she corrected. 'My brother and sister both moved away but I seemed to get stuck. More of a home bird, I suppose, and there are worse places to live,' she added, wondering why she was justifying herself to someone who hadn't shown any inclination to question her decisions.

Liz appeared with a tray and put it down on a footstool, passing Bronte a cup of black coffee.

'Help yourself to milk and sugar,' she said. 'I was devastated to hear about your mum. They broke the mould when they made her. One of a kind she was. It must have been a horrible shock, her passing so sudden like that. Dreadful.'

Bronte nodded.

'I was in bits, not making it to the funeral, but me and Rich were on holiday. I hope it went well, though.'

Bronte nodded again. 'I think Mum would have liked it,' she said.

Liz took a sip of her coffee and then eyed Bronte over the top of it.

'So, what can I do for you, Bronte?' she said.

There was a pause as Bronte considered her questions again. She had been planning to go straight in and ask about the mysterious sister, but now she was here that felt a little too blunt.

'I suppose I just wanted to hear stories about Mum from when she was young, from people who knew her then,' she said, stopping herself from mentioning that Loretta had never talked about that part of her life in case Liz got spooked.

Was it her imagination or did Liz relax a little, her body becoming a little less rigid in her chair?

'Well, now then. Let me see,' she said.

19

'We lived in Barnet. North London, as you know?'

Bronte nodded, although she only really knew the bits of London that she'd seen on a school trip – Buckingham Palace, the Houses of Parliament, Trafalgar Square. The parts where people actually lived were a mystery to her. The fact that her mother had lived there, however, was the greatest mystery of all.

'You'll have been there, I suppose,' Liz said, and Bronte shook her head.

'Mum never took us. That's partly why I'm interested,' she said.

'Well, it was a council estate but not a bad one. No high rises to speak of and we didn't have riots, not round our way. Plenty of people bought their houses from the council. It was a new thing, folks scraping together the money so they could own their own homes. My mum and dad did it, and your grandma and grandad. Like I say, it was a nice estate.'

Bronte tried to keep the shock off her face. Her mother, the way she talked, dressed, behaved, the way they lived in Ripon. Nothing about any of that spoke of the kind of humble beginnings that Liz was describing.

'Not that it was easy,' Liz continued. 'There wasn't much money. Your grandma worked in the laundrette, for pennies I should imagine, but your grandad was a welder and that brought in a decent wage. Enough to get a mortgage on the house anyway.'

Liz leaned back in her chair.

'Funny old time, the eighties,' she said. 'People these days seem to think it was all big hair, bright colours and Wham! but it wasn't really like that. We didn't have much but we were more accepting somehow. Credit cards were just for the rich. If we wanted something we saved up for it. It took an age but that made you value it more when you finally got it. But we was happy. You didn't hear half as much moaning as you do these days, people bleating on about rights and what have you. Or maybe that's my rose-tinted glasses.'

She gave Bronte half a smile.

'Anyway, we met on the first day of school, me and your mum.'

'Yes. My dad told me that. Something about you being put next to each other alphabetically.'

Liz smiled fondly.

'That's right. Liz and Loretta. Mind you, no one ever called her by her full name. She was Etta to us. Not sure how she ended up with such a posh name. Her mum must have had big ideas for her right from the start. I was always just Liz. That's what's on my birth certificate. No airs and graces for me.'

'And did you stay friends?' asked Bronte.

'We did. I left school at sixteen. Most people did. But your mum did A levels. She had to go to college for that. Our school didn't have a sixth form. But we stayed close. I liked that about her. She could have gone all snotty with her clever new mates but she didn't.

'And then she went off to university. Only kid off the estate to do that. We were so proud of her.'

Bronte was surprised.

'I didn't think she went to university,' she said.

'Oh, she went all right,' replied Liz, and then something crossed her face. Bronte saw it but couldn't identify it. All the tension seemed to come back into Liz's expression. Bronte's main question was on the tip of her tongue but she waited, hoping that Liz would answer it without her having to ask.

'You know about what happened to your grandparents, of course,' Liz said.

Bronte frowned and shook her head and then Liz looked even more nervous. She stood up and crossed the conservatory to look out at the patch of garden outside, passing her mug from hand to hand. She appeared to have clammed up entirely.

'What happened?' prompted Bronte.

'It was a terrible business,' Liz said. 'They'd gone on holiday somewhere. France, I think it was. Anyway, there was something wrong with the heating system in this place they were staying. Carbon monoxide. Killed in their sleep, both of them. Tragedy. Your mum was only twenty-one. We were having a party at theirs when the police turned up.'

Bronte was almost thirty and had barely coped with the untimely death of one parent. How had her mother borne the loss of two at such a tender age? Her eyes began to brim with tears and Liz, who had just turned back, saw them.

'Oh darlin'. You really didn't know,' she said.

Bronte shook her head.

'She never said a word about it.'

'Wanted to save you the pain, I don't doubt,' said Liz. 'That sounds like her.'

'Yes,' agreed Bronte. 'So, what happened? What did she do?'

Liz tipped her head to one side and shrugged. 'What could she do? She just got on with it. She was starting this new job so that kept her occupied. I didn't see as much of her after that. She was so busy, working shifts and what have you. And then she moved down into town and she didn't really come back up our way that often. We kept in touch though, even after . . .' Liz caught herself and seemed to change direction. 'Even after she moved up to Yorkshire. Not regularly. I've never been much of a letter writer.'

Her expression suggested that this was a huge failing, but Bronte thought of all the other ways they could keep in touch in the modern world. Her mother had eschewed social media, saying that she was too busy living her life to share the details with all and sundry, but there was always the telephone. Had the two of them not thought to keep in touch that way?

'I'm not sure Mum really kept in touch with anyone,' she said, hoping to make Liz feel better.

'No. I suppose not,' replied Liz, which Bronte thought was odd. Why wouldn't her mother have stayed close to the people she liked?

All this information was making Bronte's head swim. She had come in search of one truth and now she had so much more than she'd expected. Yet she still didn't know what she had come to find out. There could be no more beating about the bush.

'Liz?' she began. 'I know this might seem like a strange question, but did Mum have a sister?'

Liz went very still.

'Now . . .' she said, like she was having to think back, as if Bronte had asked her if Loretta had owned a bike.

Bronte stared at her. What could there possibly be to think about? It was a simple enough question.

Liz swallowed.

'I don't recall that she did,' she said. The answer was stilted, strained and quite obviously a lie.

'It's just that this woman showed up at the funeral saying that she was her sister,' Bronte continued.

Liz shook her head slowly.

'Well, isn't that odd?' she said vaguely. 'Did she say anything else?'

She was fishing. Bronte could tell from her tone.

'No,' replied Bronte. 'She disappeared at the end before any of us could get to speak to her.'

Liz's shoulders dropped a little.

'How very strange,' she said. She looked at her watch. 'Well, this has been lovely,' she added, getting to her feet, 'but I'm afraid I have a holiday cottage to turn around before three.'

She was smiling, but it was obvious that Bronte was being asked to leave. She too stood up.

'Thank you so much for your time, Liz,' she said, with as convincing a smile as she could muster. 'This has been lovely.'

'You're welcome, darlin'.' Liz's smile was genuine but Bronte thought that it might be as much from relief as anything else. 'You look just like your mum, you know?' she added.

This was true and Bronte agreed.

When they got to the front door, Bronte thanked her again for her time and the coffee.

'Oh, one more thing,' she asked as she was leaving. 'You said Mum had a job in London that kept her busy. What was it?'

'She was a reporter,' replied Liz, apparently relieved that this was a question she did feel she could answer. 'For the *Daily Chronicle*. It doesn't exist anymore but it was a big national in its day. Somewhere between a tabloid and a broadsheet.'

'Wow! I had no idea,' said Bronte, although she was getting used to these revelations.

'Yes. She was a big deal, your mum. I was so proud of her. Told everyone I knew that my mate was a reporter.'

Then Liz bit her lip and looked straight into Bronte's eyes. Something passed between them but Bronte didn't have a clue what it was.

'Be careful which stones you look under, Bronte,' Liz said quietly.

Bronte frowned.

'Some things might be best left where they are.'

Liz's words may have been cryptic but what she was telling Bronte to do was anything but.

20

Bronte started her car and drove without a clue where she was going. She just wanted to get away so she could think. She followed signs for the town centre and nosed her car into a parking spot on the quay. The tide was out and the channel was spotted with little boats all resting on the rippled sand.

She reached for her phone and rang Helen. Helen picked up on the second ring.

'Well?' she said.

'So weird,' replied Bronte. 'She told me that Mum used to live on a council estate in Barnet. And her parents both died in a freak accident when she was twenty-one.'

'Bloody hell,' said Helen. 'That's a bit rough.'

'And she was a journalist. On a national paper. How did we not know that?'

'Weird,' agreed Helen. 'But pretty cool. I wonder why she never told you.'

'And that's not all. When I asked her outright if Mum had a sister, she said that she didn't remember. They were supposed to be best mates. You don't just forget someone's sibling.'

'Er, how many have you got again?' asked Helen.

'Stop it!' laughed Bronte. 'This is serious. Don't you think that's odd?'

'Yeah. Of course,' replied Helen. 'So, she was lying. But why?'

'I haven't got a clue. But she told me to be careful what stones I looked underneath and that some things are best left in the past.'

'What have you wandered into?' asked Helen, with a touch of humour in her voice.

Bronte sighed down the phone.

'God knows. I'm going to ponder on the drive back. Do you think I should tell the others?'

'You mean your non-secret siblings?' asked Helen.

'Yeah. Them. I don't know. My gut's telling me to keep this to myself until I have more answers. Marc's bound to tell me I'm barking up the wrong tree and Annie will turn it into a five-ringed circus before I can say "mystery".'

'I agree,' said Helen. 'See what else you can work out on your own first, and then talk to them.'

Bronte paused for a moment, thinking. Helen waited and Bronte could hear her steady breathing down the line.

'Helen. You knew Mum pretty well. Do you think she was a snob?' It hurt her to even think the question, let alone give voice to it.

Helen's answer came fast and clear.

'No. Definitely not. Why?'

'Well, she had this nice middle-class life in Ripon. Dad was a partner in an accountancy firm before he retired. They had plenty of money. She was highly respected by everyone she met and she worked hard to keep it up. WI, church flowers, all of that. It occurred to me that she might have been ashamed of where she came from.'

'But who would have known?' Helen asked reasonably. 'She moved to the opposite end of the country. No need to hide anything from anyone.'

'She could have decided to reinvent herself, start again as someone different. And that's why she never mentioned her sister, because she'd ditched her and was hoping no one would ever know.'

'I suppose it's possible,' agreed Helen.

'And the woman, her sister. She looked really scruffy. She hadn't made any effort to dress up for the funeral. She could even have been living rough judging by how she looked.'

'Maybe she was a real sister but only turned up because she thought she might be able to get something from the estate.'

'That's what Marc said,' agreed Bronte. 'I don't want to come across all snobby but you do hear of that kind of thing, don't you? People who cut themselves off from their birth families because they don't want to be tarnished by them. So her sister might have assumed there was something to inherit.'

'I don't know,' said Helen doubtfully. 'If that was her game then wouldn't she have stuck around afterwards? It makes no sense to just disappear again.'

She was right. Bronte tried again.

'Well, what if she didn't want anything from us but just wanted to say goodbye? The part about Mum not wanting anything to do with her humble roots could still hold true.'

'Except for the one tiny point,' said Helen.

'What?'

'Your mum was lovely. There was no way she would ever walk out on her family, no matter how humble.'

'But there was no family,' said Bronte. 'Her mum and dad were dead. So the only one she left behind was the scruffy sister. And if Liz knew that Mum didn't want to be associated with her then it stands to reason that she would lie for her, especially now she's dead. Liz would carry on with the lie out of loyalty to Mum.'

Helen sucked in her lips as she thought about this, the sound loud in Bronte's ear.

'Maybe. But if she did want to shed her past, why keep in touch with this Liz woman? It doesn't make any sense, Bront.'

'And I've just made an eight-hour round trip and all I have is more questions and no answers.'

21

1984 – London

'This calls for a celebration!'

Loretta still had copy to file but she looked up from her typewriter to see who was wanting to celebrate what exactly. Malcolm was standing over her with his coat thrown over his arm, his face expectant. Slightly bemused, she looked from him to Mr Redpath, not at all clear about what was going on. Mr Redpath's attitude to her had mellowed since she'd started to work for him, but she still feared getting in his bad books.

Mr Redpath sighed, and then tutted, and then said, 'Go on then. It's not every day an apprentice of mine gets her own byline. But get that copy filed first.'

Loretta suppressed a grin. She might be the youngest reporter on the crime desk and the only woman but she hadn't let that get in her way. The byline wasn't permanent yet but she hoped it soon would be. She had pitched an article idea to Mr Redpath about how developments in fingerprint analysis meant that the work of comparison could be done by computers rather than by hand. The story had involved some complicated research and a couple of interviews with boffins at the Metropolitan Police but the resulting story had been informative and interesting. There had even been talk of an interview on *Tomorrow's World* although that hadn't materialised.

'Give me ten minutes,' she said to Malcolm and then dropped her head and continued to type.

Half an hour later she was sitting with Malcolm in the same pub he'd taken her to on her very first day, still so nervous back then and eager to please. Now it felt like a home from home. People had come and gone. Dave had left under a cloud, some scandal about inventing his sources, but Tracey was still there. And of course Malcolm.

'Right,' he said when they all had a glass of champagne, which had appeared from nowhere. 'Here's to Etta. Possibly the greenest apprentice we've ever had but no doubt the most courageous.'

Loretta noticed this little reference to her first day and was touched that Malcolm also seemed to remember it. She hoped that she had shown herself to live up to this claim in her three years in the newsroom.

'Hey!' she said. 'Less of the green, please. I was young.'

'You still are! Some of us have more grey hair than not these days. Seriously though, you've done good and I'm chuffed to bits for you. And a byline to boot. There are people in that newsroom who can only dream of such riches.'

'And you've stuck it out with Redpath as your boss,' said Tracey.

Malcolm raised a finger and pointed it at her.

'That'll be *Mr* Redpath to you, and he's the one who's stumped up for the fizz so let's show him a bit of respect.'

Tracey toasted the air as if Mr Redpath had died.

Loretta was touched by the champagne but not altogether surprised. Her mentor's bark was worse than his bite and she believed he had grown quite fond of her over the years. She had certainly worked hard for him, doing everything she was asked without complaint even when some complaining would have been justified. But that he had thought to provide the champagne without showing up himself was thoughtful and spoke volumes.

'And now you have a life in crime,' said Malcolm.

Loretta gave him a wry look.

'I believe you may have used that line before,' she said.

Malcolm held his hands up. 'It's a fair cop.' Loretta groaned. 'Seriously though, you should consider yourself lucky to end up working on the crime desk, Loretta. And we're a fussy bunch. We don't get along with just anyone, you know.'

Loretta had worked hard at getting along. She had listened to every piece of advice she had been given and acted on most of it. Many of her hours had been whiled away at Bow Street Magistrates' Court, looking for stories that might interest the senior reporters.

'Be nice to the staff there,' Malcolm had suggested. 'They know everything even if they pretend not to.'

So she had been meticulously polite and respectful to the black-gowned court ushers, who now smiled when they saw her and gave her tips as to where the most interesting cases were unfolding. Of course, any serious crime was passed up to the Crown Court, thus falling into the remit of the more senior crime reporters, but Loretta had been content to cut her teeth on the smaller stories until she got her break. And maybe the fingerprint story was it. She really hoped so.

After her shift finished, she made her way back home to Barnet and Natalie. She hopped off the bus and wandered up the high road, passing the Radio Rentals shop on her way. Unable to withstand the draw of the early evening news, she stood and peered in through the window and the two rows of flickering television screens. There had been a brief hiatus in stories about the miners' strike to cover the shocking gas explosion at Abbeystead in Lancashire. Loretta's head buzzed with possible content for follow-up stories now that the basic facts of the disaster had been established. She imagined sitting with the families of the bereaved, listening to the tiny details of their lives, picking though the chaff to find the grains of wheat that could become the core of a heart-wrenching story. She hadn't covered anything of national interest on her own yet but maybe her scoop was just around the corner.

Not much had changed in Solomon Street since her parents had set off on holiday, never to return, almost three years before. There was a new dog at number 21, a vicious mean-spirited creature that barked every time anyone walked within three feet of the gate. The owners, the Wrights, kept reassuring everyone that the dog had 'a lovely nature' and 'didn't mean any harm', but Loretta was unconvinced and stayed on the opposite pavement until she was well beyond the house.

Natalie was working nights and so would be in when Loretta got home. Even though Natalie was twenty-one and should be out enjoying everything the world could offer her, Loretta could guess at her whereabouts with some accuracy. Natalie was either at whichever job she was currently holding on to by the skin of her teeth, or she was at home. It was rare that she was further afield.

As she slotted the key into the lock and opened the door, Loretta took a deep preparatory breath. The strain of having to be so jolly and upbeat could be exhausting and it took some effort at the end of a busy day. Not that she always needed to dig deep. Sometimes, Natalie was almost back to her old self. She would show interest in Loretta's work, asking questions about how her news stories were developing. They would cook together and then bicker over the washing-up and it was almost like it had been before, as if their parents had just popped out to the pub or round to a neighbour's house. She could let herself forget that their parents were dead and she and Natalie only had each other.

Other weeks were not as easy. Natalie would slip back into being morose and monosyllabic. She could lose entire days simply staring into space, too low to even make herself a drink whilst Loretta was at work. Those were the times when Loretta worried for her baby sister and how she would ever get herself back on track. Sometimes it was very hard to imagine that that might happen.

'Hi Nat. I'm home,' she called out in her over-bright voice.

22

Loretta followed the sound of the television to the lounge. The curtains were drawn against the daylight and Natalie was sprawled on the sofa. Around her were scattered a couple of empty mugs and a cereal bowl in which a desultory cornflake floated in a puddle of milk. She was watching *The Tube*, an irreverent live music show where a presenter with blonde spiked hair was interviewing a musician with blond spiked hair. Loretta could tell from looking at him that he wasn't about to play the kind of music that she liked.

'Who's that?' she asked, nodding at the screen.

'Kirk Brandon. Spear of Destiny. He just said that they're the best rock and roll band in the world.' Natalie turned her head and grinned up at Loretta and Loretta's heart felt a little lighter. She loved that smile.

'I've never heard of them,' she said.

'Neither has most of the world. I think he's deluded. Bloody gorgeous though.'

Loretta moved closer to the television and peered at the screen. Kirk Brandon's hair was almost white and his skin was a flawless porcelain. If it hadn't been for the black sleeveless tee-shirt he would have looked like a ghost. He was beautiful, though. Loretta would give him that.

The music was the kind of thrashy rock that she never listened to but she focused on the sound, absorbing it. 'I liberate,' he sang over and over again, his body twitching convulsively. It was mesmerising and Loretta stood and watched until the band got to the end of the song, only pulling herself away when he reached for his guitar to play the next one.

'What time do you start, tonight?' she asked.

Natalie replied without taking her eyes from the screen.

'Six.'

Loretta looked at her watch although the gesture was unnecessary. She knew it was already gone six.

'You're late,' she said.

'Yeah,' agreed Natalie but she didn't move.

'They'll sack you.'

'I'm on a final warning already. It's only a matter of time. And there's this new place opening in Kentish Town. Apparently, they need waitresses.'

'Waitresses with no references?'

'I've got references. Just not from Chester's Chicken Shack. I don't think Chester can write anyway.'

'So, are you just not going tonight? What about your wages? You need to pick them up. Can't you wait until you've been paid for last month and then leave?'

The song had changed into something with a hauntingly militaristic drumbeat. Again, Loretta found her eyes drawn to the screen.

'No point going now,' replied Natalie. 'He'll have found someone else to cover the shift.'

There was no point arguing with her either. Loretta had done that often enough over the years and anyway, she couldn't really blame her sister. She wouldn't have wanted to do all those dead-end jobs. Endless bars, warehouses, factories. None of them lasted more than a few months and the only connecting factor between them all was that barely anyone but Natalie was prepared to do them. Loretta had to give that to her sister. There was nothing wrong with her work ethic.

The song finished and the camera panned round the crowd and on to Paula Yates, who, wearing a skin-tight red dress, was draped provocatively across a sofa. Staring at her blonde spikes, Loretta realised her own wavy shoulder-length tresses were clearly some way wide of the cutting edge.

'Don't suppose you've made any dinner?' Loretta asked, without much hope of a positive reply.

Natalie grimaced. 'I was going to . . . but I got distracted by the beautiful Kirk . . .'

She flopped back on the sofa.

'You're bloody useless,' laughed Loretta. She'd been at work all day and she was hungry and worn out, but she couldn't get cross with Natalie. What would she gain by that anyway? There would still be no dinner.

'We've got some cornflakes!' she heard Natalie shout after her.

The kitchen was tidy. Their mother would be proud of them on that front at least. They had kept the house nicely. Anything less would have been an insult to her memory and doing the housework had also given Loretta something to hang on to in the early days.

On the wall hung the photo of the four of them at her graduation. As it turned out, it was the last picture of them all together and consequently precious, although Loretta tried to ignore how it highlighted the differences between her own life and Natalie's.

She opened the freezer, pulled out a packet of Findus Crispy Pancakes and slithered a couple out on to the countertop.

'Crispy pancake?' she shouted back to Natalie.

'Are they minced beef?'

Loretta inspected the red box.

'No. Chicken and bacon.'

'Then yes please. And chips.'

Later, they were sitting at the kitchen table – eating at the table was something else that they had never let slip – their plates clean but for the lick of tomato ketchup on each.

'Let's do something tomorrow,' suggested Loretta. 'I assume you're not working.'

Natalie rolled her eyes.

'Pretty safe assumption,' she said.

'Neither am I so let's go somewhere.'

'Like go down to Camden?'

'No. A proper trip. Out of London. We can catch a bus from Victoria. Where do you want to go?'

'Stonehenge,' replied Natalie at once.

Loretta stared at her, uncomprehending.

'What?!' replied Natalie. 'I've always wanted to go there. It's so mystical. And they're making all that fuss about closing it off from the hippies. We should go before they put it all in a glass box or something. There are bound to be buses and if we get down there early we can nab a couple of seats.'

Her eyes shone and Loretta didn't have the heart to pour cold water on the plan even though it wasn't what she might have suggested for a trip.

'You'll have to pay though,' Natalie added. 'I'm skint.'

23

There was a bus to Stonehenge and they were on it. As it trundled along the motorway, they hunkered down with their knees pressed up against the seats in front. Loretta could feel the heat transferring through Natalie's jeans into her own thighs and smell the familiar musky scent of her sister, as much a comfort to her now as it was when they had shared a bed as little girls.

At moments like this, it seemed to Loretta that she and Natalie were almost like a single entity, pitched together against whatever life threw at them. It was something she'd felt even more keenly over the last few challenging years and now, when Natalie was still a little lost, they continued to draw strength from one another. Sisters against the world. That was how it felt.

Loretta told Natalie about the crime stories she had covered that week until she sensed that Natalie was losing interest. Whilst she could talk about angles and hooks and sources and follow-ups endlessly, she knew that it didn't always hold the same fascination for others.

Natalie's concentration ebbed and flowed depending on the story, but she had nothing of her own to contribute to the conversation. Her life had become so closed that anecdotes worth retelling seemed to be few and far between. Either that or she just didn't have the energy for it.

It was around midday when the bus pulled into the car park. Stretching their legs, they climbed down, thanking the driver on their way out. Loretta gave a little nod to her mother, wherever she was. She had been a stickler for manners. The driver was already reaching for his copy of the *Sun* and Loretta tried to see what they'd gone with on the front page but couldn't quite make it out without being obvious about it.

The pale-blue sky was striped with cirrus clouds, stretched thin like strings of candy floss. A small encampment of tents had been set up in the field opposite, the protesters she assumed, but there seemed to be relatively few people around the stones.

'Come on,' said Natalie, grabbing Loretta's hand and dragging her past their fellow travellers and towards the huge stone circle. 'Quick. Let's get there before anyone else does.'

It had been a long while since Natalie had done anything urgently and Loretta was happy to be dragged along. They ran hand in hand across the grass, laughing at the silliness of it. Natalie's dark hair blew away from her forehead revealing her eyes, equally dark and with deep shadows surrounding them, but something in the moment made them shine like they had done before, and Loretta felt a surge of hope that there would be a way forward for her sister.

'Do we really need to run?' she said, her breath coming in gasps. 'Those stones aren't going anywhere.'

But Natalie did need to run – Loretta could see that. And she too was enjoying the breeze on her face and having clean air in her lungs, even if they were protesting a little at the unexpected exercise. They should get out of the city more often, she realised, absorb this feeling of space and freedom.

They weren't allowed to walk in and out of the stones, couldn't touch them even. Loretta could understand the thinking, she supposed. They were an important archaeological site and needed to be protected. Then again, they had been standing there for three thousand years. She very much doubted that she could do them harm with just her bare hands.

'Can you imagine getting them here?' Natalie asked her, shaking her head in wonderment. 'I mean, how?'

'Haven't got a clue. Sheer bloody hard work and determination, I suppose. Like most things that are difficult to achieve. Photo!'

Loretta dug her camera out of her bag and Natalie posed in front of the stones. As she slipped the camera away, Loretta considered nipping across to interview the hippies in the camp about their take on it all. She was sure they wouldn't mind talking to her. She had a byline, after all!

Then all of a sudden Natalie stood stock still. She put her hands up, palms wide, and closed her eyes.

'Can you feel it?' she asked.

Loretta wasn't sure what Natalie was talking about. The just-there warmth of the sun? The gentle breeze on her face?

'Feel what exactly?'

Natalie's eyes flicked open but she seemed to be listening intently to some sound that Loretta couldn't pick up.

'The energy,' she said. 'The power.'

Loretta couldn't feel a thing but she could see that the moment was important to Natalie and so she played along.

'I think so,' she replied weakly. 'I mean, the stones are built on ley lines so it makes sense that we'd be picking up something here. After all, twenty thousand hippies can't all be wrong.'

She cocked her head at the encampment, laughing, but Natalie's expression remained sombre.

'Doesn't it make you feel small?' Natalie asked.

Loretta still wasn't with her. The stones were huge and towered over them. Of course they felt small by comparison. But that wasn't what Natalie meant. Loretta could see that.

'We're so insignificant,' Natalie said. 'We thrash about, thinking how terribly important we are, that what we're doing is vital, but actually that's rubbish. We get what, three score years and ten? Four score if we're lucky. Not even that for Mum and Dad. These stones have been here for thousands and thousands of years. And they're new in the grand scale of Earth. We're so very . . .' She paused as she tried to come up with the right word. 'Trivial.'

Loretta got it now. She had thought the same once as she squinted up at the night sky and tried to make out a star or two through the orange glow of the streetlights. It had struck her then just how insignificant human life really was.

'Yes,' she agreed.

Natalie's eyes glistened, a film of tears glazing their surface.

'And vulnerable,' she said, 'sitting on this planet as it hurtles through space. Our lives can be snatched away just like that. Our life is all we have and it can be gone.' She clicked her fingers. 'Just like that. Doesn't that frighten you, Etta?'

It didn't, but mainly because Loretta didn't allow her mind to veer off down that path.

'You can't think like that, Nat,' she said gently. 'What happened to Mum and Dad was a tragic accident but it doesn't mean that anything bad will happen to us. Most people live to a ripe old age. Spending your life in fear of what might be around the corner is no way to live. I know it's hard but you need to get back out there, start living again, discover what lights your fire.'

She was tempted to say that their parents would be disappointed to see how Natalie was wasting her time, but it felt like a low blow. So instead she focused on the future.

'Do you remember the summer you finished school, before the accident? You were talking about going to live abroad, grape picking or finding work in a holiday resort somewhere. Do you remember?'

Natalie shook her head, her expression perplexed as if she couldn't imagine this ever being something she had considered. Loretta pressed on.

'You did. Honestly. Maybe you could do something like that this summer. It doesn't have to be abroad—'

'Not many grapes to be picked in England,' interrupted Natalie wryly and Loretta grinned, relieved that she seemed to be taking the suggestion in the spirit in which it was intended.

'Well, no. But there are so many more interesting things you could be doing. And there's nothing stopping you. You could save some cash between now and the summer and catch the ferry to Calais, head down to the south. You might as well be doing bar work in the sun somewhere as in some dreary pub in Barnet.'

'Are you trying to get rid of me?' Natalie was teasing but Loretta knew that her reaction was a front and could see her sister's anxiety loitering in the shadows of her smile.

'As if,' she replied warmly. 'But I'm worried about you, Nat. I want you to be happy.'

'I am happy,' objected Natalie. 'I like crappy jobs in shitty places. It's why I get out of bed in the morning.'

There she was, thought Loretta with relief. The sparky sister she had missed so much. She was still in there, deep deep down.

'Seriously though, sis,' Nat continued. 'I do appreciate that you're worried about me. But I'm fine as I am. Honest.'

But you're so obviously not, Loretta wanted to shout, but she could tell that there would be nothing to gain. She had tried to plant the seeds of change numerous times over the years but none had taken root. But maybe this time things would be different, she thought. Maybe Natalie was finally ready.

'I'll tell you what, I'll think about it,' said Natalie. 'Do some research in the library. They're bound to have a book on how to go grape picking. And if there isn't I'll go and do it and then I can come back and write one.'

She grinned and Loretta saw another glimpse of the carefree sister she used to know before the accident. Then again, she thought, hadn't Natalie been directionless then too, floating on the water and waiting for the tide to dictate her direction. Maybe the loss of their parents had just highlighted what was already part of Natalie's personality.

And when she herself was so driven by her goals, it was easy to see Natalie's inertia as a failing – but was it simply that she came at life in a different way? The danger was, however, that soon too much time would have been lost. Perhaps being at Stonehenge, with all that talk of how ephemeral human life was, might jump-start something in Natalie and make her realise that life is short and time really is of the essence.

24

Yet time marched on. Natalie got the job at the place in Kentish Town and that seemed to be working out to the extent that these things ever did. There had been no more talk of grape picking. Loretta considered doing the required research herself and presenting her findings to Natalie to take the effort out of it for her. She spent a fair proportion of her time researching as part of her job so it would be child's play to pull the basics together. But her time was also scarce and somehow the task fell off her list.

Then one day everything changed. Loretta had just got back in the newsroom, having been out interviewing a family whose daughter had been accidentally caught up in a shooting. This kind of assignment was never easy but Loretta was learning how to get people to open up to her and her results were impressive. Mr Redpath, in a rare moment of positivity, had said she had remarkable empathy, which had made her shiver to the tips of her toes.

She was just settling herself back at her desk when Malcolm breezed over.

'Bit odd this one, but how would your sister like a job in Sicily?'

Loretta was intrigued.

'As I'm a reporter, I'm going to ask you for the five Ws,' she said.

'Someone clearly trained you well,' replied Malcolm with a grin. 'My wife Vicky's best friend married a Sicilian. She lives out there, near Syracuse, I believe, and is in urgent need of someone to help with the kids. There are three of the little darlings, none of them teenagers yet so not too awful. Anyway, Stella sent up a distress flare and I thought of you. Or actually I thought of your sister. I'm not letting you swan off to Sicily, you're far too valuable.'

Noting and relishing the compliment, Loretta asked, 'What does it involve? Natalie's pretty resourceful but she doesn't know much about children. She's only ever done a bit of babysitting. She isn't a trained nanny or anything.'

'At the risk of insulting Natalie's capabilities, I think Stella's only requirement is that the person speaks English and can get there PDQ! I gather she's been let down and with the summer holidays coming up she really needs someone, and fast. And I know I've never met your sister but I know you pretty well so if you can vouch for her then that's good enough for me and Vicky. What do you think?'

'I'm sure she'd be interested,' said Loretta without hesitation.

Malcolm handed her a piece of paper.

'This is Stella's number. Get Natalie to give her a ring and they can have a chat. No harm in that. If it's not for her then that's no bother but it was worth a punt.'

'Definitely,' agreed Loretta. 'Thanks, Malcolm.'

◆ ◆ ◆

'What do you reckon?' Loretta asked Natalie that evening after she'd repeated what Malcolm had told her. 'It's not grape picking but it might be fun. It'll certainly make a change from pulling pints and serving chicken in a basket.'

Natalie ran her hand through her short dark hair and frowned.

'How old are the kids exactly?' she asked. 'Boys? Girls?'

'I've told you everything I know. If you want more details then ring the number and speak to the woman. Malcolm says she's nice. And if it turns out that it's not for you then there's nothing lost.'

Loretta looked into Natalie's eyes and tried to guess what she was thinking. Natalie turned the piece of paper over and over in her hands, clearly thinking things through. It gave Loretta a moment to think too. What if she actually went? Whilst Loretta was anxious for Natalie to get out into the world as she herself had done, was sending her to live thousands of miles away really the solution? Loretta wasn't sure that she was ready to lose her only family overnight. Well, not lose her entirely, but on a day-to-day level it would be much the same.

'Well?' she asked after a few moments had passed and Natalie still hadn't spoken.

'I could just ring, couldn't I?' said Natalie. 'Find out what's involved. I'm not committing to anything by doing that, am I?'

'Not at all,' agreed Loretta. 'And if anything about it sounds like it's not for you then there's absolutely no obligation to take it any further. It might be fun, though.'

'And Sicily is in the Med?'

They took down the relevant volume of the *Encyclopædia Britannica* that their father had bought on credit one book at a time and opened it at S, leafing through until they found the entry for Sicily.

'Sicily is the largest and most populous island in the Mediterranean Sea and one of the twenty regions of Italy,' read

Loretta. 'Its most prominent landmark is Mount Etna, the tallest active volcano in Europe and one of the most active in the world.'

Natalie looked up from the page and pulled a face.

'I don't think it's dangerous,' Loretta reassured her. 'I can't remember it erupting recently.'

'It's saving itself for when I'm there,' laughed Natalie grimly.

Loretta examined her face. 'So you're considering it?' she asked.

Natalie shrugged.

'Well, I might as well give the woman a ring. What've I got to lose?'

She made the call whilst Loretta busied herself in the kitchen. When she came back into the room, Natalie's eyes were shining.

'Stella sounds really nice. It's her and her husband, Salvatore. He's Sicilian. They have three kids, eleven, nine and six. Two boys and a girl. I'll get my own room and my job will be to help with the kids over the summer. She wants me to go out a week or so before they break up so I can get the hang of everything.'

Loretta did some quick calculations. It was the end of May and the holidays probably wouldn't start until mid-July.

'So in Italy that's June. Next week,' Natalie continued.

Loretta swallowed.

'As soon as that? Wow.'

Natalie caught her bottom lip between her teeth.

'I think I want to go, Etta,' she said, although she sounded unsure.

'Then you should,' said Loretta, trying to make her voice sound as positive as she could although her heart was racing at the speed of it all. Next week! 'We'll have to get you an appointment at the Passport Office. No time to send off through the post.'

'I didn't think of that,' said Natalie. 'Is there anything else I need?'

Loretta tried to think as her mind buzzed. Natalie was leaving her. She was going to live far away and she would be on her own. In this house on her own. And, of course, this was a good thing, was everything she had been hoping for for her sister, everything their parents would have wanted for her. But she'd had no time to get used to the idea, nothing to help her prepare for it. What would she do? How would she cope on her own?

'We should get you some lire?' she said.

25

1984 – Sicily

The heat hit her as soon as she stepped out of the plane. It was warm in London sometimes, but nothing like this. Natalie felt wrapped up in it, cocooned, and couldn't square being outside when the air felt as if she were in an airing cupboard. Was the oxygen sufficient for her body's needs here? Would her lungs be able to pull in enough to breathe? It was hard to believe.

She wanted to linger on the top of the stairs and absorb the newness of it all, but the other passengers were eager to disembark, shoving her gently from behind, and so, reluctantly, she made her way down to the tarmac. A little of the tension she'd been storing for years seemed to seep out of her with each step she took. How could you be tense when you were surrounded by this nurturing warmth?

This was only her second experience of an airport, the first being Gatwick that morning, so she wasn't sure what happened next. Anxiously, she looked around, hoping to find clues, but all the signs were in Italian.

A wave of doubt flooded her head. It had been a mistake coming here, she thought. She wasn't up to it, didn't have the aptitude to deal with so much change in such a short period.

Silently, she cursed Etta for pushing her into it. Where was her sister now, when she needed help? Back in London, where Natalie's life had been small but had at least made perfect sense to her. This chaotic, hot space filled with people she didn't understand was making no sense at all.

Everyone seemed to be heading in the same direction with a unified sense of purpose, so Natalie followed them. At passport control she offered up her brand-spanking-new passport with its dark-blue cover. It had barely been opened. The guard flicked to the photo page and gave it a cursory glance before looking up at her face.

'Buongiorno,' he said.

Natalie had bought a pocket-sized Italian phrase book in WHSmith's and had practised a few words in the privacy of her bedroom, but now, faced with the real deal, she felt stupid and gauche. She smiled at him in lieu of words and he passed back the passport and looked over her shoulder for the next in line.

The airport system seemed to dictate that she collect her suitcase next. A gaggle of people were gathered around one conveyor belt and so she went to join them, hoping that they had been on her plane. When her suitcase swung round, she hefted it off the belt with not a little effort. It was the biggest case she'd been able to get her hands on and it was full of everything she thought she might need and then some. She had no idea how long she was going to be in Sicily, so she had brought almost everything she owned with her.

The other passengers had got luggage trolleys and her eyes darted around to find one for herself, spotting one abandoned not far away. As she wheeled it back to her case, a short, stocky man with dark hair and eyes spoke to her in Italian. She had no idea what he had said but from his gestures it seemed to be an offer of help. She nodded gratefully and he lifted the case on to the trolley for her and then shook one hand from the wrist as if passing comment on just how heavy it was. She smiled at him again. Yes, I'm the stupid English girl who has brought all her possessions to Sicily in one case.

Now that she seemed to have got through the formalities and had her suitcase safely back in her possession, the tightness in her chest eased a little although the overwhelming sense of being out of her depth pervaded. But it was all right, she thought to herself. She could scale this by leaping one enormous hurdle at a time.

She followed everyone else through the exit and emerged on to a bustling concourse. The enticing smell of strong coffee mingled with cigarette smoke and an underlying stench of bins. It was still very warm.

Stella had said in her letter that she would meet Natalie at Arrivals and Natalie had to assume that that was here. She had no idea what Stella looked like but then she spotted a tall, willowy and incredibly blonde woman heading her way. She stood head and shoulders above most of those around her. Sunglasses perched in her hair and a straw bag hung from her shoulder and she was wearing cut-off denims and a pale-pink vest top, her toned arms a rich mahogany. She was quite possibly the sexiest woman Natalie had ever seen.

Stella's gaze fell on her and her face broke into a wide smile. She waved her long arms wildly as if greeting a long-lost loved one, and then made her way over.

'You must be Natalie,' she said when she was close enough to be heard, and engulfed Natalie in a smothering hug. 'I'm so pleased to meet you. The kids can't wait. I left them at home with Annette. They wanted to come but I couldn't face getting them all in the car. It's like trying to herd cats, dealing with them all at once. I probably shouldn't be telling you that. They're great kids really. I just feel outnumbered most of the time. And Salvatore works such long hours so he can't help. Actually, he's not much help when he is there, to be honest. All he does is wind them up and say they can have gelato too close to bedtime. It's a bit like having four kids actually.'

She barely drew breath as she led a stunned Natalie out to a covered car park, her chatter running on from the children to how hot it had been recently and then how long it would take them to drive back to the house.

Natalie soon realised that she wasn't expected to speak and let Stella's prattling wash over her, watching the scenery fly by. They left the airport and gradually moved through the outskirts of Catania and out into the countryside. Everything looked parched and dry, which was hardly surprising if it was always as hot as this. Was it ever green, Natalie wondered, as an unexpected pang for the lush grass of the park down the road from the house in London hit her. The radio was playing softly in the car. Most of the songs were unfamiliar but one or two were Italian versions of songs she knew. It occurred to her that that reflected her thoughts. The car, the countryside, the woman sitting next to her – none of it was entirely new but nor was it what she had known before.

Finally, Stella slowed the car and pulled down a rough track. Natalie had begun to relax but now all her nerve endings sparked as her apprehension reasserted itself. What was she doing here? The only thing she knew about looking after children was that she had once been a child herself.

'You know,' Stella was saying, 'I'm so grateful you've come, Natalie. We don't have a great track record with nannies. You'd think the children were monsters and they're really not. We've just had a run of bad luck. And I've tried local girls but I so want the kids to be bilingual. The only way I can do that is to have English spoken in the house. They need to hear conversations happening around them, otherwise it's just how Mummy speaks.'

'They do speak English already though?' said Natalie hurriedly, panicking that somewhere along the line what Stella required had become confused.

'Oh God, yes. Of course. But I want it to be natural for them to hear it. That's why I have Annette.'

'Who's Annette?' Natalie asked.

'She helps me with the cleaning. I'm sure you'll like her. She's a similar age to you, the niece of one of my good friends back home. I've been calling in favours all over the place.'

Natalie must count as a favour too, she thought.

'I was so glad when Vicky told me about you. Your sister works with Malcolm at the paper, right?'

Natalie nodded.

'Vicky is one of my oldest friends. It's perfect to have such a personal recommendation.'

Natalie squirmed as she wondered how much Stella actually knew.

'I'm so glad to be here,' she said, hoping that this was enough.

This at least was true now. When Loretta had bounced in from work, full of the plan that she and Malcolm had cooked up, Natalie had been less than sure.

'I don't know anything about looking after kids,' she'd countered when Loretta put the plan to her, apparently keen.

'She's not looking for a nanny though. She'll be there most of the time. It's just an extra pair of hands that she needs. And you can be that.'

'But I can't speak Italian,' Natalie had continued, throwing up all the objections she could think of.

'But you'll learn. That's the best way to pick up a language, to live there.'

Natalie wanted to keep placing obstacles in her own way, to protect herself from change. But something had to give, she could see that. Her life had been ebbing away as she sat in their house waiting for God only knew what to rescue her.

And she knew that her being there, stuck, was forcing Loretta to stay too. Not that Loretta would have seen it like that, but Natalie knew that her own inertia was impacting on her sister. She really had no option but to take the job in Sicily and relieve Loretta from having to take responsibility for her any longer. She was twenty-one and it was about time she stood on her own two feet.

And so here she was, with a stranger, about to enter an unknown world.

They reached the end of the track and Stella brought the car to a stop under a vine-covered pergola.

'And here we are. Home sweet home. Now, let's go in and face the music.'

26

The villa at the end of the track took Natalie's breath away. Their house in London was a three-bedroomed semi. This had three floors and a huge frontage. It was rendered in white stucco but the afternoon sun made it glow gold. Natalie swallowed hard. What was she doing here when she quite clearly didn't belong? Was it too late to get Stella to take her back to the airport?

'Come in, come in,' said Stella. 'We'll bring your case in later.'

The front door stood open and there was a pile of trainers and flip-flops in various colours and sizes spread across the threshold. Stella aimed her foot at the pile and tried to push it to one side.

'Gosh, I'm sorry. I do tell them to put their shoes away when they come in. There's a cupboard over there but they never seem to get the hang of it.'

The shoes didn't seem to be the only items out of place. Stray garments and wet towels hung from every surface and the marble floor was scattered with plastic toys, balls, a single roller-skate.

'Please excuse the mess,' Stella said. 'We live like pigs!'

Natalie wasn't sure how to respond. This appeared to be true. But there was Annette. Wasn't tidying up her job? If it was then she didn't seem to be very good at it.

'The kids will be outside,' Stella said. 'They're basically feral.' She ran a hand through her hair and smiled. It seemed that having feral children wasn't something that overly concerned Stella. In fact, she almost seemed proud of it.

'You and Annette live on this floor with Danny. We have the first floor.'

Who was Danny? Natalie didn't want to ask and it seemed that she wasn't going to be shown which was her room either as Stella made straight for the stone staircase and headed upstairs.

A dark corridor led into a large sitting room. There were two French windows, which stood open, allowing a gentle breeze to cool the room. The sounds of splashing and children shouting floated in from outside.

Stella walked to a window and looked out and so Natalie followed her. Below was a huge garden dotted with stunted trees with gnarled trunks. Were they olive trees? Natalie had no idea. And there were palm trees. She hadn't expected that. As far as she knew, palm trees were confined to deserts and camels. A climbing plant with rich purple flowers scrambled over another pergola, which shaded a patio area, and beyond that was a large rectangular swimming pool. The light bounced off the turquoise water and played on the blue tiles enticingly. Natalie itched to dive in and let the water cool her and cleanse the journey from her sticky skin. Maybe being here would be okay, she allowed herself to think.

Two dark heads and one blonde one were bobbing up and down in the water and a girl with milk-bottle-white skin and ginger hair was lying on a sun bed, sheltering beneath a faded blue umbrella.

Stella raised an arm and called down to them.

'I'm back and see who I have with me. Look, everyone. This is Natalie.'

Natalie gave them an awkward little wave.

'Hi,' she said, but in a voice so quiet that it was unlikely that they would have heard.

The children took no notice. The girl with ginger hair looked up and returned the wave frantically as if she were signalling for help after a shipwreck. Natalie's sense of foreboding returned.

'That's Annette,' said Stella. There was no further mention of Danny.

'Where are my manners? Would you like a drink? Or are you hungry? I can rustle up some food. I'm sure there must be something in here . . .'

She walked across to an open-plan kitchen area and opened the fridge but there was very little inside.

She tutted to herself. 'I must get to the shops. Maybe you'd like an ice lolly?' Opening the freezer compartment, she lifted out a cardboard carton but it was empty. 'Those little rats. I'm always telling them not to put the empty boxes back. And now I have nothing to offer you. What must you think of us?'

Natalie didn't know what to think so she just smiled.

'I'm not really hungry,' she lied.

'Well, that's lucky,' said Stella as she banged the freezer door shut. 'Let's go outside and you can meet the savages.'

They went back down the dark stairway. There was no carpet anywhere, Natalie noticed, and their footsteps rang out around them. They turned the opposite way at the bottom of the stairs and out through an open door that led into the garden. It had been cool in the house but now she was back outside the temperature took Natalie by surprise again. It was delicious, the way the heat licked her skin. She could feel it burrowing into her.

'Right then, you horrible lot,' shouted Stella. 'Come and meet Natalie.'

The two dark-haired little boys didn't respond. The smallest child, a blonde girl who was a miniature version of her mother, looked briefly in Natalie's direction and then looked away again.

'This is Enzo and Gianni,' said Stella, pointing at each boy in turn. 'And that's Paola.'

It was hard to know how to greet them when the children didn't even turn to face her.

'Hi,' she said, trying to sound friendly and enthusiastic.

'And this is Annette.'

Annette was much more forthcoming. She moved across the sun bed to make room for Natalie to sit and patted at the towel.

'Hi, Natalie. Welcome to Sicily!' Her smile was wide and friendly and Natalie immediately felt grateful that she was there, a beacon in the darkness.

'Super. Well, I'll just leave you to . . .' said Stella vaguely and then she floated off in the direction of the house.

Annette rolled her eyes and shook her head slowly.

'She's lovely and all that, but she's bloody useless.'

'Who? Stella?'

'Yes. Salvatore isn't much better. He thinks he is, but he's hardly ever around so whether he's a decent parent or not is neither here nor there.'

'He's the husband?' clarified Natalie.

'Yes. He's some big-shot businessman but he works away a lot. The kids run rings round Stella when he's not here.'

Natalie must have pulled a face because Annette added, 'But they're nice really. Not mean or anything.'

Natalie wasn't entirely convinced. She knew nothing about children but she knew that they were supposed to speak when they were spoken to.

'And how long have you been here?' she asked.

'Since last August. You're the fourth nanny since then.'

Natalie wanted to say that she wasn't a nanny but she was more concerned about why the others had all left. She didn't need to ask as Annette seemed only too pleased to share the information.

'First one went home to go to uni. That was always the plan. The second one got herself pregnant. That was a massive scandal. Nobody liked that one little bit. Even Stella was a bit sniffy about it and she's as laid-back as they come. The Sicilians are very traditional. The local girls are barely allowed out without a chaperone. So when the English girl got herself in trouble, they were all delighted. Played up to all their preconceived ideas. Of course, no one batted an eyelid that it was one of the waiters from the pizzeria up the road that did the dirty. He didn't get sent anywhere. Then her replacement just upped and left without a word to anyone about a month ago. And now you're here. She'll be delighted to have found you, what with the school holidays about to start.'

She gave Natalie what was clearly meant to be a meaningful look. Natalie wasn't sure she had enough information to interpret it but she was certainly getting the picture.

'So what's your story?' Annette continued. 'Stella hasn't said much.'

Natalie wondered whether she should let on exactly how underqualified she was for the job but decided against. She had only just met Annette and whilst she seemed friendly, you never really knew. She didn't want to become lost nanny number four before she'd even unpacked.

'No story really,' she said. 'My sister works with Stella's best friend's husband. She needed a nanny at short notice and I was available. And so here I am.'

'It's such a relief to have you here,' replied Annette. 'I get so bored on my own.'

'And Stella mentioned someone else. Danny?' Natalie asked.

'Oh, him. He was Sarah's boyfriend. She's the one who went to uni. He came out to visit her on holiday and then never went home. When she left, he stayed.'

'Doing what?'

'Bit of gardening and handyman stuff to start with but now he mainly works for Salvatore. No idea what he does. I sometimes wonder whether Stella has forgotten why he came. It can be a bit like that. Everything's a little bit fuzzy round the edges.'

'Yes,' said Natalie. 'I'm beginning to get that impression.'

27

The children didn't seem interested in their new nanny and barely acknowledged Natalie's presence. Eventually, the youngest, Paola, climbed out of the pool and stalked over to the sun beds. She could only have been about six but she had her mother's long limbs and smooth tanned skin and to Natalie's mind was already aware of her own charm. Her hair was pulled back in a ponytail but long wet tendrils that had escaped the hairband hung at either side of her face.

She flopped dramatically on Annette's sun bed and then spoke to her in Italian. Annette answered her and sounded fluent to Natalie's untrained ear. Was she the only person in the house that spoke just English? It shouldn't have been a surprise but the understanding only served to make her feel even more out of her depth.

'She's asking if you've brought any make-up with you,' said Annette.

Natalie replied directly to Paola. She did speak English after all, and so there was no need for a translator.

'I have,' she said. 'Would you like to see it?'

Paola nodded.

'It's in my suitcase, which is . . .'

As far as Natalie knew, her case was still in Stella's car.

'Well, we can look at it later,' she added. Paola tutted and rolled her eyes in a way that Natalie had only ever seen adults do before. That Natalie had failed her first test was more than apparent. Paola stalked back to the pool and slid into the water like a seal, disappearing under the surface almost immediately. Natalie wasn't at all sure that she could swim when she was that age and certainly not so elegantly. She threw a glance at Annette to check whether she should be concerned that her charge was underwater, but all seemed to be well.

She and Annette picked up their conversation, swapping basic biographical details. Annette was twenty. She came from Bolton, she said, and Natalie had to concentrate hard to make out her strong northern accent, some words not being clear at all.

'I was going to uni but I didn't get the grades so I came here to learn Italian instead. I'm supposed to be travelling around Italy,' she confessed, 'but somehow I never left this place. There's always something going on. It's never been the right time to go.'

As if to prove her point, an argument seemed to be building in the pool between the boys. Indignant shouting rang out and Natalie looked up to see the bigger one bearing down on the smaller. He landed on his brother sidewards, taking his legs out from under him, and then began to push his head under the water. The smaller one was splashing in protest as he disappeared beneath the surface.

Natalie looked around for Stella but she was nowhere to be seen. This was her job now. She was here specifically to look after the children, and it appeared that if she didn't act quickly the number of her charges would rapidly be reduced by one third.

Standing up, she ran to the pool side, not sure of what she was going to do but certain that something needed to happen.

The larger of the two boys released his grip and let his brother come up for air. He rose to the surface, coughing and spluttering, and managed to draw a breath before he was once more submerged.

A range of options ran through Natalie's mind. Should she shout at them, or jump in and pull them apart? She didn't think either option would be particularly effective and she didn't want to get wet if she could avoid it.

The elder boy pushed his brother under for a third time, and inspiration struck.

'If you kill him, you'll have no one to play with,' she said in a voice loud enough to be heard over the shouting and splashing but in a matter-of-fact tone.

It was enough to make him pause, and in that gap the younger brother was able to wriggle free and torpedo himself out of harm's way. The elder boy side-eyed her, not sure what to make of her.

'Enzo or Gianni?' she asked.

'Enzo,' he said, more out of surprise, she felt, than because he wanted to engage with her.

'Well, Enzo. Think about it. You murder your brother and what are you going to do for fun around here?'

Paola, curious as to how the new person was going to deal with her brothers, joined in.

'Yeah, Enzo. If you kill Gianni, you'll be stuck with just me. Assuming Papa doesn't kill you next.'

Enzo looked at Natalie and then at Paola. He didn't seem to know what to say.

'How old are you?' Natalie asked.

'Eleven,' he said.

'And you get twenty-five years in prison for murder so by the time you come out you'll be . . .'

Gianni was circling back round towards them.

'Thirty-six,' he said. 'You'll be thirty-six when you come out. That's basically dead.'

'Very good,' she said to Gianni. 'Good maths.'

The boy must be bright, Natalie thought. It wasn't a hard sum but he had replied very quickly and he was only nine.

Enzo looked completely thrown by the exchange and it occurred to Natalie that she might inadvertently alienate him before the end of her first day.

'If you're dead set on drowning someone,' she said to Enzo, 'then you can try me, although I don't like your odds.' She flexed her muscles in what she hoped was a comical fashion. Enzo grinned. 'Although you'll have to wait until your mum comes back with my case. I'm not getting these jeans wet for anyone.'

'I could drown you, no problem,' Enzo fired back.

'Oh yeah?' Natalie goaded.

'Yeah.'

Gianni, who had clearly recovered from his recent near-death experience, joined in.

'I'll grab her ankles, Enzo. Tip her up and then you can jump on her head.'

For the briefest of seconds, Natalie doubted her strategy. How appropriate was it to encourage such violent behaviour? Then again, it was clear that the boys were taking it in the spirit in which it was intended. All was well.

Paola, who had swum over to her, pushed herself out of the water on strong little arms and sat on the edge, her wet skin glistening in the light.

'Maybe we could just drown them both,' she said. 'Who needs brothers anyway?'

28

Within a day or two of being in Sicily, Natalie was beginning to find her feet. The glorious weather seemed unbreakable. Each morning when she emerged from her cool, dark bedroom and made her way up the stairs to the family's part of the house to start work, she was struck by the perfect blue of the sky. It was like someone had painted it with great care, no corner less blue than another. She had not yet seen a single cloud, not one.

'Does the weather ever change?' she asked Annette.

Annette shook her head.

'Not really. When I got here, I felt I had to be out in it all the time,' she said. 'You know what it's like at home. Half a day of sunshine and it's a heatwave. And I was trying to get a bit of colour so the locals would stop staring at me. I know this tan is pretty crap,' – she gestured at her pale skin – 'but you should have seen me before I arrived.' She grimaced, making Natalie laugh. 'But then I realised I didn't have to bother going out every time the sun shone. The sun shines every day. And it gets hotter than this in July and August. I've even heard Sicilians complaining that it's still chilly at the moment.'

'But it's scorching!' objected Natalie.

'Not if you're Sicilian,' Annette replied drily. 'They were reaching for their furs when I arrived last September but I couldn't bear to wear my jeans until November. You do acclimatise after a bit, though.'

Natalie thought this was highly unlikely. She couldn't imagine a day when she would get up and not notice the heat or the sunshine or the deep-blue sky.

A daily structure of sorts was beginning to emerge, although she had next to no guidance from Stella. On her first morning, she was lying in bed trying to work out what would happen next when a little blonde head appeared around the door.

'You have to wake us up and make our breakfast,' instructed Paola. 'But I'm awake so it's just the boys.'

Natalie rubbed at her eyes and sat up in bed. The room was virtually dark because the shutters were so effective, and she had no idea what time it was. Reaching for her watch, she peered at the face. It was ten past seven.

'School starts at eight thirty,' Paola informed her helpfully. 'And it takes fifteen minutes to walk there.'

'Okay,' said Natalie, as she did quick calculations in her head. 'So we've got about an hour. Is that enough time?'

Surely it was. How hard could it be to get three children up, fed and out of the door? Paola nodded solemnly. 'But the boys don't like getting up so you have to tell them lots of times.'

Natalie didn't fancy getting ready with an audience.

'Why don't you go and tell them and I'll get dressed,' she suggested and Paola skipped off.

There followed some shouting, then groaning and then more shouting. Nothing here seemed to be done quietly. It was such a contrast to all the silent hours she had spent at their empty house in London. The sounds of bustling family life reminded her of the old days, which brought with it a pang but then also a frisson of excitement at this new way of living.

When she made it upstairs, Annette was already in the kitchen, the table set and breakfast cereals and milk ready on the table. Natalie was relieved to discover that breakfast looked much as it did at home, she assumed because both Annette and Stella were English.

'Morning. Sleep well?' Annette asked her as she poured orange juice into three tumblers.

Natalie wrinkled her nose. She had been awake for chunks of the night wondering what she had done by moving so far away from everything she knew, and how she had let herself be talked into it. She had lost her ability to sleep through the night when she lost her parents and it, like them, had never returned. She was used to looking at the world through a 3 a.m. filter, the sounds of the city keeping her company.

'It was so quiet,' she said. 'Not like London. Sirens and people in the street at all hours. It's like there's been an apocalypse here.'

Annette laughed, a wide-open laugh that drew Natalie to her immediately.

'It is pretty peaceful,' she agreed. 'But you'll get used to it. It took me a while but I like it now.'

Natalie wasn't sure she could ever get used to the eerie silence of the villa at night.

Paola had been right and it took three attempts to get Enzo and Gianni out of bed but eventually they appeared, tousle-haired and slightly grubby. Was she supposed to have supervised some kind of washing? Well, it was too late now and they weren't that dirty. She had definitely seen worse when she'd been at school.

They ate quickly, found lost belongings under the patient instruction of Paola, who was evidently in charge, and were on their way more or less on time.

The walk to school was easy enough – back along the track to the road and then pretty much a straight line down towards the town and the school. Paola chattered away at Natalie's side, keeping up a running commentary on everything they passed. The boys soon met up with a couple of others and barely even acknowledged her, but when they got to the school gate they turned to her before they went inside, Enzo giving her a discreet nod. He was old enough to walk on his own, Natalie thought, but he didn't appear to object to having a chaperone.

Back at the villa, Natalie helped Annette to clean and tidy up whilst Stella stayed in her bedroom, only appearing around midday. She appeared to have the life of Riley but it felt too soon to pass comment, even to Annette.

The children finished school just after lunch and she went to collect them and listened to their stories all the way home, each child fighting for space to share the day's exploits. Even Enzo wanted to be heard and Natalie had the impression that her attention was the most comprehensive they received.

After school there was the pool and then dinner, which Stella attended if she was at home. Annette seemed to cook as well as clean, but Stella had the car so the fridge was only full when she remembered to go to the shops.

There was no sign of Salvatore or Danny. Natalie questioned Annette about it.

'Danny will be here tonight,' she said. 'He was off doing some job or other on the mainland. I don't ask too many questions.' She pulled a face that suggested Natalie shouldn't either. 'Salvatore tends to show up on Fridays so you'll see him then.'

Natalie was intrigued. Apart from Enzo and Gianni, who were children and so didn't count, the household felt like an entirely female domain, as if men being present would spoil the equilibrium. It was hard to imagine any men being there at all.

That evening, she finished the letter she had been writing to Etta. Stella had said that she could use the telephone but she didn't want to be overheard, and also didn't trust herself not to cry when she heard Etta's voice. She wasn't yet homesick but she was missing Etta horribly.

In the letter she described everything that she had come across so far, including little pencil sketches of the household members, which she thought Etta would find amusing.

'I think I'm starting to win the kids round,' she wrote. 'It was hard at first. I'm their fourth nanny in ten months. It's not surprising that they were a bit reluctant to talk to me. But I think it's going to be okay.'

She wrote this because she didn't want to worry her sister by sending her anything but positive news, but as she lay in the warm darkness of her room, listening to the cicadas outside, she decided this might actually be true.

29

There was a stranger sitting at the dining table that night. Most of the household had already assembled under the pergola by the time Natalie arrived, a little delayed by putting away the children's toys in an attempt to restore order to the house. It wasn't yet dark, although the sun had dropped out of sight and the fierce heat had gone out of the day, leaving behind a gentle, comforting warmth. Cicadas chirruped, a low-level white noise that already Natalie barely registered.

The stranger must be Danny, Natalie assumed. He had his back to her, so all she registered was his broad back in a scruffy tee-shirt, mid-brown hair that hadn't been cut in a while, and a tanned neck. He was sitting in the seat that she had adopted for herself. She walked round to find another chair but Paola had her back.

'That's Natalie's seat now,' she told Danny, slipping her little hand into Natalie's and standing so close to her that Natalie could feel the warmth of her skin through her dress.

'I've only been gone for three days,' he said, turning round in his seat. 'Would you jump in my grave so quick?'

'But you're not dead,' chirped Gianni and he threw Annette a confused glance.

'It's just an expression,' reassured Annette. 'It means that Natalie took his place very quickly.'

Natalie didn't want to blush but did so regardless.

'I didn't know it was your chair,' she said, looking at her feet. 'No one told me.'

'It isn't his chair, you daft apeth,' laughed Annette. 'Sit anywhere.'

But as they had all sat in exactly the same seats at every mealtime, Natalie knew this was just Annette being kind. There were two seats that nobody had yet sat on. One of those must be Salvatore's, she assumed, but Natalie had no idea which one. She dithered, not wanting to make the wrong call for a second time. Gianni came to her rescue.

'Papa sits there so that one's yours.' He pointed at the chair next to Danny.

Natalie pulled the chair out and sat down quickly.

'Welcome to the madhouse,' Danny muttered under his breath. Not being entirely sure how she was expected to respond, Natalie said nothing.

Stella breezed out of the house carrying a huge platter of little fried fish in one hand and a basket of bread in the other. She placed them on the table and sat down.

'Oh, isn't this lovely. I do like to see a full table. Buon appetito, everyone.'

The boys dived on the food, picking the little fish up by the tail, dangling them over their mouths and biting the bodies off before dropping the tails on their plates. They were eating the heads. The idea turned Natalie's stomach but now everyone else was tucking in too.

The platter of fish was just out of her reach so Danny picked it up and passed it to her.

'No thanks,' she said, assuming that there would be something less challenging to eat next. She reached for a piece of bread instead.

Again, she heard a low voice muttering to her.

'You need to eat when there's food,' it said. 'Or you'll starve.'

For the first time, she turned to glance at Danny and found that he was already looking at her. He twisted his mouth as if to say 'You don't believe me?', and then he nodded to emphasise his assertion. Actually, from the little she'd learned about Stella so far, she could believe this to be true. But she couldn't eat a fish whole. Could she?

'Go on,' he encouraged, passing her the platter again. 'They're good.'

Tentatively, Natalie took a fish by the tail and took a bite. It was salty and crunchy and tasted of the sea. It was actually not bad if she didn't think about what she was doing.

Danny pulled a face that said 'See! Told you so', and continued to hold the platter in front of her. She took three or four of the tiny fish and he nodded his approval.

At the other end of the table the children were all telling Stella noisy stories about what had happened that day, speaking over each other in their desire to be heard. Stella appeared to be engaged, nodding and smiling as the stories came out, although Natalie wasn't sure she ever really listened. She seemed too distracted.

'So, when did you blow in?' Danny asked her. He was polishing off the little fish at quite a rate and had a large pile of tails on his plate.

'Monday,' she said. 'But you weren't here.'

He shook his head. 'I was in Naples for a couple of days. Back now.'

This much was obvious.

'Do you go away often?' she asked him, and he shrugged.

'Only when there's stuff to be done. How are you finding it at Casa Barbieri so far?'

Natalie managed a smile.

'Bit of a shock to the system if I'm honest. But everyone is really nice and Paola is keeping me in line.'

Danny grinned. It was a nice grin, one eye crinkling more than the other, which gave him a dimple of sorts near his eyebrow.

'She's a force to be reckoned with,' he said. 'She's going to be terrifying when she grows up.'

'She's pretty scary now,' Natalie replied. She meant it as a joke but Danny frowned.

'Don't let them get the better of you,' he said. 'You need to keep your wits about you around here.'

Before Natalie could ask him what he meant, Gianni started cheering and leapt down from the table. Natalie turned to look and there stood a stocky man with a deep tan. His hair was silver at the temples and he had a neatly trimmed beard that was also flecked with silver. His eyes were lost beneath thick eyebrows and his face had settled into deep lines across his forehead. He was wearing a suit in a lightweight navy-blue fabric and even though Natalie knew nothing about these things, she could tell it was expensive.

The man swept Gianni up in his arms, easily turning him over and dangling him by the ankles, Gianni squealing loudly. A general cry of 'Papa!' went up and the children leapt from their seats and swarmed around him. This must be Salvatore.

Stella stood up and wafted over to him and he immediately deposited Gianni safely on the ground and pulled her into his arms and kissed her. The kiss was long and lingering and Natalie had to look away. Her parents had been married for twenty-five years but she had barely ever noticed them touching one another, let alone seen passion like this. Thinking of her parents made her chest tighten. It had been three years, but the grief could still ambush her if she dropped her guard.

To distract herself, she looked over to Annette and caught her eye. Annette pretended to put her fingers down her throat, which made Natalie giggle. The kissing was a bit much but maybe this was the Italian way. The kids didn't seem at all fazed by their parents' intimacy and wandered back to their seats to hoover up the last of the little fish.

After what felt like an age, the couple drew apart and Stella spoke.

'Natalie. This is Salvatore.'

30

'Ciao, Natalie,' said Salvatore and held out his hand.

Natalie was sitting on the opposite side of the table. Was she expected to rise from her seat and go round to shake it? She assumed not, but Salvatore's hand remained extended and so after a second she pushed back her chair and stood up.

Her hesitation had been noted though. Salvatore withdrew the gesture and Natalie was left with the impression that she had a black mark against her.

'Hello,' she said. 'It's nice to meet you.'

Salvatore gave a perfunctory nod and took his place between Stella and Enzo. He spoke to his wife in a low voice, in Italian, Natalie thought, but she couldn't be sure. Stella replied in Italian, her voice higher in pitch and so easier to catch.

Now the chatter around the table seemed to switch arbitrarily between languages with the adults and the children seemingly happy to converse in either. Natalie felt entirely at sea and tried to follow but without much success. Salvatore never seemed to use English. Perhaps he didn't speak it at all.

'How's your Italian?' Danny asked her, again speaking quietly as the chatter continued around them so their conversation was more private.

She shrugged and looked up to the dusky sky.

'I've got a French O level. Just.'

'It'll come,' he said. 'If you let it.'

'How's yours?' she asked.

'I get by,' he replied.

'And you've been here, what? A year?'

'Nearly. I knew a bit before I arrived but I've picked the rest up since. It's easier when you hear it every day. The important thing is not to get sidetracked by the Sicilian.'

'The what?' Natalie was thrown.

'Sicilian. It's not the same as Italian, although pretty much everyone speaks both. Then there are area dialects too. But if you ever go up north speaking like they do down here, no one will take you seriously.'

'But how can I tell the difference?' asked Natalie.

Danny smirked.

'That's part of the challenge,' he replied unhelpfully.

Stella had gone back into the house and Annette began to clear up the debris of the first course. Natalie also leapt to her feet to help but Annette shooed her away.

'I clean. You do the kids,' she said.

She grinned and then took the pile of plates and fish tails away.

'Papa, Natalie has brought lots of make-up with her,' said Paola. 'She says I can try it.'

Natalie's heart sank. Salvatore didn't seem the type to appreciate make-up on his six-year-old.

'Just a little,' replied Natalie quickly. 'Maybe a tiny bit of lipstick.'

She realised that they were speaking in English, presumably for her benefit. So Salvatore did understand at least. She supposed that made sense. How could you have children who spoke a language you didn't? That was surely unsustainable.

Salvatore said something to Paola in Italian and then added, 'The young always want to grow up so fast.' His English was heavily accented but perfectly clear.

'I was the same. Couldn't wait to try on my big sister's clothes.'

'Natalie's big sister is called Etta, Papa, and she is a . . .' She paused as she retrieved the word. '. . . a giornalista.'

'A journalist,' corrected Natalie. 'That's right.'

'Interesting,' said Salvatore. His eyes lingered on her face as if he were storing up every detail. Natalie met his gaze, refusing to be intimidated. His eyes weren't as dark as she'd first thought, sitting as they were in the shadow of his thick eyebrows. They were neither blue nor brown, she saw now, but something in the middle.

She expected him to ask her something about herself but he just continued to watch her.

'You have a lovely home and family,' she said, to fill the gap.

'Sì,' he said. There was no acknowledgement of her compliment. Perhaps this was so obvious that he didn't feel it merited comment.

Then Stella and Annette reappeared, Stella carrying a steaming bowl of pasta and Annette with a ceramic jug and a bottle of red wine. Natalie wasn't fond of wine, preferring lager or cider, but at this point she would take what she could get.

The food was served and conversation sprang up again. The pasta was good, a fresh tomato sauce topped with shiny discs of fried aubergine.

'How was Naples, Danny?' asked Stella.

Something passed between Danny and Salvatore that Natalie felt rather than saw.

'Good, thanks, Stella. Got everything done.'

'Isn't it silly that it's quicker to take things yourself. The post can take an age here.'

'True. It's not like home, is it?' Danny replied, deftly spearing two pasta tubes with his fork and putting them in his mouth.

'It definitely isn't,' laughed Stella. 'And that's why we love it so much.'

'How long have you lived in Italy, Stella?' asked Natalie.

Stella pushed her hair away from her face and held it up in a topknot for a moment before letting it cascade over her shoulders.

'Now there's a question,' she said. 'I came with work so that would have been . . .' She did the arithmetic in her head. '. . . 1969, I suppose. Goodness. That sounds a long time ago. Then I met Salvatore in 1970 and we got married in '72 and I've been here ever since.'

Natalie wanted to know how they had met but this felt like a story for when she and Stella were on their own.

'And do you go back home much?' she asked instead.

'A couple of times a year, I suppose,' Stella said. 'You like England, don't you, kids?'

There was general agreement around the table.

'I like the fluffy floors,' said Paola.

'She means carpet,' explained Stella. 'Not many of those in Sicily.'

When Natalie arrived she had found the hard tiled floors cold and unwelcoming, but now she understood how impractical carpet would be, at least in the summer.

'But Salvatore's work means that we can't get away as often as I'd like,' Stella added.

Natalie cast her mind back to what Annette had told her. He had something to do with exports? Was that it? Natalie wasn't sure what that was but maybe this was a good moment.

'And what is it you do?' she asked Salvatore directly.

The atmosphere changed. There was nothing specific. No one had flinched or looked uncomfortable but something had shifted.

'My company runs a sulphur mine,' he said, his accent making him emphasise the last syllable of each word.

Natalie had only a vague notion what sulphur was used for and her face must have told Salvatore.

'We sell it for use in fertilisers,' he said. 'But it has many uses around the world.'

'They use it for matches,' piped up Gianni. 'Don't they, Papa?'

Salvatore smiled at his son indulgently.

Enzo suddenly became animated, sitting forward in his seat, his eyes twinkling.

'And guns,' he said.

31

A hush fell over the table. Natalie glanced about her surreptitiously, searching for a clue for what had caused the change in atmosphere. Was it that they avoided talking about violence in front of the children? Whatever it was, some nerve had evidently been struck by Enzo's comment.

Then Stella let out a shrill laugh.

'Now, you know that's not true, Enzo,' she said. 'Sulphur is in gunpowder but modern guns don't use gunpowder anymore.'

'They used it in the old days, didn't they, Papa?' said little Gianni, looking up at Salvatore for approval. 'In cannons.'

'Sì. È vero, Gianni. No guns. But sulphur was big business in Sicily, Natalie. Now not so much, but still we mine and export what we can.'

Natalie thought of mining at home. The year-long coal miners' strike was underway and the news had been full of how the business was no longer financially viable. Maybe sulphur was the same.

'What do your parents do?' Salvatore asked her. She saw Stella give him a tense little shake of the head. But it was too late; the question was out there.

Natalie paused. She didn't want to talk about her parents in front of the children in case they were upset by it. No one needed to know that your parents could be gone at any minute, but especially not a young child.

'Dad was a welder,' she said quickly, hoping that the children would either not notice or not question her use of the past tense.

Salvatore didn't understand and Stella quickly offered him a translation, at which point he pulled an approving face.

'Working with your hands' – he held his up and it was obvious from the smooth skin and manicured nails that he had never done any manual work – 'is honourable work.'

Natalie nodded.

'My dad helps run a shoe factory,' chipped in Annette. 'There are lots of those round where I live.'

Paola immediately ducked under the table to examine Annette's footwear and then popped back up.

'What kind of shoes?' she asked. 'With high heels?'

'Sadly not,' replied Annette.

Paola pulled a face.

'What about you, Natalie?' asked Salvatore. 'What will you do?'

People had been asking Natalie this for as long as she could remember and she never got any closer to answering it. She shrugged.

'Well, for now I'm here looking after your children,' she said.

Paola gave a little 'yippee', and Natalie smiled warmly at her.

'And after that? Well, we'll just have to wait and see.'

It was a light and flippant answer that was appropriate to the mood around the table but Natalie wished the subject had never come up. She knew she was actually running away.

'And you, Danny? What is your life plan?' asked Stella.

Danny took a breath, looked around the table and then let his eyes settle on Salvatore.

'I like it here,' he said. 'I'm learning as much as I can and then I think I want to stay and work in Sicily. I don't know what I'll do but I can't see me going back to England.'

The words struck Natalie like a bolt of electricity. It hadn't occurred to her that she might never go back to London, but maybe that was the solution. She could reinvent herself here. In Sicily she was just an English au pair. No one knew or cared about the tragedy of her parents. There was no hushing when she walked into a room, no crossing the street to avoid her because people just 'didn't know what to say'. Here she was simply Natalie. The thought of it was starting to appeal.

Then she remembered Etta. Could she really move here and leave her sister behind? Etta was like the better part of herself, the shiny side of her coin. Coming here for what she had thought would be just a few months had been a wrench. They had held each other and cried the night before her flight, each swearing to keep in touch as much as they could. Part of that was weeping for what they had lost rather than the separation that was to come.

But Etta had her life at the newspaper, which she loved, and now that Natalie was no longer at home dragging her back every evening, she might move closer to work with some of her colleagues or friends. If Natalie decided to stay, Etta would be free of responsibility for her sister – a task she had never once complained about but one that Natalie knew must be a burden. They might even sell their parents' house. The idea made Natalie's heart hurt but they couldn't stay there, cooped up together, forever.

'I like the sound of that,' she said out loud. 'Staying in Sicily, I mean,' she added.

Danny raised an eyebrow.

'It wasn't an invitation,' he said lightly.

'Not with you,' she laughed. 'I mean like Stella did. Move to Italy and live here. Permanently.'

'We can get a house together,' said Paola, jumping down from her seat and clambering up into Natalie's lap. 'I can share your clothes and your make-up.'

Salvatore turned the corners of his mouth down in a comic expression.

'What about Papa?' he asked sadly. 'You can't leave Papa.'

'Don't be silly,' jumped in Stella. 'She's not going to waste her life looking after you. She's only half Italian, you know.'

Natalie tensed, wondering if she was about to witness her first spat, but Salvatore just grinned at her.

'Of course. And I have you, amore mio. And Nonna.'

The children all laughed and Natalie was once again aware that everyone else knew something she didn't.

'Nonna. Salvatore's mother,' Danny explained quietly. 'She lives with Salvatore's sister and her family but when she comes here there are usually fireworks.'

Natalie didn't understand.

'Between Salvatore and his mother?'

'No. Between his mother and Stella. Nonna doesn't approve of the English wife.'

There wasn't time to say more without seeming rude but Natalie was dying to know all the ins and outs.

'Actually,' said Salvatore in his heavy accent, 'my mother rang today. She is coming to visit next week.'

A whoop went up from the children and Stella let out another of her brittle laughs.

'Oh, how lovely,' she said.

Under the table, Natalie felt Annette nudging her foot. When she looked up, Annette winked at her. They were in for something, it seemed. Natalie wasn't sure exactly what.

32

The days got progressively hotter and as they moved towards the end of the school year there was a palpable excitement amongst the children. They became louder and giddier and harder to control, yet a respect of sorts seemed to be building between herself and Gianni and Paola that meant that Natalie could generally get them to be compliant. Enzo was the most likely to push the boundaries and was more distant but not unreachable.

The school summer holidays were three months long and for a portion of that the family would apparently decamp to their summer home closer to Syracuse. The villa they lived in felt like being on holiday to Natalie so she couldn't understand why the family would need to go somewhere else.

'They all do it,' explained Annette. 'Everything shuts down and they move out to the coast. Bit like Wakes Week at home but hotter and longer.'

Natalie didn't know what that was either and Annette just laughed at her.

'You southerners. You haven't a clue.'

The first day of the school summer holiday coincided with the arrival of Salvatore's mother at Casa Barbieri.

'Keep your head down and you'll be fine,' advised Annette. 'She doesn't speak any English so you won't be able to say much to one another. She hates us girls being here, thinks Stella should do it all like she did. She loves Danny, though. He's a proper golden boy. Blatant sexism but what can you expect here. It feels like they're at least twenty years behind home. The food improves no end when Nonna is here, though, so that's a bonus.'

Natalie had seen the army of old women on her way to and from school. They would be there, dressed in plain black dresses with black headscarves holding back silvery hair, sweeping doorsteps and shaking out dusters first thing in the morning. On her way home at lunchtime, they were sometimes to be found sitting outside their houses on uncomfortable-looking camping chairs in groups of two or three, putting the world to rights. Natalie would notice their voices drop as she walked past although she had no hope of understanding, especially if they spoke in Sicilian.

When Salvatore's mother arrived, she matched the stereotype exactly. A car door banged shut outside and Annette, who was sorting laundry in the large airy family room, looked up.

'Stand by your beds. Nonna is here.'

'What do I call her?' asked Natalie. 'Not Nonna?'

'Her name is Maria-Teresa but we're most definitely not on first-name terms. I avoid calling her anything but if I have to then it's Signora Barbieri.'

'Where's Salvatore's dad? Does he come too?'

Annette put a finger to her lips.

'We don't mention him. I tried once and got my head bitten off.'

'That's weird. What did he do wrong? Leave her?'

'No clue. But whatever it was, he's most definitely persona non grata. And don't try going into the kitchen when she's here,' added Annette. 'That's her realm.'

'I've got no problem with that. Anything else?'

But before Annette could reply they heard Stella chattering away in Italian to someone on the stairs, her tone unnaturally bright. Annette swept her laundry up into the basket and cast her eye over the family room, checking for anything out of place. Natalie found herself smoothing down her dress as if she were about to meet royalty.

Then Signora Barbieri came in with Stella following behind. The contrast between the two women couldn't have been more stark, Stella fair, long-limbed and elegant and the older woman very short and round. She was dressed in a plain black dress that came to just below her knee. Her legs were covered by thick black tights that made Natalie sweat just by looking at them and her shoes, also black, were stout. A black headscarf completed the look. She reminded Natalie a little of Grandma from the Giles cartoons.

Stella gestured to Natalie and introduced her. Even with her inadequate Italian, Natalie got the gist. She smiled broadly at the older woman and resisted the urge to curtsy. Signora Barbieri held out her hand and Natalie took it. Her palm was dry and cool. As she shook it, Signora Barbieri looked Natalie directly in the eye and gave her a tiny nod. Salvatore took after her, Natalie thought. They had similar not-quite-a-colour eyes. She must have been a good-looking woman in her youth.

Annette greeted her in Italian and got a curt response back and then Stella was whisking her off along the corridor towards the family's bedrooms.

'So there you go,' said Annette when they had gone. 'The indomitable Nonna.'

'She seems okay,' said Natalie. 'I mean, I can see why she's suspicious of us. We're looking after her grandchildren. She's bound to be worried that we aren't up to the job.'

Annette tutted.

'I'll just be glad when she's gone,' she said.

'How long does she usually stay?'

'Weeks! But this time she's got to go back because Salvatore's sister is having an operation and she's needed to look after the kids. So I think we'll get away with only a couple of nights.'

Natalie gave her an admiring look.

'Is there anything you don't know?' she laughed.

'I just keep my ear to the ground,' replied Annette. 'It's amazing what you can hear when no one knows you're listening.'

Natalie went out into the garden to check on the children. The boys were playing in the den that Danny had built them and Paola had all her dolls arranged on a sun bed and was chatting away to them in English. No one seemed to need her in that moment so she took a beat to reflect. She had arrived here with no idea what lay in store for her. She had seen how desperate Etta had been for something to improve and so had agreed to take the job more to please her than because of any interest she had in it herself.

It wasn't all plain sailing. There were days when the old familiar darkness seemed to consume her and she had to battle just to open the shutters in the morning. At times like that, she painted on a smile and trudged through the hours hoping nobody noticed how broken she was feeling inside.

Once or twice she had almost opened up to Annette but something held her back. What would she say? 'My parents died three years ago and I'm still living in a very deep pit.' It sounded so pathetic.

Her doctor had talked about clinical depression, but he was the only one. No one liked to acknowledge mental illness. It wasn't something you either confessed to or talked about. Natalie was just 'down in the dumps' or 'a little out of sorts' to anyone who witnessed her misery and tried to describe it. Whilst she liked Annette, she couldn't risk sharing anything that would make her treat her differently.

It was hard, though, carrying the weight of her melancholia without Etta's understanding. Some days after work she fell on her bed, exhausted by the sheer pretence of it all.

But not every day. That was an improvement. She could see small signs of change and feel herself beginning to open up. The warmth undoubtedly helped. It was hard to stay buried inside yourself when the heat made you unfurl like a flower.

She thought it had something to do with the children, though. Through them, she had found something she was good at. She'd had next to no experience of kids, a fact that Stella had seemed prepared to overlook in her desperation to find someone to help her, but it didn't seem to matter. She was discovering that she knew what to do instinctively. She had won them over quickly and now there was a kind of trust between them. Even Enzo, older and so more worldly-wise than his siblings, was prepared to listen to what she had to say.

On top of this was this new idea that she didn't need to go home. At least, not for some time. The thought had ambushed her at the dinner table, but she was now finding that she wasn't uncomfortable with it. What was there at home anyway, apart from Etta? She had allowed her friends to drift away. Even Chrissie had eventually given up with her. She had been a project that no one had managed to complete.

Things were different here. She had found a purpose and was good at it, and she was amongst people that she liked. There were definitely worse things in life.

33

2022 – Ripon

Bronte had the makings of a mystery novel without the first idea of how to move beyond the opening chapter. This was going to require serious thought, which she would rather not do alone. Chatting things through with someone else was generally how Bronte came to sensible conclusions. When left to her own devices, it was easy to talk herself out of anything that felt unlikely or difficult to achieve.

That tendency of hers had been born of years of Marc dismissing her ideas and Annie showing no interest in them. When Bronte was feeling robust, she knew that she was just as likely to be right about something as her siblings. It was on her less than robust days when the self-doubt would smother her confidence.

Yet this mystery was too important to let go. She felt that in the deepest part of her core. The depth of the emotion coming from the woman at the funeral, Liz's shadowy memory of things she would never have forgotten, Bronte's own gut instinct. It all pointed to something that needed to be got to the bottom of. She just needed help to make sure she didn't add two and two together and come up with five.

But who should she talk to? It was clear from their previous conversations that her father knew no more than he'd already told her, or if he did he wasn't aware of what he knew, which was much the same thing.

Her siblings should have been the obvious choice but Marc would scoff and Annie was in London. She might scoff too, and Bronte also didn't want to have the conversation over FaceTime, or worse, by the emoji-riddled WhatsApp messages that were Annie's preferred method of communication.

So that left Helen, who had the dual advantage of already knowing as much as Bronte herself did and of being the person who Bronte would have chosen to confide in anyway. She rang her.

'Hi. It's me. Can you come round on Saturday night? I'll cook and we can do a cute film or something and talk about my secret aunt.'

There was a pause.

'What you actually mean is, can I come round on Saturday to talk about your secret aunt,' replied Helen.

'Yeah. Can you come? I will cook, though. Promise.'

Helen turned up on Bronte's doorstep with two bottles of rosé and a bag of Cadbury's Chocolate Buttons.

'To soak up the rosé,' she said.

Bronte hadn't cooked.

They ordered in Thai.

'Okay,' said Helen once the food was plated and the wine poured. 'What do we know so far?'

Bronte bit into her spring roll and thought about it as she chewed.

'Mum had no sister but someone claiming to be her sister showed up at the funeral,' she began. 'Mum apparently went to university even though she told us she hadn't. She was a journalist on a national newspaper. Her parents died when she was twenty-one—'

'Should we be writing all this down?' interrupted Helen.

Bronte found a new notebook and made a numbered list of points under the heading 'What we know'.

'Also, she lived on a council estate in Barnet and went to a school with no sixth form yet still got her A levels and went to uni, the only person from her estate to do that.'

Helen crunched into a tempura prawn.

'That's pretty impressive, you know,' she said. 'It's not easy to do something different to everyone else around you.'

'Mum was an impressive woman,' reflected Bronte. She could feel tears starting to prick but she blinked them away. 'And Liz was definitely lying when she said she couldn't remember a sister. She couldn't have looked more shifty.'

'Yeah. That's super weird.'

'She was weird about a few things, actually,' continued Bronte. 'It was like she was being really careful not to say the wrong thing. One minute she was all open and forthcoming and the next she'd totally clammed up.'

'She must know more than she's saying too. A woman of mystery!' replied Helen with a comical raise of her eyebrows. 'And is that everything?'

Bronte nodded. 'I think so.'

'Then the main question is, why?' said Helen. 'Why did your mum lie about having a sister and why did she go to such great lengths to cover up her past?'

Bronte took a mouthful of her wine. She wasn't comfortable with describing her mother's actions as lying, but really that was just semantics. Loretta had both lied and lied by omission. There was no getting away from it.

'I've been thinking about that. Either she was ashamed of where she came from, or someone did something that she didn't want to associate herself with.'

'A fair assumption,' agreed Helen. 'And that person would have to be . . .'

Bronte nodded.

'Her sister. With her parents dead there's no one else.'

'We don't even know her sister's name, do we?' Helen asked, but then her face lit up. 'But we could find out. Couldn't we do one of those ancestry search things? A census report would tell us who was in the family. Do you know your mum's maiden name?'

Bronte nodded.

'It was Hamilton,' she said. 'And Loretta's not that common a name. It shouldn't be hard to find her.'

'No. Easy-peasy. Where's your laptop?'

Bronte fetched it and Helen started to search, but an hour later, with the food gone cold in its aluminium trays, they were no further forward.

'Are you sure that's her name and her birthday?' asked Helen as yet another search drew a blank. 'There's no one of the right age in Barnet or anywhere else for that matter, let alone someone with a sister. Maybe you could ring Liz back, ask her.'

Bronte pulled a face.

'I don't really want to admit that I don't even know Mum's real name. I mean, that's what we're talking about here, isn't it? We can't find her because she must have changed her name.'

'It certainly looks that way,' agreed Helen.

'But why?' wailed Bronte. 'Who does that?'

'Someone who wants to leave something behind,' said Helen. 'The more I think about it, the more it starts to look like your mum was ashamed of where she came from. Maybe she came north to start a new life and then when she met your dad she didn't want to . . .'

'Want to do what, Helen? Admit that she'd come up in the world? It's hardly a state secret. So she grew up on a council estate in north London. Big deal. Why would it matter? And anyway, she had that job as a journalist. That's something to be proud of, not something to bury.'

Helen eyed her thoughtfully.

'But your dad doesn't know she had a career before coming north, that's what you said, right?'

Bronte nodded.

'As far as I know,' she said. 'He's never said anything that didn't fit her story and he's a stickler for honesty. He's always said you can't be a decent accountant if your integrity can be questioned. I can't see him being happy lying for her, especially not to us.'

'Okay. So, let's assume your mother never told him either and he's as much in the dark as the rest of you. That would mean that it's not just her background that she was trying to hide. It was everything about her old life in London. Your mum came north to reinvent herself, to start over. She left it all behind her.'

Bronte flopped back in her seat and sighed. They were going round and round in circles.

'But why?' she groaned.

34

Bronte had got as far as she could go without any new information. The mysterious 'sister' had disappeared in a puff of smoke, all online searches for her mother had come to nothing and the only person who seemed to know anything wasn't talking. She had run into a brick wall. She would just have to wait until something else happened.

As the days got warmer, the numbers of tourists to Ripon began to increase and the little bell over her door jangled more often. Her shop attracted a particular kind of customer. They had to be curious to have wandered away from the roads that came off the market square like spokes on a wheel. And then they had to be fairly confident to step inside what looked from the street to be a dark and slightly foreboding interior. Bronte sometimes looked with envy at other shopfronts, the ones painted in muted shades of duck-egg blue or sage green, with tempting displays of baskets and throws tumbling out on to the street to encourage passers-by to venture over the threshold.

But her place wasn't like those. She didn't sell tokens of a sought-after lifestyle to dreamers. Her bric-a-brac shop was a little dark and quite dusty, like Dickens' old curiosity shop. It had shadowy corners and an air of mystique that attracted a very different type of customer. And anyway, she couldn't afford a new paint job.

She had regulars, some who liked to browse what was new in but rarely bought, others who she suspected bought from her and then sold on with a mark-up. She didn't mind. It was all part of the trade. Everyone had their eyes open for a deal and if you didn't appreciate the true value of something you had then it was fair game for someone else to capitalise on it.

One of her favourite customers was Tom. He was an older gentleman in all senses of the word. He always wore a jacket and tie and often a beaten-up trilby as well. When he'd first come in several years before when the shop was new Bronte had been suspicious, assuming he was a rival trader come to spy and maybe buy to sell on. However, he rarely bought anything and eventually he stopped pretending that he might. He was more interested in Bronte's company and now she flicked the kettle on as soon as she saw him in her doorway.

This was his first visit to the shop since the funeral.

'Now then, Bronte,' he said as he stepped inside. 'How's thee doing?'

Bronte gave him a genuine smile, pleased to see him in the midst of all the other, suboptimal aspects of her life.

'Fair to middling, I think, Tom,' she replied.

'Aye. Well, you can't expect better than that. She were a grand lady, your mother. She'll be missed, not least by you I don't doubt.'

Bronte had heard almost nothing but platitudes of this type, but somehow coming from Tom it felt more sincere.

Niceties out of the way, he looked around him and asked, 'What's new?'

He meant in the shop, but there was plenty new in her life too. Bronte decided to stick with the stock.

'Those came in yesterday,' she said, pointing at a velvet box with a satin lining in which nestled a set of eight silver-plated fish knives. 'From a house clearance over near Thirsk.'

Tom plucked one of the knives from its soft bed and turned it over appreciatively.

'Nineteenth century, ivory handles, silver plate. Sheffield,' he said.

'Very good,' replied Bronte, 'although it says Sheffield on the blade so I don't think I can give you that one.'

Tom ran the knife's flat edge across his palm and then placed it carefully back with the others.

'And that hatbox,' Bronte added, tilting her head at a black Second World War cardboard hatbox decorated with blowsy red roses.

'No one has use for a hatbox these days,' he said, despite the hat on his own head.

'People like the aesthetics of them, though,' she said. 'Like to have them on display. A nod to a previous age.'

Tom shrugged.

'Nowt so queer as folk,' he said.

Bronte made the tea and handed Tom a steaming mug.

'Ta,' he said, settling himself down in a mid-century Parker Knoll chair. She had bought it intending to have it reupholstered and then sell it on, but Tom and her other visitors had taken a liking to it so now it had a 'Sold' sign on it to put off potential purchasers and was a permanent fixture.

'Hear there was an uninvited guest at your mother's funeral,' he said.

Bronte's spine stiffened. Was the whole town talking about it or was this just Tom's way of asking without seeming nosy?

'Well, you were there, I assume,' she said. 'Did you not see her for yourself?'

Tom shuffled in his seat.

'I were at the back, couldn't see owt.'

Bronte took a sip of tea as she worked out what to do with his enquiry.

'You hear correctly,' she said. 'A woman came and sat in the family pew with us. Marc asked her to leave but she wouldn't go.'

It was Tom's turn to take a drink. Bronte waited patiently for him to make his next move.

'Funny thing to do,' he said. 'Make out like you're family at a funeral.'

How did he know that that was what the woman had done? Bronte was desperate to know what he knew, but she had to play by Tom's rules, dancing around the subject rather than asking directly.

'How do you mean?' she asked, hoping that an open question would draw him out.

Tom lifted his hat and scratched at his scalp.

'Sat on front row,' he said. 'There's not a soul alive who don't know that only family sits there. Funerals, christenings, weddings. It's all the same.'

Bronte deflated a little. So he didn't know any more than she did. Should she tell him what the woman had claimed, confide in him? In the moment, she couldn't think of a valid reason not to.

'Actually, she told us she was entitled to sit there because she was Mum's sister,' she said, trying to make it sound like this was of no particular interest to her. 'My brother thinks she was an attention seeker, or a fraudster.'

Tom pulled a face, taking this in and considering it.

'Never heard your mother had a sister,' he said.

Why he would ever have heard about her mother's family should have surprised her but of course it didn't.

'She didn't,' replied Bronte, 'not as far as we know.'

'Bit strange then,' said Tom.

'Yes. Really weird.'

'Did she look like your mother?'

This was something Bronte had not thought about. Was there any family resemblance that might help convince her of the truth of the stranger's claim? But she had seen her so fleetingly, had been far more interested in making sure her father was all right than taking in the stranger's features. She only had the vaguest idea of what the woman had looked like and that was mainly based on the way she was dressed and her severe short hair.

'I don't know. I didn't get a good look at her,' she said. 'And then at the end she just slipped away before I could talk to her.'

Tom lifted his hat and ran his hand over his bald pate.

'Mighty peculiar,' he said, more to himself than to her. 'Right then.' He stood up and handed Bronte his mug. 'Best be off.'

And then he shambled out of the shop, leaving Bronte smiling after him.

35

On Sunday, it was her nephew's birthday party. Barnaby would be three and was having his party at a soft-play centre in Leeds, and Sara and Marc had invited them all over. Annie had declined the invitation on the basis that it was too far to travel, but as it was less than an hour from Ripon, Bronte felt that she ought to make the effort. She offered to take Garth.

'I'm not sure I have it in me,' he said feebly, 'but your mother would never forgive me if I didn't fly the flag for the pair of us, so a lift would be most welcome. Thank you, Bronte.'

He patted her gently on the arm. He still had the air of a man bewildered by where he had found himself. It was early days, Bronte knew, but she found herself wishing her old father would return sooner rather than later. Somewhat selfishly, she felt that his grief was impeding her own recovery. In the absence of her mother, she needed her father to be strong or, at the very least, not quite so feeble.

In the car on the way to the party he was very quiet and so rather than sit in sad silence, Bronte put on *The Archers* omnibus on Radio 4. She wanted to tell him about her trip to see Liz but something stopped her. It was bad enough that her mother had been evasive about her past. If Bronte thought her father was also hiding things from her, she wasn't sure how she would cope. She had never before had any reason to think that their family wasn't entirely honest with each other and she wasn't at all sure she liked this redrawing of their boundaries. As she drove, she wondered if the others had secrets too. Maybe she was the only one without any.

The play centre was on an industrial estate, which was deserted but for the cars delivering the party guests, who seemed to swarm like bees round a hive. Bronte had to park some distance from the entrance. How many friends could a three-year-old have accumulated?

This might have been her, she thought. Delivering her offspring to parties on a Sunday morning. Waving to the dads she knew, sharing intimate little eye rolls with the mums. Uttering mock complaints that the children seemed to have better social lives than the adults and how did that happen, but all knowing they wouldn't have it any other way and were too exhausted by parenting to have much left for their own entertainment in any event.

The life she had imagined for herself was no longer on the cards. She tried not to think about her relationship with Joel as time wasted, but it was hard not to when the clock had been ticking all the while they were together and she was now back at square one, five years older and no closer to having a family of her own.

Usually, she could keep these thoughts at bay, but faced with dozens of little family units made that harder. A little girl with blonde curls and a pink party dress that twinkled as she moved ran past her, anxious to get inside. Her little pink shoes had rosebuds stitched on to the straps. She was so beautiful that Bronte felt like congratulating the parents for having created such a perfect child, although that was silly. All children were perfect, especially the ones you didn't have.

The child's mother caught up with her daughter and grabbed her hand, reprimanding her for running in a car park, and Bronte stopped watching. She sucked in a deep breath and straightened her spine. This morning wasn't about her. It was about her gorgeous nephew and his birthday. She would have to deal with her shattered dreams on her own time.

Gathering their gifts for Barnaby, including the one Bronte had bought for Annie, who had left it too late, she and her father made their way inside, where their senses all came under fire at once. The play centre was huge and unpleasantly warm, and the rank odour of hot bodies, fried food and popcorn hung in the air. Music blared out, the tune indistinguishable but the bass resounding through the soles of their feet. Children of various sizes ran, jumped, climbed and slid down vast curling tubes of primary-coloured plastic. Many were crying but more were squealing with delight or shouting to be heard over the din.

Garth turned to Bronte, his expression somewhere between astonishment and horror.

'Good Lord,' he said, eyes wide.

'Let's go and find Marc,' she suggested and set forth purposefully into the fray.

It was quickly apparent that these weren't all her nephew's party guests. The centre was open for business to all parents who needed something to entertain their offspring on a Sunday morning, but down one side Bronte noticed three enclosed rooms, one of which had 'Barnaby's Party' chalked on to a noticeboard on the door.

Through the smeared windows she could see a long trestle table set with party hats and paper plates and cups for around twenty. The room was empty but in the far corner lay a pile of discarded clothing, an array of boxes wrapped in cheerful paper and ribbon and a baby-changing bag.

'This is the place,' she said to Garth. 'Let's drop these presents off and then we'll see if we can find them!'

She assumed that they would be in one of the lower play areas but then she caught sight of Marc at the very top. He waved at her.

'Bronte! Up here!' he mouthed, although she couldn't hear him for the engulfing noise.

A conversation of sorts took place based mainly on gesticulation and pointing, from which she deduced that Sara and her younger nephew, Felix, were to be located in the toddler area at the back of the room.

'Come on, Dad,' she said, but Garth was looking up. She could see a flicker of his old self in his eyes.

'I think I might go up there,' he said, more to himself than to her. 'It looks fun.'

He set off towards the bottom of a scramble net.

'Dad! Your shoes!' she called after him. He stopped, slipped them off and then carried on.

She watched him negotiate the netting and then a tube and then she lost sight of him. This was her old dad, or at least the dad he had been when encouraged by her mother. She was heartened to see that he hadn't entirely disappeared. It gave her hope for the future. She took the shoes back to the party room and then went to find her sister-in-law.

Sara was sitting in a ball pool with one-year-old Felix. He had a blue ball in his little hands, which he was trying to eat. Sara had to keep knocking it from his hands – 'No, Felix. Dirty' – at which point he just picked up another and tried again.

'I hate these places,' she said as Bronte settled herself in the ball pool. 'So unhygienic.' She pulled a face. 'I can't even imagine what's lurking under these balls.'

The thought hadn't occurred to Bronte but now the idea was in her head she wished that it wasn't.

'Stray socks,' she suggested. 'The odd dummy. Maybe a virus or two?'

She grinned but Sara remained stony-faced.

'Barnaby insisted on having his party here. My sister Claire had her eldest's here too and since then Barnaby's been obsessed.'

'It's great,' said Bronte, looking around her. 'I used to love these places when I was little. I don't remember them being as high as this though.'

She looked upwards into the cavernous space above them. The children playing at the very top looked like little specs of colour.

'I know. And Marc insisted on taking him straight up there, said it'd be good for his confidence. He's far too young.'

'Dad has just gone up to find them,' Bronte said.

Sara's jaw dropped.

'No! Well, there you are. It's official. All traces of madness definitely come from your side of the family.'

At last there was a smile and Bronte grinned back, eager not to lose momentum. She had always found Sara hard work but a stressed Sara was the worst of all to deal with.

'How can you keep track of his little chums?' Bronte asked.

'It's a total parental supervision party. It's the only way.'

Sara then proceeded to complain almost non-stop until a tannoy rang out.

'Will everyone attending Barnaby's party please make your way to the party room, where lunch is being served.'

'That's us,' she said and rolled her eyes. 'Food fights and spilled drinks all the way.'

She really was a bundle of joy, Bronte thought.

36

The meal was a joyful chaotic cacophony. The guests, most around the same age as Barnaby and a few a little larger, all took their places around the vinyl-covered table. Parents hovered at shoulders, ready to leap in with extra ketchup or to rescue teetering drink bottles. Barnaby sat at the head, paper hat at a jaunty angle, and laughed as if this was the most fun he could ever imagine having. Bronte couldn't help but smile, despite her own disappointments.

Her mother would have loved this, she thought. All of them together to celebrate her elder grandson's birthday would have gladdened her heart. Loretta hadn't been one of those children-centric women whose entire life was focused on her kids, but family had meant everything to her. Bronte had always assumed this was because she had had no family of her own, but now it was starting to look like she had chosen to cut loose from her own relations. Did that put a different slant on how her mother had been with her own children? Bronte wasn't sure.

Thinking about her mother's absence brought a wave of grief that threatened her good mood, and she squeezed her lips together to stave it off. She looked over at her brother, standing proudly behind Barnaby and chatting to a dad to his left. Felix was nearby, seated in a highchair with Sara crouched at his side trying to encourage him to eat tiny portions of carrot and cucumber whilst the older children tucked into chicken nuggets and chips.

Marc sensed her looking and met her eye. They exchanged a look in which Bronte congratulated him on what he had achieved and he accepted her good wishes.

Next came the cake and singing and then it was time to say goodbye to the guests and leave. Barnaby handed out his party bags, proudly passing a brightly coloured paper bag to each guest. The guests in their turn were prompted to thank first Barnaby and then Sara for the party. Bronte noticed how Marc didn't really get a look-in. That was the way of things, she supposed. Mothers took the credit for both of the parents. An image of Joel at her side popped into her head before she could stop it. He would probably have made a terrible dad, she thought without evidence to back up the idea but pleased by it nonetheless. What did she need him for anyway? The controversial thought was barely strong enough to stand on its own spindly legs but it was a start.

When the final guest had left, Marc let out a big breath.

'That's that for another year,' he said, as if the party had been a marathon that had to be endured.

'Felix's next,' chipped in Sara.

'Yeah, but he'll only be two. We can get away with family and close friends at home for that.'

Sara opened her mouth to object but Marc didn't give her the opportunity. He turned to Barnaby. 'Did you enjoy your party, mate?'

Barnaby nodded enthusiastically.

'Can I open my presents now, Mummy?' He started to move purposefully towards the pile of gifts as Bronte wondered why gift opening needed maternal permission and not paternal.

'Hold your horses there, young man,' said Marc, grabbing him by the back of his sweaty tee-shirt. 'Let's get everything home before we start.'

Barnaby looked like he might object or even cry, but Sara swooped in with a distraction about going to recover his new light-up trainers from the shoe cubbyholes and that saved the day. This parenting lark appeared to be a complicated game of strategy and tag-teaming.

'Would you like to come back to ours for a cup of tea before you head back?' asked Sara. Every bone in her body was signalling that the correct response to this offer should be 'no' but before Bronte had a chance to oblige her, her father was accepting the offer.

'That would be most welcome, Sara love,' he said and then bent to speak to his grandson, and so missed the tightening of her lips.

◆ ◆ ◆

Back at Marc's house, tea and what was left of the birthday cake was served. The sky was an ominous grey but Sara had seated them outside on their tiny patio as if she were desperate to keep any trace of them away from her clean carpets. Barnaby opened his presents one by one, momentarily delighted by each, only to discard it seconds later and move on to the next. Sara kept track of who had brought what for the purpose of thank-you letters by taking photos on her phone. It seemed like a military operation to Bronte.

Marc went into the kitchen to fetch more milk and Bronte, seeing her opportunity to catch him on his own, followed.

'Hi,' he said as she appeared in the doorway.

'Great party,' she replied. 'He's had a wonderful time.'

'Yeah. And Dad too,' said Marc as he poured milk into a little blue jug. 'He seems to be getting over Mum pretty quickly.'

There was a barb in his tone that Bronte didn't like.

'He has good days and bad,' she replied evenly. 'Just like all of us. Listen, Marc, something a bit odd has happened. About Mum.'

'Oh?'

He began emptying the dishwasher and Bronte wished he would give her his whole attention, but some of it was better than nothing.

'You know when you were preparing the eulogy?'

'Hmm.'

'Did you start with her life with us on purpose or did you think about going a little bit further back?'

Marc stood up and turned to face her.

'Not sure what you mean,' he said.

Bronte could hear in his tone that he was bracing himself for a criticism, which he would no doubt defend vigorously. She would have to tread very lightly.

'Well, you talked so beautifully about her and her life in Ripon. It really was a gorgeous tribute. But it made me think about what was in her life before she came north. I just wondered if you'd wondered about that too.'

Marc dismissed the comment with a shrug.

'Not really,' he said. 'Mum always said her life began when she met Dad, so I took her at her word.'

'But weren't you curious? She was twenty-eight when they got married. That's older than Annie is now, quite a lot of life to just ignore.'

'I didn't ignore it,' replied Marc steadily. 'I just chose not to include it.'

Bronte leapt on to his words.

'So you did find something out?' she fished.

She was in dangerous waters again. Any hint that Marc hadn't done a thorough job and she'd lose him.

'Not really,' he said. 'I asked Dad but he got upset. And I googled her.'

'Using which name?'

'Well, Hamilton, of course. That was her maiden name, after all.'

Was it though, Bronte wondered.

'And did you come up with much?' she asked.

'No, actually. Drew a blank. But then I didn't know much about where she was born. Loretta Hamilton, London, 1959. It's a bit vague and it's like the Dark Ages googling a person from back then. Unless they're famous, there's not much to find.'

'I suppose so.' She paused for a moment. 'Do you think Hamilton was actually her name?' she said.

Marc looked at her as if she had a screw loose.

'Why wouldn't it be?'

Bronte wasn't sure how much she wanted to give away.

'I don't know. It's just that after the funeral I realised that I didn't know much about her either, so I searched too. I even looked for a birth certificate online. And the census. There was no Loretta Hamilton born in London on the right date. So either she wasn't born in London, which she said she was, or she had a different name.'

Bronte had Marc's full attention now. She watched his expression change as he processed what she'd said.

'Are you sure?' he asked. 'Could you have been searching in the wrong place?'

Bronte tried to ignore the implications of his question. She was used to the family presuming she had got something wrong or messed it up when things didn't work out the way they hoped. She had grown up with those assumptions. When she was younger she had just accepted them, assumed they must be right and she wrong and backed down as a result. But she was an adult now and she wasn't wrong. And she had done the searches with Helen so if she was mistaken then Helen was too.

'No. I'm certain,' she said boldly. 'There was no one of that name born in London on that date. In fact, I couldn't find anyone called Loretta Hamilton born on her birthday anywhere in the UK. So, I'm wondering if she changed her name. I think that's more likely than changing her birthday.'

Marc frowned, thinking.

'Have you asked Dad?'

Bronte shook her head. 'I thought he had enough to deal with. I did ask him if Mum had any old friends though, people he'd invited to the funeral.'

'And?'

'There was a woman from primary school. She was on holiday at the time so she couldn't come.'

Sara called through from outside.

'Are you coming with that milk, Marc?' she said.

'Yep. On my way.'

He picked up the jug and moved towards the door.

'Maybe you could ask her,' he said over his shoulder. 'But I can't see how it matters. I'd be tempted to let sleeping dogs lie myself.'

He went back outside and Bronte heard him asking who needed the milk. Bronte, not quite ready to go back herself, went to the downstairs cloakroom instead and locked the door. She put the loo seat down and sat.

She had intended to tell Marc about Liz and how vague she had been about her mother having a sister, but they hadn't got that far and now Bronte concluded that that was no bad thing. She didn't want Marc dismissing her discoveries or undermining her search.

It was true that she had put up with a lifetime of being the butt of family jokes, considered the under-achiever, the one most likely not to do something or to get it wrong. But her gut was telling her that this was too important. This time she mustn't allow herself to be put off her course of action. There was something here. Granted, it was something long buried, but it needed to come out of hiding. And it wouldn't do that if she just dropped it, no matter how uninterested her siblings might be.

37

1984 – Sicily

Annette had been right about the impact of Nonna's presence at Casa Barbieri – the food improved immeasurably. The woman never seemed to leave the kitchen, from the moment the cicadas started singing in the morning until the sun dropped down behind the villa at the end of the day. A constant stream of delicious aromas wafted through the house and garden. There was bread first thing, round sweet buns that the children filled with lemon-sharp granita for breakfast, tomato-based ragùs, which simmered down to the richest sauces Natalie had ever tasted, and golden arancini stuffed with oozing mozzarella.

For all that Nonna seemed intimidating, she always acknowledged Natalie as she passed through the kitchen, often offering her a spoonful of something delicious to taste. Natalie would close her eyes so she could savour the flavours and when she opened them again she would find Nonna staring at her intently.

'Buono?' she'd ask.

'Molto buono,' Natalie would reply, and she meant it. She had never tasted food as incredible as Nonna's, food that made you want to cease all conversation just so you didn't miss any part of the enjoyment. It was all a far cry from Findus Crispy Pancakes and she longed for Etta to be there to experience it for herself.

She would try to explain what she had eaten in her long letters home. 'It's pasta but it doesn't go all soggy in the pan like it does when we make it. It stays firm but it's not hard. It's like if you bit into an earlobe. I don't know what it's like to bite an earlobe but you get what I mean.' Or, 'The lemons here taste so much more lemony than at home, like thousands of little needles all spiking your tongue at once so that it's almost too intense to bear but you still want more.'

But she knew she wasn't adequately getting across what she wanted to say. The only way Etta was really going to appreciate everything was for her to come and see for herself, and as Natalie had only been there a few weeks, it felt too soon to ask Stella if she could have a guest to stay.

Etta was the only thing Natalie missed about England. The rest of her former life had just drifted away. It was almost as if it had happened to someone else. Now if she thought about the time since her parents died, she couldn't believe she had wasted so much of it in dead-end jobs when she could have been in Sicily, but she knew she wasn't being fair on herself. How was she to have known what kind of life awaited her and anyway, she'd had to wait for the stars to align. Any earlier and she wouldn't have found her way here, to this family, to this house.

It was also hard to explain in her letters to Etta just how much she was enjoying herself. Her job really didn't feel like work. The children were fun to be with. Even Enzo with all his dark brooding already had a soft spot in her affections. Cleaning up after them at the end of each day never felt like a chore because all she had to do was look around and she'd feel almost overwhelmed by how lucky she was to have landed there.

It wasn't just the children she liked. The rest of the household were equally lovely. Annette was quickly becoming someone she could see as a best friend. They seemed to share an outlook on life and had a similar sense of humour. Stella, despite being absent in both mind and body much of the time, was a fair boss. Salvatore was an unknown quantity, not giving much away – it was easy to see where Enzo got his aloofness from – and Natalie hadn't yet worked him out and was a little wary, but he seemed perfectly pleasant.

And then there was Danny.

Natalie was twenty-one and reasonably pretty, she thought, so there had always been boys around her and she'd shown interest in her fair share of them. She'd even had the occasional relationship, and had lost her virginity to a guy in the year above her at school in a heady rush of hormones and cider. Since the accident, however, her interest hadn't been piqued by anyone. She just hadn't had the energy.

But Danny was something different. Danny made her heart bang against her ribs each time she caught sight of him. Everything he said was beyond fascinating to her. If he came into a room she was in, she would rack her brain for topics of conversation that might be enough to make him stay for a while.

She stored up her questions about life in Sicily for when she saw him, even though Annette could answer them just as well. Sometimes, she actually asked the question of both of them. That way she could get the answer from Annette when she needed it, but then had the sheer joy of watching the way Danny's lips moved as he talked, the way he pushed his hair away from his forehead, that tiny dimple by his eye.

It was like an addiction. If she knew he was in the house somewhere, she could barely concentrate until she knew exactly where. Having never been particularly interested in the shapes her body made, she found herself sitting and standing in ways that she hoped showed it off to its best. When the sun burnt her forehead one day whilst she was playing in the pool with the kids, she was mortified. There was no hiding the beacon-like glow that radiated from her face at dinner that night and even in the dim dusk light she had never felt more self-conscious. She caught herself joking about it at her own expense before anyone else had a chance to comment on it.

She thought she was hiding her growing feelings for Danny well, but of course Annette noticed. They were tidying up Gianni's bedroom together and as she moved closer to the window, Natalie chanced a quick look outside to see if she could locate him.

'He's gone to Catania for Salvatore,' said Annette without her having to ask. 'I saw him leaving first thing. He'll be back for dinner.'

Natalie's shoulders slumped and she felt a blush rise up her throat.

'Is it that obvious?' she sighed.

'Only to a blind man in a dark room,' laughed Annette.

Natalie closed her eyes and screwed up her nose.

'Do you think he knows?' she asked.

'That's a trickier question. He is a man, after all. They haven't got a clue of what's going on most of the time. But yes. I think he knows.'

Natalie dropped down on the bed and hid her face in her hands.

'Oh God,' she groaned.

'What? That's okay. There's no law against fancying someone.'

Natalie looked up and met Annette's eyes.

'Ah,' said Annette as the light dawned on her. 'This is more than that.'

Natalie nodded.

'I can't help it. I think about him all day long—'

'And all night,' chipped in Annette, smirking lasciviously.

'Yeah, that too,' admitted Natalie and grinned back. 'But it's horrible. I don't know what to do with myself most of the time. Whoever said that being in love is one of life's greatest pleasures has clearly never experienced it themselves.'

She stood up and straightened Gianni's sheets, which had got themselves into an impossible tangle as he slept.

'Well, there are worse things,' said Annette with a quick raise of her eyebrows. 'You need to stop complaining and buckle up for the ride of your life.'

Voicing her feelings for Danny was the first time Natalie had opened up to Annette about anything personal but it felt good to have a confidante, someone who was on the spot and who might understand her a little. She wasn't a replacement for Etta. That would never happen. But it would be good not to have to carry everything on her own.

Before she'd had a chance to weigh this in her head, she was talking.

'The thing is,' she began, 'I'm not really used to having strong feelings.'

Annette looked at her doubtfully.

'What do you mean?' she asked. 'Never been in love before? Or in lust, at least. I find that hard to believe.'

Natalie swallowed hard before she took the next step out into the unknown.

'It's not that. It's more that I haven't felt anything, not for years. No emotion at all, just a deep kind of emptiness . . . It's hard to explain.'

Annette eyed Natalie contemplatively for a moment and then sat down on the newly straightened bed and patted the sheet next to her. Natalie obliged.

'That must have been tough,' Annette said.

'Yep.'

Having started this conversation, Natalie wasn't sure where to take it. Talking about how she felt, or didn't feel, rendered her far more vulnerable than she ever wanted to be. But Annette wasn't asking difficult questions. She seemed content just to listen.

'The thing is,' Natalie continued, 'I hit a bit of a low spot after my parents died. But then I couldn't seem to get myself out of it. It's been a dark few years.'

Annette nodded as if she understood precisely what Natalie was talking about.

'So this thing with Danny,' Natalie said. 'It's . . . well, imagine that you've been living in the corner of a very dark cave for a very long time and then suddenly someone appears with lights in all the colours of the rainbow and a massive orchestra playing your favourite music. It's incredible and you love it, but it's a lot to take in all at once. After the cave, I mean. It feels a bit like that.'

'I did wonder if there was something,' replied Annette. 'You're so bright and smart but you seemed to have a gap. None of your stories are recent. I noticed that. And you mainly talk about your sister rather than your friends, but I couldn't see why you wouldn't have any friends. You're lovely. You should have loads.'

Natalie raised her eyebrows.

'Ta. And you're spot on. I did have friends before but I let them all drift away.'

'I bet it's been tough,' replied Annette.

Natalie just shrugged.

They sat side by side for a moment. Natalie was relieved that Annette seemed to have understood what she was trying to say instinctively without asking the endless questions that she had come to dread. It felt like one of the shrouds that she'd been wearing for so long had been lifted off her shoulders. Then Annette nudged her.

'So fancying the pants off Danny has come as a bit of a shock to the system,' she said. Her smile was all-knowing and Natalie could tell that her own dark truth had been recognised and accepted.

'Yeah. Just a bit,' she replied, relieved that they could move the conversation back on to a lighter footing. 'Do you think I'm in with a chance? Is he still seeing that girl, the one who went back home to go to uni?'

Annette wrinkled her nose.

'I'm not sure. He plays his cards pretty close to his chest. But she left almost a year ago and he's only been home once in that time and he never talks about her any more. I think it might be over. Why don't you ask him?'

Natalie's stomach flipped.

Whether it was at the idea of asking the question or excitement at what the answer might be she couldn't say, but she was going to have to do something. This level of unrequited passion was more than she could bear in her newly emotional world.

38

Natalie didn't get a chance to quiz Danny about his mysterious love life until the following day. He breezed into the kitchen when she was organising a tray of drinks for the children, and with her equilibrium immediately disturbed, she had to focus hard to make sure she didn't spill anything or trip up over her own feet.

'Good day in Catania?' she asked him.

His eyes narrowed warily and Natalie worried that she'd been told his whereabouts in confidence and shouldn't have let on that she knew. But then the darkness lifted from his face and he answered.

'Yeah. I just had to drop some stuff off at the accountant's. Salvatore doesn't like using the post. It's not the most reliable.' He rolled his eyes as if this was something everyone knew and joked about, a bit like British Rail.

Natalie was nervous of criticising the Italian postal system, not being sure how much English Nonna understood, but Danny had no such qualms.

'It's like everything around here,' he continued. 'It either doesn't work or it doesn't work unless someone else is pulling the strings.'

Natalie had no idea what he was getting at but she nodded as if she understood.

Nonna had put a mound of flour on the tabletop and was forming it into a volcano with lumpy arthritic hands. She picked up an egg and thrust it at Natalie.

'Fallo tu,' she said.

Natalie wasn't sure what she meant and hesitated, looking first at Nonna and then at Danny.

'She wants you to help,' he explained.

'Okay,' she replied slowly.

Nonna nodded at the sink.

'Better wash your hands first,' said Danny. 'I'll take that tray out to the kids if you like.'

He picked it up and headed out into the garden with it before Natalie could object. Nonna was talking to her and she gathered that she was expected to crack the egg into the centre of the flour as Nonna had just done. Natalie did and then watched as the old woman began to fold the egg in without letting any of it escape. She passed the fork to Natalie and nodded at her to have a try. Natalie soon got into a rhythm. It was therapeutic, getting the egg to absorb the flour within the confines of the steadily decreasing volcano, and she did it without mishap.

'Bene,' said Nonna, nodding approvingly. Then she showed Natalie how to knead the dough until it was smooth. Finally, she pressed a stubby forefinger into the ball to test its resistance and then wrapped it in a damp cloth and put it in the fridge.

Natalie seemed to have done a good job and she was feeling momentarily pleased with herself when a cry rose up from the garden. Gianni.

'Mi scusi,' she said to Nonna and raced out of the kitchen to find what the trouble was.

She found Gianni underneath Enzo on the grass. Enzo was sitting on his chest and had his knees on Gianni's arms so he couldn't struggle. Gianni shouted and squirmed but he couldn't get himself free.

Natalie put her hands under Enzo's armpits and lifted him up. He shouted too and kicked out at her with his legs but she managed to hold him so he couldn't hurt her.

'Isn't it annoying when someone bigger than you stops you from doing what you want?' she asked him, eyebrow raised.

Gianni, seeing his chance to escape, was up and away like a mouse escaping from a cat and then Natalie put Enzo down. Enzo scowled at her, and then he glanced across to where his brother had gone, anxious to give chase but well brought up enough to know that he should listen to the adult first.

'Don't bully him,' she said gently. 'You're better than that. Use your brain to get what you want, not your body.'

Enzo didn't respond or appear to take any notice of her advice and when she had finished giving it he set off at full pelt after his brother. Natalie smiled to herself fondly. Then, seeing the tray of drinks sitting untouched on a nearby wall, she sat down and helped herself to one. As if out of nowhere, Danny came and sat next to her. Had he been there all the time? If so, why hadn't he broken up the fight?

He reached for a cup of squash for himself.

'Nicely done,' he said.

Natalie shrugged. 'I hate it when they fight,' she said. 'I only have a sister and we never fought like that.'

'It's different for boys,' said Danny. 'More primitive. A battle for supremacy.'

'But it's not a fair contest. Gianni is tiny next to Enzo.'

'Maybe, but he won't always be. Enzo is marking his territory as the elder brother before it's too late.'

Natalie eyed him curiously.

'Are you sure? They couldn't just be arguing over who gets the biggest cup of squash?'

'It's all the same,' said Danny. 'Today it's cups of squash, tomorrow it will be money, women, you name it. There'll always be something, no matter how big they are.'

'I don't get why they can't share, or just work together?' she asked.

'They can. But only when they trust each other entirely. That comes later. Just now they are testing the ground.'

'You're quite the psychologist, aren't you?' she said.

'I have two brothers. I know what I'm talking about.'

This was the first piece of information that Danny had shared about himself and Natalie quickly slotted it in to her understanding of who he was.

'Do you get on?' she asked.

'With my brothers? I suppose so. Better when I'm over here.' He grinned and his little dimple winked at her.

'Have you been home much since you arrived here?' she asked innocently, but conscious that this was her chance to find out about his love life.

'Not really. My mum wanted me back at Christmas so I went, but that's the only time.'

Natalie pressed on.

'But haven't you got a girlfriend?' she asked, hoping that her body didn't give her away with its infernal blushing. 'Annette said you were going out with the girl who used to do my job.'

'I did for a bit, but that's all over now,' he said, and Natalie had to work really hard not to smile.

'Young, free and single then,' she said with what she hoped was an alluring look.

'Yep.'

They held each other's gaze for a moment. If this were a film, Natalie thought, she would lean in and kiss him. She held her breath, let the thoughts in her head show on her face.

But this wasn't a film and she was supposed to be working, and as if to remind her of this Paola arrived and plonked herself down next to her.

'Is that my drink?' she asked and lifted a cup carefully so as not to spill any. 'What are you two talking about?'

'Brothers,' replied Natalie.

Paola gave a huge sigh and rolled her eyes. She really was six going on sixteen.

39

'Have you seen the news?' Annette asked Natalie as they passed one another in the corridor later that day.

It seemed like an extraordinary question. Natalie had been living in a bubble since she arrived in Sicily and had no interest in what was going on elsewhere. On top of that, she had been looking after the children all day, had no access to a television and her Italian wasn't yet good enough to work out what they were saying anyway. She shook her head.

'No. Why?'

Annette looked around surreptitiously to make sure they weren't being overheard.

'Another dead magistrate,' she said in a whisper. 'In Palermo. A car bomb.'

Natalie didn't understand and her expression must have told Annette so. She dropped her voice even lower.

'Cosa Nostra,' she breathed and then, when Natalie still didn't get it, she mouthed, 'the Mafia.'

'Oh.' Now Natalie understood.

She had heard of the Mafia, had rented *The Godfather* from Blockbuster's with her dad back in the day, but she hadn't thought it was a real thing.

'Isn't that just in the films?' she asked.

Annette shook her head.

'God no. It's everywhere,' she said. 'All over the island. All over Italy, in fact, but no one talks about it. You know that bakery that had the fire in town?'

Natalie nodded. She had visited the tiny shop with the children in her first week. It was barely more than a hole in the wall with the ovens on view behind the counter but Natalie had been touched by its simplicity, and the bread had been delicious.

'Burned out,' said Annette. She spoke with the air of someone for whom knowledge was power.

'No!' said Natalie, slack-jawed. 'Why?'

'I think it's usually because they won't pay for protection but it could be anything. Half the time they are sending a message to someone else entirely. The poor family concerned just gets caught in the crossfire.'

Natalie was lost for words.

'So, do you know anyone, anyone who's in it?' Her words sounded naive, gauche, but she had nothing to draw on to make her seem more streetwise. She knew literally nothing.

Annette shrugged.

'Probably. Who knows? I learned pretty quick that you don't talk about it. No one does. You shouldn't either. If you've got questions, ask me. Don't go to anyone else, just in case.'

This warning felt a little extreme to Natalie. She knew no one in Sicily to ask apart from the people living in Casa Barbieri. Unless that was precisely what Annette was telling her.

'You don't mean . . . ?'

Annette shrugged again.

'Like I say, I know nothing and I want it to stay that way. You should too. No need to get your knickers in a twist about it all, though. It barely touches us here. Just be aware. That's all I'm saying.'

Natalie heard her name being called. It wasn't one of the children but the rasping, strongly accented voice of Nonna.

'Sounds like your presence is required,' said Annette, tipping her head in the direction of the kitchen.

'Oh God, do you think I'm in trouble?' Natalie said, drawing her face down into a comedy grimace. She was only half joking. Nonna was formidable and all this talk of dark forces at work had unsettled her.

'Best go and see,' said Annette.

Nonna was standing in the kitchen with the pasta dough in her hand and she waved it at Natalie as she approached. Natalie relaxed. This was to be another cookery lesson and nothing scarier.

Nonna showed her how to roll the pasta out with a pin until it was just the right thickness. Then they spotted it with fried sage leaves, folded it over on itself and ran it through the pasta machine until they had long thin strips of yellow dough, the leaves visible inside like little black fish. Next, Nonna showed her how to measure the space between raviolis with her finger and then she spooned blobs of orangey sweet potato filling on to the pasta, sealed the joints and finally cut them into little squares. Nonna's were a work of art. Natalie's were a little wobblier around the edges but she was proud of her efforts nonetheless.

She wanted to ask how they would cook and then serve the raviolis but she lacked the language. She would just have to wait. She smiled at Nonna and said thank you. Nonna just nodded back but something about her expression made Natalie think that she had made some progress with the curmudgeonly old lady.

They ate the pasta at dinner that night, lightly dressed in a buttery lemon sauce.

'My mother says you made the pasta,' said Salvatore to Natalie. 'Brava.'

He was more casually dressed than usual that evening in jeans and a white tee-shirt but still managed to look like he had stepped off a film set. He and Stella really were a beautiful couple, the contrast between his dark rugged look and her fair willowy one making them all the more striking together.

He smiled at Natalie, making her feel like a child who had done a good job for a discerning teacher.

'I don't know about that,' replied Natalie quickly. 'But I helped a bit.'

'Nonna lets me make pasta,' chipped in Paola. 'I make the best pasta.' She quickly repeated herself in Italian and her grandmother nodded.

'Sì. È vero, piccolina.'

They continued to eat with exclamations of appreciation throughout. Natalie tried not to show how proud she was of her efforts but she couldn't suppress all her smiles. Once she looked up and caught Danny staring at her. She felt the electric shock of it run right through her. She tipped her head to one side questioningly, but he didn't speak.

When the meal was finished, the children asked to be excused.

'Ten minutes,' said Stella sternly. 'Then Natalie will be coming to put you to bed.'

Natalie nodded but she knew that ten minutes here was considerably more elastic than it was at home.

The children had scampered away and Nonna brought steaming cups of strong black coffee to the table. It was dark now, the sky above them speckled with stars and the air rich with the scent of jasmine.

'Nasty business yesterday in Palermo,' Stella said out of nowhere.

Natalie was surprised. Annette had told her never to mention the Mafia and yet here was Stella apparently discussing it at the dinner table.

Salvatore began to reply to her in Italian but Stella stopped him.

'In English,' she said. 'For our guests.'

Natalie knew that she was the only one who couldn't follow and she was staff, not a guest, but she appreciated the sentiment.

'They know the risks when they take the job,' Salvatore repeated sternly, without making eye contact with Stella.

The atmosphere had shifted and Natalie struggled to get a grip on it. Stella was staring at her husband and there was something almost defiant about her expression, as if she were wilfully overstepping some mark. By contrast, Salvatore's body language was closed. He seemed to have no intention of engaging any more than was necessary. Natalie couldn't work out if the vague conversation, such as it was, was for her benefit, to make sure that she was aware of what had happened, but she hadn't learned anything she didn't already know. And she had rarely witnessed a more awkward exchange.

'You must put the children to bed now,' said Salvatore. His voice wasn't gruff or angry but it had an authoritative air that Natalie wasn't about to ignore.

'Will do,' she said, bouncing up from her seat. Either it really was the children's bedtime or he wanted her out of the way. Natalie wasn't sure which.

40

The house was in a state of busyness as the family readied to move to their summer house for the holidays. Natalie's responsibility was to pack everything that the children could possibly require for two months away. Having never been anywhere for two months herself, she wondered if it might not be easier to take everything they owned, but they had been allocated one suitcase each so she was going to have to be more discerning.

It didn't help that for everything she put into the case, Paola added two more items. She did this not just for herself but for the boys too.

'We need beach shoes,' she said, 'because there are some caves that Papa takes us to. And Gianni needs two pairs of goggles because he always loses them. And I need my pens and lots of paper and Enzo needs old tee-shirts to swim in because he stays in the water too long and his shoulders burn.'

Natalie listened to the long list of requirements and tried to make sure she had everything covered, although there were surely shops nearby if she forgot anything. By the time she came to a basic first-aid kit the cases were too full to close so she slipped the kit in her own case, removing a pair of trainers to make room.

Nonna was going back to Salvatore's sister's house before they left and they all gathered outside to say goodbye. Danny hefted her case into the back of the car. He was to drive Nonna as Salvatore was at work and it didn't seem to be acceptable to either party for Stella to take her.

The children all hugged their grandmother. Even Enzo gave her a proper squeeze. She kissed them each in turn, putting her wrinkled hands on their smooth cheeks and lifting their faces towards hers. She spoke to them all softly, giving instructions on how they should behave until next they met.

Finally, she turned to Natalie.

'Arrivederci,' said Natalie. 'E grazie.'

The old woman accepted her thanks with a single nod. Then she met Natalie's eyes. If you looked beyond the crinkles in the surrounding skin, they were the same as her son's: sharp, intense and missing nothing.

'Be careful,' she said to Natalie in English, but before Natalie could ask her what she was talking about Danny was helping her into the car, leaving Natalie to wonder just how much English the old woman knew.

As they drove away, Natalie searched for meaning in the simple warning. It might just have been about the children. Having responsibility for them was an important job and care should most definitely be taken with that. She might have said it because the previous incumbents of her job had all left so quickly and Nonna didn't want the same to happen to her. They had got on well, Natalie thought, but it seemed unlikely that such a warning was necessary.

The only interpretation Natalie was left with was that it had been a warning for her own personal safety. But the old woman couldn't have meant it like that, surely. There was no danger here, if you didn't count the almost constant risk of being pushed into the pool by the boys.

Natalie had no time to ponder, however. The house needed to be ready for their departure and so she set to helping Annette with the cleaning, being able to focus on the task because she knew Danny wasn't there.

'What's the summer house like?' she asked as she followed Annette's broom with her mop.

'Huge. And much older than this place,' replied Annette. 'They had this one built when they got married. The one in Syracuse used to be an old palace or something.'

Natalie thought this house was huge. She couldn't imagine why the family needed anything bigger still. And a palace?

'That sounds very grand,' she said.

'It certainly was once,' agreed Annette. 'It's a bit of a faded beauty these days and it's got no pool, but it's in Ortigia, which is why they go. Everyone who is anyone is there in the summer to catch up with friends, be seen at the right parties, that kind of stuff.'

This didn't really accord with Natalie's understanding of who Stella was and she said so.

'It's not her choice. This is all about Salvatore's business,' said Annette. 'Stella goes along for the ride but I think she'd rather stay here with the kids. It's good for us though. There's far more to do there than there is here. Nicer bars, more restaurants. Definitely more lads. Not that you'll be interested, not with your giant crush.'

Natalie shoved her playfully.

'How's that going?' Annette asked. 'Confessed your undying love yet?'

'No. But I found out he's single so that's a good start.'

'I reckon you'll be together by the time we leave Syracuse.'

Natalie longed for this to be true and was desperate for any snippets of information that pointed in that direction.

'Why do you say that?' she chanced, trying and failing to appear casually disinterested.

'I've seen him looking at you,' laughed Annette, tapping her nose. 'I'm good at spotting the signals.'

Natalie had been searching for signals herself and had found nothing, but she was happy to take Annette's opinion as the truth rather than her own more negative interpretation of the situation. However, as far as she could tell, Danny was entirely occupied by his duties for Salvatore. There didn't seem to be much room in his life for romance.

But maybe if the opportunity for some was presented to him, he might make the time. She could, at least, live in hope.

41

Annette was right about the family summer house in Ortigia being grand. It didn't look much from the front. As with many Italian houses, it was hidden behind a plain wall and a pair of wooden gates that opened directly on to a narrow street. There was literally nothing for the passing public to see.

But once inside it was a different story. The narrow entrance opened out into a wide cobbled courtyard. At its centre was a stone fountain, the water trickling gently over a pair of alabaster dolphins caught in mid leap. Creepers twisted around many fluted stone columns and shocks of pink and purple bougainvillea blooms were everywhere. Shafts of sunlight fell like spotlights on to the cobbles.

'Bloody hell,' said Natalie under her breath. She had travelled with Stella and the children, who were squeezed into the back seat and desperate to pop out of the car like corks from bottles.

'Well, here we are,' said Stella. Her voice had something slightly false about it, as if being here wasn't quite what she wanted. 'Let's go in and see if Gabriella is ready for us.'

Natalie had no idea who Gabriella was but guessed she too was staff of some kind. There were certainly plenty of those around.

Stella released the child locks and the children burst out of the car and raced straight towards a set of wide stone steps that Natalie assumed led up to the house.

'This is some place,' she said, getting out and opening the boot to get the cases.

'It's horribly grand,' replied Stella. 'Totally over the top for what we need but Salvatore insisted on buying it. He loves it. And the children enjoy coming,' she added, which made Natalie think that Stella didn't. 'It'll be lovely to have you young people with us too. Salvatore's business types can be a bit stuffy and I don't always fit in as well here as I do at home. I'm not quite their cup of tea.'

She linked arms with Natalie and pulled her in close as if they were friends and not employer and employee. 'Right. Into battle we go. Don't worry about the cases. Gabriella will do that. Let's go up and I'll show you around.'

They climbed the stone steps, following after the children, the dappled shade making the air pleasantly cool.

'I know I've barely seen you since you arrived,' Stella said as they walked, 'but I'm so glad to have you with us, Natalie. You're doing a great job. And the children adore you.'

A glow pulsed through Natalie. It had been so long since she had been praised by anyone – not counting Etta, of course, whose approval of her had been constant and well-meaning but totally undeserved.

'I adore them too,' she said, and meant it. 'They're so sweet and all so different.'

This was true. Enzo with his serious determination, carefree Gianni and bossy little Paola, they were each tiny prototypes of the adults they would become. Was this what it meant to have children, to create fascinating miniature beings out of parts of their parents that ultimately grew into their own selves?

'They're certainly that,' replied Stella with a tinkling laugh. 'Enzo is so like his father and Gianni is a free spirit like me. I'm not sure where Paola came from but I wouldn't be without her.'

'Me neither,' agreed Natalie. 'She's my primary source of information.'

'I'll bet she is,' smiled Stella indulgently. 'She's wise beyond her years, that one. But honestly, Natalie. I don't know what we'd do without you.'

Natalie muttered her thanks because she could feel her throat start to tighten and she didn't want Stella to know how affected she was by her kind words. But she stored the moment away so she could take it out later and enjoy it again.

Moving to Sicily, taking that leap into the unknown, had been exactly what she had needed. For years she had been floundering around in what felt like deep water, not knowing how she was going to get herself out. It had taken everything she had just to keep afloat, never mind swim to the warm shallows.

This, though, this family, the way they had opened up their lives and accepted her in. It felt like a new start to Natalie. The beginning of the next part of her life. She wasn't trying to replace Etta or her parents but she did need more than them alone. She needed something that she had created herself, that she could be proud of but also could build her future on. And here in Sicily she believed she might have found it.

At the top of the stairs was a grand wooden door standing ajar and next to it a slender woman with black hair pulled up into a bun. She was wearing a white cotton housecoat – a uniform, maybe – and greeted Stella with a broad smile and a tumble of Italian. They hugged and then a stream of information was quickly exchanged, Natalie barely following what was said. Eventually, Stella introduced her, and Gabriella nodded and smiled before bustling off. So that was four of them, if you counted Danny. Four full-time staff, plus a gardener or two. The Barbieris must be even wealthier than she had thought.

And then they went into the house and everything she was beginning to realise about the family was confirmed. Stella showed her through room after room of what clearly was a palace. The ceilings were high and vaulted and painted with frescos of cherubs and clouds. There were trompe l'oeil cornices and pillars painted on to the cream walls in a delicate duck-egg blue. There were even painted archways containing painted statues so realistic that Natalie wanted to touch them just to convince her brain that they were really two-dimensional.

Even the furniture was ornate. Every table had intricately carved legs, every lamp a frilly shade. Huge silk curtains pooled on polished parquet floors. Natalie had been to Windsor Castle on a school trip once. This place reminded her of that.

'I see what you mean about it being grand,' she said to Stella. 'You'll have to tell me where the children aren't allowed to go.' As she spoke, Natalie was already worried about how she would stop the boys from ruining everything.

'Oh, it's open all areas,' said Stella. 'It's their home, after all, and if you look closely you'll see that it's all taken some wear and tear. The whole house could do with a revamp but we're waiting until the children are a bit bigger. So there's no writing on the walls or playing football in the ballroom in case they break a window, but apart from that . . .'

Natalie thought of their little terraced council house in Barnet. If only Etta could see her now.

42

The bedrooms for both family and staff were all on the first floor and Natalie found herself in a room next to Danny's. After the grandeur of the reception rooms, the bedrooms were a little more down to earth, or at least hers was. It had simple white walls, a high double bed, and mismatched wardrobe and drawers in a black lacquered wood. Natalie was relieved. She wasn't sure she was up to all that splendour all the time. Down the corridor was the bathroom, which she would share with the children.

The room had a tiny balcony looking out over the courtyard with the dolphin fountain, and there were the ubiquitous wooden shutters to keep the light and heat out of the room. A gentle breeze lifted the white organza curtain and then set it down again. The room smelled fresh and clean and someone, she assumed Gabriella, had put a jam jar of mock orange stems on the bedside table. It was such a thoughtful gesture and Natalie pushed her nose into the flowers and breathed in their heady scent.

A cursory knock sounded on her door and then in bounded Paola.

'We're going for ice cream with Mummy. Come on.'

And that was it. They were going out.

◆ ◆ ◆

'Ortigia is an island,' Paola explained as they wound their way through the narrow streets. 'That's why there aren't many cars. Cars aren't allowed, are they, Mummy?'

'Not many cars, no.'

'But we're in Syracuse?' clarified Natalie, confused by how they seemed to be in two places at once.

'Ortigia is part of Syracuse. The nicest part,' said Paola.

Stella threw her a look as if to say that a little modesty wouldn't go amiss.

'Well, it is! Papa says that too. That's why our house is here.'

'Okay, but it's not nice to show off,' said Stella.

'And our favourite ice-cream shop is just down there.'

The street opened out into a wide square. At its centre stood a huge fountain, jets of water shooting out at a statue of a goddess with a bow and arrow in the centre. She was surrounded by mermaids, giant fish and other mythical creatures, and the sun lit the whole thing so that it shone like gold.

'Wow!' said Natalie.

'That's Diana, isn't it, Mummy?'

'You're so boring, Paola,' complained Gianni. 'No one cares.'

'Actually, I'm very interested,' corrected Natalie. 'This is my first time here, remember. I don't know anything.'

'I can't remember what she's goddess of,' said Paola, her brow furrowed into little lines of frustration.

'Hunting,' said Enzo as he fired an imaginary arrow from an imaginary bow directly at his brother.

'The ice-cream shop is just here,' said Paola. She took Natalie's hand and dragged her across the square to a side street. 'I'm going to have stracciatella. It's my favourite. Do you know what that is?'

Natalie hadn't got a clue, so Paola pointed at the mound of white ice cream. It had tiny little black bits in it. They looked like dead thunder flies, Natalie thought, but she assumed it was chocolate.

Stella ordered the ice creams – chocolate for the boys and a lemony sorbet for herself. Natalie chose strawberry. There would be time to be more adventurous later. She had all summer.

They wandered through the alleyways with their ice creams. Cats lounged on black leather Vespa seats that had been warmed by the sun, and washing hung languidly from first-floor windows.

After a while they reached a broad promenade with tall houses on one side and the sparkling ocean on the other. The water looked so inviting.

'Is there a beach?' asked Natalie.

'Yes, but the nicer ones are a little drive or boat ride away,' replied Stella. 'Don't worry. You'll have seen them all by the time we go back.'

'Can we go today?' asked Gianni enthusiastically, walking backwards on his tiptoes so he could face his mother.

'We've only just got here. Let's get unpacked first.'

'Tomorrow?!' he asked hopefully.

'We'll see,' smiled Stella.

A memory of her own mother using that holding device sprang into Natalie's mind but instead of suppressing it, she let it play out and was surprised that it didn't hurt as much as she'd assumed it would. Now that she was an adult, she could see the expression for what it was – a way of responding without committing to anything. Whether whatever it was ever came to fruition depended on who was saying it. With her mother, it had invariably been a build-up to a no, a way of letting her and Etta down gently. Lack of money or time meant that she could rarely say yes to exciting plans. But Natalie had the impression that when Stella said it, the activity really was a possibility. Her 'we'll see' was a way of teasing her children, of eking out the pleasure of what was to come.

Satisfied, Gianni turned round and continued walking. He also knew what his mother meant.

'So, what do you think?' asked Stella.

Ortigia seemed small and cramped after the wide-open space around the other villa but Natalie hadn't seen enough to get a grip on it and so she happily told Stella that she thought it was lovely. Stella seemed gratified.

'There are some old Greek remains over in Syracuse, caves and an amphitheatre. We can go there one day.'

Enzo rolled his eyes, uninspired by the trip, which he had no doubt done every summer, but Stella let it go.

'That sounds great,' said Natalie.

Stella kept using 'we', which made Natalie wonder exactly how much of the childcare she was expected to do on her own. Less than she had been doing, perhaps. And would Salvatore be around more if this was their summer holiday? She didn't want to ask, worried that it might be seen as a criticism of his general absence, but also she wasn't sure she wanted him there. She felt far more comfortable around Stella and Annette and the children than she did with the watchful Salvatore. He made her anxious, she realised. When he was there she felt awkward, ignorant, a little bit stupid. His long silences intimidated her and the way he seemed to take everything in was disconcerting.

He would be around though, she decided. It stood to reason. And that meant Danny would be around too, which could only be good news.

43

That evening was the first for a while when Natalie had enough time to herself to write Etta a letter. Stella had said that she could use the phone whenever she wanted and Natalie knew she meant it, but she didn't want to be overheard. There were also the telephones in a couple of the local bars and she had bought some gettoni so she always had one in her purse in case of an emergency. However, there was something about a letter. It was as if in setting things out on the page she was also formulating her own thoughts.

She found the airmail pad she had bought from the post office on the estate at home and dug a Bic biro out of her bag. Sucking the end for a moment or two, she thought about what had happened since she had last written and then she began.

Dear Etta
Hello from sunny Sicily. We've moved – well, for the summer at least. (I'll get the address for you.) The family has this holiday house in Ortigia which is an island off Syracuse. It's incredible. I'll take some photos. The ceilings are all decorated like a church or something and there are statues painted on the wall. It's like being on a film set. Am getting on great with the kids. They're hilarious. Stella is warming up a bit too. I think she likes me. And

I can make proper Italian pasta now. I might train as a chef! (Only joking!!)
Annette has been telling me about the Mafia. Apparently it's a real thing here although I've not seen any signs. I suppose it's a bit like the Krays were but no one talks about it much – it's all taboo – but now I'm getting a bit more tuned into things, I'm noticing everything that doesn't get said. It's all just out of sight, behind closed doors. If Annette hadn't mentioned it I probably wouldn't have even realised. No need to worry though. If you keep your head down you're perfectly safe.
BIG NEWS! I've got a bit of a crush. It's been a while but there's a guy here. He's about your age. English. His ex-girlfriend did my job for a bit. He lives with the family too – they are so loaded – and helps Salvatore with his business. Did I tell you he has a sulphur mine? Must be more like a gold mine given how much money they have!!! Anyway Danny, that's his name, is gorgeous. Annette says I should make a move but I'm not sure what to do. I know this is 1984 but I'm not asking him out. He seems to like me though so that's a start. I haven't a clue if he fancies me. Watch this space!!
It's weird, Etta, but since I've been here everything's starting to make more sense to me. I think I got myself a bit stuck in a rut at home, with the accident and everything. Now that I'm away from the house and all the stuff that happened there I feel a bit more in control of my life. Do you understand what I mean? I talked to Annette and she gets it. She didn't make me feel bad about it all which makes a change.
It's not that I don't miss you. God I do! Every day!! But it feels like the world is finally opening up for me. I know

that happened for you a while ago with your work and everything but I think I got left behind.

Anyway, I'm catching up fast! I'm even thinking that I might not come back to England right away. I hope that's not a shock but I think there's more for me here. I can learn Italian and then when Stella doesn't need me anymore I can go and work for another family or maybe get a real job. Salvatore might give me some work at his mine, in the offices or whatever – not down the actual mine! But if not, I'm sure there will be other jobs for someone who can speak English and Italian. (I know I can't speak Italian yet but I'm learning!)

But that's all a long way off, and I know you. You'll be thinking I'm trying to run before I can walk. Maybe I am a bit, but the thing is, Etta, this is the first time since before the accident that I've even thought about walking – let alone running!

Anyway, write soon and tell me what's going on there. And say thanks again to Malcolm for thinking of me for this job. I owe him one.

Loads of love.

Nat. xxxxxx

PS I'm getting a great tan!

PPS Those new sandals I got from Dolcis do give me blisters. I should have listened to you!

PPPS When can you come and visit?

Natalie read the letter through, added a couple of extra kisses to the end and then slipped it into an envelope and licked it shut. Then she wrote Loretta Halliday on the envelope and printed the address in small, neat letters. There were no pangs of homesickness as she formed the words.

She was just thinking about getting ready for bed when she heard a light tapping on her door. She slid down from the bed and went to answer it. There stood Danny in a pair of cut-off Levis and a sleeveless vest, black espadrilles on his feet.

'Fancy going out for ice cream?' His smile was tentative. 'I asked Annette too but she wants an early night.'

Natalie immediately thought of what she must look like. She had no make-up on and she wasn't sure she'd brushed her hair all day. Why couldn't he have given her a bit more notice? She could ask him for ten minutes to get ready but he might change his mind about going, and anyway he'd seen her now. She looked him up and down. It wasn't as if he had made much effort either.

'Can you go dressed like that?' she asked. 'I thought this place was posh.'

'Who cares? They all think the English have no style anyway,' he said. His grin was broad now. Had he been nervous about asking her? Was this a kind of date? Natalie tried not to let her imagination run away with her but she didn't have to be asked a second time.

'I'll just get my bag,' she said.

44

1984 – London

'How's your kid sister getting on in Sicily?' asked Malcom. 'All going well?'

Loretta and Malcolm were sitting in the Crown Court waiting for the jury to return its verdict on a particularly nasty hit-and-run case, which had attracted press interest because the driver had knocked the victim down and then gone back and reversed over the body before driving off at speed. The job didn't really need them both but it was a slow news day and Malcolm wasn't showing any interest in going back to the newsroom.

'Great!' replied Loretta. 'She's thriving. In fact, she said to pass on her thanks to you for setting it all up.'

'I was just the messenger,' said Malcolm, 'but I'm glad it's working out. Stella can be a bit of a space cadet but her heart is in the right place.'

A man in a donkey jacket with a leather satchel slung across his body and a newspaper under his arm was making his way across the foyer towards them. He lifted an arm in greeting and Malcolm responded.

'Who's that?' whispered Loretta.

'Smales. *Guardian*,' replied Malcolm. 'Bit of a plodder.'

'Hi, Frank. How are you doing?' he said to the newcomer. 'Have you met Loretta Halliday?'

'Never better,' replied the man. 'Nice to meet you, Loretta.'

Loretta was used to being looked up and down by pretty much all the men she met on the job, but this one didn't seem interested in her. His mind was on other matters. 'Listen, Malcolm,' he continued, 'have you heard anything about this hit-and-run?'

'The Turnbull case? We're just waiting for the verdict now,' replied Malcolm. 'Not sure which way they'll go. They've been out since last night.'

'Did you sit through the evidence?' Smales asked.

'Young Loretta here caught some of it. Why?'

Smales looked over his shoulder and then bent in towards them and dropped his voice.

'Was there anything . . . you know . . . out of the ordinary?'

Malcolm pulled a face.

'Apart from the guy reversing back over the poor bloke to make sure he'd done a proper job, you mean?'

'Yes. Does it smack of something else to you? Something with a whiff of the . . .' Then he seemed to think better of it and straightened up. 'Anyway. Nasty business all round. Nice seeing you, Malcolm. I'll catch you later,' he said, and scuttled off towards the door.

'What was that all about?' asked Loretta.

Malcolm watched Smales go, a frown on his face.

'I don't know,' he said slowly. 'But whatever it was, he wasn't up for sharing.'

The hairs on the back of Loretta's neck stood to attention. This was what she loved most about the job, that moment when she sensed that there was more to something than met the eye.

'What do you think it might be?' she asked. 'I did a background check on the defendant and the victim and nothing came up.'

Malcolm tapped his fingernail on his teeth. 'Nothing at all?'

'Nope. I even spoke to your mate at Bow Street police station, DS Thompson. He told me neither of them were on the police's radar. Said it was probably a domestic.'

'Yeah, that's what I heard too. Victim shagging the driver's wife,' said Malcolm. 'And that's what came out in the evidence, right?'

Loretta nodded. Malcolm ran his hand over his chin, a gesture that Loretta associated with cartoon baddies.

'So what does Smales think he knows, then?' he mused, more to himself than to her.

'You said he's a plodder,' said Loretta. 'How likely is he to be on the trail of something?'

'I'd have said not at all, but he was definitely fishing, trying to find out what we knew. Which appears to be nothing. What are we missing here, Loretta?'

Loretta had no idea but she was keen to find out.

'Do you want me to go back to the police station, see if I can get anything else out of DS Thompson?'

Malcolm shook his head.

'No. Let's hang on here for the verdict, see if there's anything in that. We can have a sniff around afterwards. He's probably just stirring up trouble, planting red herrings. Either that or he's got the wrong end of the stick.'

Malcolm's eyes scanned over towards the door. Loretta turned too and saw Smales heading out into the street beyond.

'Not hanging around for the verdict, though,' said Malcolm thoughtfully.

'It might be nothing,' said Loretta.

'Yeah, probably. Old Smales was never one to set Fleet Street alight.'

Just then a court usher dressed in a flowing black gown appeared at the door to their courtroom.

'All those with an interest in the Queen versus Turnbull. The jury is about to deliver its verdict.'

'They're coming back,' said Malcolm. 'Let's go and see what they've got to say.'

The courtroom was cool compared to the stuffy foyer. The barristers and their instructing solicitors were already in place when Malcolm and Loretta slipped into the press bench at the rear. Loretta took out her shorthand pad, ready to make a record of exactly what was said. There weren't many other people in there. A woman in a denim skirt and yellow tee-shirt who was sitting in the gallery sniffed loudly. Loretta wondered if she was the wife of the victim or the defendant.

The jury filed back in. Loretta generally played a game with herself, trying to guess whether juries were going to find the defendant guilty or not guilty by their body language. She was right about ninety per cent of the time. It was to do with the way they looked at the defendant. There was a certain smug righteousness that jurors gave off when they had found them guilty and something more conspiratorial when they were innocent, as if they wanted to reassure the defendant that he would be going home that night.

This was definitely going to be a guilty verdict, judging by the set of their jaws. One woman sporting a tightly permed blue rinse gave the defendant a particularly filthy stare. She really didn't like him. It wasn't surprising. The evidence Loretta had heard against him had been both compelling and appalling.

'All rise,' said the clerk and everyone sprang to their feet.

'Fifty pence says he's guilty,' said Malcolm.

Loretta shook her head. 'I'm not taking that bet,' she said. 'I reckon he's a goner too.'

When the jury were asked the question, their foreman declared that Richard John Turnbull was indeed guilty as charged of the murder of Kevin Smith. The woman in the yellow tee-shirt howled but Loretta couldn't tell whether it was in anguish at her husband going to prison for life or in revenge for her loved one's premature demise.

Malcolm was getting to his feet. 'Okay?' he asked. 'Got everything you need?'

Loretta ran her eyes down her notes and then nodded.

'Right. I'll get back to the office and see if I can dig out anything we've missed. You go back via Bow Street, see if DS Thompson is on duty.'

45

Loretta had become used to the inside of police stations. They were busy, noisy places with a distinct whiff of testosterone in the air. She had been intimidated at first, feeling vulnerable and exposed as she tried to get the attention of the harassed officers, but now she had the measure of them.

Her technique differed to her male colleagues'. Where they made straight for the front desk to ask their questions, Loretta was more subtle, watching and waiting first to see what she could pick up without alerting anyone to her presence. It was easy enough to do with all the comings and goings. Only when she had drained that well of information did she announce herself.

Today, the front desk area was relatively quiet so Loretta went straight up and rang the bell. A WPC about the same age as her came to answer it.

'Good afternoon, madam. Can I help you?'

It felt absurdly comical to be addressed in this way by someone so young, but Loretta kept a straight face. She and this policewoman were both doing what was necessary to get on in a man's world.

'Yes. Loretta Halliday, *Daily Chronicle*. Is DS Thompson on duty and, if so, could I have a word, please?'

Loretta gave the woman her most winning 'we're both in this together and I'm on your side' smile, but it was not reciprocated.

'I'll just check for you,' replied the woman in a dull drawl. Then she disappeared into a back room, giving Loretta time to think about exactly what she was trying to achieve here. She had already spoken to DS Thompson about what was a grisly but not at all mysterious crime. What reason could she give for wanting to talk to him again without mentioning tip-offs from competitors or journalistic hunches?

The woman reappeared.

'He'll be out in a mo,' she said and then turned her attention to the person waiting behind Loretta, a French tourist who had had her bag snatched in Soho by the sounds of it.

Loretta sat down on a moulded plastic chair to wait. She ran her eyes over the various dog-eared posters that adorned the walls. Most of them warned the unsuspecting public about thievery – pickpockets on the Tube, the need to lock or lose your bicycle, making sure windows were shut. To look at them you'd think London was a den of vice, but then again, maybe it was.

After ten minutes or so, DS Thompson emerged. He was around the age her father would have been, a stout man with thinning fair hair and round pink cheeks like a cherub's.

'What can I do for you, Miss Halliday?' he asked.

He came and sat down next to her and his plastic chair creaked in protest.

'Good morning, DS Thompson. Dave. Can I call you Dave?'

DS Thompson gave her a look that suggested he wasn't sure whether this would be in order or not, but Loretta had heard Malcolm calling his police contacts by their first name and she wanted to build the same level of rapport that he had.

'I've just come from the Crown Court,' she began.

'Ah.' DS Thompson nodded knowingly. 'The Turnbull case. Nasty business, that.'

'Just so,' replied Loretta. 'The thing is, I was wondering just how nasty . . .'

Loretta paused and looked him straight in the eye so she could see if there was anything he was hiding, but if there was it was currently buried pretty deeply.

'I'm not following,' said DS Thompson.

Loretta tried again. She had to tread carefully. All she had was the merest suggestion from Smales that there was more to this case than met the eye, but she was totally in the dark as to what that might be.

'Well,' she began slowly. 'The case was pinned as a domestic, a scorned husband . . .'

DS Thompson was nodding along.

'But I was just wondering if there might have been another motive for the murder. Could the affair story have been a smokescreen to keep the real reason hidden?'

How feasible did this sound? Loretta wasn't sure and from his expression it appeared that her police contact wasn't that convinced either. He did look intrigued though.

'And what might that have been?' he asked.

Loretta shrugged.

'That's just it. I don't know. It's just a feeling, a hunch if you like, that there's more to it than meets the eye.'

'What did the jury decide?'

'Guilty as charged,' said Loretta. 'He's going down for life, no matter what.'

She paused, knowing she was on delicate ground, and looked directly at the police officer in what she hoped was a trustworthy way.

'Dave? Do you suppose anyone looked into whether he was really having an affair with the victim's wife? More than just speaking to him and then to her, I mean.'

DS Thompson shifted in his seat and the plastic groaned ominously.

'A thorough investigation will have been carried out,' he said, trotting out the party line.

Loretta lowered her head and looked at him through her eyelashes.

'Yes, but between you and me . . .' she said.

DS Thompson rolled his eyes and then sat a little forward in his chair so that their heads were almost touching.

'Between you and me,' he said, 'if Turnbull said he was having an affair with the deceased's wife and the wife confirmed it then there's a chance that no one looked much further. Just a chance, mind you. I'm not saying that that's what actually happened.'

'So might there be more to it?' she fished.

DS Thompson stared at her dumbly and Loretta tried to get her jumping thoughts in order.

'Could the dead man have been targeted specifically?' she asked. 'Maybe for something other than the alleged affair.'

The policeman frowned as if this hadn't occurred to him, but he was beginning to look interested.

'Or maybe,' she said, now enjoying herself as the ideas sparked, 'might he have agreed to take the rap for something in exchange for some other benefit?'

'I suppose so. But why would he?'

This was a perfectly reasonable question and Loretta had no answers, but the things that Natalie had said in her letter about the Mafia and the Kray twins were flying round her head. There was an outside chance that she was really on to an angle that no one else, except maybe Smales, had spotted.

'You can't think of anything?' she asked. 'I read somewhere that with organised crime, individuals sometimes sacrifice themselves for the greater good?'

DS Thompson grinned. 'You've seen *The Godfather* too then?' he said. 'Not sure we're a hotbed of organised crime here, but I suppose it could happen. Particularly if the person pulling the strings had something valuable to offer. Or had threatened to make life worse for Turnbull than the prison sentence itself.'

Loretta considered this for a moment, but it wasn't making a whole lot of sense. She tried to hold exactly what he had just said in her head so that she could make an accurate note when she left.

'Like hurting his family, for example?' she asked. She watched his face carefully but he didn't seem to balk entirely at the idea. She pressed on. 'Can you think of anyone that might have that much power?' she asked.

DS Thompson bit at his upper lip as he thought.

'I mean, the Corleones aside,' he said with a wry smile, 'there was the Firm, you know, the Krays and all that, but that was the sixties. They all went down in '69.'

'And no one has stepped up to fill their boots?' asked Loretta.

He stuck out his lip and then shook his head, flights of fancy dismissed.

'Nah. There are a few small-time players but no one like them. Whatever you think you're on to here, I reckon you're barking up the wrong tree.'

'I'm not sure I'm on to anything at all,' replied Loretta. 'But I'm curious, that's all.'

DS Thompson threw her a warning look.

'And you know what curiosity did, Miss Halliday,' he said.

46

Loretta wasn't sure what she had after talking to DS Thompson. She sat on a wall near the police station to scribble down exactly what she could remember from their conversation and then reread it over to herself. Could this really be something to do with organised crime? Was that what Smales thought he was on to? It all felt a bit far-fetched to her but then she knew nothing about it. She had been just a child when the big Kray twins trial had hit the headlines and it wasn't something that had crossed her path since. All that stuff felt a bit like a Hollywood film to her. It was hard to equate the stories with the London that she occupied.

Still, she was a crime reporter so maybe she had better make it her business to find out if there was something in this. Even if there was nothing more to uncover than appeared on the surface, it couldn't do any harm to do a bit of background work. As being on the crime desk was to be her future then she should know something about organised crime.

She made her way back to the newsroom and found Malcolm already at his desk, flicking over that day's editions.

'Learn anything?' he asked optimistically as she approached.

Loretta shook her head.

'If there is something to know then Dave Thompson definitely doesn't know it,' she said. 'Have you turned anything up?'

Malcolm shrugged.

'No. Nothing in the papers. Can't find anything on Turnbull before this. He seems clean. I rang my pet policeman and asked about the victim. He was a bit more interesting, had some form. Nothing major but he went down for two years for driving the car at a post office hold-up. They didn't get away with anything and it was his first offence, so the judge was lenient.'

'Ironic, given how he died,' said Loretta.

Malcolm rolled his eyes.

'Maybe your *Guardian* mate was just teasing us,' suggested Loretta. 'Making out that he had some bigger story just to wind us up.'

Malcolm pulled a face.

'Maybe,' he said, 'but I think there was something. We'll keep our ears to the ground, see what crawls out of the woodwork.'

But nothing did, and Loretta returned to visiting the court each day and filing stories about the more interesting cases that she came across. She was ready to listen if anyone mentioned organised crime but no one did.

She kept digging though. She borrowed a book on the Krays from the central library. They seemed to have been more celebrities than gangsters, although the descriptions of what they did to some of the people they killed made Loretta feel queasy.

One quiet afternoon, she decided to dig out any relevant cuttings. That involved a conversation with Mrs Brayshaw in the cuttings room.

Mrs Brayshaw had been at the *Daily Chronicle* since before time began, if the popular gossip was to be believed. She had the memory of Mnemosyne and an encyclopaedic knowledge of her realm. She had cultivated a slightly scatty old lady look so that she reminded Loretta of Miss Marple. She was both disarmingly polite and exceedingly sharp at the same time.

Loretta hadn't wanted to draw attention to her investigations, such as they were. This was more of a background study than a deep dive into something specific, but when she found herself in the cuttings room for the third time, Mrs Brayshaw's curiosity came to the fore.

'Are you looking for anything specific, dear?' she asked as Loretta took another file down from the shelves and started flicking through it aimlessly.

Reluctant as she was to give anything away, Loretta knew the value of using the resources available to her.

'To be honest, Mrs Brayshaw, I don't know that I am,' she said.

Mrs Brayshaw smiled at her benignly, apparently knowing that if she just bided her time more information would be forthcoming. She wasn't disappointed.

'It's probably nothing,' Loretta continued, 'but I've been trying to make connections.'

Mrs Brayshaw raised a shapely eyebrow.

'There's just been a case recently. A man murdered another by running him over. Twice. He went down for life.'

'Richard Turnbull, yes,' nodded Mrs Brayshaw.

'Someone hinted to me that the case wasn't as straightforward as it seemed and I've been wondering why.'

'And you landed on researching the Kray twins? Might that be a bit of a stretch, dear?'

Loretta could feel her cheeks go a little pink.

'Probably,' she said. She should give this up. She was clearly on a hiding to nothing.

'But the Turnbull case isn't the only one,' Mrs Brayshaw said. 'Example of men being killed like that, I mean.'

Loretta was listening.

‘There was something similar in Brighton in 1974 and another in Watford in ’80. And now this one. It’s starting to look like a pattern.’

‘And were the victims knocked down and then run over again, like this one?’

Mrs Brayshaw nodded. ‘Exactly like this one, dear.’

Loretta could feel excitement building in her chest.

‘Could you get me the clippings?’ she asked. She wasn’t sure what this was but it might be something and it certainly merited digging into.

‘By all means. One moment.’

Mrs Brayshaw was up and down her library ladder like a young girl, despite her advanced years, and soon Loretta had three files in front of her. She sat down at one of the tables and began to read.

Half an hour later she sat back in the chair.

‘You’re right,’ she said. ‘Those cases are all basically the same.’

‘I thought so,’ replied Mrs Brayshaw with an air of someone who had known she was right all along.

‘But I suppose,’ mused Loretta, ‘that because they all happened in different places, the police never connected them.’

‘You’d have to ask them that, dear.’

Loretta looked at the old lady quizzically.

‘And was there anything else that struck you as odd?’ she asked. This was part flattery and part fishing but there was no harm in asking.

Mrs Brayshaw drew her eyebrows together and tipped her head to one side in a gesture that was almost coquettish.

‘Well,’ she said thoughtfully, ‘there was the fact that the victims all came from Hackney. That struck me as a bit of a coincidence.’

Loretta’s story radar was well and truly vibrating now. Her thoughts raced as she tried to piece together what this might mean.

It felt very hazy but she was certain there must be some significance to it all.

'Was there anything else, Mrs Brayshaw?' she asked, hopeful that the old lady had been sitting on yet more theories and just waiting for someone to ask. But she was to be disappointed.

'No,' Mrs Brayshaw said with a little sigh. 'Just that.'

Loretta opened her pad and began to scribble down notes so that she would have all the details to hand when she told Malcolm. Then she thanked Mrs Brayshaw and raced back to the newsroom.

47

'So, Mrs Brayshaw thinks the killings were all some kind of gangland vendetta,' said Malcolm doubtfully.

'Well, she didn't say that exactly.' Loretta didn't want to put words in Mrs Brayshaw's mouth, but the old lady had clearly thought that something was amiss. She pressed on. 'But I've been thinking. What if there was someone in charge? The three victims had all done something wrong or knew something, so the boss tells someone he can trust to get rid of them. And if they're caught, they will go down for murder. You can't claim accidental death when you reverse back over the body once you've hit it. But maybe the boss said he'd make sure that their family is provided for if they do get caught.' Her mind was racing with the possibilities as she spoke. 'Or more likely Turnbull and the others would have been terrified the boss would come after their families if they didn't do it. Either way, we have three men from the same patch of east London all killed in the same way. Only Turnbull got caught, but maybe that was just bad luck.'

'Or maybe Turnbull killed all three but got away with the first two,' added Malcolm, but the corners of his mouth turned up in a barely suppressed grin. He was teasing her.

Yet Loretta wasn't ready to let it go. There was something here. She could smell it.

'Do you think that's what Smales knew?' she asked.

Malcolm pulled a face. 'He was just casting around for an angle. There's been nothing since that day we saw him. No stories. Not even a hint of anything like this.'

'Maybe they haven't got enough to run with it,' suggested Loretta.

'Or decided it was a dead duck,' said Malcolm. 'It's all a bit circumstantial, Loretta. I'm not sure we've got much either.'

Loretta could see his attention beginning to wane and his eyes flickered to the other papers on his desk. The story did have some holes in it, that was true, but she could investigate, tease out the troublesome details. She was growing tired of writing up court reports. She longed for something meaty to get her teeth into, to show Mr Redpath what she was really capable of.

'So, what shall I do?' she asked.

She could feel her initial excitement starting to fade in the face of Malcolm's lacklustre reaction, but she wasn't prepared to let it go. She had hoped Malcolm would say she had the makings of the story of the decade but something about his expression told her that she was going to be disappointed.

'Keep a watching brief,' he said instead, and she felt herself deflate a little further. 'I doubt there's anything in it. And the police aren't stupid. If there were connections to be made, someone would have done it. But don't waste any more of the paper's time on it. I need you and your notepad at the court.'

Then he turned his attention back to his typewriter.

Loretta returned to her own desk and tried to look busy, but her head was full of possibilities. What if she became the paper's expert on organised crime? Even if this wasn't *the* story, one would come along before too long – and when it did, she would be ready. She could do this quietly, without fanfare. No one needed to know what she was up to and Malcolm had told her to keep a watching brief so that meant she wasn't completely off-piste. She would find the story here, no matter what.

◆ ◆ ◆

In the meantime, the rest of her life continued. The family house in Barnet was too big for her now that Natalie was in Sicily and filled with too many ghosts for her to live there by herself. So they had agreed to let it out on a short-term basis and she moved into a bedsit in Clerkenwell, which put her closer to the centre of things. Each day she would walk down to Fleet Street and the courts with her nose in the air, sniffing out the stories around her. Her head buzzed with 'what if' questions, her imagination conjuring up the scenes behind closed doors. She knew that on a practical level her actual job was just reporting on what she saw each day in the courts, but in her heart she felt that her big-break story was just around one of those corners and she wanted to be ready to write it.

Out of the blue she had a phone call from Liz, her oldest friend from school. Personal calls weren't really allowed at work but given how easy it was to pretend that any call was something to do with work, it was a rule that was roundly flouted.

Loretta had felt herself drifting away from most of her friends from Barnet. Her life was so different to theirs now and she had started to wonder whether they would ever have anything in common again. But Liz was different. They had been friends since the very first day of primary school and Loretta would always make time for her.

'Hi,' she said down the phone, glancing around to make sure that no one was listening in. 'How are you?'

'Same old same old,' said Liz. 'I'm stitching knickers for a living now. There must be more to life than that. Fancy a night out? A proper old knees-up? There's a fundraiser for the miners at the club.

A bit of a band. A disco too. Wondered if you might want to come for old times' sake.'

The club was the working men's club on the estate, scene of many of Loretta's notable firsts. It wasn't really her kind of place anymore but she loved Liz and the evening did sound fun. Plus supporting the poor miners was a cause she could put herself firmly behind.

'Yes!' she said. 'When is it?'

'Tomorrow night. Do you want to call round at mine first and then we can walk down together?'

Loretta mentally ran through her diary. She was on earlies at work and there was nothing else pencilled in for that night – no reason at all why she couldn't go.

'Great. Pick you up at seven?'

Loretta heard the payphone that Liz must have been calling from start to make a pipping sound. Her money was about to run out.

'Yes. And bring your . . .'

But Loretta would never know what she was supposed to bring because the call was cut before Liz had the chance to tell her. She guessed it would have been her dancing shoes.

48

Loretta had only been gone from the estate for a short while but already it felt like it was no longer a part of who she was now. As she got off the bus and walked up the high street towards Liz's parents' house, she could feel the smallness of it, all its parochial undertones. It seemed silly to call a part of the sprawling metropolis that was London 'small'. Millions of people lived in this borough. Yet to Loretta's mind, the people who had settled in this tiny corner of it, the people she had grown up with, had never looked beyond its borders, never asked themselves what else there might be for them. They were content in their little patch and weren't seeking more.

There was nothing wrong with that, Loretta was sure. It had been enough for her parents and their parents before them. But it wasn't for her. She had pushed out into the open sea and left them all behind without so much as a backward glance. Like the Jumblies in the Edward Lear poem, she thought, setting sail against all advice to discover what else there was out there.

Looking now at the tatty shopfronts, the off-licences with their barred windows, the greengrocers with broken pallets and cardboard boxes piled head high outside the door, it didn't look so very different to the part of Clerkenwell where she was living. But it *was* different and that was the point. Some of these people had never moved more than a mile from where they were born, some of them never would. But Loretta wanted more and she was going to make that happen.

For tonight, though, an evening out with Liz would be great. She made her way up Liz's road, just one along from where she had grown up, and knocked on the door. Liz's mum answered it.

'Oh, Etta, darling. How are you? Come in, come in. Not seen you for donkey's. How've you been? How's Nat? I heard she'd gone off to live abroad somewhere. That right, is it? And don't you look lovely. Life doing you proud, is it? Liz won't be a minute. She had to wash her favourite top. Assumed I'd done it. I said to her, "What do you think I am? Your skivvy?" Been trying to dry it with her hairdryer. I ask you! A hairdryer!'

Liz's mum rattled on like a machine gun, barely drawing breath, and Loretta just smiled and didn't even attempt to interrupt her but followed her through to the front room, where Liz's dad was sitting on the sagging sofa watching *Play Your Cards Right*. Bruce Forsyth was whipping the studio audience into a frenzy as they tried to predict the next card to be turned over.

'Lower, you stupid mare,' Liz's dad muttered. 'Lower.'

'Look who's here, Jim. It's Etta. Say hello, then.'

Jim pulled his eyes from the screen, saw Loretta and toasted her with his can of Watney's.

'All right, Etta.'

'Hello, Mr Young,' said Loretta.

He reached down the side of the sofa and grabbed the last can from a four-pack, the plastic that had held them together still dangling round its neck. He offered it to Loretta but she smiled and shook her head.

'No thanks,' she said, just as Liz arrived dressed in a checked shirt, a pair of baggy jeans and her Doc Martens, a twisted scarf holding her hair away from her face.

'Stop trying to fob that crap off on Etta,' she said. 'We're sophisticated women, I'll have you know.'

'That'll be blackcurrant in your lager then, will it?' deadpanned Mr Young and Liz glared at him, but it was an affectionate glare.

Liz's mum was looking in her handbag and she pulled out her purse and fished out a pound note. She offered it to Liz.

'Stick this in the collecting bucket from me, would you. It's the wives and kiddies I feel for. None of this is their fault but them's the ones suffering.'

Liz took the note and stuffed it in her pocket.

'You take care of that, my girl,' said her mother sternly. 'Money doesn't grow on trees, you know. And mind that makes its way into the collection. Don't you be spending it on drink now.'

'Cross my heart hope to die,' replied Liz, running a finger in a diagonal cross over her chest.

'You're a good girl, Etta. You make sure she doesn't spend it herself.'

'Will do, Mrs Young,' said Etta with a grin.

'Let's get out of here,' said Liz, whipping a key up from a bowl on the sideboard. 'Anyone would think we were fifteen, not twenty-four!'

'Lovely to see you both,' said Etta as Liz dragged her away from the house.

'God, don't parents drive you mental,' said Liz as she pulled the front door closed behind them with a healthy slam. And then she stopped, standing stock still, her hand over her mouth. 'Shit, I'm so sorry, Etta. I didn't think.'

Loretta shrugged it away.

'If mine were here they'd drive me mental too,' she said, and she was sure it was true.

They could hear the music pulsing on to the street as they approached the club. Someone had made a banner using a bed sheet. 'Suport the Miners' was daubed across it in black letters. The spelling error leapt out at Loretta but Liz didn't mention it and Loretta wondered if she hadn't noticed. She kept her mouth shut.

Familiar faces stood around the door, one with a bucket that had coins and the odd note sitting in the bottom.

'Coming in, girls?' said a man who Loretta had known since childhood. 'It's fifty pence each and there's a raffle inside.'

'Certainly are, Sean,' grinned Liz. 'And look! I've even fished Etta out of her posh new life to come along.'

Loretta felt the colour rise up her throat. She had wanted to leave but she didn't want people to think badly of her. She knew they probably did.

'Hi, Sean,' she said. 'Are you well? And Margi?'

'Fine, darlin',' he replied and held his bucket aloft.

They both dropped fifty pence in. Liz held back her mother's pound.

'Not putting it in there,' she said under her breath as they walked in. 'I don't trust Sean not to siphon off all the notes for his beer fund.'

Inside, the air was heavy with cigarette smoke and smelled of beer and hot bodies. A string of multicoloured light bulbs had been hung over the bar and there was a roadworks light flashing orange in one corner. The closed doors didn't quite manage to disguise that it was still light outside. The room was filling up, though, with enough already there to show promise for a good night ahead.

They made for the bar. A 'Coal Not Dole' collecting tin was chained to one end and Liz curled the pound note into a tube and fed it into the narrow slot.

'There. Now. What are you drinking?'

49

Loretta was having a great time. The DJ was doing a fantastic job and the floor-fillers just kept coming. They had danced to every song that he played: Blondie, Wham!, Elton John, Abba, The Jam. Each time the style of music changed they looked at one another, brows furrowed, until they recognised the tune and then set off again with renewed vigour, breaking off only to go to the bar.

Loretta bought a strip of raffle tickets – it was all in a good cause, after all – and then stuffed them in her jeans pocket, forgetting all about them, but around ten thirty the lights came up and the DJ asked for hush whilst the raffle was drawn. Sean had appeared next to the DJ with a plastic tray of chops, sausages and bacon. Loretta wondered how long it had been out of a fridge.

'And the lucky winner of the top prize, a tray of choice cuts from our very own Wainwright's butcher's, goes to . . . drumroll, please . . . and it's a green ticket. Green twenty-seven.'

Everyone checked their tickets and groaning came from various parts of the room.

'I never win anything,' someone said, and, 'Could have done with bagging that,' said someone else.

'Come on. Which lucky person has won this amazing prize? Who is it?'

Loretta fished her tickets out of her pocket. They were green and she scanned down the numbers. The winning ticket was amongst them. Quickly, she screwed the strip up and stuffed it back into her pocket.

'Not you?' asked Liz.

Loretta shook her head and tried to look disappointed. What was she going to do with a tray of meat? Carry it back with her on the bus? Winning meat at the club wasn't part of who she was now. It was better to let them redraw and have the prize go to someone who wanted it, or needed it.

'Okay. Number twenty-seven must have gone home. Let's go again.' The DJ stuck his hand back into the bucket of tickets. 'And it's pink. Lucky for some, number thirteen.'

He held the ticket aloft and a middle-aged woman with a blonde perm squealed.

'It's me! It's me!!' she shouted, waving her ticket. She strutted across the floor, her white court shoes tapping as she went. She turned and gave a little bow and everyone cheered.

The ticket was exchanged for the tray and Loretta thought again how far she had travelled from where she'd begun.

'Drink?' asked Liz.

Loretta nodded. 'And a sit-down. My feet are killing me.'

They got the drinks and found a table over near the flashing roadworks light. The Formica tabletop was sticky, ringed with the traces of previous glasses.

'What a laugh!' said Liz, leaning back in her chair, her face glowing from the dancing.

'Yeah. Thanks for inviting me. Best night out in ages,' replied Loretta.

Liz raised an eyebrow but didn't pass comment.

'And it's going well, the being a reporter thing?' asked Liz.

'I like it,' nodded Loretta.

'Got any big scoops yet?'

Loretta shook her head. 'No, but if you happen to have any big stories you'd care to share . . .'

They laughed, running through events from their childhoods and recasting them as news stories.

'Actually,' began Loretta, 'I've been doing a bit of background on crime families. You know, like the Krays and the Richardsons.'

'Find anything?' asked Liz and then, 'You do know the Youngs are the most feared family in Barnet?' Liz flexed her biceps and Loretta shook her head in mock despair.

'No. Not really,' she replied. 'There doesn't seem to be much to find.'

'Nasty world though,' said Liz. 'I heard that if you cross these blokes they'd think nothing of kneecapping you and ditching you out at sea. No body, no crime.'

'What, still? I thought that all ended years ago.'

Liz shrugged. 'It's just what you hear,' she said. 'They're pretty scary.'

'Who are?' Loretta's story antennae were twitching.

'I don't know. And if I did, I wouldn't tell you. I quite like you, Etta. Don't want you ending up in a concrete coffin at the bottom of the Thames.'

'Nat says there's Mafia over where she is in Sicily,' Loretta said.

Liz blew her lips out. 'Now, they're the ones you really want to be scared of, by all accounts,' she said. 'They don't mess about. They make our British villains look like playground bullies. And they can hold a grudge. If they want you dead, they don't forget. It can go on for decades.'

Loretta's eyes opened wide.

'How do you know?' she asked. She hadn't spent much time with Liz for almost ten years now. Maybe she had got herself caught up in something in that time, something that Loretta knew nothing about.

'Have you never seen *The Godfather*?' Liz laughed.

Loretta's shoulders slumped. 'Oh, for God's sake,' she said. 'I thought you were serious there for a minute.'

'Crime families? Round here? Give me a break. It's more likely that old Sylv over there will stop dyeing her hair.' She nodded at the woman who had won the tray of meat.

And then the opening bars of 'Oops Upside Your Head' came on. People stopped dancing and sat on the floor, one in front of the other in long snakes. Liz grabbed Loretta's arm and pulled her to her feet.

'Come on!' she said and within seconds Loretta too was sitting on the tacky floor, legs wide. Liz was behind her, her arms holding on to Loretta's waist, and a man her dad used to drink with was in front of her. Loretta could see his bald patch, visible despite the efforts he'd made to hide it with a comb-over.

Soon the whole row was rowing backwards and forwards in time with the music and then spreading their arms and tipping from side to side like manic little aeroplanes. It was surprisingly hard work.

'You see,' Liz shouted in her ear, 'this is what a good night out looks like.'

Loretta had to agree.

50

2022 – Ripon

Bronte was in her shop. She liked the way being there soothed her as she pottered around working through boxes of other people's rubbish, sorting the wheat from the chaff. What she could sell changed with the seasons, just like fashion did. Recently, there had been a huge demand for small items of rattan furniture, then macramé. At the moment, it seemed to be mismatched vintage crockery. Part of the fun for Bronte was trying to stay one step ahead of the trends so that she could foresee the next Instagram-fuelled craze and be ready with suitable stock accordingly.

She pulled out a little shoebox that she had just acquired. Its contents slid around heavily as she handled it. Whatever was inside hadn't been carefully wrapped. The box had a red lid and the Start-Rite logo on the side of two children wrapped up well and walking down a tree-lined avenue. Bronte had seen plenty of these vintage shoeboxes and had often wondered what the logo really had to do with shoes other than the fact that the children were walking.

She lifted the lid. The box was full of little Whimsy animals, mass-manufactured pottery figurines with a high-shine glaze in realistic colours. This lot had no doubt been somebody's pride and joy back in the sixties or seventies. She could almost visualise someone running a duster over them. It wasn't a full set, she noticed in dismay, but a mixture of animals, presumably whichever ones had caught the collector's eye. A couple of them were chipped. Bronte wondered if they had been intact when they were unceremoniously swept into the shoebox for disposal, not that it mattered. They weren't valuable and could be found in house clearances the world over. Someone could enjoy them again, though. She would give them a second lease of life.

She picked out a little ginger kitten, posed with its head tipped coyly to one side, and smiled at him. They were quite charming in their own way. She put the little pottery animals on a shelf, carefully arranging them first by colour and then, when that didn't please her, by species.

'Ah, Wade Whimsies,' said a voice from behind her. 'Nasty little wastes of clay.'

Tom stood in the doorway, blocking the light like a stranger rolling into town in a Western. He was wearing a three-piece suit, despite the warmth of the day, and his battered trilby on his head.

'Don't be so unsentimental, Tom,' chided Bronte gently. 'People still love them.'

'More fool them,' Tom said dismissively.

'Tea?' she asked as he settled himself into the Parker Knoll.

'That'd be grand,' he replied.

He kept his own counsel until she returned with the drinks and then he spoke.

'She's not left town, then? The woman?'

Immediately, Bronte was on high alert.

'Which woman?' she asked, hoping that she knew exactly who he was talking about.

'Your woman. Her from the funeral,' he said. 'Saw her up by the cathedral. In the graves. Reckon she was looking for your mother. She's not there though, is she?'

Bronte shook her head, but the details of her mother's burial were not what was salient here.

'When was she there?' she asked urgently. 'Did you see her?'

It took Tom an irritatingly long time to reply.

'Aye,' he said just as Bronte was about to repeat herself. 'Saw her there just this morning as it happens.'

Bronte could feel her adrenaline spiking. It hadn't occurred to her that the woman might have stayed after the funeral. If it had, she would have been out there searching for her herself.

'What was she doing?' she asked again. 'Did you speak to her?'

Tom shook his head.

'Not one for speaking out of turn,' he said slowly, and Bronte's heart sank. How was she ever going to find the woman now? She couldn't stop her shoulders sagging with disappointment.

Tom stared at the contents of his mug. 'But I might have mentioned you and this place,' he added. 'Just to be friendly, like.'

Bronte sat forward in her chair.

'You told her about my shop?' she asked, almost giddy with excitement. 'What did you say?'

'Just that if she were looking for any of Loretta's family then you're Loretta's kid and you have a shop in town.'

The pace of Tom's delivery of this information couldn't have been more exasperating, but Bronte knew she needed to be patient.

'And . . . ?'

'And that was it,' he said. 'She wandered off and I went about my business.'

'But did you tell her my name, or the name of the shop, where it is?' she asked desperately. She could see this one opportunity to speak to the woman slipping away from her.

Tom gave her a look that said everything that was on his mind, but then he replied as well.

'I may be old, Bronte, but I'm not daft. How's she going to find you if all she knows is that you have a shop in Ripon? It'd take her until kingdom come to track you down.'

Bronte smiled at him, grateful and relieved.

'Yes, sorry, Tom. Of course you did. And did you get the impression she might come and say hello?'

'Not much point turning up at the funeral and sitting in the family pew if you don't want to be part of the family,' he said.

'I suppose not, but then she disappeared without speaking to any of us.'

'Happen she lost her nerve. You're a pussy cat, Bronte love,' continued Tom, 'but that brother of yours. He can be enough to put anyone off their stride.'

Bronte remembered how dismissive Marc had been of the woman. If he could have physically shooed her away without looking like an idiot in front of the whole congregation then he would have.

'And she didn't say anything else?' she asked.

She was desperate for a little more information, anything at all. If she didn't know when the woman – her aunt – was going to turn up then she would have to bring a sleeping bag down to the shop. She couldn't risk her arriving when Bronte wasn't there to meet her. She might never come back and then the opportunity of finding out who she really was and where she had been for the last forty years would be lost.

51

Bronte was like the proverbial cat on a hot tin roof for the rest of the day. She couldn't settle to anything. Every time she thought she heard a noise in the passageway outside the shop her head turned towards the door, hoping that she would be there. But no mysterious would-be aunt appeared.

She thought about keeping the shop open a little later than normal just in case, but she decided against it. Unless the woman had been living under a rock all these years, she would know the hours that shops were generally open in a tiny place like Ripon. It was hardly the metropolis, with places open all hours. There really was no point staying beyond six o'clock.

The cathedral bells sounded the hour and Bronte reluctantly picked up her bag and left, but she looked up and down the narrow street as she turned the key in the lock to see if there was anyone out there watching her. There wasn't, or if there was they weren't making themselves known.

She thought about calling in on Helen on the way home, bursting to tell her what had happened and to do a deep dive into what it might mean, but the two of them had arranged to run together that evening so she decided her news could wait until then.

She made her way back to her terraced house feeling hyper-vigilant and constantly checking behind her, peering in shop doorways and generally behaving in what must have looked like a most suspicious manner to anyone who might be watching her.

But there was no one there. And why, Bronte thought as she closed her front door behind her, would the woman sneak about anyway? If she wanted to talk, surely she would just come forward and make herself known? What was to be gained by skulking in the shadows?

Bronte just had to accept it. The woman wasn't going to show up tonight. After all, unless she had followed her home then how would she even know where Bronte lived? No, Bronte would just have to hope that she put in an appearance the following day.

An hour later she was standing on Helen's doorstep, dressed in her running gear. She knocked on the door and moments later Helen appeared. The top part of her body was dressed in a high-visibility orange running vest but below that she was wearing nothing but her pants and one sock.

'Come in, come in,' she said. 'I'm ready. I just need to . . .'

Helen fell on to her sofa with her legs high in the air and stuffed one foot and then the other into a pair of leggings.

'Good day?' she asked as she stood up and jumped up and down, pulling at the waistband of the leggings until they were sitting where she wanted them.

'Not bad,' replied Bronte, not wanting to launch into her news until they were on their way. Doing otherwise would probably result in no run, and she really needed to clear her head a bit.

They left Helen's house and began to run down Boroughbridge Road towards the wetlands nature reserve. Bronte let Helen chatter first, telling her about her day and a boisterous class of year nines who had made it their life's work to make Helen's days as challenging as they could. Bronte had heard so much about this particular class that it was beginning to feel like she knew some of the individuals personally.

'I had some news today,' she began when Helen's tales had come to an end. 'Apparently, the woman from the funeral is still in Ripon. Tom saw her up at the cathedral today.'

Helen stopped running and Bronte was forced to do the same.

'No way!!' Helen said. 'And?'

Bronte, who was still jogging on the spot, set off again and Helen did the same.

'And nothing, really. Tom spoke to her, told her that I was Mum's daughter and the name of the shop and then he left her to it.'

'Okay,' replied Helen, 'that's good. So now she knows how to get hold of you if she wants to. And I think we can assume that she does want to, or why else would she still be here? The funeral was a few weeks ago. Do you think she went away and came back, or has she been kicking around all this time looking for you?'

'She must have gone away, surely. It would only take a handful of questions for someone to direct her to me, or Dad. She can't possibly have been looking for us all this time. Unless she hasn't spoken to anyone until Tom approached her today.'

'God bless Tom, eh,' puffed Helen as their path took them up an incline.

'Yes, nosy old so-and-so. But yes, if he hadn't recognised her and said hello then she might have gone on for weeks not knowing where to find us.'

'I'm not buying that she couldn't have found you if she'd wanted to,' said Helen. 'I bet she's known exactly where you are. She was probably just biding her time, waiting for the right moment to come forward.'

'You mean like a stalker, watching but never saying hello?' The idea made Bronte shudder. Another thought struck her. 'You don't think she's dangerous, do you?'

'No! If she'd wanted to harm you, she could have done it a dozen times by now,' reassured Helen. 'It's more likely that she's been building up the nerve to speak to you.'

This did seem more likely.

'Maybe she's nervous about broaching whatever it is that was going on between her and Mum?'

But Helen scoffed.

'Sorry to be blunt here, Bronte, but your mum is dead and you've never heard of this mysterious aunt. Whatever it was that's been keeping her away, it can't possibly be relevant anymore.'

This was true and Bronte acknowledged it as such.

'And what's next?' asked Helen as they reached the turning point on their run.

'I just have to sit in my shop and hope she turns up,' replied Bronte. 'What else can I do?'

Helen turned her head to look at her as they ran and pulled a face.

'Sometimes I just want to shake you, Bronte,' she said.

'Why?!'

'Stop being so passive! Make something happen. You're more than capable but you don't ever give yourself permission to take the initiative.'

Helen was probably right. That was something Bronte could think about at a quieter moment. But right now she had literally no idea how she could control the situation.

'Okay, Einstein,' she said, laughing. 'Exactly how do I make a woman I don't know turn up in my shop on demand? By using the power of my mind?'

Helen grinned back.

'Okay. Maybe you can't actually do anything about this situation,' she said grudgingly.

'Exactly. I just have to wait.'

52

Bronte couldn't resist the urge to get to the shop early the following morning, even though it seemed unlikely that her putative aunt would turn up before nine.

Summer was a couple of weeks old and, as was so often the case in June in England, it was making a pretty good job of being summery. Generally, on warmer days, Bronte let the shop door stand open. Potential customers were more likely to wander in if they didn't have to push at a closed door, but it also meant that visitors could enter the shop without setting the doorbell jangling.

So Bronte busied herself at the front of the shop but no one out of the ordinary came in all morning. Each time a shadow fell over the threshold she felt her scalp tingle in case this was her, followed by a wave of disappointment when it wasn't.

Usually when lunchtime rolled around, she would pop into the baker's up the road to buy herself a sandwich or a jacket potato. It wasn't very economical but it at least gave her the chance for a little human conversation, which could be sorely lacking in the shop on a quiet day.

Today, though, she had brought her lunch from home, not wanting to attach her handwritten 'Back in Five Minutes' sign to the door in case the woman chose those very five minutes to visit.

And, of course, she was just biting into her egg sandwich when she heard someone clearing their throat.

Bronte looked up.

Even though the woman's features hadn't settled in Bronte's mind during their brief encounter at the funeral, she recognised the pixie haircut and the black dog-walking fleece, surely not needed on a sunny day like today.

The woman stood on the threshold of the shop, as if she couldn't quite commit to stepping inside. She was slim, with hunched shoulders and a careworn face. If she really was her mother's sister, then she must have been the elder. Loretta had been sixty-two when she died but this woman looked a good five years older. Bronte peered at her face; she could see the similarities, the line of her nose, something around the eyes.

Her left hand was covering her mouth and she was worrying at her nails with her teeth. They were bitten so short that the tips of her fingers were red and swollen. Her eyes darted around the shop nervously as if she were wanting to take everything in before coming inside.

It was like coaxing a timid animal out into the open: no sudden movements or loud noises. One wrong step and the woman would bolt. Bronte tried to relax and offered her most welcoming smile.

'Hello again,' she said.

The woman replied with a tight nod of acknowledgement but didn't return the smile.

'We didn't really get a chance to introduce ourselves at the funeral,' Bronte continued. 'I'm Bronte, Loretta's middle child. And you are?'

There was a pause. The woman took a quick glance over her shoulder and then peered into the back of the shop as if there might be some danger lurking there. Then she looked at her feet, at her hands, and eventually back up at Bronte, but she didn't make direct eye contact.

'Natalie,' she said, her voice so quiet that Bronte almost missed it. 'I'm Loretta's sister.'

Bronte wanted to mark the uttering of this sentence somehow. It was huge. This was her aunt, her mother's long-lost sister, and even though she had no idea why they had become estranged, the mere fact of her was hugely significant.

Normally, she would have embraced Natalie or at the very least let what she had said settle before she spoke again, but it was clear she had to keep the fragile momentum of the conversation going so that her aunt didn't flee.

'I'm so pleased to meet you,' she said instead.

She held out a hand but Natalie merely stared at it and then stuffed her own hands into the pockets of her fleece.

'Yeah, me too,' she muttered.

Bronte had nothing but questions, but this moment clearly needed careful handling.

'Would you like a cup of tea?' she asked. 'I can put the kettle on and I think there are some biscuits somewhere.'

Natalie's eyes dropped back to the floor.

'That'd be nice,' she muttered. 'Thank you,' she added as an afterthought.

'Great!' Bronte waved an arm at the shabby Parker Knoll chair. 'Please, sit down.'

Usually, she would have showered a visitor to her shop with polite enquires but nothing about Natalie welcomed questions of any kind, and so Bronte busied herself with the kettle in silence.

She could hear the woman wandering around rather than sitting as invited, and she positioned herself so she could watch her as she made the tea. Natalie stopped at the shelf with the

Whimsy animals. She picked up the ginger kitten, turning it over in her fingers.

'I'd forgotten about these,' she said, her voice barely more than a whisper. 'Etta collected them.' Then she looked up sharply. 'These aren't . . . ?'

Catching her meaning and horrified that she might think Bronte was selling her mother's possessions so quickly after her death, she said, 'God no. I didn't even know Mum had any. If she did, I never saw them.'

Natalie put the cat back down.

'No. I suppose she had to leave them all behind when she left.'

The questions that Bronte was desperate to ask were starting to stack up now. Where had her mother left, and why? And how come she hadn't packed her things up before she went?

But she sensed that this was not the time for any of that. Natalie was as nervous as a wild rabbit. One false move could send her scuttling out of the shop and out of Bronte's life.

'Did she?' she said instead. 'I didn't know that about Mum.'

'No. I suppose not,' replied Natalie. 'I suppose there is a lot you didn't know.'

Bronte wanted to say that until Natalie had shown up at the funeral, she had thought she knew everything of any importance, but again, this didn't feel like the moment for that.

'Yes, so it seems,' she said instead. 'Milk and sugar?'

'Just black,' replied Natalie, and then added another quick 'thanks'.

Bronte poured milk into her own tea and then carried the two mugs over to the chairs. She passed one towards Natalie and then, when she showed no sign of taking it, placed it down carefully on a coaster on the antique desk she used to serve customers.

'So,' she said as she sat down. 'Where shall we begin?'

53

Natalie took a sip of her tea, winced slightly at the temperature and then took another. She opened her mouth to speak, closed it again, dropped her gaze to her lap. Bronte watched her. She had rarely seen anyone look quite as uncomfortable as her aunt did right now. Whatever there had been between her and Bronte's mother, it was clearly a huge deal.

Bronte was about to break the silence with a mundane question when Natalie spoke.

'I'm sorry about the funeral,' she said. 'I shouldn't have just shown up.'

Well, that was as good a place to start as any, thought Bronte.

'It was fine,' she replied soothingly. 'It was just a bit of a surprise for us. We didn't know Mum had a sister.'

'No,' said Natalie. 'I suppose not.'

There was no shock in her expression. That her nephew and nieces didn't know of her existence didn't seem to be news to her.

'If we had,' Bronte continued, 'then obviously we would have invited you. But it was just a bit of a bombshell, you turning up like that. And Marc, he's my brother, well, he can be a bit . . .' Bronte searched for the word. She didn't want to put Marc down, but he had been very dismissive of Natalie in the cathedral. 'Well, it was a stressful day for us all,' she said. 'And then when you disappeared at the end . . .'

Bronte let her eyes rest directly on Natalie's face, giving her an opportunity to explain her behaviour, but Natalie's lips were drawn into a thin line.

'Anyway, you're here now. That's the main thing,' Bronte stumbled on, but it was hard work, like drawing blood from the proverbial stone. Maybe the small talk thing wouldn't work. Perhaps she needed to dive straight in with the real questions. Then she had a better idea.

'Let me tell you something about us,' she said brightly and began to paint a full picture of her father and the three children. She described where everyone lived and what they were all doing, talked about Marc and his children, Natalie's great-nephews, and Natalie looked interested, nodding at the details and smiling a little. The smiles felt like a breakthrough although they were tight and short-lived.

'I did know some things about you all,' she said. She picked at a bobble on her fleece. There were plenty to go at. 'I knew that Etta had children and that she lived in Ripon. That's how I heard she had died, from the local paper. A headline popped up on my phone.'

Bronte's mouth fell open.

'Oh God, that must have been awful,' she said. 'Hearing like that.'

Then she remembered that she didn't know why her aunt wasn't in her mother's life. If they had fallen out then perhaps she didn't care that she had died. Yet she had been at the funeral and was here now. All love was evidently not entirely lost.

Natalie swallowed and brought her mug to her mouth, although she didn't take a sip, and Bronte had the impression that she was using it as a kind of mask.

'Yeah. That was a bit shit. I always thought, maybe one day . . .' She shrugged. 'Too late now.'

This statement brought a punch of emotions to Bronte that she had to brace herself to withstand. She closed her eyes to concentrate on maintaining control, but Natalie was right. It was too late. It was all too late.

The wave of grief left Bronte feeling less sympathetic to this stranger.

'So why did Mum never tell us about you?' The words were out of her mouth before she had weighed them up.

Natalie shrugged again as if she had no idea why the split had occurred. But that couldn't be true. You didn't just stop keeping in touch with your sister for no reason.

'Was there an argument?' Bronte pressed. 'Was that it? Some kind of falling-out.'

'I never fell out with Etta,' Natalie said simply. 'I loved her.'

This was making no sense and Bronte began to feel exasperated as she tried to unravel the story behind it all. She remembered what Liz had said about the family's humble beginnings. Could that be the key to unlocking this mystery? Bronte hated to even consider it, but was the answer simply that her mother had chosen to ditch her old life and leave her family behind? She stared at her aunt in her scruffy jacket, with her bitten fingernails and face lined from a hard life – harder than the one her mother seemed to have had, at least. She supposed it wasn't inconceivable.

Bronte decided to change tack.

'Why don't you tell me about you?' she said. 'You're older than Mum?'

Natalie shook her head.

'No. Etta was my big sister. Three years older than me.'

Bronte tried not to let her surprise show on her face but she was apparently unsuccessful. Natalie ran a hand through her cropped hair and shuffled in the chair.

'It's been tough.'

'What has?' asked Bronte bluntly, in case being blunt and not gentle was what was required to move the conversation forward.

For a moment Natalie looked as if she might actually tell her but then the shutters seemed to come back down and she didn't reply. Maybe she wasn't going to tell Bronte anything at all.

'Where do you live?' Bronte tried. Surely that couldn't be a controversial question.

Natalie paused for a moment, as if deciding how to answer.

'I was abroad for a long time,' she said. 'Italy first. Then France, Spain, Greece. I've moved around a lot.'

Bronte smiled encouragingly.

'That's cool,' she said. 'I've always wanted to travel but somehow I've never really left Ripon. And now? Do you live in the UK?'

Natalie nodded.

'I've been back for a while. Scotland. Wales. I like remote places. Not too busy. Safe. I tend to do best by myself. I'm pretty self-sufficient.'

A flicker of pride crossed her face.

'I'm the opposite,' said Bronte. 'I need people around me. I've never been much good on my own. When we were kids, Marc, that's my brother, he used to abandon me in places so that I could make my own way home. He was always telling me how I'd never get anywhere in life if I didn't learn to stand on my own two feet. I don't have any gumption, apparently. He's probably right. It would explain why I've never wandered far from the nest.'

Natalie pulled her eyebrows together into a deep frown that made the wrinkles on her face even more severe.

'That's bollocks,' she said, and the vehemence of her reply made Bronte start. 'Look at this place,' Natalie continued. 'It's great. This is just you, isn't it? No one else?'

'No. Just me.'

Natalie opened her hands as if to signify the accuracy of her point. QED.

'You shouldn't let people put you down like that, Bronte,' she said, her voice suddenly fiery. 'Don't get caught up in someone else's agenda. Marc saying that tells me more about his faults than any you might have.'

This was the longest sentence she had uttered since she arrived and she looked almost as surprised by her outburst as Bronte was.

'Yes,' said Bronte. 'You're probably right.'

'It sounds like he needs to make you feel rubbish so that he can feel better about himself. But that's his crap, not yours. Don't ever forget that.'

A flush began to spread over Natalie's cheeks and she lowered her gaze again.

'Sorry,' she muttered. 'None of my business.'

Bronte considered her, this stranger with her secrets and her forthright opinions. Who was she really? Where had she been and what did she want now? Bronte was still none the wiser.

And yet here she was, sticking up for Bronte as if she had always been a part of her life. For years Bronte had been the butt of her siblings' jokes, the middle and slightly inadequate child. It was so refreshing to feel as if someone had her back, just like her mother had always done.

'Well, it is kind of your business,' Bronte said. 'After all, you are my only aunt.'

54

1984 – Sicily

Natalie had been in Ortigia with the family for two weeks and she now knew her way around the tiny island. The wider city of Syracuse was still a mystery but as they tended to be either on Ortigia or at one of the nearby beaches then that didn't matter. She already had a favourite bar, the one where she and Danny had been for a drink on that first night, and she knew which shops sold the nicest bread, the freshest fish, the sweetest fruit.

She, Annette and Paola seemed to be in charge of buying food and Stella, who had never excelled in this area, seemed happy to relinquish control. Cooking had become a bit of a cooperative affair with all the women claiming a signature dish or two. Even Paola could make a mean pollo alla cacciatora with a little bit of help. The family also ate out in the evenings a lot, which left Annette, Danny and Natalie to have free run of the kitchen. Gabriella, the housekeeper, didn't live in and as long as they left the kitchen clean at the end of the night she was happy too.

That evening Natalie had made a tomato and mozzarella salad, drenching everything in thick green olive oil and finishing with a generous grind of black pepper. Annette had fried some fish and they'd eaten it with fresh bread and washed it all down with a bottle of red wine, which was Danny's contribution. Now they sat on a first-floor balcony overlooking the town and enjoyed the evening's warmth.

Annette, sprawled in a chair with one leg slung over its arm, took a packet of cigarettes out of her shirt pocket and lit one before offering the packet around. Natalie had never been a smoker, but Danny helped himself, lighting it with an old brass Zippo that he always had on him. He took a long luxurious drag, closing his eyes as he let the smoke travel deep inside his lungs. He didn't look anything like James Dean but the way he moved, so languidly, reminded her of him. She found it hard not to stare and only just looked away in time when he opened his eyes again.

There was still nothing going on between them beyond a kind of slightly aloof friendship. They didn't even indulge in harmless flirting. There were no looks that held a second too long, no accidental brushes of each other's bodies with stray hands.

But there was something there. Natalie could feel it, a tension between them that would make no sense if it wasn't gilded with sexual chemistry. He was biding his time. Natalie had no idea why but she could feel his restraint as strongly as if he had physical bonds holding him back.

Well, she could wait. Not forever – she wasn't a doormat. But until he got over whatever it was that was making him cautious. And there was something quite exciting about it, trying to work out what was going on in his head, although she was no clearer on that score. Annette had said she should just take matters in hand herself, kiss him first to force something to happen, for good or bad, then at least she'd know. But that wasn't Natalie's style, and anyway she did know. She just didn't know why he was being so hesitant.

This evening, they were tipping over into being drunk. That wasn't something that often happened. Natalie had to be up with the children and generally bowed out early, which tended to bring Annette to a stop too, but this evening the first bottle had quickly slipped into a second and now they were on to the Strega.

Natalie tipped her head back and looked up at the velvety sky. The moon wasn't more than a slither of light and she couldn't see as many stars here as she could at the villa because of the lights all around them, but the sky was definitely clearer than it had ever been in London. She let out a sigh of contentment.

'This is the life,' Annette said, blowing smoke rings. 'So tell me, Danny,' she continued, as the latest curl of white smoke floated off into the night. Her words sounded thicker and less crisp than they usually did.

Natalie opened her eyes wide, signalling that Annette most definitely should not ask Danny what his intentions were regarding her, but that didn't seem to be what Annette was interested in.

'Uh huh?' replied Danny, flicking his ash into the scallop shell that sat on the table for that purpose.

'When you go off doing "jobs" for Salvatore . . .' She flapped her hands to make loose air quotes around the word. 'What is it that you're actually doing? I mean, it's all so bloody mysterious.'

Danny shrugged.

'Not that mysterious,' he replied. 'Usually I'm delivering documents for him, stuff that needs to get there fast or that he doesn't want to risk in the post.'

'Yeah, yeah,' said Annette. 'I know all that. But what is it *actually*?'

'It's actually that. No mystery.'

Annette turned to face him, narrowing her eyes as she sucked on her cigarette.

'Okay. So what's in the documents to make them so precious?' she asked.

Danny shrugged.

'How am I supposed to know? I don't read them. They're in sealed envelopes.'

'And you never have to deliver anything else,' Annette persisted. 'Stuff that isn't document shaped?'

Natalie hadn't given any thought to what Danny did for Salvatore.

'Why does it matter?' she asked. 'Who cares what he's delivering?'

'It's just weird, that's all,' replied Annette. 'Sneaking off here, there and everywhere and then not saying what he's up to.'

'I do not sneak,' said Danny, sounding affronted now.

'So why not say what you're up to?' persisted Annette.

'I don't not say!' Danny's frustration was showing in his tone. 'I say I'm delivering documents for Salvatore. There's no mystery, no sneaking.'

'Humph,' said Annette.

'What are you getting at, Annette?' asked Natalie. 'What is it you want him to admit to?'

Annette slumped back in her chair, the fight gone from her.

'I don't know,' she said. 'But don't you think it's weird though?'

Natalie wasn't following.

'I don't get you. Weird how?'

Annette opened her mouth to reply, closed it again. Then she shook her head with exaggerated movements.

'Nothing,' she said. 'Ignore me. I'm going to bed. See you two tomorrow.'

And then she stubbed her cigarette out in the scallop shell and weaved her way into the house.

55

Natalie watched Annette leave and then looked back to Danny.

'What was that all about?' she asked.

Danny shook his head slowly and blew his breath out noisily.

'God knows,' he said. 'She's got a bee in her bonnet though. We've had that same conversation before, her and me. I think she thinks Salvatore is up to no good.'

The conversation Natalie had had with Annette about the car bombing and the burned-out bakery came into her mind. Annette had warned her about mentioning anything to anyone but this wasn't anyone. This was Danny.

'You mean, she thinks he's got something to do with the Mafia?' She lowered her voice on the last word but it came out like an exaggerated stage whisper. Danny didn't flinch.

'Pretty much,' said Danny. 'Or at least, that's what I'm guessing.'

Natalie thought about Salvatore dressed in his expensive suits, the way he watched everything and never gave anything away. Then there was this house and the villa and who knew what else. She supposed it might make sense that the money for it all came from something shady. Then again, it might just as well have come from the sulphur mine business. People did make money in Sicily without it being done through the Mafia, she assumed.

'He hasn't, has he?' she asked.

She couldn't think what difference it would make to her to know one way or the other, but the question slipped out anyway.

Danny threw her a look that made her wish she hadn't asked.

'Of course not,' he said, his tone sharp-edged.

Natalie suddenly felt very small and stupid.

'Well, I didn't think he would be,' she added weakly.

'Don't you think I'd know?' he said. 'If I was working as a delivery boy for a Mafia boss?'

'I suppose so,' she replied.

But if you were, you're hardly likely to tell me, she thought. In fact, denying it is exactly what you'd do. These thoughts didn't have time to play out much further because Danny was leaning towards her and taking her hand in his. His hand was cool and smooth. Natalie looked at it and then up at him, confused by the sudden change of direction.

His face was very close to hers now. She could smell the Strega and cigarette smoke on his breath.

'You know that I like you, Natalie,' he was saying. 'I like you very much.'

And then before she could reply, he was kissing her. Her eyes closed automatically as she concentrated on the sensation of his lips on hers. She had thought about it so many times but his touch was gentler than she'd imagined. Slowly she opened her mouth and felt the tip of his tongue beginning to explore, and then she was lost.

The kiss seemed to go on for eternity and when he finally drew away, she opened her eyes and looked directly into his.

'Wow,' she said.

'Wow indeed. I've wanted to do that for so long.'

It was such a corny line, she knew it was, and if she had been recounting the scene to Annette their comments would have been mocking; but somehow, now that it was being said to her, it felt like the most romantic thing ever. All the sloppy films she had ever seen flashed before her eyes and here she was, the star.

'Me too,' she said dreamily. Then a little of her senses returned. 'So why didn't you?' she asked with a frown.

Danny looked as if the question had taken him by surprise, but he quickly rallied.

'I wanted the moment to be exactly right,' he said. 'And I wasn't sure you felt the same way. I didn't want to make a tit of myself by pouncing on you only for you to reject me.'

He grinned at her, his little dimple winking at her, and she was lost again.

'Well, we should probably make up for lost time,' she said and leaned in for another kiss.

Around eleven o'clock the big front door banged downstairs and Natalie heard voices echoing around the house. Enzo and Gianni seemed to be arguing about something, Stella trying to calm them. She and Danny pulled apart.

'You'd better go to bed before they catch us,' he said, giving her nose a playful tap. 'I'll tidy up here.'

Natalie didn't have to be told twice. If she was still awake no doubt Stella would rope her into getting the children to bed, even though she was technically off duty, and that was the last thing she wanted. All she wanted right now was to lie in the dark in her bed and replay her first kisses with Danny, the first of many, she felt sure.

'Thanks,' she whispered. 'See you tomorrow.'

'You bet,' said Danny. He reached for his cigarettes, ready to look as though he'd been here by himself just contemplating the night sky after she and Annette had retired to bed.

Natalie moved quickly along the corridors and into her bedroom before anyone could see her. Not wanting to suggest that she was awake, she operated without putting the light on. She wouldn't be able to use the bathroom until the family had all gone to bed but that was all right. It wasn't as if she was going to be asleep any time soon. She had far too much thinking to do.

She lay on top of her sheets in the dark, not even bothering to close the shutters in case she made a noise. She ran the pad of her finger over her lips, retracing where Danny's had been minutes before, and her stomach somersaulted deliciously. What was this? The start of whatever had been brewing between them? Natalie felt sure that it must be. She closed her eyes and then she fell asleep, still fully dressed.

56

When she woke up, thirsty and her teeth a little furry against her tongue, Natalie's first thoughts were of Danny. Had he really kissed her? Of course, she knew that he had. She hadn't been that drunk, but it was still hard to believe. She had been hoping for that moment ever since she first arrived in Sicily, and now, all of a sudden, it had happened out of the blue.

She let her mind replay what she could remember of the build-up to the kiss. She had to admit that that part was a bit hazy, but there was nothing vague about the kisses themselves. They were now imprinted on her memory.

The wooden shutters were still tucked back against the wall and so the sunlight streamed into her room. She glanced at the travel clock on her bedside table. It said six thirty. Paola would be in any minute, bouncing her awake with her questions and enthusiasm for the day ahead.

Natalie sat up abruptly. Paola couldn't find her like this, in her clothes from yesterday and the bed slept on rather than in. Quickly she stood and stripped, letting her clothes fall to the floor. Then she retrieved her nightdress from under her pillow and was just dropping it over her head when she heard the tapping on her door.

'Come in,' she said, moving quickly towards the shutters so Paola might think she had just opened them.

Paola appeared wearing a pair of pink shortie pyjamas, her blonde hair a tousled bird's nest. Natalie cast a quick look in the mirror but luckily any make-up she had been wearing yesterday had worn off. She might get away with it if Paola didn't check her teeth!

'Why are you out of bed?' Paola asked at once, eyeing Natalie suspiciously.

'I woke up! Is that against the law?' Natalie replied in mock indignation.

Paola considered this for a moment and then conceded that it wasn't. They both settled on Natalie's bed, leaning back against the headboard with Paola snuggling in against Natalie. Natalie snaked an arm around her little shoulders and pulled her close.

'How was your evening?' Natalie asked her. 'Did you have a lovely dinner?'

Paola pulled a face.

'There was lots of boring grown-up talk but we did get ice cream on the way home. I had two scoops, stracciatella and zuppa inglese. That's got wine in it but Papa said I was old enough to have some.'

Paola stretched her neck proudly and Natalie rubbed her tangled hair.

'That is very grown-up,' she said. 'And did the boys have a nice time?'

Paola screwed up her nose.

'They did but then they got into a fight about Enzo's Top Trumps so they weren't allowed any ice cream. And today Papa has lots of important people coming for dinner and so we have to be quiet and not get in the way. Shall we go to the beach?'

'That sounds like an excellent idea,' agreed Natalie. 'I'll speak to Mummy and see what she says.'

Paola shrugged as if this were a foregone conclusion and she wouldn't have wasted her time on asking the question.

'I'm going to wear my bikini with the strawberries on,' she said and then wriggled out of Natalie's grasp and away.

Natalie got herself showered and dressed and then went down to see if she could add any more details to the sketchy plan that Paola had provided. There did appear to be some unusual activity in the house. Gabriella was there, directing men in the moving of furniture. It seemed Salvatore and his friends would dine in a room that Natalie had not yet seen used. It was long and thin and a scene of cherubs and stola-clad maidens in a flower-filled garden was painted on its ceiling. The walls were a delicate pink with the usual trompe l'oeil columns snaking up them.

The extension flaps of a highly polished dining table had been opened out so that it was now at least three times as long as it was the last time Natalie had seen it, and two men were bringing in antique dining chairs to set around it. It was clearly going to be a grand affair.

Not wanting to get roped into helping, Natalie skirted round the men and into the kitchen, where she began pulling breakfast together for the children, grabbing a bowl of cereal for herself as she went. She had the faintest traces of a hangover but she ignored it. It was worth it for all the fun she had had with Danny, although she hoped he would have kissed her anyway without the assistance of the wine and Strega.

The children appeared one by one. Enzo and Gianni seemed to have forgotten their argument of the night before and today the debate was about which of the local beaches they should visit. Gianni favoured the one that had rock pools to explore whereas Enzo preferred somewhere different because of its beach café.

In the end, Stella settled the discussion by opting for the beach with the most comfortable sun loungers and so that was where they went, with Stella driving, Natalie sitting next to her and the three kids bunched into the back seat.

It took a little while to establish themselves on the beach. Stella rented three sun loungers and an umbrella from the café. The third lounger was for Paola, who would come and drape herself over it from time to time, wanting to play at being a young lady, but then scamper back off into the water or to find her brothers after a few minutes.

Stella lay on her sun lounger at its flattest setting but Natalie kept hers upright so she could watch the children. Technically, Stella trumped her on childcare responsibilities when they were both there and she was terrifyingly relaxed about her children's safety so Natalie could have been too, but that didn't sit well with her. And so she sat up and kept alert.

They had been there a while when Natalie brought up the subject of the impending dinner.

'I gather there's a bit of a do at the house tonight,' she said. 'I saw them setting up the table before we left.'

Stella was lying on her back with her eyes hidden behind a pair of Ray-Ban Wayfarer sunglasses, which Natalie secretly coveted.

'Yes,' she said. 'Nothing to do with me though. They're all Salvatore's cronies. I'm only expected to show my face when they arrive, smile graciously and then make myself scarce. Thank God. Those dinners are so dull. And they will insist on speaking in Sicilian, so I can't understand most of what's said anyway. I'll have dinner outside with you and the kids.'

Natalie's mind took her back to Annette's questioning of Danny the evening before.

'Is it work?' she asked, trying to sound innocuous. 'Something to do with the mine?'

'God no,' replied Stella with a flap of her wrist. 'It's the summer. That's all closed down until September. No, this is his friends. Actually, not friends. They're part of some group or other that he's in. I've never quite got to the bottom of what it is, but he meets them at various venues once a week. This week it's his turn to host.'

Natalie's imagination went into overdrive but what could she do? She could hardly ask Stella if this cosy men's group was actually the Mafia. She would sound ridiculous, and it might be an insult; she wasn't sure of the etiquette here. And Danny had been adamant that Salvatore wasn't involved.

Thinking of Danny whisked her away into a little daydream again and as Stella toasted herself in the heat of the sun, Natalie watched the children play and thought about his lips on hers.

57

They arrived back from the beach, sticky and tired, around six thirty and Natalie took the children straight upstairs to get clean. Downstairs, Danny and Annette were pulling together the evening meal, and by the time she and her little tribe of fresh-smelling angels arrived in the kitchen everything was ready. The meal turned out to be spaghetti in a plain tomato sauce with grated cheese and some bread. There wasn't even an accompanying salad. Annette's hangover must have been worse than hers, Natalie thought with a grin.

They served the food on the table on the patio and just as it was ready Stella wafted in in a cotton kaftan that made her look even taller and more willowy than usual. She didn't seem to notice the simplicity of the meal and soon they were all tucking in, the children sharing details of their day at the beach.

Natalie kept glancing towards Danny, hoping to catch his eye, but either he wasn't looking her way or her timing was off as they never seemed to connect. Natalie tried not to read anything into this. Maybe he wanted to keep their private business private. She could definitely see the sense of that and in the end she stopped trying.

The old familiar dark thoughts were never far away, however. Who was she anyway? Why did she imagine that this good-looking guy would be interested in her? She knew it was ridiculous. A couple of kisses when they were drunk. It was hardly the basis for a romantic tryst. She should probably stop getting carried away and remember who she was, which was most definitely not a person who would attract someone like Danny.

Then again . . . those kisses. She hadn't imagined that spark.

When the children's bedtime arrived – it was a very moveable feast, particularly in the holidays – Natalie, relieved to have something to do other than gawp at Danny, gathered her charges and ushered them upstairs, Stella promising to follow them up and tuck them in.

Forty-five minutes later, Natalie made her way back downstairs, hoping to find the others, and particularly Danny, still at the table. However, the table was cleared and the patio deserted, Stella, Annette and Danny all having repaired to somewhere else.

Disappointment stabbed at her. She had hoped that Danny would have waited for her. She stood and listened to see if she could locate them in the large house. All she could hear, however, was the low rumble of male voices – Salvatore's dinner party, she assumed.

She set off towards the stairs to go to the balcony they'd sat on the previous evening. This involved walking past the long dining room and as she reached it, she paused. She wasn't eavesdropping – what would be the point? She had no hope of understanding what was being said, but she was still curious about what was going on behind the door.

Just then, the voices inside became more animated and then positively heated. One voice in particular was louder and more insistent than the others. Others spoke across him and then it sounded as if there were several people all talking at once. The volume went up and the tone seemed to become more aggressive, even though Natalie had no idea whether they were arguing or if this was just the usual Italian banter that she was getting used to hearing.

But then she heard one word that she could translate. 'No.' It was uttered clearly and emphatically, leaving no margin for doubt. And then another. 'Basta!' It sounded as if a chair was being pushed back along the floor with some force and then seconds later the double doors into the dining room burst open and a stocky man with a shining bald head stalked out, gesticulating as he went.

Natalie leapt back, embarrassed to have been caught right outside the door and aware that it looked as if she had been snooping.

'Mi scusi,' she mumbled as he stormed past her. He stared at her then, his almost black eyes scrutinising her face, his lips turned up in a scowl. He muttered something she didn't catch and then strode off in the direction of the front door, his shoes clattering on the marble floor.

Natalie watched him go. Shock at the suddenness of his appearance made her heart thud against her ribs. Then she looked into the room. Most of the men were still sitting round the dining table. Some were standing in small groups. Everything looked very tense.

Then Natalie's eyes settled on Salvatore, who was seated at the far end. He was wearing a beautifully cut jacket in a not quite navy blue with a crisp white shirt and a very stern expression. His wary eyes caught hers and he frowned. Then he raised his eyebrows at her and she knew at once that she was expected to close the door and go on her way. Feeling flustered, like a child caught misbehaving, she grabbed for the handle and pulled the door shut. Behind it, the sound of muted voices continued to rumble.

Natalie rushed away. She wanted to put as much distance between her and the room of men as she could. She wasn't sure what had just happened but she did understand that she wasn't supposed to have witnessed it.

But what had she seen really? Some men having a minor disagreement in a language she didn't understand. It was hardly anything to concern her. And yet she did feel concerned. Something about the way the man had barged past her, the look that Salvatore had given her as she closed the door, it suggested that all was not quite right.

Whatever it was that she had just seen, she was certain that she shouldn't have.

58

1984 – London

After her night out at the miners' fundraiser, Loretta decided to change the direction of her research. She hadn't abandoned the idea of finding a new London crime family. She would keep looking for clues on that front and if anything started to emerge, she would be the first to put the pieces together to form the whole picture.

But what Liz had said had struck a chord, even if it had been a joke. If the Mafia were the original gangsters then she should research them too, and if she understood something about how they worked then that might help her understand what could be going on in London.

She decided to start with the library. Mrs Brayshaw and her elephantine memory were all well and good but she didn't want to alert anyone to what she was doing. The newspaper was a small world inhabited by men all searching for the next big scoop. A single misplaced word could mean the whole project being snatched away from her.

She borrowed Mario Puzo's novels from the library as a place to start. Yes, they were fiction, but they surely had some truth in them. Even if Puzo had no personal knowledge he would have done his research, and that was what Loretta was doing.

She learned that the organisation seemed to run on loyalty and respect. If you were given a favour, the loyalty required that it had to be repaid and you could be asked to do pretty much anything. The most important thing of all was to protect the man at the top from anything that threatened him. In the Puzo novels, perceived slights could turn into hugely complicated acts of revenge, which was definitely a dish best served cold, it appeared. And woe betide anyone who got in the way. Whilst the code of honour seemed to suggest that innocent people, and particularly women and children, should be left alone, they could become collateral damage if necessary.

For the first time, Loretta began to worry a little about Natalie, but she tried to rationalise her concerns. Nat was working for a lovely family. The mother was English and the best friend of Malcolm's wife. It wasn't very likely that her husband was a Mafia boss. But maybe Loretta should just warn Natalie to be careful the next time they spoke. She wouldn't put it in a letter, she thought. You never knew who might read it. Then she chastised herself for her paranoia.

There was much going on in Sicily, however. A magistrate who had taken a stance against the crime families had been killed by a car bomb in Palermo. Journalists investigating the Mafia had disappeared without trace and there had been something called 'mattanza' – murders – almost daily, the bodies dumped on the streets outside police stations without any attempt to hide them. The Mafia meant business and they didn't care who knew it.

Most of the violence seemed to take place in Palermo. Loretta pulled out an atlas to see how far that was from where Natalie lived. Sicily was a big island but the distance between the two places looked frighteningly small.

The most recent stories speculated about the possibility of supergrasses, former mafiosi who switched allegiance to give evidence against their erstwhile bosses. The commentators seemed to think that this would be entirely foolhardy and therefore unlikely to happen. Who would want to bring the wrath of the most dangerous and widespread organisation in the world down on themselves? No matter how effective the witness protection schemes might be, a chink could always be found and exploited. How could anyone be safe?

She found herself scanning each report for the name of Natalie's boss but it was never there. He was simply a businessman. There really was no reason to worry.

59

It was around this time that Loretta met Paul. She was in the pub after work one night with her colleague Marty, unwinding after a busy day in the newsroom. Marty worked in the accounts department rather than on the actual paper but there were so few women that they had gravitated towards one another and found that they got on well.

'Don't look now,' said Marty, 'but those two blokes over there are watching us.'

Marty signalled with her eyes and Loretta tried to take a discreet look, but when she turned one of the men raised his glass to her. So much for being subtle. She smiled at him and then turned back to Marty.

'Not bad,' she said. 'I don't fancy yours much.'

Whilst the man who had toasted her was quite attractive, his friend most definitely was not. Marty flashed her left hand, the diamond engagement ring twinkling.

'I'm spoken for,' she said quietly to Loretta. 'But you help yourself.'

They went back to their conversation but a little time later the barman appeared with a bottle of champagne in a silver cooler and two flutes.

The first time this had happened to her, Loretta had been delighted. Having drinks sent over by a total stranger was like something out of a film and she hadn't been able to believe that it ever happened in real life and certainly not to someone like her. When she had started work at the paper, she had never even tasted real champagne. It wasn't a drink that had ever featured in her life and she had raced home, desperate to tell Nat about this strange new world she found herself in.

These days, she was a little more blasé about being sent drinks by men she had never met.

'From the gentlemen over there,' said the barman, pointing in the direction of the attractive man and his friend.

Marty raised an eyebrow and Loretta grinned back before turning to wave their thanks to the men. They had been left alone to enjoy the champagne but as the men left, the handsome one – Paul, as it turned out – put a business card on the table in front of her.

'Ring me,' he said and then he was gone.

Loretta picked the card up and read it out loud. 'Paul Laker. Investment Banker. Well I never.'

'Looks like you've pulled yourself a yuppie,' laughed Marty. 'Will you ring?'

She did, and a date was arranged in a wine bar in Knightsbridge. Paul was a couple of years older than her, from Nottingham, and was either making an obscene amount of money in the City or was putting himself hideously into debt by pretending that he was, judging by how generous he seemed to be. He never mentioned exactly how much he earned and Loretta took this as a sign of his good character.

They had fallen into a regular pattern of dates – dinner on Fridays, sometimes a film on Saturdays and long walks in the royal parks on a Sunday.

'How's your week been?' he asked when they met for dinner that week in a little family-run Chinese restaurant.

'Difficult,' she said. 'I had to doorstep a family whose kid fell from a balcony.'

'Dead?' asked Paul with a grimace.

Loretta nodded.

'Did they speak to you?'

'The dad wouldn't, but then he went to work and the mum invited me in.'

'And you were still there?' asked Paul. 'Just hanging around their front door? Wasn't that a bit gruesome?'

Loretta had grown used to this kind of criticism. You had to have a thick skin in her world.

'That's what I'm paid to do,' she replied. 'And I had a feeling that the mother would change her mind. There was something about the way she looked at me when she answered the door the first time. Just an impression that she might want to talk. It turned out that the railings on the balcony had been dodgy for a while. The dad was supposed to have rung the landlord but he hadn't got round to it.'

'Shit. No wonder he didn't want you there,' said Paul. 'I'm not sure how you ever get over something like that, losing someone you love in an avoidable accident. And a kid too.'

Loretta knew exactly how difficult that was but she kept her experience to herself.

'I got the story though,' she said. 'The mum really opened up to me. The dad was actually the stepdad. I don't think it was a match made in heaven. I reckon she'll kick him out after this. I could almost see her making her mind up as she told me the facts.'

'How old was the kid?' Paul asked.

'Six. A little boy. Ryan.'

Paul blew out a breath and sighed. It was hard to take in.

'Will you go back?' he asked. 'See how she's getting on?'

'Definitely. The paper wants me to write a follow-up. And she asked me to go to the funeral.'

Paul gave her an admiring look and Loretta smiled bashfully.

'You really are something special, Etta. Anyone else would have had the door slammed in their face and yet you end up being almost a friend.'

Loretta shrugged.

'I just try to understand,' she said simply.

They ate their sweet-and-sour chicken quietly for a moment or two, lost in their own thoughts.

'Have you heard from your sister this week?' he asked after the waitress had been over to check that everything was okay.

'Yes, she rang. The object of her affections made a move.'

'Finally!' laughed Paul. 'What happened?'

'Not much so far, but I'm pleased for her. She's had her eye on him since she got there. She said something about a meeting and an argument but she ran out of money before she could explain.'

'She had an argument?' asked Paul.

'No. I don't think so. They had some visitors or something. I didn't really follow. And then she was gone.' Loretta sighed. 'I miss her so much. I'm thrilled she's having such a great time but I hate that I know so little about her life out there. I can't even visualise where she is because I've never seen it.'

'You should go,' said Paul. 'Visit her.'

'I'm going to. I've never been to Italy. It sounds amazing. But they're away at the holiday house right now. Nat said it'll be better to go in September when the children go back to school.'

'That's not too long to wait. The time will fly by.'

But Loretta knew that it wouldn't. The days without Natalie trudged by. She was kept busy at work and there was Paul too, but when she turned her light off at night all she wanted was Nat. She missed their chats long into the night. She missed how they could finish each other's sentences and she hated not knowing anything about the day-to-day details of her sister's life when they had been such a huge part of her own.

'Have you told her about your Mafia research?' Paul asked.

Loretta shook her head.

'I don't want to scare her. I don't think she has any idea about what's going on in Palermo and she really doesn't need to know. I read that the Mafia isn't really in the Syracuse area and that's where she is.'

'Maybe you could get the paper to send you out there on a research trip?' suggested Paul, spearing the last of his chicken pieces with his fork.

'I doubt it. There's nothing to research, and anyway I'm a lowly crime reporter. Expenses beyond the odd cup of tea for a witness are definitely above my pay grade. I'll just save up and pay my own way there.'

She thought for a moment that he was going to offer to help and was relieved when he didn't.

'My biggest dread is that she decides not to come back. I don't know what I'd do without her.'

It was something she hadn't considered when Natalie had taken the job but now the thought had started to keep her awake at night.

'She's all I have in the world,' she added.

Paul pulled the corners of his mouth down in mock dismay.

'You know what I mean,' said Loretta. 'She's my only family. I can't bear the idea of life without her.'

She could feel her eyes pricking and she blinked fast.

Paul reached over the table and laid his hand on hers, squeezing gently.

'Now, that's never going to happen, is it?' he said.

60

1984 – Sicily

Natalie thought the atmosphere in the house was decidedly odd. There was a tension that she could neither place nor explain but it was definitely there. She asked Annette if she could feel it too but Annette just gave her an odd look and shook her head.

'Not sure what you're on about,' she said.

Natalie tried a different tack.

'Who were those men who were here the other night?' she asked.

'Salvatore's dinner party, you mean? I don't know. Something to do with work?'

But Stella had told Natalie that the dinner wasn't anything to do with the mine. The whole secrecy business was annoying. Natalie was used to people being straightforward. She and Etta told each other everything. Nothing between them was ever hidden and so all this cloak-and-dagger stuff got on her nerves and made her feel unsettled just when she was starting to fit in.

And Danny was no better. After their initial kiss he had as good as disappeared on her. Natalie was forced to conclude that the evening had been a one-off, fuelled by alcohol perhaps, and that he didn't intend to repeat it. She was hurt, then angry, and eventually a low-level disappointment settled over her, but it appeared that she and Danny weren't going anywhere – or not together, at least.

She gave up wondering about him and focused her attention on the children. They were much easier to read and their days together fell into an easy pattern until, before too long, the summer was over and it was time to return to the villa and school. Natalie was happy to go. She liked Ortigia well enough but the house, with its huge rooms and ornate grandeur, lacked the warmth of the family home.

The night before they were due to leave, Salvatore had another of his odd gatherings. Again the furniture was rearranged ready for the evening but this time Stella and the children were going out to say goodbye to some family friends. Stella asked Natalie if she wanted to go with them, but something about the offer felt unconvincing and so she said that she would stay behind on her own. She could make a start on the packing. The children had scattered their belongings far and wide and it was going to be a challenge to get everything back into the cases they had arrived with.

She and Annette made themselves a simple supper but then Annette also went out. She had been having a summer romance with a local boy and wanted to spend as much time as she could with him before they went back. There was no sign of Danny, which left Natalie alone, apart from the dinner party downstairs. From time to time she could hear raised voices as someone made a point with more vigour than the others, but most of the time it was just a low murmuring drifting up the stairs, or no sound at all.

But then she heard someone running, their footsteps echoing on the marble floor. Natalie was used to hearing running. The children ran pretty much everywhere. But the children weren't there and anyway this sounded different, the heavy steps of an adult, not a child.

Natalie was in her bedroom but went quickly to see what was happening. Then she heard shouting, voices raised this time more in alarm than anger.

Determined to investigate, she made her way to the staircase and headed downstairs. She was almost at the bottom when she heard the crack, a distinct sound that cut through the air. She had never heard that noise in real life but she knew exactly what it was. A gunshot.

She froze. The room where Salvatore's party was happening was just in front of her and the double doors stood open. She could see the backs of men running, fleeing from the room, the house. Chairs were pushed away from the table; some lay on their sides where they had been knocked over. Each place had a plate of half-finished food, as if the diners had been called away mid-meal.

Salvatore was still sitting at the head of the table, alone and calm among the chaos. Thank God, Natalie thought. He would take charge. This was his house. He wouldn't let strange men run amok with guns.

But as she watched, Salvatore slumped in his seat, his head lolling to one side, and a blood-red rose began to bloom on his crisp white shirt.

A tiny cry escaped before Natalie could stop it. What was going on? Should she go and help him? Should she ring for an ambulance? Of course she should do both those things, but where was the man with the gun?

And then she saw him. The gunman was still in the room with Salvatore, moving with confident strides to the head of the table. He looked tall and slim with tanned skin and neatly cut dark hair. He had very high cheekbones. Natalie noticed this because it was unusual to see such a patrician look in Sicily. He was still holding his gun.

He reached Salvatore's side, raised his gun and touched it to Salvatore's temple. And then he pulled the trigger.

Natalie watched as the bullet tore through Salvatore's skull. Her eyes closed instinctively but not before the sights and sounds of what she was seeing had lodged themselves in her head. When she opened her eyes again, the man with the gun was staring straight up at her.

For a second their eyes met. He's seen me, she thought. He knows that I've seen him. She knew she should run but she was frozen to the spot. She wasn't even breathing. This was it. She was a witness to a shooting and now she was going to be shot too. Her mind raced but her body was completely inert. What was the point of running? He would shoot her in the back and she would rather face her fate.

They stared at each other for what felt like forever. Then the man lifted his gun and aimed it straight at her. Natalie watched in horror. She knew she should call out to him, beg for mercy, but when she tried to speak her voice refused to make a sound, her terror gripping her vocal cords tight.

She was about to die. This was going to be her last moment on earth, murdered by a stranger in a country where she couldn't even speak the language. She wanted Etta, needed her to be with her as she died. She had to thank her for everything she had done, tell her how grateful she was, tell her how much she loved her.

But Etta was hundreds of miles away and she was alone.

She closed her eyes so she couldn't see him pull the trigger.

And then a voice was shouting, cutting through the silence and jarring with the moment of peace that she had created for herself to die in. Her eyes sprang open.

'Amuninni!'

Let's go, almost the only word of Sicilian that Natalie knew for sure.

The moment shattered around her. Instead of taking the shot, the man tucked the gun into his jacket and then ran out of the room and towards the front door. As he passed Natalie, he threw her a final murderous look as if to say that this was unfinished business, and then he was gone.

The front door banged and then the house fell silent.

61

The silence was eerie. Most of the time the house echoed with the sounds of the children running or laughing or the adults calling to one another. But now there was nothing except Natalie's heart thumping in her ears.

What should she do? She had no idea. If she were at home she would have called the police, but how did she do that here? Did you call 999 or was there a different number? And if she did get through, how would she explain what had happened? Her Italian vocabulary was made up of words like ice cream and beach. She didn't know how to say gun or shot or dead.

One thought kept pulsing through her frightened mind. She had to protect the children. She couldn't let them see their father broken and bleeding like that. She had been haunted by mental images of her own parents lying lifeless in their hotel room in France. The pictures had been the work of her imagination alone and that had been bad enough. If the children saw what she had then they would never strike that from their little minds.

On shaking legs, she made her way down the remaining few stairs and forced herself towards the dining room. Then, without looking inside, she closed the double doors and let herself slide to the floor, her back pressed up against them to guard Salvatore from she knew not what, but it felt important that she kept what was left of him safe now.

She sat there for a long time, trying not to think about what was behind her. She was desperate to telephone Etta and tell her what had happened but she didn't dare leave her post. What if the children came back whilst she was away and rushed in to tell Papa about their evening? It was inconceivable.

So instead she tried to remember the details of what she had witnessed so she would be able to repeat it convincingly to the police, but her mind was a fug and nothing seemed to hold together. The incident presented itself as a jumble of sounds and stark single images rather than a coherent record of events.

That was because of the shock, she knew, but also the fear. She had been seconds from death. The man had turned his gun on her. If he hadn't been disturbed by another man, he would certainly have pulled the trigger and then the children would have come back to two bodies rather than one.

A sound cut through her thoughts.

A door opening and closing.

Footsteps.

Panic surged through her. Was the gunman coming back? Should she run, hide? Every sinew tensed ready for flight or fight, yet flight was her only option. What could she do against a bullet?

But her legs wouldn't move. Her brain seemed to be unconnected to her muscles. So she stayed where she was. If this was her fate then so be it.

The footsteps came closer and Natalie held her breath, hoping that this would somehow make her invisible.

But it wasn't the gunman coming back to finish what he had started. It was Danny, and when he saw her sitting on the floor, pressed up against the door, he laughed.

'What on earth are you doing there?' he asked.

Natalie looked up at his familiar face and she let out the breath she had been holding. Her bottom lip began to tremble and she bit it to keep it still. This was no longer just her problem. Danny would help. Before she could stop herself, the relief made her burst into tears.

Danny dropped to his haunches so that his eyes were level with hers.

'Hey, hey. What's all this? What's up?'

And then his face fell and his expression became serious.

'Shit. What's happened?'

Natalie's jaw quivered as she tried to speak.

'A man shot Salvatore,' she managed. 'I saw it. I saw the man. He pointed his gun right at me, but then another man told him to leave and he ran off.'

Shock filled Danny's eyes as he took in what she was telling him.

'Shit. Are you okay? He didn't fire at you?'

Natalie shook her head.

'No. The other one made him leave.'

'And Salvatore. Is he . . . ?'

Natalie moved her head minutely, her eyes dropping to the floor.

'He's dead. They shot him in the chest and then . . .' The images of what the bullet had done to Salvatore replayed in her head and she felt vomit rising and then she was sick at her feet. Horrified, she wiped her mouth with the palm of her hand, even then concerned about how she behaved in front of Danny, but he barely seemed to have noticed.

'What about the other men, Salvatore's friends?' he asked, his voice calm but urgent.

'They all left when the first shot was fired. There's only me here. But the children. We can't let the children see.'

Danny didn't seem to register what she'd said.

'He should never have met them here again,' he said, more to himself than to her. 'It was stupid. Stupid!'

Natalie didn't understand.

'Who's stupid? Who are you talking about?' she asked.

'Salvatore. His bloody ego. He was always so careful, especially recently, but he couldn't resist showing off this house. There were two of them?'

Natalie nodded.

'Who were they?' she asked. 'Why did they shoot Salvatore? What had he done?'

All kinds of ideas were running through her head. She remembered what Annette had said, how she had warned her not to talk to anyone else about . . . And now Natalie found that she was so frightened she couldn't even form the word in her head.

But that was ridiculous. Salvatore was an ordinary businessman. The Barbieris were an ordinary family. Why would anyone want to come into his home, his private sanctuary, and shoot him dead?

She had nothing but questions and she deserved some answers after what she had just witnessed. There could be no more pussyfooting around. She had to understand what was going on here, what she had unwittingly become part of.

'Was Salvatore involved with the Mafia?' she asked bluntly. 'Did they do this?'

She thought of the man she had seen, the cool calmness with which he had pulled the trigger. This had been no spur-of-the-moment violence or a robbery gone horribly wrong. He had come to the house to do a job and he had carried it out efficiently and effectively.

'I think they did, yes,' replied Danny. 'But Salvatore wasn't part of it.'

Natalie was confused.

'Then why . . . ?'

Danny put a hand over his eyes, rubbed at his forehead and seemed to consider for a moment. Then he spoke.

'I don't suppose it matters now,' he said. 'Given what's happened, but you might as well know. Salvatore was leading a consortium of businessmen who want to end the stranglehold that the Mafia has. They were working with the magistrates in Palermo.'

'Like the one who was killed by the car bomb?' asked Natalie.

Danny nodded.

'Salvatore wasn't naive. He knew the risks. But they didn't think anyone would know what they were talking about way out here where there's virtually no Mafia presence. But someone must have passed something on. And now . . . God, what a mess.'

'What do we do?' asked Natalie. 'The children mustn't see.' This was fast becoming the only focus of Natalie's mind.

'I'll ring the carabinieri,' Danny said, getting to his feet to go to the telephone.

And then he stopped as a thought crossed his mind.

'Wait. You said he saw you, the gunman?'

She thought of the moments in which she and the man with the high cheekbones had locked eyes with one another, how he had raised his gun and pointed it directly at her. His features were fixed in her memory, so she had to assume that hers were in his.

She nodded.

'Shit. Then you're not safe here. He might come back for you. We need to get you away, for now at least. Go and pack a bag. I'll talk to the carabinieri, tell them it me who saw everything. You have to go.'

This was all moving too fast for Natalie's mind.

'But where?' she asked. 'I don't know anyone except the family.'

'We have friends,' replied Danny. 'You can go to one of those and lie low until we see what's going to happen next.'

'But why don't I just talk to the police myself?' Natalie asked. 'Surely they can keep me safe. I can describe the gunman and then they'll find him and arrest him and . . . and . . .'

But Danny was shaking his head.

'Oh Natalie. You've got a lot to learn.'

62

So, Natalie did as she was told. She went back to her bedroom and resumed her packing. Her hands shook so violently that it was hard to pick things up and her head swam as she tried to focus on what she needed. Should she take everything? She had no idea if she would be coming back. Maybe she should be travelling light so she could move fast.

What she did know was that every minute counted. She needed to be away from the house before either the gunman or the family returned. She didn't want lengthy explanations to Stella to delay her departure, but the thought that she was running away exactly when the family most needed her made her feel ashamed to her very core.

Maybe there was no need to run. It felt like an extreme response. Surely the police would protect her. Then again, who had protected Salvatore? Thinking of Salvatore made her think again of Stella and the children. Paola was so small, the boys barely any bigger. How could anyone begin to explain to them what had happened here that night?

She could help them, be there for them all, yet Danny said she had to run. She didn't know who was right or what to do for the best. Could she trust Danny? Could she trust anyone? Natalie had no idea.

It didn't take long to finish her packing as she had already done the bulk of it earlier in the evening. It was hard to remember that time now, a time when everything had been normal, with nothing more serious to worry about other than whether Danny would ever kiss her again.

But now her safe little world had been thrown into chaos. Her breath was coming in short sharp bursts that hurt her chest and she tried to steady herself. It would be okay. The gunman had no idea of her name, an anonymous English girl who would have been gone from this house within a couple of days anyway. And what was she going to do? She had only seen him for a couple of seconds, hardly enough to reliably identify someone.

She would be able to identify him, though. Natalie knew that and he would know it too. For that single moment there had been nothing else in the world – just him and her. And they had both seen something that they would never be able to unsee. She tried to banish the image of Salvatore slumped in his chair, the bloom of bright-red blood on his crisp white shirt.

And then the other one . . .

But the second image was too disturbing. She focused on the first, trying to make that the one that stayed with her. It was bad enough but at least his body had still been intact. He might have been sleeping if she hadn't looked too closely.

A quick rap on her door made her start and then freeze as if whoever it was could see her through the wood.

'It's me,' came a voice. 'Danny.'

She let her breath go and opened the door cautiously. Danny stood there, a pair of her trainers in his hand, collected no doubt from the pile by the back door.

'Ready?' he asked.

She wasn't. She needed more time to process. She wanted to speak to Etta, hear her calming voice on the other end of the phone. Etta would know what she should do.

But there wasn't time for any of that. She had to leave and *now*, before the man with the high cheekbones was sent back to finish what he had started.

Instead, she nodded, zipped up her case and hefted it from the bed. Danny grabbed it, grimacing slightly at the weight.

'My friend Marco is coming to pick you up. He'll take you to his place. You'll be safe there for now.'

'Who is he?' asked Natalie, suddenly feeling suspicious of someone whose existence she knew nothing of a few seconds before. Was this how she would be now, nervous of anyone and everyone, unable to trust?

'A friend. He works . . .' – Danny corrected himself – 'worked with Salvatore. He'll understand and you can lie low there for a few days until this blows over. He's outside.'

Natalie hardly dared ask the next question, but she needed to know the answer.

'Am I really in danger?'

He was going to say no. He was going to say that what had happened wasn't ideal but that the man who had blown off the head of her employer had far bigger fish to fry than her, and would assume she was just a frightened little girl who would run and hide and never even try to describe what she had seen other than in the vaguest of terms.

But what he actually said was, 'I'm not sure.'

This wasn't what she wanted to hear. Not at all.

He must have sensed her terror because he added, 'Don't worry. Marco will know what to do. You've got your passport, haven't you?'

She had.

'Yes, but I can't leave Sicily,' she objected. 'What about the kids? They'll think I walked out on them like all the other nannies.'

'Don't worry. I'll tell them you had to go and visit someone.'

'And what about Stella? She's going to need me. Her husband is dead.'

The family's life was never going to be the same again. Natalie knew exactly how it felt to have a bomb explode at the heart of a family's world, knew what that would do to them all.

The thought pulled her up short. What was she doing? She couldn't just run away. She had to stay and help.

'I can't leave,' she said emphatically.

'You don't have any choice,' snapped Danny as he dragged her case towards the stairs.

Part of her wanted to object. She wanted to say that she would stay and face the consequences so that she could comfort the children and help Stella when she needed her most. She wanted to make sure that no one thought badly of her for running.

But she was terrified. She had just watched a man have his life snatched away from him by someone who hadn't thought twice about doing the same to her. If he hadn't been disturbed, she would be dead. If she was going to be of any use to the family in the future then she had to protect herself for now.

Turning, she took one last look at her bedroom and then she followed Danny down the stairs.

63

They moved quickly through the dark house and Danny led her to the back door.

'We'll go out this way so no one sees you leave,' he said.

Natalie followed blindly, hardly registering where they were going. They crossed the courtyard, ignoring the path to the main gates, and made their way to a narrow alley at the back of the house that was too small for cars. A man was waiting there for them, a baseball cap pulled down over his eyes.

'Ciao, Marco,' said Danny. 'Grazie mille.'

The other man nodded but didn't say anything. Natalie hoped he spoke some English. She had so many questions. Then Danny turned to her, resting his hands gently on her shoulders. Before that night she would have hoped this was a precursor to a kiss, but now she just wanted him to hold her to stop her trembling.

'Go with Marco,' he said. 'It'll be fine. Lie low. I'll tell the police what you told me and we can keep you out of it. The men won't come after me because they don't know anything about me and you will be gone. It'll be fine.'

Tears were streaming down Natalie's face but she wasn't sobbing, was barely even aware of them.

'I'll see you soon?' she said, more of a question than a statement.

'Definitely,' he replied. 'Now go.'

He pushed her gently towards Marco, who picked up her case and led her silently away.

His car was parked at the end of a warren of alleyways so twisting and convoluting that Natalie lost her bearings, but when she looked up they were by the bridge that led from Ortigia to Syracuse. He threw her case into the boot and opened the back door. There was a picnic blanket on the seat, a cheerful red-and-yellow check. It seemed so incongruous next to the horror of the evening.

Marco nodded at it. Was she supposed to get underneath it? Wasn't that a bit extreme? It was dark and it seemed unlikely that anyone would be watching. But Natalie did as he suggested and sat low in the footwell, pulling the blanket over her head. It smelled faintly of petrol and it made her feel queasy again.

The car started up and Marco drove steadily, taking care on the corners so that she wasn't thrown about in the back. Natalie had no idea where they were going but that wasn't important. The main thing was that they were putting distance between her and the destroyed body of Salvatore.

She stayed under the blanket, not knowing whether she was supposed to or not. She wanted to ask that, and how far they were going, but Marco maintained a stony silence and so she did too. It couldn't be far because Marco had appeared very quickly after Danny had summoned him. It occurred to her that Marco might have been at the dinner and already on the scene. Perhaps he had seen something and could share her terrible burden.

As she thought about it, however, she remembered that the guests had all fled as soon as the gunman appeared. She had heard them running in their panic. She alone had seen what happened next.

She was the only witness. Cold tendrils of dread began to coil around her all over again and she hunkered down into the darkness beneath the blanket.

Eventually, though, she needed fresher air and chanced a peek out. The evening light had faded now and it was totally dark. They must be in the depths of the Sicilian countryside. Surely, the further they got from Ortigia, the safer she was. This thought calmed her a little until she remembered what she had seen and then suddenly she was frightened again.

She wasn't safe.

She wasn't sure she would ever be safe again.

After about half an hour the car began to slow and then came to a stop. Natalie stayed where she was under her blanket, waiting for further instructions.

'We're here,' said a man in English. 'Let's go inside. Quick.'

Tentatively, Natalie raised a corner of her shroud but couldn't see much. It was dark and there was no street lighting, only the car's dim interior bulb. She unfolded herself, her body stiff from crouching, and got out. Marco was retrieving her case from the boot.

'Come,' he said.

They were in a hamlet, a collection of a few stone-built cottages. He led her to the nearest and opened the door, flicking on the light as he went inside. Natalie followed him. The door led straight into a tiny kitchen furnished with a rustic wooden table and chairs. A woman with short dark hair was sitting at the table and she leapt up when Natalie appeared. Natalie flinched at the sudden movement but the woman spoke softly.

'Benvenuta,' she said. 'Welcome.'

Natalie tried to smile but her lips were stuck to her teeth.

'Grazie,' she managed.

'Sit.' The woman gestured to one of the chairs. 'Drink? Coffee? Water? Strega?'

Natalie shook her head. She was suddenly too exhausted for anything. Her shoulders slumped and tears began to slip down her cheeks.

The woman didn't speak but came and put her arms around Natalie. Natalie leaned into the embrace and sobbed.

64

Somehow Natalie slept but when she awoke, feeling calmer than she had the day before, she had questions about where she was and what was going to happen next.

She dressed quickly and went to the kitchen, hoping to find Marco or the kind woman from the night before. Someone must be able to tell her what was going on.

But the house was deserted. She called 'hello' as she came down the stairs but no one replied. A pot of coffee was on the hob in the kitchen. Natalie touched it and it was hot, freshly made. There was a new loaf of bread on the table with a butter dish and some cheese and tomatoes. Were these for her? Natalie had to assume so and she cut herself a hunk of bread and cheese and ate quickly, suddenly more hungry than she had realised.

She tried to remember what Danny had said the night before. He'd said she would see him soon, she was sure of that. Would that be at this house, or had he envisaged that she would be able to go back to the villa with the family? Natalie wished she had a firmer grasp of the plan.

Etta would know what to do. She always did. Suddenly, Natalie needed to speak to her sister more than anyone else in the world. There had to be a phone here and surely Marco wouldn't mind her using it in the circumstances. She could pay him back for the call.

Taking a hunk of cheese with her, Natalie went in search of the phone and found it in the tiny sitting room. She lifted the receiver and heard the unfamiliar dialling tone. Then she rang Loretta's number. It was Sunday but she was an hour ahead so whilst Loretta would be in, she might still be asleep. However, after a few rings the line connected and she heard Loretta on the other end.

'Hello?' she said. She sounded a little bit sleepy but more concerned about who might be ringing her this early on a Sunday.

'Etta. It's me.'

'Nat. How lovely. How are you? It's bloody early, or have you not been to bed yet?'

Natalie could hear the lightness in her sister's voice and wished she could reciprocate.

'Etta, listen,' she said. 'Something's happened. Something bad.'

'Oh my God, are you okay?' Etta's response was gratifyingly quick and anxious.

'Yeah. I'm fine,' she said quickly. 'But it's Salvatore. He was shot last night at the house. I saw it happen.'

There was a silence on the other end as Loretta processed what she had heard.

'Shot? Is he okay?'

Natalie squeezed her eyes tight shut.

'No. He's dead. They killed him. And I saw it. Or part of it, at least.'

'Wait. Nat. You're not making any sense. Who shot him?' Loretta said, her tone urgent now.

Natalie swallowed. It felt as if by voicing what had happened, she would make it more real somehow, which she knew was silly. It didn't get much more real than this. She lowered her voice to a whisper.

'The Mafia. Salvatore was trying to stop them and they shot him.'

The whole thing sounded beyond far-fetched to Natalie but somehow Loretta seemed to have got the point straight away.

'Shit,' she said. 'Tell me exactly what happened.'

So Natalie explained what she had heard and then what she had seen. As she described the second bullet, her voice cracked and she began to cry again. Then she told Loretta what Danny had said about the business consortium and their aims, but Loretta only seemed interested in the shooting.

'And he saw you, the gunman? You're sure he got a clear look at you?'

Natalie nodded and then realised that Loretta couldn't see.

'Yes,' she said in a tiny voice. 'He pointed his gun right at me. I was so scared, Etta.'

Loretta's tone changed.

'The Mafia is seriously bad news, Nat,' she said. 'There are all kinds of horrible things going on over there. People are being murdered every day. It's carnage. Where are you now?'

Natalie had no idea.

'In the countryside somewhere. At a friend of Salvatore's,' she said. 'Danny fixed it up.' She felt calmer as she said Danny's name. Danny understood it all. He would look after her.

But Loretta seemed doubtful.

'What friend? Who are they? How do you know you're safe? And what about Danny? How can you be sure you can trust him? For all you know, he might have set up the shooting in the first place. He could have taken you away so they can get rid of you in their own time.'

Even to Natalie's confused mind this sounded unlikely. She knew Danny. He'd only been in Sicily for a year or so. How could he possibly have worked his way into the Mafia in that time? And anyway, she did trust him. He had known exactly what to do last night. And the woman here had been so kind to her. They had left her some breakfast, for God's sake. Were those the actions of someone who was planning to kill her?

Yet Loretta sounded so sure that she was still in danger. And Loretta was always right. She always had been. Even before their parents had died Loretta had been the smart one, the sensible one. She had always known what to do. And now, it seemed, she knew about the Mafia too. She knew everything and Natalie knew nothing.

'You have to leave,' Loretta was saying. 'You have to leave now. Take a change of clothes and your passport. Have you got any money?'

'A bit. And I have some traveller's cheques.'

'Good. Take those too. And then run. Get as far away as you can.'

'But, I'm not sure . . .'

'Just do it, Nat. We can worry about the rest when we know you are safe. Get a train to the mainland and head north. They won't be able to find you on a train. There's no passenger list. Trust me, Nat. I know about these people. I've been researching them here. You have to run.'

And so Natalie ran.

65

1984 – London

Loretta sat, open-mouthed, the phone receiver still buzzing in her hand, as she tried to take on board what Natalie had just told her. A gunman. A shooting. Her boss dead and Natalie on the run. It was like something out of a film. Loretta couldn't take it in.

She ran through the options in her head. Her first response was to fly straight to Sicily and rescue her baby sister. But how could she do that? She didn't even know where Natalie was and had no way of getting in touch with her unless she rang again. And anyway, hadn't she just told Nat to run for the hills and never look back? That meant there was definitely no point going. By the time she organised herself a seat on a plane, Natalie would hopefully be back on the mainland and putting as many miles between herself and the danger as possible.

Was this her fault, she wondered. It had been through her, via Malcolm, that Natalie had got the job in Sicily in the first place. It hadn't occurred to her that she might be putting her sister in harm's way, but should she have known? She was supposed to be a journalist. She should have researched the situation before she pushed Natalie out there and into danger. Natalie was all she had in the world and now she was at risk and there was precisely nothing that Loretta could do to help her.

She felt sick. She thought of the research she had done. The Krays and anything that had happened in London was small fry compared to the stories coming out of Sicily. There, they seemed to be shooting people in broad daylight. Clearly, what had happened to Natalie's boss was evidence of how out of control the situation was. And Natalie was a witness to a terrifying crime. She had to be at risk. And it was all Loretta's fault.

Loretta rang Paul. It was early and he might still be asleep but she needed to talk this through with someone else. The phone rang several times before it was answered. Paul sounded groggy and confused.

'Hello?' he said.

'Paul, it's me. Something awful has happened. It's Natalie. Her boss was shot by the Mafia, and she saw it happen. She nearly got shot too. Her friend has smuggled her out of the house but I've told her to run. I mean, how does she know who to trust? And this "friend", she doesn't know anything about him really, and what if . . .'

There was a pause as Paul processed what he had just heard.

'Hang on,' he said. 'You're not making much sense. Run where exactly?'

'I don't know!' wailed Loretta. 'But she can't stay where she is. It's not safe.' Loretta's heart was pounding. 'They could find her. She's a witness.'

There was another pause, slightly longer this time.

'Do you think you might be overreacting?' asked Paul.

Heat rose in Loretta's chest.

'God, no! Definitely not. I know what I'm talking about here. I've done all that research. You know I have. And they're dangerous people, Paul, really dangerous.'

'But they're not going to care about Natalie. She's just one girl who may or may not have seen something she shouldn't. What can she do to them?'

Loretta was becoming more frustrated. She wanted Paul to grasp the seriousness of Natalie's situation but he was being wilfully obtuse.

'She can identify the killer, that's what!' she snapped. 'Do you think they are just going to let her get away with that? Of course not. They're going to want to finish what they started, tie off all the loose ends. And they have contacts everywhere, feelers all over the world. It won't take them two minutes to find out her name and then they will be able to track her wherever she goes. Nowhere will be safe!'

Loretta was almost shouting down the phone now but still Paul didn't seem to understand.

'I'm sure she'll be fine,' he replied calmly. 'She should go back to where she was and tell the police everything that she saw. This is their job. They aren't going to let any harm come to her.'

Loretta's anger, which had been steadily mounting through the conversation, boiled over.

'Oh, you just don't get it!' she shouted and then slammed the phone down.

What was the point of talking to him when he clearly had no concept of the magnitude of what they were dealing with?

When Loretta looked back at how everything had panned out over the following years, she could see that this morning had been the catalyst, the turning point for it all. If she had reacted differently when Natalie had rung her, if she had responded more calmly or listened to Paul when he tried to inject some common sense into her thinking, then none of the rest of it would have happened. But she hadn't and she couldn't turn back time.

And in her own defence she had genuinely feared for Natalie's safety then and for the years that followed. Through snatched phone calls with Natalie and a sketchy following of the unfolding Mafia super-trial in Palermo, she had hung on to the belief that Natalie was in mortal peril for far longer than logic dictated.

And by the time she finally came to her senses and realised that the perceived danger had only been illusory, it was too late. She had thrown her own life up in the air and Natalie's grasp on reality had become so tenuous that there was no bringing her back.

66

Loretta didn't hear anything from Natalie for two days. It was torment. She couldn't concentrate on her work. She sat in the court's press gallery, her shorthand pad open on her knee, but whole speeches were delivered without her hearing a word. Sometimes it was only the scraping of chair legs, marking an end to the proceedings, that brought her back to herself and the realisation that she had missed yet another judgement without even registering it, let alone making a coherent note.

Malcolm noticed that her output was down and questioned it, but Loretta told him there hadn't been much happening that was newsworthy and then promised herself to concentrate harder the next day.

She thought about confiding in Malcolm but decided against it. He would hear what had happened in Sicily soon enough when his wife learned the news from her widowed friend, but she couldn't be the one to tell him. She had to protect Natalie at all costs and whilst she couldn't explain why it felt dangerous to explain the situation to him, she knew instinctively that it was.

Being at work was hell. She didn't know if Natalie would have her work phone number with her and so she had to assume that Natalie would ring her at home. She bought herself an answerphone so she might never miss a call and then worried that somehow leaving a message might incriminate Natalie, as if whoever was chasing her could somehow listen in on her line.

Some part of her brain knew this was all madness, that there was no way anyone could trace her sister by locating Etta, and yet she remembered the books she had read about how organised crime was exactly that – highly organised. And if they really wanted to find Natalie then they would do that by going after her family, which was her. She was all the family Natalie had. She was the obvious weak link.

By the time Natalie finally rang her, frightened and not making much sense, Loretta had talked herself into being as paranoid as her sister clearly was.

The phone trilled in the evening and Loretta pounced on it.

'Hello? Natalie?'

There was a pause. She could hear someone breathing on the other end, ragged and uneven.

'Natalie,' she said again. 'Is that you? Are you okay? Where are you?'

'I'm okay,' Natalie replied.

'Where are you?' Loretta repeated.

There was another pause, longer this time.

'They might be listening,' said Natalie eventually.

Even though Loretta had had similar thoughts herself, somehow hearing it coming from Natalie sounded ludicrous.

'Are you on your own?' she asked. 'Can anyone overhear you?'

'They're everywhere,' whispered Natalie. 'I hadn't realised, but the more I think about it the more I get it. And they know everything.'

'Does anyone know where you are?' asked Loretta.

'No. I haven't spoken to anyone and I'm making sure that I'm not being followed. But I'm worried about you. Are you safe? I've been thinking. They can trace you. You're a journalist and they'll find out that you've been investigating them. You are as much at risk as I am. You should leave too, Etta. Get out now before they find you.'

This wasn't something that Loretta had contemplated and it didn't sound terribly reasonable. There were no grounds to upend her own life. Natalie would get back to England and Loretta would look after her. It would all blow over. They would look back on this in a few months' time and laugh at themselves.

'I'll be fine,' replied Loretta.

Natalie's voice changed then, the whisper gone and replaced with a manic wail.

'No! You have to leave, Etta. Promise me you will. They can't get you too. I'd have no one left.'

The wail was so loud that Loretta had to hold the receiver away from her ear. She hoped Natalie was in a quiet place where no one could witness her outburst. She tried to be practical.

'Have you been in touch with Stella?' she asked. 'What have the police said?'

'Don't be bloody ridiculous.' Natalie's voice was hushed again now. 'Of course not. I can't ever go back there. That's the first place they'll look.' She sounded terrified and Loretta backtracked quickly.

'Okay, okay,' she said.

'But I'm worried about the children. They're going to be hurting so much. You remember what it was like, Etta. We know. We know.'

'Well, maybe that's a reason to go back,' tried Loretta. 'Then you can help them. You know what they're going through. You understand.'

But Natalie was shouting again.

'Are you stupid?! If I go back, I'll lead them straight to the children. What if he shoots at me and it hits one of them? What if Paola runs out and he shoots her instead of me. What if Enzo thinks he can take the gunman on? He might, you know. He's a brave little soldier and he'd do anything to protect his baby sister.'

Natalie was ranting and for the first time Loretta started to worry about something other than the Mafia.

'Nat. Are you okay?' she tried again. 'You sound . . .' She paused to choose her words carefully. Her sister sounded deranged, paranoid. In just a couple of days she seemed to have lost all sense of proportion. Loretta changed tack. 'Listen. Come home. Have you got enough money? Get yourself a train ticket to Calais and then a ferry over to Dover. You could be back here by tomorrow and then we can contact Stella and the children from here.'

There was a pause. Loretta could hear Natalie chewing at her fingernails.

'I can't do that, Etta,' she said eventually. 'I can't lead them straight to you.'

And then the line went dead.

'Nat, Nat!' Loretta shouted down the phone, but it was no good. Her sister had gone, evaporated back into hiding.

67

As was inevitable, the news of the shooting reached Malcolm on the Tuesday. Loretta knew it had done as soon as she saw his face.

'Have you heard about Salvatore?' he asked. His tone was concerned and not accusatory. 'Stella rang Vicky last night. She's in pieces, as you'd imagine.'

Loretta nodded. There was no point pretending that she didn't know.

'Natalie rang,' she said. 'It's dreadful. How is Stella doing? And the children?'

'Devastated, obviously.' His eyes narrowed. 'She said that Natalie has disappeared. She just took off. No one knows where she's gone.'

Loretta's mind was racing. What should she say? How much did Malcolm know? She wasn't sure how to explain why Natalie had fled without revealing that she had seen the gunman, and something told her she needed to keep that to herself. Wasn't that the whole point of Natalie's fleeing? But without that part of the jigsaw, Natalie's actions were impossible to interpret favourably. To anyone who didn't know, it would just look as if she had left at exactly the time that Stella most needed her.

'She rang me,' she said again, vaguely. 'She was scared and just ran instinctively.'

Malcolm cocked his head on one side.

'Bit odd,' he said.

Loretta nodded. What could she say? It was odd but she could hardly tell Malcolm either why Natalie had run or that she had fuelled that fire with her own ill-advised paranoia.

'I'm sure she'll go back,' she said weakly. 'I think she just got a bit spooked. It must have been terrifying having armed men in the house.'

Now Malcolm nodded.

'I imagine so. It's a bloody business. And poor Salvatore was only trying to do some good and lost his life for his efforts. Where's the justice in that?'

The next time Natalie rang, she was even more disturbed. She still wouldn't tell Loretta where she was but insisted that she was safe. Her focus now seemed to have switched from her own safety to Loretta's.

'Why are you still at your flat?' she kept asking. 'You know how dangerous it is, Etta. You have to leave. You have to leave today. The longer you stay, the easier you make it for them. You have to promise me that you're going.'

Loretta took a deep breath.

'Nat, sweetheart. Please calm down. It's not as bad as you think it is. I'm perfectly safe. Come home and you'll see.'

'But you don't understand,' wailed Natalie. 'I can never come home. Not while you're still in London. They'll find you and use you to get to me, and then we'll both be dead.'

Loretta closed her eyes and tried to work out what she could say that would convince her sister, but she was out of her depth. Natalie seemed to be in the clutches of some kind of delusional paranoia and nothing Loretta could say would help. She remembered the dark days after their parents had died, Natalie's tenuous grip on reality. Her world had fractured then and now it appeared that it had done so again, but this time there was no one with her to counterbalance the workings of her broken mind.

'Look, Nat,' she said calmly. 'Just tell me where you are and I'll come and get you. I'll fly to the nearest airport and then we can sort this out, get you home, get you safe.'

'But can't you see?' yelled Natalie. 'I will never be safe. Never. And I can't come home. London isn't safe. You have to move. You have to make yourself impossible to find. If you don't do that, Etta, then I'll be running forever.'

68

Loretta had no idea what to do next. Of course, what Natalie was asking of her was ridiculous. She couldn't possibly just uproot her life. Everything she knew and everything she wanted was in London. Her job, her home, their parents' house – all of it.

But her sister, the only family she had, was trapped Lord only knew where. She was in a hideous kind of limbo of her own fabrication. It was a catch-22 situation. She needed Natalie to come home to get some treatment and understand that there was no threat to either of them, but she wouldn't come home until Loretta convinced her that there was no threat and the only way she could do that was by leaving London.

What was she supposed to do?

She had to talk it through with someone, someone sensible who could convince her that she wasn't being unreasonable. She would have chosen Malcolm. As her mentor in most things, he was the obvious candidate. But he was too involved. His wife was Stella's best friend and his loyalties would lie there. Natalie had deserted the family in their hour of need and that was bound to colour his judgement.

Then there was Paul, but after a couple of awkward dates when he had accused her of behaving ridiculously over the little that he knew of the situation, a rift had opened up between them. Loretta hadn't felt able to explain it all to him and he already seemed to think that Natalie was unhinged. She let his calls go unanswered and sensed that he was drifting away. She found she didn't care. She had far more important things to focus on.

Her confidant needed to be someone who knew both her and Natalie well and understood enough of their past to know what they had been through to get to this point.

She rang Liz.

They arranged to meet at Loretta's flat. Liz had never been and was enthusiastic to see where her friend was living, and Loretta was anxious that they shouldn't be overheard, even though she knew this made her as paranoid as Natalie was.

Liz arrived clutching a bottle of Liebfraumilch.

'Thought we might need this,' she said. 'God, this is nice. Look at you with your own front door. I'm so jealous. I reckon I'll be living with Mum and Dad until I'm forty. Longer, probably.'

She pulled a face and Loretta felt compelled to laugh despite everything.

Loretta found two glasses and a corkscrew and they flopped down on her sofa.

'Right,' said Liz. 'Are you going to tell me what's going on?'

Loretta took a deep breath.

'You're never going to believe me,' she said. 'It's the maddest story you've ever heard.'

'Try me,' replied Liz.

She listened carefully as Loretta explained what had happened.

'And so now Nat has convinced herself that I'm in danger and that she can't come back whilst I'm in London. And that's obviously rubbish, but I have no idea where she is and I can't get her to see sense. I can't speak to her until she rings me and every time she does she sounds even more delusional. I'm scared that if I don't do as she wants then I'll lose her completely.'

Liz stared off into the middle distance for a moment, apparently considering the situation, and Loretta waited.

'Let's look at the facts,' said Liz. 'What's the most important thing here? Your life in London or Nat?'

Loretta didn't hesitate.

'Nat,' she said.

'And what do you have that's holding you here? Your parents' place and that's rented out, and your job.'

Her job. The thing that Loretta loved the most in all the world except her sister, the thing she had worked so hard to get. She nodded.

'What if you told them at work that you had a family crisis, that you needed, say, three months off. Unpaid. You could sell the house. That would keep you afloat for a bit. Then you can move somewhere out of London, get Natalie to come home, and then when you've calmed her down you can come back home and pick up where you left off.'

Liz took a gulp of wine, and then raised the glass to her own suggestion.

It wasn't the worst idea, Loretta had to admit. She imagined it would be hard to convince the paper to hold her job open but if she didn't ask for any pay they might do it. And her tenants had asked if they could have first refusal if she and Natalie ever wanted to sell so they might be prepared to buy quickly.

'Where would I go?' she asked.

'Wherever you like,' replied Liz. 'Far enough away to convince Nat that you're safe.'

Loretta felt as if her world was being torn apart. In fact, it *was* being torn apart, but what choice did she have?

'What would you do if you were me?' she asked Liz.

Liz stared up at the ceiling for a moment or two. She was Loretta's oldest friend and suddenly whatever she was about to say carried more gravitas than anything else.

'Natalie is the most important thing in your world,' she said. 'She's broken and she needs your help. If I were you, I'd do what she wants. I don't see that you have any choice.'

69

Where did you go when you could go anywhere except the one place you wanted to be? Loretta had no idea. She knelt on the carpet with her father's battered AA road map in front of her and considered her options. They were pretty much endless. Great Britain was a big place when you looked at it in terms of places to move to.

She would have to narrow things down. It had to be somewhere that was far enough from their home in London to be convincingly safe for Natalie, but not off the beaten track entirely. Loretta was a city girl and had no experience of living otherwise. How far north could she go before basic amenities dried up? She was assuming there was running water and electricity all the way up to Scotland. She smirked at herself. She was joking, but only just. She really had no idea what lay beyond the GLC's domain.

Her finger traced its way up through the brightly coloured counties. Bedfordshire, Northamptonshire, Derbyshire. She was sure all these places had their merits, but her finger kept moving north. One county was significantly bigger than the others: Yorkshire. Well, she supposed, if she wanted to disappear maybe it was best to do it somewhere big. And if it was big, it would surely have at least some of the trappings of the capital.

The only thing she knew about Yorkshire was the names of its football teams. She had fond memories of her father listening to James Alexander Gordon reading the match results on a Saturday evening. Her finger stopped on Leeds. That was as good a place as any. She would head to Leeds and see what happened.

◆ ◆ ◆

And that was how Loretta Halliday ended up in a temping agency on The Headrow. The woman behind the desk was small and pointy with huge glasses that completely swamped her tiny features. *Coronation Street*'s Deirdre Barlow had a lot to answer for, Loretta thought.

'Name?' asked the woman, the 'a' sounding longer than Loretta was used to.

'Loretta . . .' she began. Then she remembered that she was supposed to be incognito and switched Halliday for Hamilton. She felt a little thrill at the naughtiness of it.

'Typing and shorthand?'

'Of course.'

'References?'

Loretta paused. Malcolm would give her a reference for temporary work. It didn't mean she wouldn't be going back to her real job. She nodded.

'We have something at Ashton & Brown. They're accountants a few doors down. One of the partners' secretaries has glandular fever, going to be off for a couple of weeks, maybe longer. Can be nasty, glandular fever.'

She looked up at Loretta, her eyes huge through the huge lenses of her glasses, and Loretta nodded sympathetically. The woman wrote an address down on a compliment slip.

'Take this,' she said. 'Out of the door, turn left. I'll ring them, let them know you're coming.'

And that was how it began. The partner in need of assistance turned out to be Garth, who asked her out for a drink on her last day, stumbling over his words and assuming she would turn him down even before he had finished his question. She went because she had little else to do, and enjoyed herself more than she thought she might. He was seven years her senior, with a serious and earnest soul, so different to anyone she had met before, but he was attentive and concerned for her well-being in a way that no one had been since her childhood. She found herself falling for him and his straightforward ways.

She continued to temp around the city. Malcolm had promised to hold her job open until she managed to persuade Natalie that it was safe to come out of hiding, but that was proving hard. She had sent her contact details to the most recent post office box address that she had for her, but had to wait for her to get in touch. Natalie's phone calls were sporadic and she categorically refused to say precisely where she was. All Loretta could do was to check that she had enough money, reassure her that everything would be fine and try to encourage her home. As she had no way of contacting Natalie, she was powerless to do more.

As the months rolled on, Loretta began to feel settled in Leeds. The people were friendly, and the fluidity of temping kept her on her toes. It wasn't the same as the buzz of the newsroom but the constant switching and changing meant that she didn't get bored. She'd had to change her name officially to match the stories she'd told, and doing that had felt so disloyal to her parents. Yet she had done it to protect Nat. She was sure they would have understood.

On top of that, and Loretta had never thought she would ever say it, but the countryside was growing on her. It was simply spectacular. Garth was an outdoorsy sort and he took her on long, bracing walks in the Yorkshire Dales at the weekends. In time, she even bought herself a waterproof coat and a pair of walking boots, although she was glad that her colleagues from the newspaper weren't there to see her and mock.

It was only when Garth proposed that she stopped to think seriously about her future. Accepting him would mean leaving London for good. There was no way Garth would move south. Loretta thought hard about what that would mean. There wasn't much left for her in London beyond the city itself. She had drifted away from the people she'd grown up with, had no family except Natalie, and the north wasn't quite as cut off and parochial as she had assumed.

The only thing she would miss about her old life was the paper. Her initial three months of unpaid leave was extended to six and then nine, but in the end she had had to write to Malcolm informing him that she wouldn't be going back. It was the hardest letter she had ever written but as there was no sign of Natalie returning, she had had no choice.

And then there were the lies she told, in the first place because what harm could it do when she would be leaving anyway, and then continued because she had passed the point when she could rectify them. She had told Garth nothing about her life before he met her. When he asked questions, she was vague on detail and that seemed to satisfy him. He was a simple soul, interested more in the moment than anything that might have happened before. Keeping her own counsel also meant that she could truthfully tell Natalie that she was still undercover. No one knew who she was or why she was in Yorkshire and she continued to hope that that would assuage Natalie's paranoia in time.

When Garth suggested they buy a house in Ripon, a pretty but tiny cathedral city within commuting distance of Leeds but also in the heart of the North Yorkshire countryside, Loretta found herself agreeing without objection. When Marc was born two years later, she gave up temping, threw herself into country life and waited for Natalie to come back.

70

2005 – Ripon

Christmas was almost upon them. It was among Loretta's favourite times of year, although she couldn't place it in the top spot because there were too many other occasions vying for that honour. Each of the children's birthdays, for a start, and the midsummer's eve treasure hunt she always arranged even though Marc was seventeen and far too old for hunting for treasure, and the day that the first apple fell from their ancient apple tree, and their wedding anniversary. In fact, the calendar was peppered with Loretta's favourite times. She should probably simply accept that she loved every part of the year and be done with it.

The children had already set off for school, Marc self-important in his suit and tie, the uniform for the sixth form at his school, and the girls, at thirteen and eleven, still sweet and biddable without any hint of the stormy teenage years that no doubt lay ahead, chattering away to one another. The house was quiet without them and Loretta tried not to think about what it would be like when they had all moved away. That was a while off, she knew, but the time would fly by.

She heard the letterbox rattle and the dull thud of their post landing on the mat, and went to investigate. Garth had beaten her to it. He stood at the door with a pile of Christmas cards in his hands.

'How come we get so many Christmas cards?' he asked, looking genuinely baffled.

'Probably because I write so many,' Loretta replied calmly.

Garth stood, shaking his head at her in amazement. 'When do you do it? I never see you at it. You really are a wonder, Lori.'

Loretta smiled at him. 'It's amazing what I can get done when you lot are all at work and school,' she replied.

'Can I open these?' Garth asked. 'Just so I can do my bit.'

'If you think you're going to get away with opening ten Christmas cards as your contribution to the festivities then you're sorely mistaken,' she laughed. 'But, yes. Go on.'

Garth took the pile through to the kitchen whilst Loretta started to attach the cards that had arrived the day before to the Christmas card tree she had fashioned. He was right. There were a lot of cards but then they knew a lot of people, or she did. From a standing start, Loretta had created not just one but a whole host of social circles in the city over the years and never was this more apparent than when all the cards arrived, each one representing a friend or acquaintance hard won.

'Who's N?' shouted Garth from the kitchen.

Loretta's heart stopped beating for a second.

'Sorry?' she called back, playing for time whilst she gathered herself.

What were the chances that Natalie's card would be in the pile that Garth chose to open? He never opened cards generally. In fact, Loretta couldn't ever remember him doing it before.

'N,' he said again. 'There's a card here from someone who has just signed themselves N. No message or anything.'

He came through to where she was, brandishing the card in one hand and the envelope in the other.

'It's got a foreign stamp.' He peered at the envelope. 'France, by the looks of it. Funny to go to all the effort of sending a card from there and then not writing a message in it.'

She could tell him, Loretta thought. Right now. She could simply explain everything and have the whole silly situation out in the open. Finally. It was ridiculous that it was still a secret anyway. Natalie no longer believed that she was under any threat, or at least so Loretta thought. It was hard to know exactly what Natalie thought when they spoke so rarely, but surely she had moved beyond that now. It had been twenty years. Twenty years of Natalie living on the move, never settling anywhere for long, using post office boxes rather than addresses.

A couple of times over the years, Loretta had gently suggested that Natalie would be safe by now and that no one would still be searching for her, but Natalie seemed lost to reason. Loretta wondered if her sister actually preferred to live as she did, with no ties and almost no commitments, and she herself had grown used to it as well. It was just how things were between them.

However, Natalie's wishes, unreasonable as they might be, were not the only factor at play here. She and Garth had also been married for nearly twenty years and in all that time she had never once so much as hinted that she might have a sister. How could she tell him now and expose her huge betrayal of his trust?

She couldn't predict how he might react, but she knew that integrity was written through him like 'Blackpool' in a stick of seaside rock. That was why he was such a trusted accountant. His clients could see his decency and scrupulousness and they respected that. Indeed, his practice had built its reputation on the back of it. Not all firms could say the same but at Ashton & Brown integrity was guaranteed. So what would he do if he discovered that his own wife didn't match up to his standards? It was a question that Loretta simply couldn't answer, but she did know one thing for certain. She had too much at stake to risk it.

And then there were the children. She and Garth had brought them up to be honest as well, modelling their father's values to a fault. How could she tell them that she had been lying to them all by omission for their entire lives?

In the split second between him asking about N and standing in front of her, the card in his hand, she reached the same conclusion that she always did. It would be better for all concerned if she just kept her mouth shut. No damage could be done by a secret kept. She would tell him one day, she felt sure, but it would be in her own time and not because her hand had been forced.

Garth held the card up and read its contents aloud.

'"To L. With all my love N xx". So who's N?'

Loretta could feel a pink heat starting to burn in her cheeks.

'Erm,' she began, but Garth was staring at her, his eyes on hers, his forehead creased in confusion.

'You must know,' he said. 'It's come from France, for goodness' sake. How many people do we know in France? Or do you know?'

Garth wasn't a jealous man. That wasn't in his nature, but from time to time he had questioned why someone as young and vivacious as Loretta had been would have wanted to accept his offer of marriage. That she had done so had always seemed to trigger some insecurity in him that challenged his self-worth.

'Could be Nigel from school,' Loretta blurted. Why had she picked a man's name? Her mind had gone blank and Nigel was the first idea she'd had as she struggled to avoid saying Natalie.

Garth examined the card again, the line between his eyebrows deeper still.

'Then why not write Nigel?' he asked. 'And what are the kisses about? Was he an old flame of yours?' He was smiling now, although some of the insecurity that Loretta knew he was feeling was still visible in his eyes.

'No. Can't be Nigel,' she said. 'Not from France. Must be Nicky back from when I was temping. She sends a card every year. I wonder what she's doing over there.'

'Bit of a waste sending her a card then, if she's not at home to receive it,' said Garth, handing her the card. 'Right, I better be gone or I'll be late. See you tonight?'

Loretta nodded. 'I have a governors' meeting at seven thirty, but you'll be back before I leave?'

'Should be. Have a good day.'

Then he placed a chaste kiss on the tip of her nose and departed.

As the front door closed, Loretta leaned back against the wall and closed her eyes. Garth was so sweet, so entirely trusting that she was telling him the truth although her hastily cobbled-together story had barely been coherent, let alone plausible. What was she doing, keeping secrets from the man she loved? It was unthinkable. But then, it had been going on for so long that what choice did she have?

71

2022 – Ripon

Natalie had been in Bronte's shop now for almost an hour, but Bronte didn't feel she knew much more than she had done before she arrived. Natalie fidgeted, picked at her nails, fiddled with her cuffs. She took hold of things, twirling them round in her fingers and then putting them back down in a different place. She seemed reluctant to make eye contact. Bronte couldn't remember ever meeting anyone who was quite as agitated.

'Shall we go for a walk?' Bronte said suddenly. 'It's a lovely afternoon. I'll shut the shop and we can wander down to the canal. Or a pub? Would you rather go for a drink?'

'A walk,' replied Natalie. 'I don't drink much. Not at all really. It never seemed wise.'

'Why not?' asked Bronte. Under normal circumstances she wouldn't have been so direct, but it felt that every time Natalie opened her mouth the mystery of why she had been missing got deeper.

'At the start, I needed to keep my wits about me,' she said. 'And then, well, I was on and off medication for a while.'

Despite her frustration, Bronte didn't feel she could ask what the medication had been for, but she stored the detail up for examination later.

'A walk it is then. Just give me a minute to get locked up.'

Bronte closed the shop without leaving a note of explanation. If anyone came, they would just have to be disappointed. Getting to the bottom of things with her aunt was more important than any potential lost sale and she still had the feeling that Natalie might bolt at any moment if she wasn't careful. She couldn't risk turning her back for even a second.

They stepped out into the bright street and headed away from the market square and down towards the canal. With the traffic noise and the busy pavement it was difficult to talk, so they simply walked side by side in silence. When there wasn't room for two abreast Bronte took the lead, resisting the temptation to keep checking behind her that Natalie was still there. However, once they got to the canal they could stroll along the quieter towpath, which was much more conducive to conversation.

The time had come, Bronte felt, to be honest. If her questions scared Natalie away then so be it, but they couldn't keep dancing around one another forever.

'Why don't you just start at the beginning,' she suggested, 'and tell me all of it.'

And to Bronte's surprise, Natalie did. She told her of the summer when her parents, Bronte's grandparents, had died. And then about Loretta going to work on Fleet Street, how proud Natalie had been of her but how she had struggled to pull her own life back on track. After that, she had taken a job looking after some children in Sicily. She talked about how she thought she had found her place in the world, how much she loved the colours of Italy after the drabness of London.

'It sounds idyllic there,' said Bronte wistfully. 'I'd love to live abroad. Don't suppose I ever will though.'

'You're only twenty-nine, right?' asked Natalie.

Bronte was taken aback that her estranged aunt would know this detail, but she nodded.

'Then how can you say that you'll never live abroad?'

Everything that Bronte knew about herself told her that the idea of living anywhere other than Yorkshire was preposterous. However, Natalie didn't know the first thing about her.

'It's just not very likely,' she began. 'There's the shop, and Dad, and, well, where would I go? I don't speak any languages and I'm not that practical. I can't see how it would ever work.'

'So you've written it off. Closed your mind to the possibilities?' Natalie said baldly.

Had she? Wasn't it rather that she was being pragmatic? Bronte had always liked to think so. She was nothing if not realistic, but now she began to wonder whether she might not be using practicalities as an excuse. After all, if she had really wanted to live abroad, what had been stopping her?

'Maybe,' she conceded. 'I haven't really thought about it, but yes. I suppose you might be right.'

They walked on in silence, Bronte very aware that nothing Natalie had told her about her past so far would explain the apparent estrangement. The dark waters of the canal lay very still and the reflections of the clouds scudded across its surface. On the opposite bank a duck quacked noisily, shattering the tranquillity.

'And why did you and Mum lose touch?' Bronte asked.

'Well, we didn't,' snapped Natalie. 'We never did. But it wasn't safe to come out into the open. I had to protect her.'

Then Natalie explained and Bronte listened, her incredulity barely hidden. The story sounded like something out of a novel, running from the Mafia, hiding out for years, for decades. That

Natalie hadn't been well was clear, but what struck Bronte was the extraordinary lengths her mother had gone to, to make Natalie feel safe. Then again, hadn't her mother always done that, for everyone she met? She had been so loved because she made everyone feel that they were the most important person in the room. Why wouldn't she have done this for her own sister too? Viewed in those terms, what Loretta had done did make a crooked kind of sense.

'And you had no idea that I existed?' asked Natalie.

'None,' replied Bronte. 'She never said a word.'

Natalie stared off towards the distant hills.

'She kept my secret for all those years,' she said, shaking her head slowly. 'What I made her do was farcical, looking back, but she did it anyway. And she never complained. Not once. She loved that job at the paper, but she gave it all up because I asked her to. Demanded, really. And now she's gone and I can never say thank you.'

Natalie's voice cracked and Bronte glanced across at her aunt. Tears glistened on her cheeks and Natalie wiped them away brusquely with the flat of her hand. Bronte swallowed down the lump in her own throat.

'It took me years to see that I had made a mistake,' said Natalie. 'I was so convinced that I was right, running and hiding, moving on every few months before I could put down any roots. Etta kept telling me that it was safe, that I was safe, but I didn't believe her. I made her move north – well, my paranoia did. She gave up everything for me.

'And then I suppose it became a habit, the running. Once I'd started, I couldn't find a way to stop. I've always been a bit of a drifter. Even when we were girls it was Etta that had the drive.'

'Really? You kept hiding for all those years,' countered Bronte. 'That takes guts and determination. It looks to me like you both had your share of gumption.'

Natalie grinned at her.

'Do people really still say that?' she asked. 'You've said it twice. Isn't it really old-fashioned?'

Bronte raised one shoulder.

'I'm an old-fashioned kind of girl,' she said. 'But I'm right. You didn't give up. That shows massive resilience.'

It was Natalie's turn to shrug.

'Maybe,' she said. 'I've never thought of it like that.'

Bronte let her mind float to her own self-image, how she was still shouldering the things that had been said to her as a girl as if they were true. And it seemed that Natalie had done the same, believing that she was somehow adrift and directionless when her entire life gave the lie to that idea.

'But then Etta met Garth and had you three kids,' Natalie continued, 'and eventually I stopped feeling so guilty. She made a real life for herself away from London, here. That cathedral was packed. All those people there to say goodbye.'

An image of Loretta came into Bronte's mind. She was smiling. Her mother was always smiling as she threw one hundred and ten per cent of herself at everything she did. Bronte had assumed that was just who she was, but now she had a new idea. Could it be that her mother had been overcompensating for the loss of her old life, for what she had left behind?

'She had a wonderful life,' Bronte replied. 'She was amazing. No one had a bad word to say about her. She gave so much to everyone.'

'And the journalism?' Natalie asked. 'Was she a journalist up here too? That was her real passion. All she ever wanted to do really.'

Bronte shook her head sadly.

'I had no idea that Mum had ever been a journalist until I tracked down her friend Liz after the funeral.'

Natalie's head snapped round.

'Liz? Liz from school?'

Bronte nodded.

'Dad found her address when he was sending out the funeral notices. I went to see her. She didn't tell me much and she's a terrible liar. It was obvious that something wasn't adding up. I just didn't know what it was.'

Natalie's face lit up in a grin.

'God bless Liz,' she said. 'I always liked her.'

When she smiled, she looked so much like Bronte's mother that it took Bronte's breath away. She thought of Marc and his conviction that Natalie was an imposter, but when you saw her smile like that there could be no question that she wasn't a relative.

Thinking of Marc gave Bronte an idea.

'You should meet the rest of us,' she said. 'Marc and Annie and Dad.' Then another thought crossed her mind. 'How did you know how old I was?'

'I know quite a lot about you all,' she said. 'I've usually had a post office box, or the equivalent in whatever country I was in, and I always made sure Etta had the address, just in case . . .'

Natalie tailed off, as if she couldn't imagine what emergency her sister might have needed to tell her about.

'She used to write to me every month, tell me what was going on. I didn't always read the letters,' she added sheepishly. 'It depended where I was in my head. Sometimes it was too much. There were times when I didn't check the box for months on end and the letters just piled up. It could be overfacing. I threw quite a lot away unopened. I regret that now.'

They were passing a run of moorings for the long narrow houseboats that stayed on the canal. Usually, Bronte liked to try and peep in, a fascinating window on to a way of life that was so entirely different to her own. But today they walked past, barely even registering that the boats were there.

'I always thought I had more time,' said Natalie. It sounded as if she were talking to herself now rather than Bronte. 'I thought I would get well and come home, and me and Etta could just pick up where we'd left off before I got ill. And then, this.'

The tears were streaming down her face now. Bronte stared at her and tried to work out how she felt. She didn't really understand what had gone on between the sisters, but from what she could gather so far, this woman had made her mother blow up her life, give up on the one thing she loved and move to a place where she hadn't known a soul. And all for something entirely illusory.

Should she be angry, lay into her aunt for what she had done? She felt certain that that was what Marc would do, maybe Annie too. But she found that she had only empathy. Whatever had happened, it was clear that Natalie had been punishing herself over it for years. What was to be gained by Bronte taking a pop too? But she didn't want to carry this, whatever this was, on her own any longer.

'I think you should meet the others,' she said firmly. 'You probably owe them that.'

72

Bronte didn't ask where Natalie was staying. If she asked, she would feel obliged to invite her to stay with her instead and Bronte didn't feel ready for that. Her confidence that Natalie wouldn't disappear overnight had grown a little, although she couldn't be sure. She would have to trust that her aunt didn't lose her nerve and disappear. If she did then Bronte would be in exactly the same position her mother had been in for all those years with no way of getting in touch, simply waiting for Natalie to make contact. It wasn't an ideal way to proceed but it was all she had.

Natalie said she would leave Bronte to make the arrangements with the family and would call back to the shop to find out what they were. She didn't say when she would call, unable to break the habit of the best part of a lifetime, it appeared.

As soon as Bronte's front door closed behind her, she dived on her phone and opened the family chat. Without her mother to drive the conversation, the group had been much quieter than usual. Bronte wanted to kick-start it back into life, but she didn't want the others to think that she was trying to step into their mother's shoes. However, they didn't seem to think it was their place to step up either and so the chat remained quiet.

But that was all about to change.

'BIG NEWS!' she began. 'The woman from the funeral turned up at the shop. She's definitely Mum's sister. I think we should all get together with her for a proper conversation.'

She waited for a response, desperate to share what she knew but concerned about the reaction.

Annie was first to reply.

'WTAF??????'

'It's true. She's the dead spit of Mum.'

'Where the hell has she been?'

'It's complicated. She's been ill. Mum was protecting her.'

'What from?'

'Not sure. All in her head I think. Can you come up, Annie?'

'Yeah. Maybe. Need to check. Did Dad know?'

Their dad wouldn't reply to the chat. He was the sort who had a mobile phone for emergencies and then left it switched off in the kitchen drawer. They could be pretty certain he would never see their conversation.

'I'm not sure. I've not spoken to him yet but I don't think so.'

Marc appeared in the chat.

'What does she want?'

Bronte rolled her eyes. The question was so typical of her brother.

'She hasn't said she wants anything.'

'Not yet. Funny how she's targeting you.'

As the weakest link? That's what he was not so subtly saying.

'Bron's shop has her name over the door. Easiest to find.'

Bronte smiled gratefully at her sister in her absence.

'Exactly that. She asked around and found the shop.'

'What are you proposing?'

Bronte stopped typing to think. What was she proposing?

'Invite her to Dad's? Hear the story?'

'I can come up tomorrow night if I cancel something else. Can stay until Saturday night. OK?'

'What about you, Marc?'

'Are we talking Saturday p.m. then? I can do that. Am reserving judgement. Still reckon she's up to something.'

'I'll tell Dad.'

◆ ◆ ◆

So it was arranged. Now Bronte had to hope that Natalie would come back to the shop in time for her to let her know. It was too complicated to factor Natalie's uncontactability into the plan, but it would be awful if Annie came all the way back and Natalie still hadn't shown up to be invited to the family meeting.

That just left her father. Bronte knew that she couldn't ring him. This was a conversation that needed to happen face to face.

She abandoned any idea of cooking tea. She wasn't hungry anyway after the excitement of the day. Instead, she walked the short distance to her parents' house. It was less than a mile. That was how far Bronte had strayed from where she had been brought up.

As she walked, she thought about Natalie, who had left everything she had ever known when she was just twenty-one to go and live with strangers in a foreign land and had never made it back home. The thought made Bronte feel inadequate, her life small and unfulfilled. Marc had gone to university, Annie too. But Bronte had stayed close by, working at small, safe jobs until she had taken on the shop. That had been a brave decision, she was prepared to acknowledge, but it had been her mother's doing. Left to her own devices, Bronte would probably still be the receptionist at the dentists' practice just up the road, a job her mother had arranged for her by calling in some favours.

She remembered how vehemently Natalie had leapt in to defend her each time she had put herself down. The response reminded Bronte of her mother, but with Natalie it had been a little different. Instead of trying to protect Bronte, she had been empowering her.

Her father was in the garden, pottering. He had a pair of secateurs in his hand but there was no evidence that he had used them. He was lost, Bronte knew, his tethers untied, leaving him floating without direction or destination. He had always imagined that he would see out his days with Loretta at his side. For her to die first had been on no one's agenda.

'Hi, Dad,' Bronte called over to him. She was aware that she was making her voice brighter than usual, still overcompensating.

'Ah, Bronte. How lovely.' Her father's reply was equally cheerful, belying the melancholic air that lingered around him. When he smiled it no longer showed in his eyes as it had once done, and his shoulders were more hunched as if the weight of his grief was bending him in half.

'How are you? Listen. I have some news.' She wanted to get it out first before she lost her nerve. But her father also had news.

'Me too,' he said. 'Shall I go first?'

He seemed keen to do so and as he hadn't been interested in much lately, Bronte let him take the stage.

'Mine is a little odd,' he said once he had her attention.

I bet it's not as odd as mine, thought Bronte.

'Go on,' she said.

'Well, I found your mother's will. It was in her desk filed under "Will", as you'd expect. But there was a letter with it. A most interesting letter.'

73

Bronte held her breath. Would the letter be about Natalie? She hoped with all her might that it was and that it would rescue her from having to explain her own news.

'That sounds intriguing,' she replied. 'What does it say?'

'Come inside, come inside. You can read it for yourself. It's addressed to me, of course, but I can't see the harm in *you* reading it, Bronte.' He emphasised the 'you' as if there might be harm if anyone else were to.

She followed him into the house, pleased to note that the place was still as ordered as it would have been had her mother been there. Her father was holding things up at his end.

'Now, it's in the kitchen,' he said, more to himself than to her. 'Let me see. Ah yes. Here.'

He plucked a cream envelope from the table and passed it to her. Bronte looked at the envelope in her hand and then back at her father.

'You're sure?' she asked.

He nodded and so she lifted the flap and slid the contents out. The letter was written on the thick parchment notepaper that her mother favoured and when Bronte saw her mother's bold, confident handwriting there was a little break in her breath. Then she began to read.

My darling Garth.

I have something I must tell you. If you find this after I've gone then that means I never found it in myself to tell you whilst I was alive. That was entirely cowardly on my part but also, I hope you'll understand that there was a larger issue at stake – a question of loyalty that I couldn't disregard lightly.

I have, and have always had, a sister, Natalie. She is three years younger than me and I have barely seen her since she was twenty-one. There was no falling-out. This is not one of those silly family feuds. But she witnessed a terrible crime and it caused the balance of her mind to lose its equilibrium. When you and I first met, I had sworn never to reveal my connection to her. She feared for my safety and I, for better or worse, went along with her wishes.

And then, as the years went on and the lies that I had told both you and then the children grew, I simply lacked the courage to explain. I always intended to tell you that I wasn't quite who I had led you to believe. Several times over the years it almost came out. Do you remember the anonymous Christmas cards and the occasional unexplained gift for a child? Those were from my darling Natalie.

I have only a post office box address for her, which I include below. This changes as she moves around and so I hope I can remember to update the details here. She knows all about you and the children so don't be surprised if she gets in touch one day. But likewise, don't be surprised if she doesn't.

I'm so sorry, Garth. I hope you don't think any less of me for keeping this secret from you for all these years.

Hopefully by the time I die I will already have confessed and this letter will no longer be required.
With all my love,
Lori x

Bronte could sense her father's eyes watching her as she read and as soon as she reached the end, he spoke.

'So you see. That woman who was at the funeral. She really was your mother's sister. Or I assume that was her.'

His eyes searched out Bronte's and she saw hope in them that she would tell him how he should feel. Bronte couldn't do that. She barely knew what she felt herself.

'I've met her,' she said. 'She came to the shop. That's why I'm here. I've spoken to the others. We thought we could invite her here on Saturday night to talk it all through. Is that okay with you, Dad?'

Her father looked quite excited, for him.

'Well, yes. Of course. What is she like?'

Bronte thought for a moment as she tried to pick le mot juste for her aunt.

'Fragile,' she replied. 'But fierce.'

Natalie turned up at the shop again the following day and so Bronte was able to tell her the plan and give her the address of her father's house.

Natalie took the piece of paper and rather than putting it away somewhere straightaway, she held it out and stared at it.

'Etta's house,' she said. 'She never really mentioned it in her letters. I think she was sensitive to me having nowhere that I counted as a home. But I didn't mind. I know I didn't have a choice at the start, that my lifestyle was thrust on to me, but as the years passed I got used to always moving on. I quite liked it. I would have loved to hear more about where she lived.'

'Well, now you can see it for yourself,' said Bronte. 'And my dad will be there, of course. And Marc and Annie.'

Natalie stared off into the middle distance.

'I'm probably wrong,' she said, 'but I've always wondered if your mother named Marc after Marco, the guy who helped me to escape on the night of the shooting. It's an unusual spelling in England. I wondered if it was her way of saying thank you. Not that he'd ever know. I never saw him again after that first night. Etta told me to run and so I ran. I always did what she told me. She was always right.'

Natalie was silent for a moment.

'Although sometimes I've wondered . . .'

74

Bronte would have been lying if she said she wasn't a little nervous about the forthcoming meeting between her family and her estranged aunt. She felt like the go-between, the conduit between them all, with her at one end and Marc at the other. And where did Natalie stand in the line-up? Bronte wasn't sure. When she had first met her, with her nervous tics and anxieties, she would have placed her aunt close to herself, but on reflection perhaps she was closer to Marc than she had appeared.

Not that there was anything wrong with her brother. He was a typical firstborn child – determined, a rule follower, bossy, and with a tendency to believe he knew best that was often proven to be correct. If he was cautious of Natalie it was only because he was looking out for the rest of them, a role he seemed to be taking even more seriously now that their mother wasn't there to do it.

That all said, however, she really wanted him to get along with Natalie, to listen and try to understand.

They were all in place when Natalie arrived. That had been inevitable. Garth lived there and Annie was staying with him. Marc was pathologically early to everything and Bronte had to be certain of being there when Natalie arrived and so was early too. This meant that Bronte couldn't avoid telling them Natalie's story, at least in outline, before she arrived.

'So she saw a man shot, and then decided that she had to go into hiding for nearly forty years,' scoffed Marc when she had finished with her story.

'I'm not sure it was quite as straightforward as that,' replied Bronte, 'but that's the essence of it.'

'But it's ridiculous. Ludicrous. No one in their right mind would do that.' He sat back in his chair and folded his arms as if that proved his point.

'I think that's kind of the point,' said Annie. She was sitting with her legs draped over the arm of the sofa, twirling a lock of her hair around her finger and swinging one foot so that her Birkenstock sandal clung on precariously.

'And she was only twenty-one,' added Bronte, keen that they shouldn't start assassinating Natalie before she had even arrived. 'Seeing your boss shot by the Mafia. It's a lot at any age.'

Marc shook his head. 'I'm not convinced,' he said. 'It all stinks to high heaven to me.'

The doorbell rang and they all jumped.

'That's her,' said Bronte unnecessarily. 'I'll go and let her in.'

Annie pointed a forefinger at Marc.

'Play nice,' she said.

Bronte opened the door and was relieved to see that it was actually Natalie standing there. She looked clean but was still dressed in her scruffy clothes. Bronte wondered again where she had been staying but now wasn't the time to ask.

'Come in,' she said. 'We're all here.'

She led Natalie through to the sitting room and her father got to his feet at once and held his hand out to shake.

'Natalie. So good to meet you.'

'Finally,' muttered Marc. Bronte glared at him.

'I'd say we'd heard so much about you, but alas . . .' Garth smiled kindly.

Natalie stepped forward and took his hand.

'Nope. I travel under the radar,' she said, and when she returned his smile Bronte heard Annie let out a breath.

'God, you look like Mum,' she said.

This seemed to please Natalie. She put her hand through her pixie-cut hair and raised one shoulder coquettishly.

'I always wanted to be like Etta,' she said. 'She was my idol when we were growing up.'

'Please, sit down,' said Garth, indicating the far end of the sofa that Annie was sitting on. 'Can we get you a drink? Tea, perhaps?'

Natalie shook her head. She seemed to be shrinking before them as she retreated back into herself. Now she looked frightened again, just as she had done when Bronte first met her. Were they really that scary? Bronte was trying to be welcoming but perhaps that wasn't enough to put Natalie at her ease. She broadened her smile.

'I'm sorry I didn't stay after the funeral,' Natalie said. 'I wanted to but it all got a bit . . .'

'And Marc was hardly that welcoming,' said Annie, rolling her eyes at her brother.

Marc opened his mouth to defend himself and then closed it again.

'Well, you're here now,' said Garth. 'That's the main thing.'

Nobody spoke and the atmosphere became more charged with each anxious breath.

Marc was the one to break the silence, firing questions at her as was his style.

'And now?' he asked. 'You're doing what? Settling in Ripon?'

Bronte could see that he was building up to an accusation. She wanted to defend Natalie but what could she say? For all she knew, that was exactly what Natalie was planning.

Natalie raised her head and looked squarely at her nephew.

'No,' she said. 'I'm not really the settling kind. I'm devastated about Etta and she would have wanted me to meet you so here I am, but then I'll be moving on.'

A panic began to rise in Bronte. She had only just found her aunt. She didn't want to lose her so quickly and not on the back of losing her mother.

'Will you stay in this country, though?' she asked, aware that her tone sounded desperate.

Natalie shrugged. 'I don't know yet. I need to look at the options.'

'But you could stay nearby,' she blurted. 'Not in Ripon if that's too close, but maybe not far away.'

'Are you here legally?' asked Marc. 'Or did you sneak back under cover of darkness. Like a ninja.'

'For fuck's sake, Marc,' said Annie. And then, 'Sorry, Dad, but honestly.'

'It's pretty much impossible to sneak into anywhere these days,' replied Natalie. 'Or don't you watch the news?'

Annie raised her eyebrows in acknowledgment of Natalie's point. Bronte half expected her to start keeping score.

'Well, tell me this then,' said Marc. 'Why did you appear now, after all these years? Forgive me, but it all feels very convenient to me. Long-lost aunt is reunited with her family and worms her way into everyone's affections before making off with the family silver. Not that there is any, by the way. If you were hoping for untold riches then you picked the wrong family to crash.'

'She's not crashing,' said Bronte. 'She *is* family.'

'Stop being such an arse, Marc,' said Annie. 'Let the woman get to know us. Where's the harm? Although why she would want to get to know you on present form is beyond me.'

'Look,' said Natalie. 'You're suspicious. I get it. God, I've spent all my adult life being suspicious. *Of course* I get it. But you've no need to be. My past is my business. Mine and Etta's. I would like you to be a part of my future but that's up to you.'

Bronte stood up, an all-consuming need to express her view propelling her to her feet.

'I want that,' she said. 'I want you to be part of the family.'

Everyone turned to look at her and Bronte suddenly felt awkward, her dramatic gesture out of place.

But then her father spoke.

'Absolutely. Who are we to judge your past? What happened was between you and Lori.'

Annie chipped in.

'Well, I'm up for that . . .' she said.

They all looked at Marc. He shrugged.

'Of course no one wants to drive you away, Natalie,' he said in a tone that suggested he was very far from feeling conciliatory. 'But you have to understand our caution.'

Natalie raised her chin and stared at her nephew defiantly, her eyes fiery.

'And mine,' she said. 'Trust is a two-way street.'

Was there going to be a stand-off, Bronte wondered. She had to prevent that. The last thing she needed was for Marc to drive Natalie away.

She opened her mouth to try and placate them both but before she could speak, her father interrupted.

'I took the liberty,' he said rather grandly, 'of looking out some old photo albums. They're in the kitchen. Would you like to see them?'

The look Natalie gave him was brimming over with gratitude.

'That would be great, Garth. Thank you.'

75

Six months later

It wasn't too difficult to find them. Bronte pieced the information together from the stories that Natalie shared, each coming out piecemeal over the following months. And then it was the work of a moment. Social media meant that most people were only a couple of clicks away, which was ironic, given how hard Natalie had worked to stay under the radar.

Paola Dempsey (née Barbieri) had the privacy settings on her page sufficiently open so that Bronte could see she had married an Englishman and was now living in Hertfordshire with two blonde, long-limbed teenage daughters and a German shepherd dog called Rocco.

Bronte focused on the images even though the faces meant nothing to her. Paola looked happy, but then didn't everybody look happy on Facebook? It was part of the myth of social media. Maybe there was residual hurt hiding beneath that beaming smile.

Natalie had talked of the guilt she'd felt at leaving the children to deal with the death of their father alone, but Bronte had no idea how the children themselves had reacted to that abandonment. There was a good chance that resentment about Natalie's decision had never gone away. Paola might well ignore her approach or even tell her precisely what she could do with her vicarious olive branch.

But it was worth a try – for Natalie's sake, and for her mother's.

She typed a message.

> *Dear Paola*
> *You don't know me but I'm the niece of your former nanny, Natalie. Natalie doesn't know I'm messaging you but I know how much she regrets what happened in 1984. She has had a troubled . . .*

Bronte paused, deleted 'troubled' and continued.

> *. . . complicated life and I think she would love to try and put things right with you and your brothers. I was wondering if you could find it in your heart to reply to this message. If you can't ever forgive her then I totally understand but I think it would mean the world to her if you could.*
> *Kind regards,*
> *Bronte Ashton.*

Bronte reread the message, checking for typos and tone. It seemed okay but she still hesitated. Should she be doing this? She had grown close to her aunt over the months since they first met but that didn't stop this possibly being seen as an act of betrayal. She knew that Natalie was haunted by abandoning the children to save herself but was it *Bronte's* place to act on that, to try and right a wrong that had nothing to do with her?

She knew if she asked Natalie for permission to contact Paola, she was likely to say no. But that was her aunt's guilt and shame speaking. If you cut through those emotions, was it still the wrong thing to do? If nothing else, it would explain what must have been a huge mystery for the Barbieri family. Surely they must have wondered whatever had become of Natalie, maybe not in the immediate aftermath of their father's death, but afterwards, as they grew.

What the hell? At this stage, she wasn't betraying any confidences. Paola might never see the message, or choose to ignore it. Or she might reply with nothing but animosity towards Natalie and if that happened then Natalie need never know. It wasn't as if she was ever going to have social media accounts of her own. Why any right-minded person would choose to share even the most basic of personal details was a mystery to her after she had spent her whole life hiding them.

Bronte took a deep breath and clicked send. Then she closed down her phone and tried to forget all about it.

A message pinged back almost at once. Quickly, Bronte opened it, her heart in her throat.

Oh my God, the message read. *You have no idea how long I've waited for a message like this. How is she? I would love to see her. For a long time, she was my favourite person on the planet (family excluded). Where are you? I'm in Hertfordshire but I have a car. I can go pretty much anywhere.*

P x

Bronte reread the message and then read it for a third time. There was no room for misinterpretation. Paola was certainly keen.

She swallowed her last remaining doubts and began to type.

76

2023 – Ripon

She had stopped running. She had never thought the day would come but it had.

It wasn't all perfect. Panic frequently overcame her. Sudden movements, loud noises, crowds – they all had the power to send her into a spiral of fear and anxiety. A man had run towards her down a country lane recently and she had instinctively thrown herself into the roadside ditch, hoping that the long grass would be sufficient to hide her from view. As he thundered past, shouting the name of what she assumed was a wayward dog, she had felt foolish, but there was nothing she could do to control herself. It was what it was.

But other than hurling herself into the undergrowth, her life was the closest it had been to 'normal' for decades. She had a room of her own in a shared house. Bronte had taken her to the bank and opened an account, her old one having been closed as dormant long ago, and she had transferred her small savings into it. The bank clerk had looked with horror at the scruffy roll of euros and pounds, held together with an elastic band, that she placed on the counter as her first deposit. She had registered with a doctor and a dentist. Bronte wanted her to apply for a place on the electoral roll but that was a step too far. In her heart, Natalie knew that no one was looking for her, but she couldn't help but be cautious.

She was enjoying having family around her. Bronte was wonderful. Kind, thoughtful and attentive, there was so much about her that reminded Natalie of Etta. She didn't have Etta's self-assurance though. In fact, she had barely any confidence at all, but Natalie was working on that with her. It was so much easier to see the failings in someone else and try to fix them than to do the same for yourself.

The rest of the family was growing on her too. Garth was a sweet old man – not at all the type that she would have seen Etta marrying but then again, that was the old Etta before Natalie blew up her life for her. Annie and Marc were busy people so she didn't see as much of them and that suited her. She didn't need so many people after a life of having no one.

It was a Saturday, so she had a day off from her job at the old people's home where she worked in the kitchens. Bronte wanted her round at her place and had been most insistent. Natalie had a feeling she was about to be ambushed for something but that was okay. After years on the move, she could deal with Bronte's kind of ambush.

Bronte had told her to arrive at two o' clock and not before. All very cloak-and-dagger, and it was one minute past as Natalie strolled up the street of little terraced houses. Bronte's friend Helen was in the front garden of her house and waved at Natalie as she walked by. Natalie waved back, still unsure about people knowing who she was but quite enjoying the feeling of belonging that it brought.

She reached Bronte's house and knocked on the door. It opened almost at once, Bronte standing there, her eyes shining and a huge smile across her face.

'Look who's here!' she said before Natalie had even crossed the threshold.

Natalie looked beyond Bronte and saw a blonde, willowy woman standing in Bronte's living room.

Natalie's heart stopped beating.

Stella.

Stella was standing in Bronte's front room.

She put a hand out to steady herself against the doorframe. But then she recalibrated. This couldn't be Stella. Stella would be at least seventy years old by now. So that meant it had to be . . .

'Natalie!' exclaimed the woman who wasn't Stella. 'It's me. Paola!'

Natalie felt light-headed, as if the oxygen was suddenly sparse in the room. Now she looked more closely, she could see that it wasn't Stella, although Paola certainly had her mother's colouring and physique. But she had something of her father about her too, a darkness about the eyes, a depth that Stella had lacked.

Paola was across the tiny room in an instant. She threw her arms around Natalie and held her for a long time, weeping quietly into Natalie's neck. Natalie held her tightly. Her hair still smelled familiar after all the intervening years.

Eventually, Paola pushed away from her but held her at arm's length, examining her in such depth that Natalie wanted to shy away from her. She was unused to scrutiny of any kind, let alone as intent as this.

'It's so good to see you,' Paola said. 'I worried about you for the longest time. I never stopped worrying. You just disappeared. Danny told us he'd taken you to a safe place until everything calmed down after Papa, but then you just ran away and we never heard from you again.'

Natalie hung her head, swallowing back her tears.

'I'm sorry,' she whispered, her voice barely audible. 'I let you all down. I wanted to come back and look after you all. You were so small. And Gianni. And tough little Enzo. Your world had collapsed and I knew you'd need me there, or I hoped you would.' She swallowed, gulping down air. 'But I was so scared that if I came back I'd put you all in danger. And I was scared for my sister back at home. And I was scared for me too.'

Natalie began to tremble and then shake as something of that fear found its way back into her body, although it had never really left her.

Paola wrapped her arms around Natalie again and held her tight.

'You protected us in the best way you knew how,' she said. 'You led the danger away. It was brave and fearless and loyal and I loved you for it even though I missed you more than you could possibly imagine. I was quite cross with you to start with though.'

'I'm so sorry,' Natalie said again. Questions were firing in her head. 'And how are the boys? And your mum?'

'The boys are great. Still in Sicily and with families of their own. Mum's still there too. And Danny runs the mine now. He's godfather to one of my kids.'

Paola was grinning at her and Natalie felt her heart lighten.

'Although,' Paola continued with a touch of the mischief that Natalie remembered, 'I'm still not sure I've entirely forgiven you for abandoning us. Perhaps if we spend a lovely afternoon together, and possibly dinner . . .' She glanced over to an anguished-looking Bronte, who nodded at her vigorously. 'And have a proper catch-up about everything, then maybe, just maybe, I might find it in my heart to pardon you.'

Paola was laughing now and Natalie could see the forthright little girl that she had been in the elegant woman she had become. And all at once, she knew she was safe.

ACKNOWLEDGEMENTS

Years ago, a friend told me a story about a previously unheard-of relative showing up at a funeral. (You really do have to be careful what you say to authors!) The details have long since left me, but I remembered the idea and how it made me feel – the shock that there could be a close blood relation that no one knew about. This happens quite often, I'm sure, but I knew that I wanted to write about sisters for whom being apart was a choice neither of them wanted to make.

I also knew from the very start that this was a book about loyalty, about carrying someone else's burden for them. I just had to work out what and why. I wanted to set part of the story in Sicily and for that I drew a little on my own experiences. I spent a few weeks there in my teens and early twenties and whilst the characters in the book are all invented, I have very strong memories of my first time in a country where the sky was blue every day, which I hope have come across on paper.

As ever, I had help in writing this book. I read lots of fiction set in newsrooms but I also spoke to Nick Rennie, who began his long career as a journalist in the eighties and who generously shared his experiences with me. Some of what he told me didn't suit my story so forgive me for the liberal application of artistic licence in places.

On a writers' retreat I met wonderful chef Massimiliano Giovannoni, who showed me how to make the ravioli that Natalie makes and shared stories of his own nonna in his kitchen as a child. Thanks go to him too.

I want also to thank the wonderful team at Lake Union and in particular my fabulous editor Victoria Pepe, and also Arzu Tahsin, who brought her considerable wisdom and experience to help me get the book to where it needed to be.

Thanks, as ever, to my family, who are the biggest supporters of my work. My mum died as I was editing this book so she must have a special mention too. Back when I was first learning how to write a novel, my mum paid for an editorial report on what became *Postcards From a Stranger*. It was the positive response contained in that report that encouraged me to press on and publish and so I owe everything that has followed since then to her.

Finally, and most importantly, thank you to you, my readers, both for the trust you show in me when you open one of my books and give me some of your precious time and also for your loyalty in coming back over and over again. I can never express how grateful I am.

If you enjoyed the book, please consider leaving a review on Amazon and Goodreads, which will help other readers to find it too. If you are interested in my work then you can read more at https://imogenclark.com/ where you can sign up for my monthly newsletter and find links to my social media accounts. I also write as Izzy Bromley and you can find links to those books on my website too.

With very best wishes,

Imogen.

IN A SINGLE MOMENT

Why not read another book by Imogen Clark? Turn the page for an extract from *In a Single Moment* – out now.

1

1976

It was the heat. It bore down on her, forcing its way into her already burgeoning body. Sweat trickled from her hairline and across her face. She could feel it pooling in the hollows at her collarbones.

She longed to fill her lungs with cool, crisp air but there was only the stale sort that felt as if it had already been breathed in and out a hundred times. She tried to visualise a mountainside, fresh green grass sparkling with dew, a crystal-clear brook babbling its way down to a deep lake where the water was so icy cold it would take your breath away.

But then the image was snatched away from her, and the oppressive, heavy atmosphere filled her nostrils again. She could smell the sharp tang of antiseptic and beneath that hot bodies, no doubt washed less frequently than usual due to the effort of collecting water from the emergency standpipes along the street.

And then another wave crashed over her, and all thoughts were washed away as she focused entirely on the pain of the contraction.

'That's it, Michelle,' she heard the midwife say. The voice sounded distant, as if the woman was speaking to her from another room. 'Try to keep your breathing nice and steady. It won't be long now.'

Michelle wanted to scream at her that she was doing her best but this was as steady as she could manage. It was her fourth baby and she'd got the measure of her labours, so she knew the midwife was right. It would be over soon, but the awful, overwhelming heat was shifting all the goalposts. She really wasn't sure she had the strength to keep going. One minute she felt as insubstantial and limp as a damp rag and the next a rigid poker of pain seared through her, making every muscle in her body as solid as steel. The rhythm of it was relentless.

The pain subsided again, and Michelle felt her aching muscles sag. Dean would be in the pub now, celebrating the birth of his child before he even knew it had happened. She pictured him, pint in hand, laughing with his mates without a care in the world whilst she . . .

The thought of the pub made her realise just how thirsty she was. Her tongue was sticking to the roof of her mouth and her lips felt as if they might crack if she smiled, not that there was any danger of that.

'Water,' she croaked.

It came out more dramatically than she'd intended, like something from *Lawrence of Arabia*. The midwife passed her a half-filled tumbler and Michelle craned her head up and took a gulp. The water was tepid and unsatisfying but it would have to do.

And then the pains were at her again and this time she knew it was nearly all over. She gritted her teeth and pressed on.

Michelle and Dean had first got together at school where neither of them had been convinced about the importance of a solid education. They had married in haste to avoid scandal,

Michelle's bouquet hiding what it could, and Carl had come along four months later. After that Tina and Damien had followed in quick succession and then there had been a merciful hiatus before Michelle unexpectedly found herself once again pregnant at twenty-five.

She had been horrified at first. What would they do with another child? Where would it sleep, for a start? The house was already rammed full. And then there were food, clothes, all the other stuff kids needed. Dean brought in a decent wage from the garage, but without what she earned at the engineering works she knew they'd struggle to make ends meet. But how could she hold down a job and bring up four kids? It was impossible.

But as the baby began to grow inside her, Michelle had known that they would muddle through somehow. Even though they might never have got married but for the accidental first child, she and Dean made a strong team. He wouldn't let her down. And he hadn't. When she'd told him that five were soon to become six, the fear on his face had been fleeting, and swiftly replaced by a not-unconvincing grin.

'Well, there you go,' he'd said, with a lascivious raise of an eyebrow. 'There's plenty of lead left in my pencil!'

She'd swung her handbag at him, bashing him gently on the side of his head and he'd swept her off her feet and squeezed her tightly. She'd known then that she truly loved him and always would.

But right now, she could cheerfully saw off his head with a plastic knife and feed it to the seagulls on the Brayford. And why was it so hot? Did they not have fans in these places? How could she possibly be expected to give birth when she couldn't actually breathe? The window was open but its pale green curtain dangled limply with no hint of a breeze to move it. The air felt stifling, cloying, sticky on her already sticky skin. She needed to get this baby out just so that she could have a shower. They had water in hospitals, she assumed. No standpipes here.

And then the pain changed again and the primal need to push overtook her.

ABOUT THE AUTHOR

Photo © 2022 Carolyn Mendelsohn

Imogen Clark is a bestselling author of contemporary fiction delving into the complexities of family dynamics. Her novels have captivated readers worldwide, with almost two million copies sold and eight Kindle chart-toppers to her name. *Where the Story Starts* was shortlisted in the UK for Contemporary Romantic Novel of the Year 2020.

After initially qualifying and working as a lawyer, Imogen left her legal career behind to care for her four children and then returned to her first love – books. She went back to university, studying English literature part-time whilst the children were at school. It was a short step from there to writing novels.

Imogen's great love is travel and she is always planning her next adventure. She lives in Yorkshire. You can explore her world of unforgettable stories by visiting her website, https://imogenclark.com, where you can sign up for her monthly newsletter and follow her on social media. She also writes as Izzy Bromley.

Follow the Author on Amazon

If you enjoyed this book, follow Imogen Clark on Amazon to be notified when the author releases a new book!
To do this, please follow these instructions:

Desktop:

1) Search for the author's name on Amazon or in the Amazon App.
2) Click on the author's name to arrive on their Amazon page.
3) Click the 'Follow' button.

Mobile and Tablet:

1) Search for the author's name on Amazon or in the Amazon App.
2) Click on one of the author's books.
3) Click on the author's name to arrive on their Amazon page.
4) Click the 'Follow' button.

Kindle eReader and Kindle App:

If you enjoyed this book on a Kindle eReader or in the Kindle App, you will find the author 'Follow' button after the last page.